To the Deckers, the alien was as short as Chisel, as hairless as Crowbar's head, and green, which surprised them not in the least. Obviously, he came from Mars.

"Yes, I do understand your language," responded the beige communicator box clipped to Trell's belt. "My name is Trell, I am a technician. Do not kill me and I will serve you faithfully to the best of my meager abilities."

He grovels well, noted Hammer as he hooked a thumb inside his studded belt. Must do it a lot. The street tough smiled appreciatively. He liked that in a person.

The ganglord gestured at Crowbar to release the alien, which the biker did gratefully and wiped his fingers on his grimy T-shirt. Yuck! Crowbar thought. The rubbery little creep felt like a dirty chalkboard. The biker was unaware that the alien crew member thought the same about him.

In elegant simplicity, Hammer waved his Colt at the rows of strange, glittering weapons sealed inside the cabinets of unbreakable plastic and said, "Unlock those or die."

"Fair enough," replied Trell, and he opened the first of the display cases with his master key.

Other TSR™ Books

ILLEGAL ALIENS

Nick Pollotta
and
Phil Foglio

Cover Art
PHIL FOGLIO

TSR, Inc.

To radio plays, common interests,
mutual respect, and a five year
friendship going on forever.
Yeah, what the hell.

ILLEGAL ALIENS

This book is protected under the copyright laws of the United States of America. Any
reproduction or other unauthorized use of the material or artwork contained herein is
prohibited without the express written permission of TSR, Inc.

Distributed to the book trade in the United States by Random House, Inc. and in Canada
by Random House of Canada, Ltd.

Distributed in the United Kingdom by TSR UK Ltd.

Distributed to the toy and hobby trade by regional distributors.

DRAGONLANCE is a registered trademark owned by TSR, Inc. FORGOTTEN
REALMS is a trademark owned by TSR, Inc. TM designates other trademarks owned by
TSR, Inc.

First Printing, February, 1989
Printed in the United States of America.
Library of Congress Catalog Card Number: 88-51727

9 8 7 6 5 4 3 2 1

ISBN: 0-88038-715-7
All characters in this book are fictitious. Any resemblance to actual persons, living or
dead, is purely coincidental.

TSR, Inc.
P.O. Box 756
Lake Geneva, WI 53147
U.S.A.

TSR Ltd.
120 Church End, Cherry Hinton
Cambridge CB1 3LB
United Kingdom

The Milky Way Galaxy

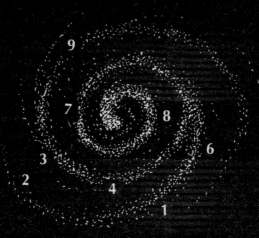

1. Terra/Earth
2. RporR
3. Darden
4. "Oh, Yeah?"
5. Gee (classified)
6. Koolgoolig
7. Big
8. Star System no. 553646 (declassified—nicknamed Buckle)
9. Unnamed Dyson Sphere

BOOK ONE
ON EARTH

DRAMATIS PERSONAE

THE UNITED NATIONS FIRST CONTACT TEAM

Prof. Sigerson Rajavur: Icelandic diplomat in charge of the FCT.
Brigadier General Wayne Bronson: American soldier assigned to the UN team.
Dr. Yuki Wu: Chinese physicist, scientific advisor to the FCT.
Dr. Mohad Malavade: India's top philologist, an expert in interspecies communication.
Sir Jonathan Courtney: Scottish sociologist and self-made millionaire.
Comrade General Nicholi Nicholi: Soviet soldier in charge of the Earth Defense Forces.

THE BLOODY DECKERS

Hammer: ganglord.
Drill: his lieutenant.
Whipsaw: legbreaker.
Crowbar: ex-biker.
Chisel: knife expert.
Torch: alley mugger.

THE ALIENS

Idow: leader.
Gasterphaz: protector.
Boztwank: engineer.
Squee: communicator.
Trell: technician.

THE GREAT GOLDEN ONES

Avantor: the guardian of Sol III.
The 17: her primary assistant.

THE REST

Amanda Jackson: lieutenant, New York Police SWAT.
Robert Weis: colonel, NATO forces.
Delores Bolivar: receptionist.
Francis McDougherty: Accounting Dept. manager.
Hector Ramariez: an accountant.
William Peterson: chief of police, Manhattan Central, NYPD.
Emile Valois: secretary-general of the United Nations.
NATO: North Atlantic Treaty Organization.
Agent Taurus: a living nuclear weapon.
Agent Virgo: a nuclear counter-agent.

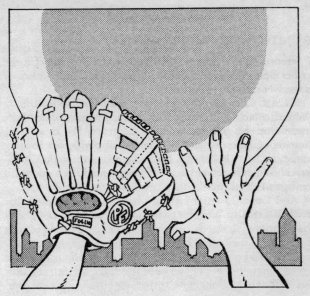

PROLOGUE

CRACK, and the rocketing softball dwindled into the blue New York sky as the grinning batter dropped his stick on home plate and took off for first base like a man with his pants on fire.

"I got it! I got it!" cried Hector Ramariez, his skinny legs backpedaling him furiously into the weedy grass of center field. His teammates, relaxing by the trees that edged the Central Park ballfield, stridently voiced their differing opinions on this matter, as Hector was the pariah of their team, a well-meaning, but ineffective weeny.

Like a leather radar dish, the cost accountant's never before used softball mitt tracked the white ball until it became lost in the glare of the August sun. This was the last game in the summer play-offs between the different departments of the Gunderson Corporation, and to everyone's unmitigated surprise, the Accounting Department (Hector's team) was in the lead, with the score at 2-0, the bases loaded, and two outs in the bottom of the ninth. The Accounting Team captain, Francis "Scrooge" McDougherty, had been so sure of a win that the old skinflint had already phoned in an order for their victory pizzas—using his own quarter.

Then disaster struck, in the form of a fly ball to Hector.

With a feeling of impending doom, Ramariez licked salty sweat from his lips and scanned the empty sky above him. Somehow, he could feel McDougherty's piggy eyes burning into him like twin lasers; it made the poor accountant's stomach churn with nervous acid. If Hector made this catch, his team won. If he didn't, they lost. It was that simple.

And Ramariez knew just how badly his boss wanted that company trophy. With his own arthritic hands, McDougherty had retrieved a wooden display case from the dungeonlike basement of their office building, and painstakingly scrubbed, painted, and polished the box back into its original pristine condition. Gleaming like an oiled jewel, the wooden case now sat in front of McDougherty's office, eagerly awaiting the company's silver loving cup.

Oh, my goodness gracious, thought Ramariez in genuine panic. Mr. McDougherty will blame me personally for this disaster and there is no telling what he might do. Why, he might even send me back to . . . Payroll! The accountant felt himself grow faint.

The Payroll Department. A fate worse than death.

Dancing about frantically in the dry weeds, Hector hopelessly tried to align himself under a falling ball that he couldn't even see. Where was the gosh-darn thing anyway? he thought to himself.

The ball had vanished. It was nowhere in sight. A monumentally shy man, Ramariez had not been under such unrelenting pressure to perform since his mother had given him twenty-four hours to learn how to dress himself before he left for college.

In his over-vivid imagination, Hector could feel the tension in the air as if it were a static electric charge. He half expected sparks to start crackling off him. Blood pounded in his temples and an agonizing knot formed in his chest. Ruefully, he smiled. Weren't those the symptoms of a heart attack? Perfect! Death before dishonor! Anything, rather than incur the wrath of Mr. McDougherty, and be the fool in front of Ms. Bolivar.

Delores Bolivar was the beautiful receptionist for the Gunderson Corporation who had actually agreed to have a drink with the timid accountant after the game. But, would the sultry Ms. Bolivar still wish to share a soda with the bumbling fool who dropped the game-winning catch and brought shame and disgrace upon the Accounting Department? Hector seriously thought not.

The annoying catcalls from his fellow employees got noticeably louder. Bravely trying to ignore them, Hector prayed for salvation . . . and there was the ball, plummeting toward him from the sun. Hastily, the accountant scrambled into position, his stiff leather glove raised for the game-winning catch. Watch this, world! he thought. A hero at last! Hector Ramariez saves the day. Ticker tape parades, lunch with the mayor, a date with Delores, nothing was too good for—

Suddenly, the impolite noises from his coworkers changed into raw-throated screams of terror, and hurriedly both teams began fleeing the park like roaches from bug spray. Puzzled, Hector squinted skyward at the source of their disconcertion. There in the air above him, ever expanding in size, was the missing softball. He blinked, and the ball swelled to the size of a stove . . . a truck . . . a house! A harsh buzzing sound filled the air. The pale hair on his skinny arms stiffly rose. Then darkness enveloped Hector as the impossible sphere eclipsed the sun.

Ramariez glanced down, and found that he was standing dead center in an ever-widening pool of black shadow. Quickly, he performed a short algebraic equation ($v \times d \times N = Y$ are you still here?), and then began running for his life, sprinting for that thin line which separated merely contemplating Heaven from finding out about it in person. All thoughts of the game, his job, and even Delores were totally replaced by the primordial urge for self-preservation and the overwhelming desire not to be crushed to death by a giant flying softball in Central Park, New York.

Unaccustomed to physical exertion, Ramariez was soon gasping for breath as he raced for the shadow's boundary, but it eluded him with nightmarish speed. In raw desperation, he cast his glove away and dashed forward in a last, frantic burst of speed. But it was too little, too late.

Like the fist of God, the titanic white globe slammed directly onto the pitcher's mound, displacing tons of dirt in an earthy tidal wave that swept the screaming accountant off his feet and hurtled him through the air, tumbling debts over assets, to jarringly crash in the top of an old elm tree more than four blocks away.

Bruised, battered, and broken in spirit, Ramariez awoke dangling from a branch. Howling like an animal, the crazed accountant clawed his way through the crushed foliage and fell sprawling to the still trembling ground. Without a moment's hesitation, Hector Ramariez dashed pell-mell down one of the park's numerous bike paths, made it to the traffic-filled street, and disappeared into the concrete canyons of New York City, never to be seen or heard from again by the civilized world.

* * * * *

Like a white Ping-Pong ball sitting in the grass, the gargantuan sphere towered over the tall Central Park trees, completely filling the space allocated to the recreational field. The highly polished hull of the ship glistened like a pearl in the bright afternoon sun. There it sat, this strange white invader, and did absolutely nothing for thirty terrestrial minutes. Slowly, a crowd began to form about the base of the staggeringly immense globe, the brave and the foolish leading the way.

Ironically enough, it was Delores Bolivar who first discovered the invisible force shield encircling the alien craft. She did this empirically, by bouncing her face off of it. Tears flowed unchecked past her bruised nose, and comfort was offered to her by sympathetic members of the crowd. Sympathy that rapidly changed to moral outrage when they realized what she was pointing to on the other side of the transparent barrier—a mangled baseball mitt that lay pitifully half-buried in the rubble beneath the monstrous ball.

The force shield had the feel of lightly padded steel and proved to be quite invulnerable to the delicate fists of Delores, the pounding baseball bats of Hector's teammates, and the .38 bullet fired from a rookie patrolman's service revolver. Yes, New York's finest had at last arrived, after some unsung genius dialed 911 and reported a *very* illegally parked vehicle.

Soon the police swarmed in by the dozens, valiantly trying to control a crowd that poured in by the thousands. SWAT team helicopters battled with TV news choppers for air space supremacy above the killer spaceship. Forcibly the multitude was pushed back and a safety perimeter established around the ship to the great annoyance of the unauthorized onlookers. The crowd started to turn ugly and shouting matches began. But then the street venders arrived and quickly restored a semblance of order to the gathering with their overpriced hot dogs, ice cream, and I SAW THE ALIEN SPACESHIP T-shirts.

* * * * *

Meanwhile, deep within the bowels of the mountainous craft, weird machines of crystal and silver began to stir. Hot power poured through molecular cables, complex circuit cubes instantly relayed multiple commands, unnameable alien devices did unnameable alien things, and finally a robot sensor awoke to focus its attention on the tumultuous assemblage outside. A translucent energy ray lanced out from the top of the starship, and the alien machine proceeded to scan that emotional human sea much the same way that a lighthouse fans the ocean with its beacon of light.

Unseen and unfelt, the ethereal sensor probed the nearest humans, paying scant attention to the sobbing Delores, the grim police, the aghast pizza deliver boy, the shocked, the frightened, and the astonished. Steadily, the beam extended its zone of inquiry, testing hundreds after hundreds of human beings, but all were found wanting. Then at last, the probe came to a group of six individuals who viewed the great ship dispassionately, apparently without fear. A small island of calm in the bubbling emotional soup. Dutifully, the machine paused on them, allowing its beam to seep into their living minds and read their secret innermost thoughts. When satisfied, the alien machine withdrew its unfelt probe and sent a priority message to its masters, who had been impatiently waiting for its report.

"These?" asked the robot of Those-Who-Command.

A conversation was held.

A question asked.

A decision made.

"Yes," came the answer. "Them."

Instantly, the six humans were bombarded with space-twisting forces—compared to which a nuclear explosion would be a candle to the sun—and they vanished in a burst of light that seared ghostly afterimages into the retinas of everyone near them.

Most of the distant crowd mistook the flash to be a reporter's camera, but those closer knew better, and Central Park became a madhouse as thousands tried to flee at the exact same time. Clothes were ripped. Women cursed. Strong men fainted. Fistfights broke out left and right. The park degenerated into a riot. Pandemonium ruled!

Serenely indifferent to the screaming hordes just outside its force shield, the starship began to broadcast a message on every frequency of the electromagnetic spectrum. A signal of such tremendous strength that it was received by televisions and radios even if they were not turned on. A message so startling, so fantastic, that most of the listening world began to chuckle, believing this to be a juvenile rehash of an old classic science fiction radio program.

But then the incredible broadcast repeated . . . repeated . . . repeated. . . .

1

In imposing silence, the committee sat around the heavy oak table reviewing plastic-coated documents of extreme importance. At the head of the table was a scholarly gentleman, a gray-haired diplomat from Iceland in a neat navy blue suit, the permanent leader of this special task force. To his left was an American general, splendid in his decorated uniform, with only a hint of ash on his right lapel, deposited there from his ever-present cigar. Across from him was his Soviet counterpart, possessing the solid body of a peasant heritage and a brilliant military mind that had earned him this position on the council. Next to him was a Scotsman, impeccably dressed in a tailored, gray three-piece suit that fit his bearing as a self-made millionaire and prominent sociologist.

Adorning the end of the table was a beautiful Chinese physicist in a soft summer dress decorated with a floral design, her long black hair worn loose about her shoulders. It was she who spoke first, breaking their somber concentration.

"Gimme two."

"Nothing for me."

"Give me the limit."

"I'm pat."

Comrade General Nicholi Nicholi sneaked a peek at his fellow players from behind his cards. Their attention was where it should be, on their poker cards, and not him. The three of them were calmly sitting there waiting for Nicholi to start the betting. Coolly, the Soviet general pretended to rearrange his cards while he studied their faces. Had they guessed? Did anyone know, that he, Nicholi Nicholi, had the ultimate in poker hands? A royal flush!

Always a cautious player, the gray-haired Prof. Rajavur had already folded from this game and was over by the kitchen unit of the command bunker, making himself a cup of the bitter Icelandic coffee he loved so much. Nicholi grimaced. And some people complained about Russian food!

The lovely Dr. Wu, though, was smiling contentedly at her cards. That meant Yuki was going to bluff again. Nicholi knew her tricks. Brigadier General Wayne Bronson was, as usual, unreadable, and Sir John Courtney was contentedly stroking that ridiculous little moustache of his. A bad sign that. The Scotsman must have an excellent hand indeed for him to be so complacent.

Nicholi grinned secretly. What matter? His royal flush was unbeatable.

The final member of their group, Dr. Mohad Malavade, a noted linguist from India who seemed to dress purely as a matter of convention, was on duty watch right now in the operations room, and thus unavailable to partake in the game they knew so well. For these six—Nicholi, Rajavur, Bronson, Wu, Courtney, and Malavade—were the United Nations First Contact Team: that august group of people designated to be Earth's official representatives when, if, or ever beings from another star system came to our fair, green orb.

Their fortified command bunker was located twenty-stories below the furnace room of the United Nations building in

Manhattan, New York. Despite its somewhat undignified position, the underground complex had a strong spacecraft feel to it, with cool metal walls, indirect lighting, and softly humming life-support machinery. This wasn't very surprising, since NASA had designed and built the place, using its proposed lunar base as a model.

Theoretically H-bomb-proof, the subterranean bunker was divided into three basic sections: a storage room fronted by a central corridor with private sleep rooms on each side; a full kitchen with a dining/recreation area; and beyond an iron pipe railing, down a short flight of steps, an operations room, with a TV monitor the size of a movie screen spanning the front wall. Grouped before the monitor were five desklike control consoles, the center console twice as large as the others. Over in the distant corner, sat a lone sixth console that jarringly faced back into the room, almost as if it had been placed there as an afterthought, or as if the console had a radically different function from the others.

Spacious and homey, the underground complex was equipped with everything the FCT needed to remain constantly on their "saucer watch." Which they did, on a three-out-of-four-week rotating schedule, with a floating pool of replacement personnel to cover whoever was absent. Today, by chance, the six original team members were present.

The bunker had cost millions to build, and the FCT had twice the national income of Belgium invested in them via training, training, and more training. They were deemed fully capable of handling any possible situation—from the crash-landing of an alien lifeboat atop Mt. Everest with its crew in dire need of medical assistance, to the invasion of Earth by radioactive mutant Chihuahuas. Nothing was considered too far-fetched. The FCT was overtrained to handle it. Yes sir.

But, in the fifteen years since the team's founding, despite countless sightings of UFOs, the First Contact Team consistently never found anyone to contact. They were fast becoming like the first aid kit you carry in the trunk of your car: as good as ever, but starting to gather a little dust, and sometimes you just plain forget it exists. The team found that they needed something to keep from going crazy(ier), and that something was poker. Straight, stud, draw, anaconda, and one hundred thirty-seven other versions that they had invented over the years.

In point of fact, the FCT held the *Guinness Book of World Records* entry for the longest-running non-stop poker game: eight straight years, easily beating the four-year-long crap shoot of the Buckingham Palace cleaning staff, and dwarfing into insignificance the 18-month-old baccarat game of the Hong Kong Freelance Bodyguard & Assassins Union.

Nicholi tucked his cards together to hide them from any stray glances. "Twenty dollars," said the Soviet, confidently betting the maximum.

Suspicious, General Bronson glared at the communist general across the table from him and shifted the position of the unlit cigar in his mouth. Twenty, eh? the American thought. Now what did that crafty Red bastard have up his sleeve? Sigerson was on the sidelines brewing coffee, Yuki was going to bluff, and Courtney had nothing, so this hand is solely between the two of us. But Nicholi is indecipherable; his craggy Russian face never shows anything he doesn't want it to. Thoughtfully, Bronson chewed on the end of his panatela. What the hell, he decided. It's time to separate the men from the boys.

"Okay by me," drawled the American. "And another twenty." Ha! That'll teach Comrade Showoff who's in charge here.

"Fold," said Dr. Wu, putting down her cards. The scientist had been planning to bluff again, but Yuki could see that her two generals were working up a head of steam, so she prudently got out of the way of their forthcoming collision, saving herself four thousand yen in the bargain. Besides, there was always the next hand.

Tantalizingly, the smell of coffee tickled her nose and Wu glanced at the kitchen behind her. Nattily dressed in a two-piece blue suit and crisp white shirt, Prof. Rajavur was at the bunker's electric stove brewing a pot of his outrageously potent coffee. Before joining the FCT and engaging in their twenty-four-hour poker-fests, Wu had only thought of caffeine as an inferior medical stimulant. Now, it was like the staff of life.

"Care for some?" offered Rajavur, gesturing carefully with his brimming mug, an extra-large tan ceramic cup marked: "TAKE ME TO YOUR LITER." When the secretary-general of the UN had last visited them on his yearly inspection tour, Sigerson had been forced to explain the joke to the pompous Frenchman.

The woman smiled gratefully. "Thank you, yes."

Politely, the physicist excused herself from the table and left for the ladies' room before joining the professor in a cup of his acidic brew. In private, Prof. Rajavur thought it a sin that Yuki added milk and sugar to the coffee; but since no other member of his team would even go near it, he forgave her that tiny perversion of Icelandic cuisine.

"Twenty is fine," said Courtney, only a faint Scottish burr rounding his words. "And I raise you twenty more."

A millionaire even before he had inherited his uncle's estate, high stakes meant nothing to Sir John; but taking these soldier boys down a peg or two did. The sociologist had a blockbuster of a hand—four nines, and he was highly doubtful that either of his associates could beat that. Confidently, he pulled crisp bills from a money clip bearing his family crest and added them to the growing pile of cash on the dining/poker table.

Recreational space was at a premium in the bunker, and almost everything had to serve two functions. Even the precious poker cards often became twirling spaceships that invaded somebody's inverted hat during an impromptu strategy meeting.

Blatantly, the Scotsman left his money clip there on the table, signifying that he was in for the duration. Bronson ignored the bit of bravado, and Nicholi tried to do the same, but failed miserably. Sir John saw the Soviet struggle with inner turmoil and incorrectly read the emotion as fear. Had he treed the old bear again?

"Well, my friend?" grinned the sociologist, positive that he smelled a kill.

Nicholi pretended to think about the bet, while internally he was cackling with glee. Czar's Blood! They think I am bluffing. Me! Bluffing! I can probably squeeze one more raise out of them before lowering the boom, but this has to be done carefully. No amateurs these.

Coyly, General Nicholi shuffled his cards around and loosened his People's Army issue necktie. It was a good thing that he was here in the United States with these cards, for back in the motherland this hand would have had him sweating blood. Three times before Nicholi had possessed a royal flush, and each had ended in disaster.

The first time was as a private, new to army life, but old in the way of cards. As he drew the card he needed to complete his winning hand his entire platoon had been ordered out to build a stupid, useless wall. Nicholi had hated Berlin ever since. Next was as a lieutenant playing poker with his men over a combat lantern, when the winning cards had been shot out of his hands by enemy fire. He escaped that night physically unscratched, though his soul was deeply wounded. The last time had been in Moscow, where, as a major waiting for notification of his promotion to colonel, he had been unceremoniously busted back to a lieutenant for playing cards on duty. His royal flush confiscated for evidence.

Ah, but here it would be different. Nothing could stop him. At last, sweet victory would be his and Nicholi Yuriavich Nicholi would finally get to *show* someone his perfect poker hand. This was it!

"*Da*, Jonathan," he happily agreed, unconsciously humming Wagner's *Ride of the Valkyries*. "And I raise you another."

Courtney and Bronson exchanged anguished glances. Ambushed! They should have known better than to trust a Red.

"Sir?" a voice addressed the room.

Everybody chorused *yes*.

Down in the operations room, visually bisected by the iron pipe railing, a swarthy man in a badly fitting suit duly pointed at Prof. Rajavur.

"What is it, Mohad?" asked the Icelandic diplomat, taking a sip from his coffee mug.

"I have been receiving some very unusual radio transmissions on the New York police channel," said Dr. Malavade, holding a tiny wireless earphone to his head.

Ice formed on Nicholi's spine and his crew cut hair threatened to leave his scalp. Oh no, he thought. The only thing in the world that could interrupt this game was—Czar's Blood, did they have to land today?

"Quiet, please!" barked the Soviet, his left hand fumbling in his uniform pocket. "Do not interrupt game. Sir John, I meet that and bet another twenty." And Nicholi hurriedly slapped his own money down, raising his own raise.

"Interesting," muttered the American, the strange double bet not going unnoticed. "Well, I'll see that. How about you, Courtney?"

"In for a penny, in for a pound," philosophized the Scot, winking to Bronson on the sly. The general shrugged in return. "Okay, Nick, what have you got?"

Returning from the washroom, Dr. Wu paused in the act of drying her hands on a government issue paper towel. Something had happened in her absence. Rajavur was hurrying toward Malavade, who was crouched over his communications console, and the remaining poker players were in animated conversation. Curious, the scientist descended into the operations room, the hem of her cotton dress billowing about the trim calves of her nyloned legs.

"Is anything wrong?" she inquired of her colleagues as they began to jointly listen to an earphone.

"There has been a landing in Central Park," announced Malavade crisply. "It has been confirmed by the traffic department of the NYPD. A unit of the National Guard has been dispatched for crowd control."

Without hesitation, Dr. Wu rushed to her console and hastily began flipping switches. Prof. Rajavur was already at his desk. Sluggishly, the liquid crystal TV monitor on the wall before them started to pulse with light as it warmed to operational temperature.

Rajavur pressed a button and a pair of small video monitors raised up from inside his control board. "Has there been any word from the—"

"Ship," supplied Dr. Malavade, hands busy on his own board. "One, round, white, approximately four hundred meters in diameter." Somebody whistled. "Yes, it is big. Reports suggest that the craft is protected by an energy screen of some kind; no one can get close. At present, there has been no announcement from the occupants." With a forefinger, he minutely adjusted a volume slide. "Just a moment, please . . ."

"*Then let's finish game!*" roared Nicholi, surprising everyone.

In the operations room, Wu, Rajavur, and Malavade jerked their heads about and stared in astonishment, while Bronson and Courtney halted on the steps to see the Soviet general still sitting at the poker table.

"Are you mad?" Sir John admonished. "There's a bloody spaceship in Central Park! Good Lord, man, this is what we've been waiting fifteen years for!"

"And this is what I've been waiting whole life for!" raged Nicholi, pounding the table with his fist. "Sit down! Will only take minute to finish game." His friends obviously could not believe what they were hearing, so Nicholi changed to a more persuasive tone. "Please? As favor to me?"

General Bronson sighed. "Well, if it's that damn important to you . . ." He returned to the poker table and flipped over his cards. "I fold. The pot's yours."

Like a gentleman, Sir John did the same.

"NO!" Nicholi howled in anguish. "Wait! Here, look at this!" Frantically, he spread out the poker cards on the table for his friends to see. They stepped closer.

"The alien ship has begun shooting people," Malavade calmly announced in his dictionary-perfect English. "Five . . . six dead. Maybe more."

2

Poker cards blizzarded into the air and fell unnoticed to the floor as Nicholi shoved the gaming table aside and sprinted for his post, with Courtney and Bronson leading the way.

Reaching his console first, the American soldier dropped into his chair, slipped on a set of earphones and deftly activated his equipment.

Each of the FCT's consoles were designed for different functions, and were alike only in general build. Basically in the shape of a horseshoe, the curved metal desks had two sets of three drawers on either side of the chairwell, and the desktop was covered with a plethora of electrical equipment. Broken into three sections, the controls were: a series of hush phones and a laser printer for hard copy on the left; a video/computer monitor and keyboard in the middle; the speciality controls, meters, switches, and dials filling the right side. If not so when they joined, every member of the FCT was by now virtually ambidextrous.

Winking telltales on the right side of the desktop informed Bronson of the status of the United Nations building above them, and of their own command bunker. He tapped a complex code onto the keyboard before him, got a warning beep, and checked the video screen to see the empty hallway outside the bunker. All clear. He then inserted a key into a slot on the desktop and turned it, setting the double pair of armored doors to their quarters cycling shut. Soon, the FCT would be physically isolated from the outside world by a meter of laminated steel, making entry into the bunker impossible, and exiting forbidden without the general's specific knowledge and consent. Voices in his ear told him that the UN was in an absolute state of panic, with the delegates alternately demanding information, not believing what they were told, and then discounting the whole incident. Bronson grunted. Damn civilians. They were about as useful as lips on a brick.

"Communications on line," said Dr. Malavade, formally following the long lost, and semi-legendary procedure manual that had "mysteriously disappeared" the day after the FCT had been given copies of the 18,000-page document.

Dr. Malavade's console was a vidiots dream come true; he could broadcast and receive messages on every level of the electromagnetic spectrum, from radio waves down to hard radiation. An expert in cryptography and codes, what languages Mohad wasn't fluent in, his computers were—from Mayan hieroglyphics, through the squeals of porpoises, to pig Latin. In a pinch the team's linguist was also a lip reader and did crossword puzzles in ink.

"Information on line," stated Courtney, sliding on his hated reading glasses, a sad result of reading too many stock portfolios and books on UFOs. His father, who thought glasses effeminate, had ordered the lad to spend more time dating women when he first got them. This the young Jonathan had gladly done. But only with rich women who belonged to the local UFO club.

Already, the teleprinter on the sociologist's right was feeding him duplicate reports from ABC, AP, TASS, NPR, the BBC,

ComStat, the *New York Times*, the *National Enquirer*, and *Grit*. His teammates may laugh, but as an expert in his field, he knew that you never could tell where the truth might be found.

"Science on line," contributed Wu, enabling her computer and linking it to the NASA, NATO, and NBC sensors en route to the park.

Yuki's equipment was so sensitive that it could track an astronaut on the moon, or analyze a ballpark hotdog—which she had done once as a test. She had immediately telexed her findings to the city's Health Department.

"Security on line," said Bronson needlessly, as everyone in the bunker felt the muffled vibrations in the floor as their only door locked shut. In grim humor, the soldier opened the drawer on the lower left side in his console and lifted out an HK 9mm pistol. Automatically, he checked the gun's clip, holstered it, and proceeded to strap the weapon about his waist. Gimme a damn gold helmet, he thought sourly, and I could pass for George S. Patton. But, regulations were regulations.

"Command on line and running," announced Prof. Rajavur brusquely, as he slipped on a throat mike and finished activating both of his mainframe computers.

As the person in charge of the First Contact Team, his console was twice the size of his associates', and infinitely more versatile. He could talk privately to any, or all of them, simultaneously. He could countermand their decisions and, if necessary, run their consoles for them, should anyone become incapacitated or unreasonable.

For psychological as well as technical reasons, Rajavur was situated prominently in front of the wall monitor. The video cameras were focused on him, with the rest of his team clustered about him like so many small moons. That is, except for Nicholi.

Comrade General Nicholi Nicholi, and not General Bronson, was the soldier in charge of the Earth Defense Forces. The American protected the FCT, the Soviet protected the world.

From the very beginning of the team, it had been decided

that, purely as a safety precaution, no alien would ever get to know of Nicholi's existence, much less see him, until their peaceful intentions had been proved beyond a reasonable doubt. Therefore, the Soviet's defense console was hidden in a corner of the command bunker parallel to the wall monitor and well outside the range of its video cameras. Nicholi had a monitor of his own, a personal life support system, autonomous lines of communication, monogrammed bath towels, and a cassette deck. He was, in fact, as independent of the FCT as they were from the rest of the world.

Hissing like an antique steam radiator, a thick sheet of bulletproof glass rose from the terrazzo floor of the bunker and locked into the acoustical tile ceiling, hermetically sealing the general in place. Only a single phone line connected him with the rest of the team.

Nicholi was the unhappy stick to the First Contact Team's carrot. If a situation fell apart so badly that there was nothing diplomatic left to try, if push came to shove, then—and only then—would Nicholi act, using whatever measure of violence he deemed proper to correct the problem—from having a sniper shoot a wine glass out of someone's hand, to the total nuclear annihilation of New York, London, Paris, or even Moscow itself. Nicholi hated his job with a passion, which was why he still had it.

Finished with his initial preparations, the Soviet gave Rajavur a ready sign, and without hesitation the professor keyed in the 'go' code on his console.

Electronically, the huge mainframe under their bunker awoke, yawned, stretched, did a few warm-up trigonometric calculations, and in the next microsecond reached out to seize control of the United Nations computer system.

With a magnetic lurch, every keyboard in the mammoth building above them froze, motionless, all non-essential programs were simply erased, and the machines subatomically bowed to their new master. Everything in the thirty-six separate and shielded computer systems became instantly available to the FCT's mainframe to do with as it pleased. Deliberately looking over the vast array of material, the machine took almost a full second to locate the correct files, access them, and process the desired data.

The transatlantic phone lines were cleared of all phone calls and NATO headquarters in Geneva, Switzerland, received an ultra-top-priority message. The lightning exchange of passwords and countersigns took another ten seconds before the military mainframe verified the information and saluted its new commanding officer. Two milliseconds later, NATO's emergency global telecommunications network exploded with signals that were the purest gibberish to anyone but the designated computer system.

Within the cavernous basement of the Kremlin, the incoming signal was shunted to a review station specifically built to prevent such a computer takeover. Already the installation had proved its worth by stopping four such acts of piracy: two from China, one from Germany, and one from the Junior Hackers' Club of Duluth, Minnesota. But this signal passed through unhindered as the construction of the review station had been supervised by a Colonel Nicholi and a young computer genius named Malavade. It was, therefore, a total surprise to their respective governments when the Eastern Block of Nations declared their allegiance to an unknown group of nobodies in the basement of the UN building.

In America, the computers of NORAD instantly complied with the proper and legal request to usurp the Pentagon, and seconds later the Army, Navy, and Air Force received duly authorized commands to go to Defense Condition One. An unprecedented move that caused moans, shrieks, groans, two heart attacks, and a promotion.

Across the globe, country after country became locked into the growing computer grid. China was the last to join, due solely to a faulty subjunction in Beijing, but join it did.

Incredibly, the problem child turned out to be Greece, as the computer operator assigned to monitor any maximum security messages that involved the safety of his nation, and perhaps the world, was locked in the supply closet sleeping off his lunchtime rendezvous with the entire secretarial pool and a bottle of ouzo.

With the activation of the FCT, many politicians became seriously displeased and threw what could only politely be called tantrums. But despite their every effort, all of the vaunted power each of them had lied, cheated, stole, and (depending upon the country) murdered to get, simply flowed through their fingers like a bride's tears. However, after a shot of brandy and a hurried reading of the FCT's original charter, most politicos accepted the inevitable and did what they could to assist.

Most, but not all.

Five minutes after pressing the button, a green light winked on Rajavur's keyboard and with the flick of a switch, he irrevocably transferred the military might of the world to Comrade General Nicholi.

Headphones on, controls live, voices began whispering to the Russian general about the launch status of NATO missiles, combat troop readiness, and the present locations of Navy-Air Force strike teams. Nicholi sub-vocalized into his throat mike, allocating five more NATO submarines to the New York harbor and scrambling an additional flight of Delta-class fighter/bombers. He already had enough atomic weapons pointed at Manhattan Island to blow it out of the history books, but he told his American CBW units to stay on the alert, and ordered his homeland to begin the careful assembly of their prototype Hellfire Bomb.

In the solitude of his truncated room, Nicholi bitterly cursed the day he learned to play poker.

"Let's hear the alien's message, please, Mohad," said Prof. Rajavur, laying aside his hotline to the White House. This was no time to chat with the president. He appreciated the man's offer of assistance, but Rajavur had infinitely greater resources at his command then the local politician.

With a nod, the linguist pressed the playback switch on his console's built-in video tape recorder.

". . . EOPLE OF DIRT, ATTENTION . . . PEOPLE OF

DIRT, ATTENTON . . ."

"Dirt?" asked Bronson, putting a wealth of questions into the single word.

"Semantically correct," explained Dr. Malavade didactically. "Though hardly flattering, I agree."

"WE ARE SCOUTS FROM THE GALACTIC LEAGUE," the strange echoing voice continued, "HERE TO DETERMINE IF YOUR PLANET, DIRT, IS SUFFICIENTLY ADVANCED TO JOIN THE COALITION OF YOUR NEIGHBORING STARS."

The rippling TV screen melted into a whirl of colors that became the picture of a blue-skinned humanoid wearing a dusky white uniform of classic military style. He (she? it?) had a formidable brow, pie plate eyes, and two mouths; although only one was in use at present. Dr. Wu touched her throat mike, commenting briefly on the oddity and the possibility of copper sulfate life-forms. Sir John made a notation on the military cut to its clothing, and requested detailed information on anything blue in nature; topaz, birds of paradise, and the music of Blind Lemon Jefferson.

"FROM THE CROWD THAT HEMS OUR SHIP . . . ,"

The facial movements of the being in no way matched the words coming from the speakers. Dr. Malavade sub-vocalized into his throat mike about translation devices.

". . . WE HAVE TELEPORTED ABOARD SEVERAL REPRESENTATIVES OF YOUR RACE. THEY ARE UNHARMED. I REPEAT, THEY ARE UNHARMED, AND ARE WITH US SIMPLY TO HELP US ASCERTAIN YOUR ELIGIBILITY FOR MEMBERSHIP IN THE GALACTIC LEAGUE."

"They're alive!" cried Sir John, his nightmares of alien invaders who eat our flesh, enslave our children, and make the stock market collapse, dispersing like a highland mist. "Alive!"

Rajavur reached for his direct line to Nicholi, but then relaxed when he saw the lights of the Russian's console blink from red to orange and the general heave a mighty sigh. The situation may still be precarious, but at least they were no longer sitting in the barrel of a nuclear gun.

"THE POPULATION OF YOUR PLANET SHALL BE ALLOWED TO WATCH THEM BEING TESTED. IF THE SUBJECTS PASS, THEN DIRT WILL BE WELCOMED INTO THE GALACTIC LEAGUE AS A NEW, BUT EQUAL, MEMBER."

Across the globe, humanity broke into wild cheering and began to dance about their TV and radio sets. Spaceships! Aliens! The stars! Whee! It was like a Saturday afternoon movie!

Meanwhile, Rajavur and company sat patiently in the air-conditioned comfort of their underground bunker, patiently waiting for the other shoe to drop.

"BUT . . . ," continued the blue being.

Thunk, thought the FCT.

". . . SHOULD YOUR REPRESENTATIVES FAIL THE TESTS, THEN WE WILL BE FORCED TO REDUCE YOUR PLANET TO A RADIOACTIVE CINDER. NOTHING PERSONAL, MIND YOU, BUT I HAVE MY ORDERS . . . THIS IS IDOW FOR THE GALACTIC LEAGUE . . . OUT."

Again, the picture on the monitor melted and swirled, changing back to an aerial view of the enormous white ship dramatically sitting on top of Central Park, the glass-and-steel buildings of the New York skyline forming a postcard background. Framing the picture was a twinkling amber bar that visibly shrank with each passing second.

"Chronometrics, Dr. Wu?" asked Rajavur, taking an educated guess as to the nature of the border.

"Fifty two minutes and counting," the scientist answered, her lithe fingers working a pocket calculator. "If that color bar is indeed a timepiece and not merely a decoration."

Bronson removed the cigar from his mouth and inspected its soggy end. "What frequency was that broadcast on?" the soldier asked Dr. Malavade.

"All of them," replied the linguist. "And as far as I can tell, it was received clearly by everyone on the planet."

Thoughtfully, the general returned his cigar to its normal position. Well, that certainly seemed to kill the hoax idea. No nation on Earth could do that. Why, to generate the crude electricity alone would require a hundred—a thousand—Niagra Falls power stations, or controlled nuclear fusion. Neither of which mankind had. Yet.

"It's a wonder we didn't pick it up on our teeth," stated General Bronson aloud, thinking about an article he had once read in a newspaper describing a truly bizarre college prank.

"Many people did," said Sir John, industriously scribbling away on his notepad. "Sixty-two feet of ferro-concrete is probably the only thing that saved us from suffering a similar fate."

Wayne grunted. The walls of their bunker were a lot thicker than that, but Courtney had never seemed very interested in concrete, in spite of those fascinating lectures on Advanced Defensive Architecture that the general had dragged him to so often. Odd fellow, Bronson thought. Becoming rich must have driven him mad. Good poker player, though. That's what mattered.

"No," stated Rajavur firmly into his UN hotline. "I'm sorry, Mr. Secretary-General, but . . . . . yes, I understand that you have an interest in this matter. But . . . I'm very busy now, sir. Look, I will talk to you later, Emile. Goodbye." And firmly he cradled the gold UN receiver between his red (Russian) and blue (American) hotline phones. Damn, he thought. The last thing I need is some frightened politico bothering me. Agitated, Sigerson ran nervous fingers through his wiry crop of gray hair, which was a sign of his heritage, not age, as the diplomat was barely fifty years old.

"Mohad, have you had any success in contacting the aliens?" Rajavur asked the team's linguist. Dr. Malavade replied no. Communications were nil. The aliens must be deliberately ignoring him.

The diplomat swiveled his chair to the right. "What is your opinion, Jonathan?"

"On what, professor?" asked the sociologist, looking up from the computer printout on emotional factor responses he was perusing.

"On the chance that this Idow and his people are a First Contact Team similar to ourselves?"

"Zero," interrupted General Bronson hotly. "Because if they are, then they're doing a damn poor job!"

Behind his glass wall, Nicholi nodded in heartfelt agreement. Yes, the aliens must be either insane or fools. The status lights were crimson again, and his American CBW unit had just volunteered to do a suicide attack on the invaders.

Irritably, the Soviet general stretched out his cramped legs. Damn consoles were designed for midgets, he decided. Probably built that way to literally keep him on his toes. Ha!

Mentally switching tracks, Nicholi wondered what the man in the street was doing. He knew there would be no trouble with his NATO troops. They were good soldiers. Tried and true. The best. But what was the population of Earth doing right now; laughing, screaming, running around in circles? Only Sir John knew the up-to-the-minute details, and he relayed his findings through Sigerson. Rajavur alone got the whole picture—good or bad. With a loud buzz, the NATO hotline broke into his chain of thought and Nicholi resumed his more pressing work, deciding for the moment to forsake his attempt to out-guess Man, a thing that God himself had trouble doing.

Concurrently, Prof. Rajavur bowed his head in thought. If Courtney's preliminary report was correct, then the Earth was in terrible shape, what with most of humanity laughing, screaming, and running around in circles. And things could go from bad to worse, when the aliens commenced broadcasting again in forty-seven minutes. But, until then. . . .

The diplomat suddenly noticed how quiet the bunker had become and clapped his hands together. "To work, people!" he cried, and the room bustled with activity.

3

While the FCT prepared to investigate, study, and defend, the population of the world reacted as it always has in times of trouble: inconsistently.

TV reporters dashed out of their air-conditioned buildings to buy an old-fashioned newspaper. Newspaper reporters hid in the bathroom and turned on the dreaded television. Survival groups, who had been patiently waiting for nuclear war, decided that this was good enough and went to their secret mountain shelters, taking their family, neighbors, pets, and TV sets with them. Alcoholics swore off the sauce forever. Junkies ordered more of whatever it was they were taking. In California, Unitarians built, and then burned, a giant question mark. In New York, landlords with buildings overlooking Central Park put them up for sale, then changed their minds and instead, doubled the rent.

The real-life landing of an alien spacecraft on Earth caused UFO clubs to disband, six science fiction movies to be can-

celled, and twelve more to be initiated. Video tapes battled it
out with aspirins for record sales. History-making traffic jams
clogged the arteries of the world's highways, as drivers: (A)
parked their cars and ran for the hills; (B) drove for the hills; or
(C) fainted in their cars, bringing the unknown word
"gridlock" to such places as Tasmania, Nova Scotia, and Outer
Mongolia.

In the United States of America, the FAA ordered the
nation's airways cleared of all traffic immediately. Every non-
military plane in flight was given fifteen minutes of grace in
which to find someplace, anyplace, in which to land. Helicopters dropped like stones straight to the ground. Small planes
landed on any flat, open land—farms, parking lots, or football
fields. One unfortunate 747, with time running low, was
forced to make an emergency landing on an interstate high-
way.

Gunning his engines to warn motorists of the approach, the
jetliner swooped low over the roadway, neatly hopping over
underpasses and a rest stop. With smoking tires the giant
plane touched down and throttled to a squealing, roaring halt
only meters away from a hastily evacuated toll booth. As a ragged cheer arose from the onlookers and passengers, some damn
fool in a Cadillac behind them started blowing his horn for the
colossal aircraft to clear the way. Heroically, the 747 pilot
refrained from firing up the #2 engine and melting the idiot
into slag.

In Lebanon, the PLO demanded to know if the aliens were
Jewish. Zurich asked if they valued gold. Hollywood begged
for the rights to film their life story. New Zealand longed to
hear their favorite lamb recipes. Poland asked how many of
them it took to change a lightbulb.

At first, the Pope declared the alien beings devils, then
angels, then devils again, then Protestants, and then he
became unavailable for comment.

The independent countries of South America found themselves in a quandary. The aliens had landed in the much-hated
United States of America. If the creatures proved hostile, this

might be their big chance to help destroy the filthy Yankee pigs. But if the aliens were friendly, America might receive advanced technology that could make them undisputed masters of the world, someone you don't want mad at you. How they should act was solved by the brilliant political strategy of aligning themselves with Switzerland. Eagerly, the always neutral Swiss bankers accepted this commission as they had so many others, positive that, somehow, they could make a buck out of it.

Ireland got drunk.

England ordered out for tea.

Italy got drunk.

Japan sent out industrial spies.

France paid its UN dues.

In a small Arab nation, a fanatical Moslem leader stood on the balcony of a tall minaret and told his faithful followers assembled below that while they could handle the evil American devils, blue monsters from space was an entirely different matter. And so, in order to save his nation, he would have to destroy it with a hydrogen bomb. He raised the detonator switch for all to see. Oddly, the crowd in the courtyard below didn't react very favorably to this idea.

While they were breaking down the locked door to the minaret, their ex-beloved leader said a prayer and pressed the detonation switch. This only resulted in a loud click as his aides had long ago stolen the plutonium from the bomb and sold it for drugs. When the howling mob of outraged Arabs finally reached the top of the prayer tower, the Moslem zealot saved them from the messy task of tearing him into bloody gobbets by simply diving over the ornate metal railing of the balcony and falling to his death.

*   *   *   *   *

Meanwhile, orbiting high above the troubled Earth was a large golden rectangle about the size and shape of an industrial packing crate. Skimming along the very edge of the planet's atmosphere, the strange box passed unnoticed by the incredible profusion of spy satellites that filled the sky, and the ground-based military radar installations that stared directly at it, unseeing with their electronic eyes.

Those who had placed the enameled machine in orbit had been assured by their research staff that the box was, on the exterior, a perfect reproduction of a scientific device made by something called Westinghouse Industries, and this was true. But the design had come from the wrong division of the international conglomerate. The golden rectangle was the exact duplicate of a Westinghouse refrigerator; from the exposed cooling grid on the back to the price tag on the door handle. (The technical staff had wondered about the function of those items, but had included them anyway, in the noble interest of Science . . . and to promote job security, a basic urge in most sentient beings throughout the known galaxy.)

At present, that refrigerator-shaped device was receiving some very curious transmissions from the normally peaceful world below. Hungrily, the machine consumed the incoming signals as fast as it could, chewed up the data into byte-sized pieces, digested them thoroughly, and then burped out a most unappetizing answer.

Crystal programming cubes—nestled in multi-compartmental ionized tin power trays—became activated and the box began to rotate, until it was facing away from the Earth toward the distant stars. Then, the door opened wide and out erupted a mighty tachyon particle beam, unwavering at fourteen seconds of arc above the orbit of Pluto. The refrigerator's message was terse, concise, and left nothing to the imagination.

Soon, the golden light beam terminated and the enameled door closed with a soundless thump. Then, tiny jets flared from underneath the waterdrip pan, and the golden box moved off to relocate itself above the North American continent, in a geosynchronous orbit that would hold it relatively motionless above the source of those extremely disturbing transmissions.

The Eighty-first Street ballfield of Central Park, New York.

4

Leader Idow reclined in his formfitting chair and scowled at the viewscreen before him, his hairy face a sober study in blue. The first contact with an alien species was always a ticklish job at best. So far, everything had gone well. He could only hope that succeeding events would justify this expedition.

The control room of the starship *All That Glitters* flowed around the humanoid being like a sine wave, with the ship's leader placed at the apex of his pristine, high-tech domain. This position gave him a comfortable feeling as his primitive ancestors had often perched in the top of trees, dropped onto unsuspecting creatures traveling below, and blithely sold them insurance.

Glitters was a modified Mikon #4 space module, exactly four hundred meters in diameter. Precisely the same size as your average Mikon. Powered by their justifiably famous exothermic reactors, the spacecraft had a mean cruising speed of light to the twelfth power, making the ship just about the fastest thing in the galaxy. Only a single planet had faster ships, and those were not for sale at any price. The twenty-four levels of the vessel varied in height and width, depending entirely upon their owners wishes and intended use. Only the control rooms were standardized.

On the curved walls aft of Leader Idow were the tech-stations of his crew: protector, engineer, communicator, and technician. The latter station was rarely used, and was situated here in the control room only because of the irrefutable fact that the damn thing had to be somewhere. An armored security door closed off the base of the room and provided the sole means of entry into this, the nerve center of the starship. At present that door was ajar. This permitted a glimpse of the outside corridor, whose seemingly endless walls were lined with a multitude of wires, pipes, and junction boxes.

The control room and its furnishings were composed entirely of multiple shades of white. Only the operating beings themselves added splashes of color—blue, gray, brown, green—and even those were toned down by the ivory uniforms the crew wore. Every tech-station aboard the *All That Glitters* had an independent viewscreen, but at present Idow had them slaved to his so that each showed the same unremarkable scene.

Amid the stark white immensity of the test chamber that occupied the entire middle portion of the starship, there stood a handful of figures, the tremendous distance making them appear weak and frail, which, in every probability, they were. Idow could see them marching up and down, shaking angry limbs at the ceiling. No doubt shouting questions, threats, and pleas. All the usual things. But the audio pickups in the chamber had yet to be activated, so their verbal barbs never reached the ears of Those-Who-Command.

Besides, Leader Idow liked to watch the test subjects first. It helped him to better evaluate their chance of success. Furthermore, being pointedly ignored seemed to drive most primitives into a splendid frenzy, and these Dirtlings showed every indication of running true to form. Why, at this moment, the largest Dirtling was attempting to tunnel through the cushioned floor. His fellow subjects appeared to be cheering him on, although with alien species it was often difficult to tell exactly what they were really doing. Ah! Now a hairy subject pulled the big male to his feet and struck him several times in the face with the flat of a hand. For some reason that calmed the large male down and he demurely rejoined his companions. The hairy Dirtling stayed apart from the group, though, and they began addressing their comments to him.

So you're their leader, observed Idow coldly. Then as one to another, *I greet you, brother*.

A hand of living granite descended weightily upon the blue alien's shoulder, and Idow glanced up into the immobile face of his starship's protector.

"So much for your 'rule by strength' contention," rumbled Gasterphaz, his atonal voice sounding like rocks mating. "Obviously, you were wrong."

"How can you say that?" asked Idow in surprise. "You saw the hairy male beat the big male into submission. Thus, they have rule by strength, as I surmised."

The stony giant blinked. *Click-click*. "That? Beat? Why, that was but a caress. More likely they are lovers."

Leader Idow smiled inside himself. Gasterphaz was a Choron, a huge, heavily muscled, rock plated species of fantastic strength. The protector could easily rip the control room's security door right off its hinges with his bare hands. His mountainous race was so powerful that it had trouble identifying anything short of a Warobot armed with an X-ray laser as an actual attack. This aloof attitude infuriated some of the more excitable races in the galaxy, and in fact, the formidable Chorons were presently engaged in at least two wars of which they were blissfully unaware.

"Trust me," Idow reassured him. "These Dirtlings are sufficiently primitive for our needs. I am sure that they will do fine in the forthcoming tests."

"Primitive garbage!" screeched a high-pitched voice in disagreement. The two beings turned to see Boztwank, the ship's engineer, gliding toward them, the invisible force field legs of his electronic pot noiseless on the ship's soft plastic floor.

"Garbage!" repeated the petulant mushroom, his fronds aquiver. "And useless to us! Those . . . ?" a translucent hand gestured at the figures on the viewscreen. "Why, they won't even pass the first test, much less all three!" Located on his stalk, the fungi's diminutive face contorted with frustration. "Let's leave this wretched place and find us a real planet, with some real people to test!"

And better tasting dirt, too, no doubt, added Idow privately. The analysis had shown the dirt here to be high in hydrocarbons, metallic salts, and animal urine. While the latter was a nice touch, it was not enough to satisfy Boztwank. But then, his fungoid race lived in an almost perpetual state of seething annoyance at the universe in general. This emotional upheaval eventually culminated in a pyrotechnic display of fury which caused the enraged mushroom to literally explode, scattering spores for over a kilometer. Most likely, Boztwank's vociferous species would have long ago been eradicated by the galaxy at large just because of a near universal desire for peace and quiet but for the fact that their pre-sentient young were considered a delicacy by almost every being that possessed the sense of taste, and by several who merely had a fine sense of propriety. It was only his superior ability as an engineer that kept Boztwank from getting stuffed into the starship's reactor core for fuel.

Idow frowned. The mushroom did have a point, though. On the whole, the Dirtlings appeared to be a pretty unimpressive lot. But, as leader, the blue being felt duty bound to defend his decision to come here.

"Nonsense," he began in a friendly tone. "They—"

"They still call their planet Dirt!" raged the engineer. "How stinking primitive can you get?" The fungi's sprayers chose that moment to moisten his dome and stalk with a watery pink fluid. Idow took the opportunity to continue.

"Every race calls its home planet 'Dirt' in the beginning, Boztwank," he explained patiently. "You know that."

"But they've had over four thousand solar revolutions in which to change it! What in the Void are they waiting for, the Prime Builder to name it for them?"

"Terra," interrupted a dry voice. "They call their planet Terra."

Annoyed, the mushroom closed his lipless mouth and Squee, the ship's communicator, waddled forward, his enormous atrophied tail dragging behind him along the floor.

Squee was the last known surviving member of his lizardoid race, the rest of his home world population having gone on to evolve into a higher species while he was touring the galaxy with Leader Idow. Nowadays, Squee, in a valiant attempt to resurrect his old species, seduced and mated with every egg-laying, cold-blooded female he could find. Current medical theories claimed that such interspecies breedings were impossible. Yet, Squee succeeded again and again in impregnating his alien lovers, and they subsequently gave birth to tiny duplicates of Squee—who promptly evolved into a higher species. This bothered the poor lizard to no end.

Suspicious, Boztwank squinted at the communicator. "Everybody calls it that?" he demanded rudely.

Squee stopped the perpetual scratching at the scales on his tail. The limb didn't itch, the act was just something he did absentmindedly—the way humanoids rubbed their chins, or bloopoids hit themselves with a fish.

"Well, no," admitted the lizard honestly. "Not everybody."

"And what is the root word for this 'Terra'?"

"Earth," he answered proudly, and the mushroom scowled, a difficult thing for him to do.

Leader Idow was unmistakably pleased by this exchange. Plainly, Squee had done an excellent job of analyzing Dirt's primary tongue.

Furious at being thwarted in anything, Boztwank rallied to the attack once more. "And in their major language, 'Earth' translates into . . . what?"

Squee bit his forked tongue. He had hoped they wouldn't ask that.

"Well?" demanded Boztwank.

"Dirt," sighed the communicator sadly. "It means dirt."

"Ah HA!" cried the mushroom in righteous victory. "I told you so! I told you so! I told you so!"

With true lizard dignity, Squee turned tail on the engineer and waddled back to his station, where his instruments lit up, overjoyed to see their scaly master again. A vegetarian, from a race of vegetarians, Squee wondered what Boztwank would taste like. Probably bitter as stinkweed, the nasty old mushroom.

Idow, too, eyed the jubilant fungi with disfavor. Boztwank had many bad habits, being a poor winner among them. And didn't the name of his home planet translate into something like, "The Place That Holds Our Roots in Safety"? Hmm . . . Hmm . . .

"Is it true, Idow?" asked Gasterphaz, resuming the original line of conversation. "Might they be too primitive a race for us to use?"

"No," stated the starship's leader firmly, crossing his legs and meticulously straightening the cuff on his dusky uniform. "They are not. Dirt has a planetary government, crude space flight, and a world communications system. These alone prove that they are sufficiently advanced for our needs."

"Acceptable then. We have dealt with worse."

"And we have dealt with better," cried Boztwank irritably. "Let's go home!"

"BUT WE ARE HERE NOW," thundered Idow, using his throat of command. "And it was quite an effort to get here now, so we will test these . . ."

"Humans," interjected Squee.

". . . Dirtlings," Idow continued unabated. "And simply hope for the best."

Grumbling to himself, Boztwank directed his floating pot back to his tech-station, where he ordered his squirter to splash him with more of the pink liquid. But it didn't cheer him up a drop.

Idow returned to his viewscreen, the picture on it the same

as before. The test subjects had hardly moved a foot. What was wrong with them? No curiosity? He flexed his eyebrows in pique. "How much longer, Squee?"

"Three hundred seconds."

Void, Idow cursed silently. "Is everything ready for the broadcast of the test?"

"Of course, my Leader."

"Fine. Oh, did Trell ever get around to replacing that broken camera in the test chamber?" As he spoke, Idow's viewscreen shifted to a different angle of the humans. "Acceptable. Gasterphaz?"

The mighty Choron rotated his head without bothering to move his shoulders. "Yes, Idow?"

"Do try to keep your warobot under better control this time. We only have so many of those cameras with us, you know."

"Affirmative."

"Why, only yesterday Trell was telling me that . . . ," Idow paused here and glanced about the room, noticing the absence of the technician for the first time. "Where is Trell anyway?"

Boztwank muttered something inaudible.

"What did you say, Engineer?"

"Maintenance. He's doing some maintenance."

"Oh, really?" inquired Idow swiveling about. "And just what is broken on my starship?"

"Broken?" hedged the mushroom. "Why . . . ah, nothing's broken. He's just doing some minor repair work . . . you know . . . here and there . . . a ship this big . . ."

"Where is Trell?" asked Idow using his throat of polite conversation. Again Boztwank answered vaguely, so the blue being switched to his throat of command. "WHERE IS TRELL?"

"Core. He's in the reactor core."

"WHAT?" throated the ship's leader, rising from his chair.

Talking fast, Boztwank had his pot retreat from the furious humanoid. "No danger! Trell is in no danger, Leader! The power levels are at 9/9 and steady. He's completely safe—as if he were in his mother's mandibles!''

Idow considered the statement, knowing that the cowardly mushroom wouldn't dare lie to him, and grudgingly sat back down. True enough. Nine over nine was well within the technician's radiation tolerance level. It would merely be very uncomfortable for him. But why would Boztwank send Trell to the reactor just as they were about to start the all-important tests? Surely he wasn't still angry about . . .

"You're still angry about that mistake he made last trip," Idow accused the engineer.

Visibly, the mushroom steamed. "He confused my pink for the window cleaner again! I won't stand for that!"

Lizard and rock roared with laughter, while Idow openly smiled this time. Yes, it had been a near tragedy. Only time had made the incident funny. "Okay, Boz, you may do with Trell as you wish, but there are to be no mysterious power surges through the core which would fry our technician into carbon ash. IS THAT CLEAR, ENGINEER?" The fungi heard the change in throats and got the hint.

"Yes, my Leader. Of course, my Leader. Whatever you say, Idow." And Boztwank stealthily turned down the power dial on his control board that he had been inching upward.

Satisfied that Trell was safe for the moment, Idow returned to the business at hand. "Time?" he asked Squee.

"One hundred seconds, Idow."

Close enough. "Squee, please activate your translator; I wish to converse with our . . . guests." A slim rod extended from beneath the viewscreen at his station and Idow cleared his throats. "Attention, your attention, please." The translator hummed to itself, and relayed his words to the test chamber.

Startled by the voice from nowhere, the six humans jumped off the floor and started shaking belligerent fists at the ceiling.

"They wish to know what you want of them," said Squee, his instruments whispering to their beloved master.

"Nothing more?" asked Gasterphaz, shifting position in his steel slab of a chair which groaned in protest.

"Well, I am simplifying it a bit," admitted the communicator, with a shy smile.

"So I would assume," added Idow coldly. "What else do they say?"

"Ssss, challenges to show ourselves, demands for immediate release, numerous death threats, and multiple references to procreating with our own mothers." The latter confused the lizard. Didn't everyone love their mother?

Leader Idow was dubious as to the accuracy of the translation and told the lizard so. "Let me speak to them directly," he instructed.

Daintily, Squee taloned the switches and dials on his control board, and Idow's viewscreen spoke: ". . . CONSUME WASTE PRODUCTS, YOU UNCLEAN OFFSPRING OF UNMAR-RIED PARENTAL UNITS! YOU MALE INFANTS OF FEMALE CANINES! MAY THE PRIME BUILDER CAST YOU INTO THE VOID! MAY—"

"Be quiet," said Idow in a conversational tone as he thumbed the volume switch on his microphone to maximum. His amplified voice resounded in the test chamber and the humans rocked beneath the sonic assault. "Behave your-selves," he ordered them, resetting the switch to its normal position. "There is no need to shout. I can hear you quite clearly."

"Negative waste products," said the female test subject, and the rest of the group concurred.

Puzzled, Idow looked at Squee.

"An expression of disbelief," translated the lizard.

"Ah."

"Primitive trash," muttered Boztwank to nobody in particu-lar. Why couldn't everybody understand that he was always correct, one hundred per cent of the time, no matter what the facts were?

In the test chamber Idow's voice boomed out with: "YOU SIX HAVE BEEN BROUGHT ABOARD THIS STARSHIP AS A SAMPLING OF TYPICAL DIRTLINGS."

"Dirtlings?" asked a small male.

"Your mother was a dirtling!" shouted the large male.

"Cease your mindless discourse," ordered the hairy male, and his cohorts swiftly obeyed.

"BEFORE THE PEOPLE OF YOUR WORLD, YOU WILL BE TESTED TO SEE IF YOUR RACE IS READY TO JOIN THE GALACTIC LEAGUE."

A brief silence followed.

"Is . . . is that anything like the major league?" asked the small male.

Idow looked at Squee again.

"Their ruling planetary body," explained the communicator.

"YES . . . EXACTLY . . . OUR LEAGUES WILL BECOME UNITED IN FRIENDSHIP . . . UNLESS YOU SHOULD FAIL THESE TESTS . . . THEN DIRT WILL BE DESTROYED."

"That inhales!" cried the female.

"That exhales," added a male.

"I smell most unpleasantly on tests," wailed the small male.

"Forcibly place the garments of your feet in your mouth, anal orifice," snapped the hairy male, and the small male cringed. Thoughtfully, the leader of the six surveyed the gigantic white room, remembering how they had gotten here. "Because I would wager that they can do it, too," he whispered.

"YES . . . WE CAN."

In an indecipherable human gesture, the tall hairy male spread his arms wide. "Agreement, then," he said to the ceiling. "So pray, inform us, what will these tests consist of?"

"An intelligent question at last," rumbled Gasterphaz, sounding pleased. "Why don't we show them?"

"Yes," encouraged Boztwank eagerly. "Let's show them! Show them!"

Idow cut his microphone. Why not? They certainly were a boring group. Maybe some visual stimulation would make them more physically active. "As you wish," he agreed. "Squee, see if you can contact the representatives of their Major League and inform them that we will begin the tests immediately."

"At once, my Leader," said the communicator, working the controls of his tech-station in preparation to send off the communique. It really was a shame, thought the lizard privately. This had been such a pretty planet.

5

The First Contact Team had been working like madmen at their consoles, the command bunker a maelstrom of activity, as fifteen years of preparation paid off in forty-seven minutes.

Hastily, the crowd around the spaceship had been forced outside the park by the National Guard, who were then replaced by crack NATO troops. Any buildings that faced the alien craft had their rooftops lined with every weapon and sensor that modern science admitted to, and a few it didn't. The Eighty-first Street ballfield of Central Park was a battle zone, merely waiting for official authorization to become a disaster zone.

And everywhere in Manhattan, people were disappearing.

Under the United Nations emergency act A-Zero-A (informally known as Snatch-and-Run), all important civilian personnel were being evacuated from the greater metropolitan area. Whether they wanted to be or not.

Prof. Gregory Ketter, a particle physicist of world renown,

was whisked out of his Park Avenue penthouse and flown off to Washington, D.C.

In Mt. Sinai Hospital, Dr. Michael Walsh was stopped in front of his operating room and was dragged off to a police car. He left behind his startled assistant, who was only the second best brain surgeon in the United States of America, and a prepped patient waiting in the operating theater.

A highly embarrassed team of FBI agents removed Dr. Daniel Lissman from New York's most infamous house of ill-repute, failing to bring along his Frankenstein mask, his whips, or his tutu, but retaining the doctor's battered briefcase that contained his latest treatise on Biological Warfare Counter Weapons.

Specially appointed federal agents, many of whom had been ordinary firemen and police officers just minutes before, went scurrying every-which-way throughout the Big Apple, tracking down their prey any-which-way they could. By bribery, blackmail, or busting heads. Time was important, not method. The agents had forty minutes to find one hundred people and get them two hundred miles away from New York. It was a mad scramble from the start, but they did it, and by dint of what Herculean efforts only their fellow agents knew.

And in lower Manhattan, a fleet of Federal Depository Bank trucks with an escort of heavily armed Army helicopters was discreetly pulling away from the Metropolitan Museum of Art, its last stop on a frightfully long list, racing off for Canada and safety, carrying a paltry few hundred paintings and statues, and leaving behind far too many. One poor, half-crazed curator had to be forcibly restrained from throwing any more Rembrandts into the back of the last truck.

The immense United Nations building stood deserted but for a squad of U.S. Marines left behind to deter looters. On every floor, doors gaped wide, furniture was overturned, and the warm, black ashes of hastily burned secret documents billowed along empty corridors like autumn leaves. The entire cadre of attending delegates was already at Kennedy Airport, being herded aboard specially commandeered SSTs and flown off to Geneva, Switzerland, the UN's alternate headquarters. The FCT was left quite alone in its sub-sub-sub-sub-basement command bunker. Even its honorary security guards were gone, leaving the external hallway unattended.

Seated shoeless at his defense console, Comrade General Nicholi Nicholi finished the arduous procedure of keying in his identification code, and The Button lit up on his board, its glaring red light leering at him like the eye of some demented devil from Hell.

Parcheesi, he thought. Why couldn't I have learned Parcheesi for God's sake!"

Prof. Rajavur doggedly held the blue phone to his ear, the pained expression on his face telling a story that Julius Ceasar would have understood completely, even though it wasn't March 15th. *Et tu, Secretary-General?*

"Mr. Secretary, how did you get on the White House hotline?"

"I have friends, Rajavur," said Emile Valois rudely. "Friends in important places who do not want to see you usurp my authority. The first contact with an alien species must logically be the responsibility of the United Nations."

"I agree, sir."

"Then give me back my goddamn computers and stop ordering NATO around like a bunch of ribbon clerks! I run the UN, not you. This nonsense must stop! These creatures are a threat to mankind and must be eradicated."

"No, sir," Rajavur said firmly. "I agree that the situation should be handled by the United Nations, and it is. The FCT is a duly chartered division of the UN Security Council, answerable only to ourselves once activated. Please try to understand, sir, that we have been waiting and training—"

"And playing poker!"

"And playing poker," conceded the diplomat, "for nearly fifteen years. We know better than you the seriousness of the matter. And there is nobody else on Earth better qualified to handle it than us. Personally, Emile," said the professor, switching tactics, "I am shocked by this petty grab for glory on your part. Heaven knows your psychological profile indicated no such tendencies prior to this."

"*How the bloody Hell did you get your hands on my psych file?*"

Prof. Rajavur refused to oblige him. "Mr. Secretary, you shall remain with the rest of the delegates, in Geneva, until this matter is resolved, or we are dead. End of discussion. Good-bye, sir." Displaying incredible restraint, Rajavur gently cradled the phone receiver, but under his breath, the professor muttered a biting Icelandic phrase that dealt with the dire consequences of fat people skating over thin ice.

With perfect timing, the digital clock on his console blinked a new time and started beeping at him.

"That's the ten-minute warning," he told his team. "Let's have your reports, please."

General Bronson turned off his teleprinter in acknowledgment and placed a fresh cigar in his mouth. His supply of them seemed endless.

"Central Park has been cleared of all non-military personnel, and NATO troops have it cordoned off," he said, reading from the top sheet of light green computer paper. "The adjoining rooftops are manned and armed. Snatch-and-Run was completed without any newsworthy incidents, and I still have no idea who the aliens have in their ship." Bronson started to light his panatela, then decided against it. "What I do know is that some poor bastard by the name of . . . Hector Ramariez is under the damn thing. Dozens of eyewitnesses saw it land right on top of him. He was . . . let me see . . . a bachelor, an accountant, and a Baptist."

"One dead," sighed Rajavur sadly. "God grant that there are no more. Dr. Wu?"

Primly, the Chinese scientist stood, as she always did when making a report. "So far we have been unable to penetrate the force shield that domes the ship. Conventional armament has proven useless. Neutron steel drills can find no purchase in which to operate. Magnetic keys yield nothing, and radiant energy stops dead at the surface, not bounces off, mind you, but stops, so the shield is probably H-bomb proof. Did you hear that, Nicholi?"

The Russian general waved her on, engrossed in his work.

She shrugged. "At present we're trying lasers, since the shield does pass visible light, and we have moved up"—here Wu tactfully coughed—"an ion cannon. I believe that may work."

Tea sprayed out his nose as Nicholi gagged in mid-swallow. Czar's Blood, so that's where the damn thing was! Here he was trying to find somebody in the Kremlin who would even admit that the weapon existed, and Yuki already had it positioned in Central Park running tests! Mopping his console with a handkerchief, Nicholi could feel his face turn red as the woman passed Prof. Rajavur a sheet of paper covered with mathematical equations—probably the operational figures on the top secret device. The Russian general smiled in spite of himself. Efficient wasn't the word for it. Magic was. Nicholi suddenly had the feeling that if Yuki wanted his uniform for a test on the ship, he would miraculously find himself sitting buck naked in his chair, with absolutely no idea how he got that way. Good thing she was on their side.

"What's the public reaction, Jonathan?" Rajavur asked the team's sociologist.

"So far, so good," announced Courtney, folding away his reading glasses and tucking them into a pocket. "The lunatic fringe is up and running, claiming a million different things, very few of them making any sense. But they're just a two per cent factor and we can safely disregard them. Interestingly enough, twelve per cent to fifteen per cent of the population is denying the whole incident and have turned their TV sets off. The classic 'Turtle in the Shell' syndrome. Fascinating, really." Nobody commented. "Well, I think it's fascinating. Anyway, the rest of the world is apprehensive and under some appreciative tension, but nothing they can't handle. In summation, Earth is not in very much worse shape than, say . . . America, on a Superbowl Sunday."

General Bronson whistled. "That bad, eh?" Yuki quickly

hushed him.

The diplomat turned to his left. "Mohad?"

"Hmm?" said the linguist, his unfocused eyes staring off into space. Constantly, the man readjusted the audio controls on his communications console. The FCT knew that if the bunker was on fire, the best way to inform Mohad of the fact would be to announce the news over the radio.

"Dr. Malavade!" shouted the diplomat.

"What? Oh!" The Indian philologist removed the earphones from his head, and tried to straighten his rumpled jacket, a procedure as useless as spitting on a volcano. "At present, communications are nil. The aliens will not respond to anything I say, except to acknowledge that they do receive my transmissions. Most infuriating. They ceased to broadcast some fifteen minutes ago. The picture you see on the wall monitor is from a NATO surveillance camera." Mohad twirled a dial on his console and the scene zoomed in and out from the white ship.

"One curious piece of information I have is about their original message." Dr. Malavade consulted his notebook. "In North America the transmission was in English, in South America a polyglot of Spanish and Portuguese. Europe received a mixture of Russian and German. Asia got Chinese, most impolite of them. In Africa it was Swahili, and in Australia . . . French."

"French?" chorused everyone.

Mohad gave them the most imperceptible of shrugs. "At least it proves that they are not infallible."

Just then, the NATO telephone on Malavade's console began to ring, and as the linguist reached for the receiver, Prof. Rajavur instructed him: "If that's the secretary-general, tell him we're out for lunch."

Unexpectedly, the wall monitor dimmed and the picture on it changed from a ground view of the white ship to an aerial view of the white ship.

"They're back," observed Sir John dryly.

"Minutes early," contributed Dr. Wu.

"Lunch," said Mohad, hanging up the phone and starting his video recorder.

With a swirl, the picture melted and refocused into the stern visage of the alien, Idow.

"PEOPLE OF DIRT, ATTENTION . . . PEOPLE OF DIRT, ATTENTION . . . THE TESTS TO DETERMINE THE LIFE OF YOUR WORLD ARE NOW ABOUT TO BEGIN . . . WE WILL ALLOW YOU TO WATCH AND THUS BETTER UNDERSTAND THEIR NATURE . . . HERE IS THE CHAMBER OF TESTING, AND THE DIRTLING SUBJECTS THAT WE HAVE CHOSEN." Again the monitor performed its Technicolor gymnastics.

"About time," growled General Bronson, from behind his cigar. As few as they were, one of his virtues had never been patience.

Slowly, the wall monitor focused into the picture of a blinding white room, thousands of meters square, and in the midst of that snowy acreage were a half-dozen tiny figures. As the camera, or its alien equivalent, dollied in, the six humans filled the TV screen with their presence—and their faces, hair styles, and mode of dress clearly announced to the world exactly on what rung of the social ladder they belonged.

"More aliens!" cried Mohad, aghast.

"No," Sir John corrected him. "They're a street gang! A bloody New York street gang!"

"Perhaps you are correct," recanted the linguist. "Creatures from another star would most likely dress with better taste."

Prof. Rajavur did a double take. Considering the source, this was without a doubt the strangest thing he had ever heard. But, diplomatically, he said nothing.

"The NYPD computer just called in a positive ID on the gang," Bronson announced, scowling at a flax from his teleprinter. "The kids call themselves . . . geez . . . the Bloody Deckers, and they're supposed to be the worst street gang ever to plague this city."

"I think they stole my car once," said Dr. Wu, scrutinizing the monitor closely. "Yep, it was them."

"Mohad!" barked Rajavur, making everybody jump. "Contact Idow immediately and tell him that he's made a terrible mistake!"

Tense minutes followed as Dr. Malavade tried once more to break through the aliens' radio silence. As the communications expert waged his private brand of electronic warfare, the FCT, and the rest of the world, carefully studied the six gang members.

They were all young, in their early twenties, yet each bore scars testifying to battles hard fought, and won. Five men and a woman, their hair styles ranged from crew cut, to ponytail, to bald. They wore boots and denims like a uniform, and everyone sported a black leather jacket, dripping in chains, with the back of each adorned with a vividly painted toolbox splashed with crimson. Underneath that was the name of the gang, boldly emblazoned in shining steel studs: THE BLOODY DECKERS.

Malavade snapped his fingers for attention. "I have been talking to an entity named Squee, and he assures me that a road maintenance crew is perfectly acceptable to them."

"Road maintenance crew? A street gang!" Rajavur groaned aloud. "Mohad, make him understand that—"

"Too late," stated Bronson, and it was.

The transmission from the ship had shifted to a wide angle view, and inside the test chamber something was happening. Close by the street gang, a section of the floor had dilated and a column rose into view, bearing four metal lumps—blue, gray, brown, and green, each resembling an army helmet. Hesitantly, the Deckers took a step forward but Idow's voice stopped them.

"THIS IS THE FIRST OF YOUR TESTS . . . WITHIN SIXTY SECONDS, THESE FOUR DRONES WILL BE ACTIVATED . . . THEY WILL INSTANTLY TRY TO KILL YOU."

Defiantly, the Bloody Deckers sneered, the FCT frowned, and the rest of humanity leaned eagerly into their TV sets. Hot dog, action at last.

"DESTROY THESE DRONES OR DIE . . . HEY."

The "hey" was because the street gang was already in action. Their leather jackets flapping like bat wings and howling their name in a battle cry, the six youths leaped upon the inert drones smashing them to pieces under their heavy motorcycle boots. The largest gang member grabbed two and ground them against each other. Fragments of wire and plastic sprinkled to the floor. A slim male produced a motorcycle chain and viciously whipped it down, sending bits of drone flying everywhere. The remaining drone was drop-kicked into its component works by a hulking third gang member, while two more Deckers moved in and systematically stomped into junk anything they could find. The sixth member of the street gang, a tall, hairy male, watched the carnage with a bored expression and kept checking his watch.

As the end of the minute approached, he whistled them to his side and on the sixty second mark, one tiny chunk of drone stirred. Bravely, it gave forth a fierce hoot, and a shining steel blade emerged from the broken shell of its body. The smallest gang member scuttled over to the dying drone, snapped off the blade and happily tucked it into his sleeve. The lord of the Bloody Deckers nodded approvingly at this act and then turned a murderous grin toward his unseen audience of five hundred million.

"So tell us," he asked smugly. "What's next on the game plan?"

*   *   *   *   *

Leader Idow yipped and hit the switch killing his microphone. Spinning about, the blue being found himself staring at his equally flabbergasted crew.

"GAME!" throated Idow using both of his mouths. "Did he say *game*?"

Nervously, Squee rubbed his claws together. "Yes," the lizard hissed. "There is no chance of translation error. The hairy Dirtling definitely said the word 'game.'"

Gasterphaz rumbled in amazement, "But, how . . . how did they know?"

6

"A test?" demanded Dr. Wu, her voice peaking on the last syllable. The scientist's almond eyes flashed in anger, and she radiated such violent moral outrage that the printed flowers on her white, cotton dress almost wilted. "What the hell kind of a test was that?"

Dr. Malavade undertook to answer the woman's clamorous question. Calmly, the linguist postulated that it may have been a test *of* us, not *to* us.

Yuki had to think about that. "So, you believe the drones would not have attacked? That this was merely a test to see what humans would do when threatened?"

"You must admit, that is a possibility."

Dr. Wu frowned. A possibility? Yes.

With a gentle whine, Sir John's teleprinter started duplicating copies of the latest news bulletins on the world's reaction to this unforeseen development. Swiftly, the sociologist began writing notes in his personal style of shorthand as the computer paper unfolded from his console with ever increasing speed.

Prof. Rajavur sat with his chin resting in the palm of his left hand. Blankly he stared at the picture of the strutting street gang. Lost in rumination, his keen mind absorbed everything the screen displayed, but drew no useful conclusions. Insufficient data. What was it Sherlock Holmes had said about that? Oh, yes. *Data, Watson, data! I cannot make bricks without clay.*

How true. Thought, then action, was the formula for success. Generally at least . . . general . . .

"Who are they?" he asked Bronson, coming out of his reverie and returning to business.

"The gang? Just a second." The security officer of the FCT retrieved his clipboard from under a code book. Bronson had been busy accessing the data files on the gang from the New York police computers and found the work hard going. His console could take in information a hundred times faster than theirs could disgorge, and some complex maneuvering had been necessary to interface the two systems. "Ah! Here we are, ah . . . Hammer, Whipsaw, Crowbar, Drill, Chisel, and Torch."

"Those are their names?" asked Sigerson, in a stunned voice.

"The only ones they'll answer to."

Prof. Rajavur scowled. "Identify them, please."

Bronson fiddled with the controls on his console until a green circle appeared on the monitor. He moved the marker until he had haloed the face of the tall man in the center of the milling gang. "That hairy fellow there is Hammer," he said loudly for everybody's benefit. "The leader of this rat pack. His rap sheet reads like the encyclopedia of crime, with no convictions. A real smart operator. The police consider him dangerous with a capital D."

With the turn of a dial, the marker moved a bit. "The big guy next to him is Whipsaw— also considered dangerous. The guy's a nut case. A homicidal maniac who is totally under Hammer's control. Whipsaw is loyal to the street gang only because Hammer is in charge."

"Interesting. And how does the ganglord perpetuate this control?" Rajavur asked.

"He feeds him."

"Drugs? Sweets?"

"Innocent bystanders."

Pause. "Oh."

Proceeding onward, the marker came to a devilishly handsome man and the general continued. "Smiley over there is Drill. He's the locksmith for the gang. Gets them into places so they can steal everything not nailed down. Supposed to be pretty good at it, too. Apartment doors, car trunks, store gates. They say he goes through them like a . . ."

"Drill," supplied Dr. Wu, impatiently tapping a pencil on the metal edge of her console. "Okay, Wayne, we get the idea. Who are the rest of these charming people?"

Bronson flipped over a page on his clipboard. "The ugly bald kid is Crowbar."

"The girl?" asked Dr. Malavade in surprise. He had heard of such outlandish tonsorial effects, but had never personally encountered anybody who shaved their head solely for fashion. But then, he didn't really get around much. Aside from the FCT, he mainly associated with fellow scientists, librarians, and the occasional Swedish airline stewardess.

"No, the ugly bald kid with a moustache is Crowbar," answered the unflappable American. As a soldier, he'd seen worse, but only because his nephew was in a punk rock band. "We really don't have too much on this guy. He's only been in New York for a few months. Moved here from Chicago. Rumor has it he killed a fellow gang member out there, but we don't know for sure. The day he left town, the Chicago Police Department's computer room was blown to bits by a 'mysterious' stick of dynamite."

"A coincidence?" asked Rajavur.

Bronson stared at the man. "I—don't—think—so."

Wearily, the diplomat undid his necktie and stuffed it into the coat pocket of his blue suit. "Tell me about the girl."

"Her name is Torch," said General Bronson, shifting his cigar as if it had suddenly acquired a bad taste. "She used to mug people by dousing them with gasoline and threatening to set them on fire unless they paid her, then she'd do it anyway and dance around their flaming bodies—laughing."

Collectively, the FCT made gagging noises.

"Yeah, I agree," sighed the American, in a pained voice. "One of her victims accidentally set Torch's hair on fire, burning it off. She spent months in Bellevue hospital recovering from the burns."

"Did that change her any?" asked Sir John inquisitively, his clinical interest aroused. Often, such accidents were viewed by the mentally unbalanced as divine retribution, and the poor misguided souls hastily mended their ways.

"Change her? You bet it did," said Bronson positively. "The police report states that it made her even meaner than before, and now she uses iron baling hooks to kill people instead of no-lead premium."

Nauseated, the sociologist returned to his collating, his professional interest in the matter more than sated.

With a hop, the marker moved across the screen to a scraggly haired youth possessing remarkable beaverlike teeth. "And that's Chisel," said General Bronson, finishing his list. "Who, in my opinion, is the worst of the lot."

"Why do you say that?" asked Rajavur curiously. "The boy doesn't look like a killer."

"Part of his charm," countered the general, fishing in the pocket of his uniform for a fresh cigar. "Chisel still wouldn't appear very dangerous even as he was cutting your bleeding, liberal heart out. He's a blade man."

Born and raised in Iceland, this statement confused the diplomat. It upset them that the boy was a good skater?

"An expert with knives," explained Malavade to his puzzled chief. Bronson grunted assent.

"The kid's bad news. He's mentally retarded. Actually enjoys cutting people into pieces."

Prof. Rajavur gave a heartfelt sigh and took a sip from his

coffee mug, only to find bitter dregs at the bottom. He hoped that it wasn't prophetic. "Marvelous," he muttered, half to himself. "Simply marvelous."

From behind his bulletproof glass shield, Nicholi had been listening to the conversation of his teammates and he was less than pleased. Their situation had become even more unstable, more explosive. The fate of the entire Earth now rested in the hands of dangerous, antisocial psychopaths. Wryly, the Russian soldier grimaced. *So what else was new?*

* * * * *

Meanwhile, in the glistening white control room of the alien starship, Leader Idow remained unswerving in his conviction.

"No," said the blue humanoid to his shipmates. "They are an innocent road maintenance crew who have been abducted by strange beings from outer space and forced to fight for their lives against weird, undirtly foes. No!" Idow repeated the word for emphasis and pounded the empty air in front of him with his fists, an almost obscene gesture to his species. "They must be calling this a game simply from youthful zeal and the foolish belief that they can win. They probably also think that Right Makes Might."

Mushroom, stone, and lizard laughed heartily at that. *Snorful*! Right makes might. *Horank*! Hot Void, Idow was a funny guy at times.

"The fact that they are treating this as an amusement only serves to heighten the desired effect." Leader Idow paused here for dramatic effect. "So, I *double* my bet!"

A hush fell upon the control room, and Idow waited to see how his associates would react.

"Accepted!" cried Gasterphaz, his rocky fingers feeding the figures into the ship's computer bank. If Idow wanted to throw his money away, well, that was just fine by him! Besides, Idow could afford it. By the Prime Builder, he owned *All That Glitters*. With a bit of luck, the Choron could end up winning the starship and become Leader himself.

Leader Gasterphaz. The very thought made the Choron

feel bolder.

With a vegetable snarl, Boztwank tore a leaf from the spray of foliage in his pot and ate it, a gesture of supreme confidence on his world. "Bah! You don't really think those primitives will actually prevail, do you? Ridiculous! Pass test #2? They won't even survive it!" The mushroom braced himself here, for money was almost as important to him as . . . sex? . . . pink? . . . harassing Trell? But then, what was money for if not to enjoy taking it from others? "I double *my* bet!"

"Done!" whooped Gasterphaz, as gleefully as a Choron could. If anything, this was going to be a profitable trip! With avarice-filled diamond eyes, Gasterphaz rotated his head to glance at Squee, who was standing over by his tech-station methodically scratching at his tail. "And how about you, Communicator?" rumbled the Choron sweetly.

Politely, the lizard inquired about odds.

Mortally insulted, Gasterphaz turned away in stony silence. Odds? The nerve of some beings.

"Test two!" cried Boztwank, noiselessly stamping his invisible feet. "Let's do test #2!"

"Agreed," said Idow, for once harmonizing with his engineer. "Let the *game* begin."

Squee hissed in acknowledgment, touched the necessary controls, and Leader Idow's voice flowed into the test chamber.

* * * * *

"YOU HAVE DONE WELL, DIRTLINGS."

"Get ready," said Hammer to his gang, running nervous fingers through his long, greasy hair. Ever since the gang had been brought aboard this spaceship, he'd known that they were in for the fight of their lives. Happened often enough in the movies. On some television shows, too.

"THIS WAS BUT THE FIRST OF YOUR TESTS . . . NOW, LOOK TO YOUR LEFT."

Expecting the worst, the Deckers looked. Fifty meters away from them, a section of the curved wall was breaking apart, the pieces of white metal sliding into each other. Exposed was an ominous black door edged with silver bolts. It disengaged with muffled thuds, the metal portal swinging aside. Beyond was a dimly lit tunnel in which, in rapid succession, a spiked portcullis lifted into the ceiling, another dropped into the floor, a shimmering energy curtain faded away, and a metal screen opened wide, spreading its plates like a blossoming flower. Through this impressive array of doors, there shambled a creature, the likes of which no human had ever seen. When clear, the tunnel closed, permanently sealing the monster in with the street gang. They stared with bulging eyes at the . . . thing that came toward them with slow, sure steps.

"THIS IS YOUR SECOND TEST. . . . FIGHT, DIRTLINGS . . . FIGHT AND KILL FOR THE LIFE OF YOUR PLANET. . . . FIGHT *THE QUATRALYAN*!"

It was Chisel, having the lowest mentality of the group, who broke first. Clutching his sides, the boy fell to his knees, laughing hysterically. Crowbar smirked. Whipsaw guffawed. Torch and Drill clutched each other, hooting uncontrollably, and pointed shaking fingers at the ridiculously fat chickendog who approached them, its jelly-belly body jiggling and bouncing with every step it took. The lumpy, featureless potato-head regarded the gang curiously, and then a tiny flap of a mouth dropped open and it gargled at them, sending the gang into fresh gales of laughter.

"HA!" barked Whipsaw, the scarred mass of tissue that was his face assuming the unusual position of a friendly smile.

"W-what's it going to do?" gasped Drill, breathlessly struggling not to fall to the floor. "S-sit on us?"

"Damn thing's uglier than me!" clowned Chisel, holding his sides in pain, his wits never sharper.

"And your mama," said Crowbar, grudgingly joining in on the fun.

"I ain't laughed so hard since that ambulance crashed into the orphanage," giggled Torch, wiping tears from her eyes.

"HA!" repeated Whipsaw, as ever a man of few words.

Only Hammer did not join in on the merriment; a fact that both Gasterphaz and Nicholi found noteworthy. The street tough knew that looks could be deceiving. Nuns don't seem like much, but they're wildcats when cornered. And those crosses . . . whew!

"Whipsaw!" barked the ganglord, his eyes never leaving the alien creature for a second.

Still chuckling, the gang member wiped his runny nose on the sleeve of his leather jacket. "Yeah, boss?" he asked.

"Kill it," said Hammer.

And the legbreaker surged forward, his heavy motorcycle boots slapping loudly against the cushioned floor, pushing his three hundred-plus pounds on with astonishing speed. A freight train with a mohawk, a Mack truck in leather, Whipsaw roared like a primordial beast and closed in on the corpulent alien, his weight lifter's arms ready to block any escape attempt on its part. The street gang cackled in glee. This was going to be great! Whipsaw was three times the size of that cheesy alien mutt. This was going to be over in seconds!

It was.

As the big man reached for the Quatralyan's throat, two slim tentacles shot from the creature's feathery chest spearing him through the stomach. The Bloody Deckers' laughter died when they saw the dripping limbs fingering the back of their friend's jacket. With a dreadful cry, Whipsaw tried to pull away and the Quatralyan stabbed a third tentacle into his body. The gang member writhed in agony, blood gushing from his hideous wounds. Another tentacle lanced out and his knees buckled. Then another . . . and another . . . and another . . . and another.

Abruptly, the Quatralyan yanked its arms from the street tough's form, and Whipsaw crumpled to the floor. Daintily, the chickendog stepped over the spreading pools of red as more and more tentacles snaked out of its impossible body— ten, twenty, thirty. It became a Medusa's head of wiggling limbs on doggy paws. The living nightmare turned its potato-head toward the street gang and fiendishly gargled at them again.

"Waste that thing!" snarled Hammer, drawing an Army

Colt .45 from under his jacket and the Bloody Deckers attacked.

Razor sharp throwing stars, shurikens, appeared and disappeared in Chisel's talented hands. The Quatralyan dodged the whirling blades and came at the boy. Twin switchblades *snikked* into existence and the young blademaster circled to the left. Torch, her hands full of iron hooks, moved to the right. Drill pulled a stiletto from his boot and charged straight at the monster. Crowbar produced a motorcycle chain and twirled it to near invisibility as he deliberately stepped in front of Hammer.

"What the—? Get outta the way!" yelled the ganglord furiously, but Crowbar pretended not to hear him. Hammer tried to angle past the man, and again Crowbar stepped right in his path, preventing Hammer from using his pistol. This couldn't be any better. Right on TV he would show the world that Crowbar didn't need a gun to make him tough, and bikers would flock to him. He'd have his own gang then. Crowbar's Commandos! No more a nobody. He'd be the boss. Yeah, the time was ripe. Time for Crowbar!

Hammer eased his grip on the pistol. No way. Crowbar couldn't be stupid enough to be doing this on purpose. Got to be a mistake. The ganglord thumbed back the hammer on his weapon and tried once more for a clear shot.

With a martial arts *kia*, Drill threw himself at the Quatralyan, who hopped out of the way. Hitting the floor and rolling, Drill twisted about and came up swinging, right where the creature was supposed to be. But wasn't. Sensing a trap, the Quatralyan had darted between Chisel and Torch. Neither of them was close enough to stab it, though both tried. For an instant, the beast was in the clear.

Hammer leveled his automatic, and Crowbar again got in the way. The ganglord cursed violently. Crowbar allowed himself a quick victory grin and released his chain, the four feet of linked steel flashing across the room like a silver arrow that slammed the pudgy alien off its feet in a tangle of limbs. The Quatralyan tried to stand and failed. Weakly, it bleated in pain. Charging in from every direction came the gang.

Grinning openly, Crowbar unwound a second chain from his waist and went to help with the kill, his traditional biker's weapon expertly wrapped tight around a scarred fist.

The Quatralyan poked a lumpy head from the jumble of its body and mournfully bleated again. Oddly, no damage was showing. No blood. Hammer didn't like that and got a hunch.

"Watch out!" he yelled in warning. "The dust mop's doing a suck play!"

Not completely stupid, Crowbar heeded the ganglord and fired off his second chain in a hip shot that cannonballed toward the ropey alien. Jerking aside, the Quatralyan let the metal missile pass by, not wishing to be hit again by that strange weapon. The monster gargled nastily and ran to kill Crowbar, the closest of its enemies. Hammer tried to zero in on it anyway, and the creature moved to the far side of the gang member, as if somehow it understood what the function of a gun was.

Crowbar then unlimbered his last weapon. From inside his pants pocket he withdraw an Italian gravity knife and waited for the attack. More blade than handle, the weapon was like a butcher's axe, made for chopping. His hand held high, the grim man braced himself to cut the thing in two with a single stroke. Dr. Guillotine meets the Spaghetti Monster.

But flashing knives from Chisel bracketed the beast, forcing it back. Then, in another of his mad rolls, Drill sliced open both of the creature's hind legs. The Quatralyan screamed in real pain now—no mere bleat, but a steam whistle keen that icepicked Crowbar's head as he chopped down. Several of the monster's tentacles hit the floor, the stumps oozing yellow.

Off balance, the chickendog stabbed holes in the gang member's flapping jacket, the rigid limbs scoring bloody trenches along his ribs. Crowbar stabbed with a knife not designed for the purpose and missed. The Quatralyan reared, its snake nest body poised to strike. Death filled Crowbar's eyes, and Torch buried her iron hooks in the monster's plump rump.

The Quatralyan shrieked like a million smoke detectors, and the laughing woman jumped back, but not fast enough. Pivoting, the wounded creature rammed all of its remaining arms straight into the human. As they jerked out, blood fountained from her riddled body and the woman fell limply to the floor. Just then, the thunderous reports of the Army .45 filled the air as Hammer finally got an unobstructed view. Yellow blood and feathers sprayed into the air under the impact of the soft lead bullets and the ganglord brutally fired again and again, the heavy slugs from the booming Colt punching the screaming alien across the room, leaving oily smears on the white floor. Its death scream peaked the ultrasonic . . . and then abruptly stopped as Drill brutally slit the monster's throat with his stiletto.

Helplessly, the world watched as the mangled pile of flesh that had once been Torch reached out a hand to her chief. Hammer rushed over. Kneeling by her side, he took the woman's hand in his and gently gave it a squeeze. She raised her head to speak, causing more blood to well from her hideous wounds. Hammer bent close, and she whispered something too soft for him to hear. Then her hand went stiff in his, her body spasmed, and Torch died, laying sprawled in a pool of blood and intestines.

Tenderly, the ganglord closed her only intact eye and bowed his head in sorrow. Chisel turned away from the scene, ashamed of his unmanly tears. Stiffly, Drill walked to the Quatralyan's body, retrieved his friend's hooks and lay them next to her battered corpse. Crowbar, showing great wisdom, stayed in the background.

For a moment, nobody spoke.

Then Hammer stood, his face a cold mask of fury. He had the blood of a good friend staining one hand, and a smoking .45 in the other. The youth squeezed those scarred hands into hard fists and glared hatefully at the clean white ceiling so far, so goddamn far, out of reach.

"NEXT!" he roared defiantly.

7

"Magnificent! They were magnificent!" squealed Boztwank, beside himself with pleasure. The joyful mushroom flew across the control room to congratulate his leader. "Oh, I do apologize, Idow. You were absolutely correct. These Dirtlings are wonderful. Wonderful!"

"Yes," agreed Squee with a toothy smile. "They are very good, indeed."

But the starship's leader heard neither of them.

"A distance weapon," he muttered, faintly echoing himself. Idow leaned forward in his seat, the chair automatically adjusting itself to the humanoid's new position. "They have a distance weapon. Gasterphaz, why was I not informed of this?"

"Because I did not know," replied the Choron protector honestly. "Metal is metal, and they're covered with it. It's in their mouths, nose, ears . . . any orifice you care to name. And what is not hidden inside their clothing is holding it together. My sensors indicated no weapon-grade energy sources, so I reported them unarmed." Gasterphaz's veneer cracked. "Sorry."

Idow brushed the matter aside. "Accepted, my friend. So tell me, what weapons *do* they have with them?"

Thoughtfully, the rocky giant drummed his fingers on his control board, rhythmically denting the metal. "Well . . ."

"Thin knives, thick knives, folding knives, throwing knives, round throwing knives," interjected Squee, reading from a list that he had made during the battle. "Chains, short hooks, the projectile weapon . . . which by the way I want for my collection . . . sss . . . I believe that is everything they carry."

"One of the edged weapons is not properly a knife," sang Boztwank, his electronic pot weaving and dipping in a ritual dance of joy. "Better list it as a cleaver."

In the ensuing feeling of good-fellowship, Squee made the appropriate notation on his list, instead of ignoring anything the mushroom said as he normally did. Besides, to a collector, there was no such thing as useless information.

"And the small Dirtling stole a spike from one of our drones in the first test," added Gasterphaz, trying to salvage his shattered reputation as a protector. Though he rarely used them himself, weapons were his speciality.

Squee clamped his elongated jaw down on his forked tongue in concentration. "And he used it against the Quatralyan?" asked the lizard excitedly.

"No, he still has the spike on him."

Annoyed, Squee crossed out his last notation. Okay, maybe there was such a thing as useless information.

In reflection, Idow toyed with the silver microphone of his viewscreen. "Boztwank, is Trell still in the reactor core?"

"Yes, my Leader," replied the fungi gaily. "Why? What has he done wrong now?"

"Nothing," mused the blue being. "But get him out of there and have him send in the cleaning robot. I want the arena immaculate for the next test."

Gasterphaz perked up at this. "Suitable for recording and adding to our video library?" asked the Choron shrewdly.

Idow just smiled.

Excellent, thought the protector. The third test had always been his favorite to watch. "Then I hereby announce that the bank is closed. All bets must ride." This announcement astonished nobody, as Chorons were notoriously cheap. "And I shall prepare the warobot for immediate use. Half-speed as usual?"

"Let's try full speed this time," suggested Squee coldbloodedly, the luminescent controls of his tech-station brightening at their master's anticipation. "I think our Dirtlings can handle it."

The ship's leader had a momentary vision of small furry creatures being dropped into an active food processor and he shivered in pleasure.

Idow nodded regally, the fringe of indigo hair around his face bobbing from the motion. "Let it be done."

Upon hearing this, Boztwank scooted back to his post. Wow. Full speed. They had never done this before. Eeee! This was going to more fun than watching garbage rot.

* * * * *

His teleprinter finally at rest, Sir John removed his reading glasses and polished them with the handkerchief that jutted from the breast pocket of his tailored, three-piece, gray suit. The handkerchief was silk, monogrammed with the designer's name, and the color of the fabric perfectly matched his blue silk shirt. Then he blew his nose on the handkerchief and threw it in the wastebasket beside his console. These were merely his work clothes.

"Would you like it straight, or condensed?" the millionaire Scotsman asked the room at large.

"Would we like what, straight or condensed?" asked Dr. Wu, strips of computer paper littering the floor at her feet. The Chinese physicist had tied her console in with the computers at Cal Tech in an effort to discover how to crack the alien's forceshield. As her printer reeled off another failed equation, she ripped the sheet free, made a note of something interesting in the formula on her clipboard, then crumpled the paper into a ball and threw it in the general direction of her wastepaper basket. So far, the score was wastepaper basket—zero, floor—thirty seven.

"World reaction to the events we have just witnessed," politely explained Courtney.

"Condensed please, Jonathan. No lecture today," said Prof. Rajavur, laying aside his earphones and giving Dr. Malavade the go-ahead signal.

Enabling a never before used section of his console, the linguist started diligently tapping complex commands into a computer keyboard.

The sociologist cleared his throat. "Ahem . . . hurrah for the good guys."

Rajavur spun about in his chair. "I beg your pardon."

"Well, you wanted it condensed."

"Elucidate," ordered the diplomat.

"It's the street gang," explained Sir John, looking embarassed. "The majority of the world is cheering for them. The Bloody Deckers are heroes."

"Heroes?" stormed General Bronson, slamming down the reciever of his hush phone so hard that the instrument rang, even though it was not equipped with a bell. "They're loonies!"

"Heroic loonies," corrected Courtney. "So nobody cares."

"Well, Bill Paterson cares," countered the American soldier.

Sir John raised a questioning eyebrow. "And he is?"

"The police captain for Manhattan Central. He just issued arrest warrants on each gang member for carrying a concealed weapon. Apparently, the man has been trying to nail the Deckers for the past seven years. Captain Paterson is reported to have turned a cartwheel when Hammer pulled that gun in front of two billion eyewitnesses."

"Well, I wish him luck in serving it."

Bronson gave a half-smile. "Yeah, me too."

* * * * *

Taking their time, the Deckers went about the messy task of

placing their dead friends side by side and removing their leather jackets to cover their mutilated bodies. Afterward, Chisel scurried about the test chamber recovering most of his knives. He still had that blade he'd stolen from the little robot. A secret weapon, yeah. Cool. Crowbar offered his spare chain to Drill. It was accepted and together the two men were working the kinks from the metal lengths, getting ready for the next attack.

Meanwhile, Hammer dug fresh bullets from his pocket, loaded his clip, and slid it into the butt of the automatic pistol where it locked into place with a satisfying click. Eight more rounds and the Colt would be useless. He had to make every shot count, even though one of the bullets was on reserve. The ganglord had talked briefly to Crowbar, telling the stupid sonofabitch that if he ever disobeyed orders again, he would blow the man's freaking head off. Torch was dead because of him, and the only reason Crowbar was still sucking in air was that the gang needed every stud they had to get out of this mess alive. But, a single mistake and—pow!

The hissing noise of the arena's weird door opening made the Deckers glance up from their weapons, and though they had faced death a thousand times before, today the street gang dropped their jaws. This next test was going to be a grade A, bottled and bonded, four star mother.

Stepping away from the closing wall was a giant humanoid robot. The machine man stood at least twenty feet tall, with a shiny body made of smooth green armor. In its right hand, the awesome robot held a big metal bar. It looked like a telephone pole veined with energy cables, and there was a worn, pitted nozzle at its lower end. Nobody had to tell them that this was plainly a weapon of power.

Without any preamble, the deadly machine began to walk straight toward them.

"DECKERS!" yelled Hammer, and the gang rallied to the cry. Bravely, they charged their newest opponent, ready to fight to the death, because Deckers don't surrender.

Curiously, the cleaning robot peered down at the beings

running toward it and wondered what the problem was. The test chamber was a mess, yes, but no more so than usual.

Crowbar and Drill reached the green giant first. They arced around the machine's legs, whipping the robot with their chains as they passed. The thin plastic armor spiderwebbed under the violent blows and bits sprinkled to the floor, exposing an inner framework of struts and circuitry. The gang took heart from this and bellowed their name again even louder.

Dispassionately, the machine scanned the damage. The waterproof casing of its legs—wasn't—anymore. With a robotic sigh, the janitor laid aside its electronic mop and bent over to retrieve the broken pieces of itself.

In an overhand throw, Chisel released his pride and joy, a two and a half pound, stainless steel Bowie knife. The Texas toothpick whizzed through the air and smashed into the robot's chest, lodging firmly between a circuit cube and a power cable. Instantly, the machine flashed into overload, its control relays systematically burning out. Blind and deaf, the dizzy robot noisily crashed to its knees and sent an urgent plea for help to Those-Who-Command.

* * * * *

"They're doing *what?*" throated Idow, rising from his chair.

"Attacking the cleaning robot . . ." said Squee, his voice fading away as his shipmates scrambled to their tech-stations. Oh, nobody ever listened to him.

Angrily, Leader Idow slapped the switch activating the microphone on his control board. "Hey, you waste-heads! Cut that out!"

In the test chamber the translation came as . . .

* * * * *

"STOP, FOOLISH ONES."

As always, the Deckers paid no attention to what someone in authority told them to do. Crowbar grabbed the robot's staff and dragged the pole away, almost straining a gut in the process. Fighting to retain its balance, the mechanical man reached out a hand to steady itself. Hammer easily dodged the clumsy attack, and aimed the barrel of his .45 automatic pistol right between the sightless eyes of the rapidly disintegrating janitor.

"CEASE THESE ACTIONS . . . THAT IS ONLY THE CLEANING ROBOT."

"Bull!" roared Hammer rebelliously, pulling the trigger.

With a jolt, the mechanical's head kicked back. In vain, the machine tried to stabilize its internal systems as two more steel-jacketed rounds were pumped into the sparking remains of its face. The ganglord was gambling here, for even the street punk knew that the brain could be anywhere in a robot—the chest, legs, arms, anywhere at all.

But, in a cleaning robot it was judged most prudent to keep the machine's delicate brain as far away as possible from the caustic reagents and potentially destructive chemicals that it handled on a daily basis. So the brain *was* in the head. For protection.

As dead as it could be, the robot stiffly pancaked onto its face, the lovely green armor peeling away from its overheating nuclear stomach like the leaves of a murdered artichoke. Fat crackling sparks crawled over the broken machine, smoke poured from its joints, and a leg fell off.

Then, in crude humor, Chisel unzipped his pants and contemptuously relieved himself on the fallen Goliath.

* * * * *

Utterly flabbergasted, the aliens couldn't believe what they had just seen. This was almost beyond their comprehension. Exactly how primitive were these guys?

"By the Prime Builder's Waste Products," gulped Idow, slumping backward into his formfitting chair.

* * * * *

"Holy crap," gulped General Bronson, slumping backward into his padded swivel chair.

A prude at heart, Prof. Rajavur took umbrage at the mild profanity. "Really, Wayne, your language—"

"Is most appropriate," interrupted Dr. Wu. The scientist was utterly flabbergasted. This was almost beyond her comprehension. "Holy crap, indeed."

* * * * *

Chisel's base spectacle brought forth unexpected results. The smoke from the robot thickened, the sparks got fatter, and a vicious humming started. Justifiably frightened, the gang quickly retreated to safety.

"Hey, chief," whispered Drill, crouching low, with the rest of the gang following his lead. "You know what? I think that thing is going to—"

It did.

The starship shook as the tortured works of the broken robot whoofed into a fireball. Tendrils of smoke and shrapnel filled the air. As the force of the detonation knocked the Deckers prone, the gang gripped the floor like Moslems in Mecca. Every warning light in the starship winked on, klaxons sounded, bells clanged, power lines snapped, and the viewscreens in the control room went black.

* * * * *

Suddenly, the FCT found itself staring at the outside of the alien ship.

The word "damn," was said in six different languages.

* * * * *

As the force of the detonation dissipated, the rattled street gang slowly got to their feet.

"Everybody okay?" asked Hammer, straightening his leather jacket and checking for damage. Nyah, the coat was fine.

With a grunt, the ever-dapper Drill tucked his sweaty T-shirt back into his worn denims. "Yeah. Sure. I just love getting dumped on my butt by exploding robots."

"Me, too!" cried Chisel, in simple-minded delight. "Let's do it again!"

In a friendly manner, Hammer gave the boy a smack on the

head. "Joking. He was only joking, pinhead."

"Oh, okay."

"I'm fine, too," winced Crowbar, gingerly touching the raw scrapes on his rib cage.

Drill loftily sniffed at him. "Like, who cares if you got a hole in you or not, dude?"

The ganglord started to tell the two of them to stuff a sock in it, when an odd thought occurred to him. A hole in him? . . . The gag had worked in an old spy film he'd seen once. Maybe. Just maybe.

"Follow me!" cried Hammer, and he sprinted for the blast area, his gang close on his heels.

"What's up, chief?" asked Drill, effortlessly keeping abreast of his commander.

"Cross your fingers," said the hairy youth, and the panting Chisel did. Both hands.

Hot, acrid smoke lay thick in the area, and the Deckers had to tread carefully so as not to trip on any of the fused machine parts or chunks of green armor that littered the blackened floor. The place looked like a tuna melt left too long in the oven. And the smell was worse than a wino's kiss.

After a quick glance, Hammer grimaced. Damn, he thought, guess my idea's for snot. Vexed, he kicked at a half-melted lump of robot, and the startled youth saw the hundredweight piece of metal disappear from view, shortly followed by a loud clang. Wary of their footing, the Deckers advanced closer to the spot and, sure enough, there was a gaping hole in the floor. Through it they saw a corridor on the ship level below them. The street gang needed no further prompting. Heedless of the hot, jagged metal that ringed their escape route, the Bloody Deckers scrambled down the hole and raced out of sight.

*   *   *   *   *

Replacing the blown fuses in his control board, Squee activated the video cameras in the arena and hissed in horror when he saw the bilevel view inside the devastated test chamber.

"Gone!" he raucously informed the control room. "The primitives are gone!"

"Mrmph," said Leader Idow unintelligibly, absorbed in the task of recalibrating his navigational equipment. Gasterphaz had lifted the lid of his tech-station and was working on the internal circuitry, bent over at the waist in an angle impossible for any species not possessing an endo- and ectoskeleton as did his. "A pity," rumbled the Choron. "But that blast could have damaged even me."

Frantically, the lizard danced about. "No-no! Not dead, gone-escaped, gone!"

With amazing speed, Gasterphaz freed himself from the maze of wiring. "The primitives are loose?"

Idow dropped an electro-wrench. "*Loose aboard my ship?*" he throated, using both of his mouths.

"Alive?" screamed Boztwank. Squee said yes and the mushroom fained to swoon. This was terrible. He couldn't believe it! So the fungi pinked himself, and he still couldn't believe it.

Gasterphaz slammed shut the lid of his tech-station, switched on the anti-intruder systems and prepared for personal combat.

Squee located Trell, alerted the technician to the situation and ordered him to go hide.

Boztwank keyed the starship's reactor to 20/20, sealed the ship, and set his squirter on emergency sequence.

Leader Idow, however, calmly reclined in his chair and rubbed a pale blue hand across a pale blue cheek. Well, well, he cynically thought to himself. It appears that there was going to be a third test today.

Only this one he and his crew had to pass.

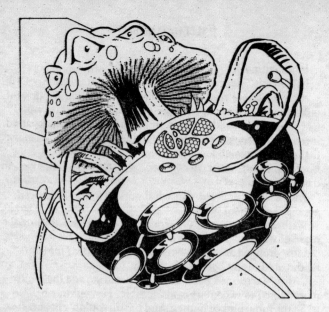

8

Slowly, a human head eased its way around the corner of a white passageway and daringly looked this way and that. Nothing was in sight but another white passageway with blank white walls. It was exactly like every other corridor in the goofy ship. The gang could have been going in circles, although they had been trying very hard not to do that.

"Clear," panted Drill, and the street gang hurried past him. At the next corner, Chisel took the point position and ventured his head into the corridor beyond.

"Clear," announced the youth, and the process repeated.

Ever since their escape, the Bloody Deckers had been dodging and ducking through miles and miles of crazy white corridors, positive that somebody must be chasing after them. But, so far nothing happened. It was a nice change from the alleys of New York, but where the hell was everybody? Hammer knew that time was short and the gang had to do something clever, fast. Every science-fiction movie he had ever seen told him that much.

"Go left," he ordered Chisel at the next intersection. "Drill, take the right. And keep your eyes peeled for an air vent. Should be easy enough to spot on these damn white walls."

"Gotcha," said the locksmith with a wink, and he departed.

Chisel, though, seemed uncertain what to do, so Hammer turned the boy about. "That way, idiot."

The young blade master toothily smiled at Hammer in thanks and tiptoed away as quietly as possible in his Army surplus boots.

"What if we don't find an air vent cause there ain't any?" challenged Crowbar in an insolent whisper, so close behind the ganglord that his bad breath actually swamped his body odor. "Then whatta we do, huh?"

Hammer glared at his personal troublemaker. "Then we keep searching till we find an air vent," he snapped. "Now shut your freaking mouth or I'll shut it for you."

Just then, Drill psst'd at them from around a white corner, interrupting the impromptu detente. "Hey, guys! Over here!"

The gang mobbed up, and sure enough, there, set flush to the white wall, was an air vent. About a meter square, the vent was covered with an ivory-colored metal lattice that was fastened shut with some kooky bolts. Drill studied them with the eye of a professional, frowned, then smiled and pulled a lockpick and a rat-tail comb from his jacket pocket. Deftly, he began to remove the bolts. During the work, Hammer and Crowbar assumed defensive positions on either side of him. Soon the Deckers would be safe, concealed inside the walls like fugitive cockroaches. The ganglord knew that the aliens would never find them there. He'd seen this trick work in a dozen movies.

* * * * *

"What do you mean you can't find them?!" screeched Boztwank, swooping over to the starship's protector and beating his fronds against the rocky giant's back. "You incompetent bungler! There are dirty stinking primitives loose in our ship, and you can't find them?"

Facing his tech-station, Gasterphaz failed to notice the leafy assault and went on viewing a panorama of pictures on his screen, each showing empty white corridor after empty white corridor.

"Well?" demanded Idow vehemently, his bushy eyebrows alternately flexing in annoyance.

The mountainous Choron sadly shook his head. "The explosion wrecked a minor junction box, and I've lost control of the cameras. I'm rerouting the system, but not even Trell could fix this quickly."

"So?"

"So, either they are moving very fast and dodging my security cameras as if they've been doing this their whole lives, which is most improbable, or else they've metamorphosed into white paint," stated Gasterphaz simply. "I cannot understand it. A road maintenance crew should not be able to do this." The rocky giant raised his hands in disgust. "If anyone thinks he can operate my equipment more efficiently, then please do so. I cannot find them."

Maintaining a firm grip on his temper, Leader Idow took a breath and slowly counted from one to eight.

"Well, they haven't physically left the ship," argued Boztwank petulantly, his force field hands twisting dials. "None of the air locks have been opened. The storeroom hasn't been entered, the engine room . . . Bah!" Boztwank hit the manual override and ordered his pot to pink him again. This was getting serious. Had the primitives evaporated into thin air?

"No attempt has been made to broadcast a message," added Squee unhappily. "So I haven't been able to triangulate on them. Besides, nothing they have could penetrate our force shield."

Idow's eyes formed crescent moons. "Are you sure?" he muttered deep in his throats. "Consider the facts: they smuggled a distance weapon aboard; they escaped from the test chamber; and now they elude us with the greatest of ease. Are these the acts of primitives?"

A coward at heart, or at the fibrous lump that served for a heart with his fungoid species, Boztwank understood the implied hint. "Not . . . the Great Golden Ones?" he asked in quaking fear.

"Perhaps."

"Foolishness," boomed Gasterphaz, his immobile face never more so. "Two of their own kind lay dead in the test chamber. Would even the Great Golden Ones—"

"Yes," interrupted Squee, with a couple of extra Ss tacked on to the word. "They would. The Great Golden Ones would do almost anything to capture us alive."

"A trap?" mused the Choron thoughtfully. That possibility had not occurred to him. But then, until his race had joined the galactic society, they had never heard of the word.

Impatiently, Boztwank rocked his pot to and fro. "The gas! We must use the Omega Gas!" he cried. "Flood the ship. Nothing can resist Omega Gas. Not even the Great Golden Ones!"

"You hope," added Squee, clutching his bare tail to his uniformed chest as if for protection. Omega Gas. Dangerous stuff. Just talking about it made him feel itchy. But then, breathing made him feel itchy. And horny. Too bad this planet was populated by mammals.

"And what about Trell?" asked Idow, casually leaning back in his chair. "Is he to die along with the primitives?"

Boztwank opened his mouth to speak, and then closed it with a snap. What a pleasant surprise! "A pity, but yes. He must become a sacrifice for the good of the ship."

"He is also the only technician we have," noted Gasterphaz practically. "Maybe you want to do every dirty little job that keeps this ship operating properly, but I do not." The gargantuan protector frowned, an act which resembled a landslide at a gravel pit. "Idow, we must save him!"

"We can try. Squee, contact Trell and have him take refuge in a gasproof compartment until we tell him it is safe to leave."

"Affirmative, Leader."

"Gasterphaz, how long will it take to warm the Omega Gas?"

"Nine hundred seconds."

"Then begin at once. Boztwank, start to seal off everything organic that the gas would destroy—clothes, food, us. . . ."

"Us, too? Oh, how clever of you, my Leader," mocked the mushroom from his tech-station. "Why, I never would have thought of that." The closing of the armored security door punctuated his words.

Eat waste products, toadstool, thought Idow hostilely. "Gasterphaz, where is your warobot?"

"Outside the test chamber. Why?"

"Ready that, too. Just in case."

* * * * *

Barely a meter square, the ventilation shaft was a cramped fit, and the Deckers were constantly bumping into each other as they crawled along the seamless metal tube in single file.

"You fart on me again and you're a dead man, Drill," growled Crowbar from the darkness at the end of the line.

Without a word, the locksmith passed gas again in retaliation.

"Why you—!"

"Clam up," Hammer told them tersely. "Or I'll beat both your heads in! Hey, Chisel!" he called to the worn denim pants in front of him. "What do ya see?"

"A room," echoed back the youngster. "Full of machines and stuff. Like a boiler factory. You want I should check it out?"

"Nyah, keep going."

The gang had been in the air shaft for only a few minutes before they started encountering dozens of vents that led to various rooms. Funny that they hadn't found any in the corridors. Each vent offered them an avenue of escape, but escape to where? The Deckers needed an exit out of the ship, access to the control room, or something useful like that. But so far, they'd only come across more rooms similar to the last one, and it had more fancy equipment in it than a high school!

Then, unexpectedly, Drill butted into Hammer, which made him bump into Chisel. Irked, the ganglord swatted the man behind him. "Watch where you're going, stupid!" he growled.

"Wasn't my fault, chief," denied the gang member with hurt innocence in his voice. "Crowbar slammed into me."

"You lying turd. I did not."

"Did."

"Not."

"DID!"

"NOT!"

Hammer clicked off the safety of his pistol, and the argument came to an abrupt halt. Ahead of him, Chisel was peeking through the next grill. The light coming through the metal lattice was bright enough for him to see that the kid was grinning like a pimp on payday. "What is it this time, pinhead?" the ganglord demanded. "Their bathroom?"

Almost bursting with excitement, the boy turned and blinked at the darkness of the air shaft below him. "Geez, Hammer, you won't believe what's in here!" he gushed happily. "I think it's their . . . their . . . ," he fumbled for the word. "You know, what the army has . . . an *armory*. It's their armory!"

Hammer quickly shouldered Chisel out of his way and peeked in for himself. Sure enough, the walls of the white room on the other side of the grill were filled with racks holding swords and spears and crazy, weird things with handles and slings. Most of the weapons he couldn't recognize, but the street punk could tell what some of them were. Rifles and pistols. Futuristic rifles and pistols. His mouth watered at the prospect.

"Jackpot!" breathed Hammer, unable to believe their good luck. "Hot damn, now we're cooking!" Briskly, he crawled aside to let Drill get to work on removing the grill.

* * * * *

"They're at it again," sighed Squee.

Idow almost fell out of his chair. "What? Who? Where?"

"The United Dirtling Welcome Committee," explained the lizard, exasperated at the natives' persistence. Why didn't they just watch the broadcast and . . . oh, he wasn't broadcasting anymore. Oops. "This must be the *Nth* time they've called. And on one of the higher bands of the electromagnetic spectrum, too. Actually, that's pretty impressive for primitives."

"Answer them!" barked a voice of command.

The aliens recoiled in surprise, because it wasn't Leader Idow who had spoken, but Boztwank. Furiously, the fungi glared at his shipmates.

"Answer them!" he shrilled, gliding closer. "Let's end this charade! The tests are ruined, primitives are loose on the ship, we're about to lose our beloved Trell . . . ," A fake tear welled from a lidless eye. ". . . so let's talk to this Welcome group, give them The Speech, and ruin their day, too! *Let's ruin everybody's day!*" finished Boztwank on a slightly hysterical note.

Using only a moment to consider the idea, the rock, lizard, and humanoid decided to go with the mushroom's plan. Yes, it was time to make the whole planet miserable.

Impatiently, Leader Idow buttoned his uniform into a more presentable appearance and fluffed his eyebrows. "Squee, are you ready to broadcast?"

The communicator grinned from gill to gill. "On the mark, my Leader . . . *ss*-three . . . two . . . one . . ."

* * * * *

"PEOPLE OF DIRT . . . ATTENTION."

Startled, the FCT raised their heads to see the alien called Idow sneering down at them from the wall monitor. General Bronson removed the cigar from his mouth, Sir John put his glasses on, and Mohad exploded from the bathroom. Holding his pants closed with one hand, he leaped over the iron railing, dashed past his teammates, and threw himself onto his console.

"Recording," he gasped breathlessly, jabbing a button.

"Get ready," Rajavur warned the linguist. "This could be what we've been waiting for."

Trying to catch his breath, Dr. Malavade just nodded. Everything was as ready as it would ever be. Now, if only luck was on their side and the equipment would perform as desired.

Fiercely, the blue being on the wall monitor scowled at the First Contact Team. His shoulders were straight, his eyes wide, his uniform misbuttoned.

He's worried about something, noted Dr. Wu, absentmindedly fingering the buttons on her own clothing. But what? Us? Must be. Surely not the street gang.

"I AM SORRY TO REPORT TO YOU THAT THE TEST SUBJECTS ARE—"

"Now!" ordered Rajavur, and Dr. Malavade hit a switch. Instantly, a high-pitched squealing replaced Idow's words. The alien continued to talk, oblivious to the fact that his words weren't reaching anybody.

A minute passed. Then two.

"Well, Johnny?" asked General Bronson.

Hesitantly, the sociologist smiled. "It's . . . yes. I believe it's working. The world is demanding to know what's going on, but no one suspects that we are jamming the alien's transmission."

Rajavur appeared greatly relieved." Then the rioting we feared . . . ?"

"Will probably not occur."

Dr. Wu let out the breath she had been unconsciously holding. "Thank God," said the scientist.

The radio jamming of what the FCT guessed to be the alien's pronouncement of Earth's destruction was Nicholi's idea. It was the old idea that what you don't know, can't hurt you. Worked all the time in Russia. If the aliens actually could destroy the Earth, then at least mankind would go out with dignity and not as a howling, fear-crazed mob. Nicholi had simply telephoned the notion to Rajavur, and the professor had immediately set Mohad to work on the plan.

Gigantic dish antennae had been erected on top of every building facing the alien ship. Satellites were shifted in their orbits, moving rather close to a certain golden refrigerator. Upon Mohad's signal, everything but the refrigerator had vomited forth a powerful electronic caterwauling that blasted the alien's transmission off the air. Their message had never left Central Park.

People everywhere were fiddling with their TV sets, wondering what the hell was going on. Damn things always broke just when you need them. A few people, exceptionally clever or paranoid, suspected government intervention and tried to do something about it, but anyone who could, wouldn't, and anyone who would, couldn't.

Down in Australia, however, the hastily appointed French translator to Parliament was having trouble convincing the government that this new radio gargling was a jamming field of some kind and not an obscure form of the Gaulic tongue. The Aussies, of course, did not believe him, having dealt with the French before.

Idow scowled at Earth for one last time, flexed his bushy eyebrows, and left the screen in a swirl of color. Mohad waited a few seconds more, just to be sure, and then let blessed silence washed across the globe.

"Do you think it worked?" asked Rajavur hopefully.

Courtney shrugged. "Impossible to say at the moment. But, I would guess—and it's only a guess, mind you—yes."

* * * * *

Leader Idow clicked off his microphone and settled back in his deliciously soft chair. So much for Dirt. Within minutes, there would be a worldwide panic, and the planet's civilization would soon begin to collapse. He had done this many times before. The Speech always worked. That's why it was *THE SPEECH*. Lovingly, it told the story of an invasion fleet coming to ray-blast Dirt into a cinder—with lava rain falling from the sky, volcanoes, tidal waves, death, destruction, famine! Whee!

The Speech was woven whole-cloth from the essence of nightmares. Idow had willingly paid a fortune to have it written for him, but as he had killed the author immediately afterward, he received a full refund, death being the only sensible way to deal with writers. Leader Idow didn't even have to read The Speech anymore. He knew it by hearts.

Ah, Idow thought happily, the poor Dirtlings must be going mad by now. There would be mass destruction, buildings on fire, warfare in the streets, rape, murder, suicide! And every brutal act would be lovingly recorded in quintaphonic 3-D for our later viewing pleasure.

Delicately, the blue being shuddered in borderline ecstasy. Of course, the mere fact that there was no war fleet, and that Idow and his shipmates could no more destroy a planet than eat it, meant nothing, since the stupid Dirtlings *thought* they could! Idow wrapped himself in warm thoughts of violent bloodshed and was on the verge of orgasm when a titanic roar woke him from his reverie.

"Squee!" thundered Gasterphaz, noticing a meter on his security board twitch. "Someone has broken into your room!"

"My room? My collection!" cried the lizard, instantly realizing the truth of the situation. "The primitives are after my weapon collection!"

Idow choked. Twice. By the Prime Builder's nose hairs, it was just going to be one of those trips, wasn't it? "G-Gasterphaz, send your warobot to Squee's room. Order the machine to kill anyone it sees. No. Anything that moves! The primitives must not get their hands on those weapons!" Even though most of them were antiques, the weapons were still in perfect working condition and some of them were powerful enough to constitute an actual threat.

"How long till the Omega Gas is hot?" demanded Boztwank, almost uprooting himself as he nervously fondled the dirt in his pot. The rich loam slid easily off the frictionless surface of his force field hands.

"Three hundred seconds," rumbled the busy protector.

"Too long!" screamed the mushroom and, spinning in place, he extended an arm to stab a button on Gasterphaz's board. Horrified, the Choron tried to pry the translucent limb away, but the force field limb resisted even his mighty hands.

"Stop, you fool!" he shouted in desperation. "The Omega Gas isn't hot enough yet!"

"Die!" screeched the engineer, completely out of what little mind he possessed. "Die-DIE-*DIE*!"

9

"Hey, slick, you dig English?" asked a hairless giant holding a projectile weapon with a bore large enough to accommodate Trell's nose. Which, at present, it did.

The alien crew member had to swallow before he was able to reply to the question. Squee had only just warned Trell that the test subjects had broken free from the arena when unexpectedly the technician confronted those very same individuals right outside the communicator's private room. Bodily, the alien had been lifted off the floor and yanked inside by a large, smelly humanoid whose only redeeming feature was that he was properly hairless.

To Trell, the four humans came in a confusing assortment of sizes, shapes, and colors. The only unifying aspect of their appearances was the space black, animal skin armor that they wore. Which Trell thought was rather pretty, until the small Dirtling with grotesquely protruding teeth turned about and he saw the decoration on the back. The technician gulped. He was in the hands of primitives indeed!

To the Deckers, the alien was as short as Chisel, as hairless as Crowbar's head, and green, which surprised them not in the least. Obviously, he came from Mars.

Trell was dressed in a ivory wraparound that left his arms bare, and a pair of calf-high soft plastic boots. A wide, beige belt covered with pouches and a sealed tan box circled his waist. Hammer frisked the alien for weapons, but if there were any hidden among the technician's tools, he couldn't find them.

"Yes, I do understand your language," responded the beige communicator box clipped to Trell's belt. It had taken the device a few seconds to translate the human speech into something that Trell could understand and then convert it into the subsonic range his species could hear.

"My name is Trell, I am a technician. Do not kill me and I will serve you faithfully to the best of my meager abilities."

He grovels well, noted Hammer as he hooked a thumb inside his studded belt. Must do it a lot. The street tough smiled appreciatively. He liked that in a person.

The ganglord gestured at Crowbar to release the alien, which the biker did gratefully and wiped his fingers on his grimy T-shirt. Yuck! Crowbar thought. The rubbery little creep felt like a dirty chalkboard. The biker was unaware that the alien crew member thought the same about him.

In elegant simplicity, Hammer waved his Colt at the rows of strange, glittering weapons sealed inside the cabinets of unbreakable plastic and said, "Unlock those or die."

"Fair enough," replied Trell, and he opened the first of the display cases with his master key. Eagerly, the Bloody Deckers grabbed the antique rifles and patiently listened as Trell told them how to fire the weapons. A brief test on a bulkhead proved that he told them the truth. Twist this, turn that, pull the trigger, and a bolt of polychromatic fire spat from the rifle's muzzle, vaporizing a fist-sized hole in the metal wall. Lovingly, the gang caressed their new death-dealers. Wait till the Ninety-fifth Street Commanches saw this! For the brief period that the rival gang survived the experience, they'd sure be impressed.

The Deckers took as many of the weapons as they could, with two of the antique lasers strapped to each man's back and a third held in their hands. The gang was armed for war. Chisel, though, was given Hammer's automatic pistol, the ganglord wisely recognizing the boy's limited ability to acquire new knowledge.

Checking over the display cases for anything interesting, Drill asked the alien technician about grenades. It took Trell a while to absorb the novel concept of portable throwing explosives, and then he replied in the negative. No such anti-personnel devices were available.

On Hammer's command, Crowbar poked his head into the corridor outside the armory to see if the coast was clear, and when he wasn't attacked by anything, the street gang left the room. Drill paused in the act of shutting the door to spray the display cases with his laser, destroying everything in sight so that none of the antiques could be used against them.

"Where now?" Crowbar asked his boss, *pro tem*.

"The bridge," decided Hammer, knowing that must be where their alien tormentors were hiding.

"The . . . what?" asked Trell adjusting the controls on his translator. There were no artificial constructs for crossing waterways aboard this ship.

Hammer gestured vaguely. "The bridge," he repeated. "You know, the . . . ah, front desk, the head office . . . the driver's seat . . ." The street punk was clearly at a loss. How could he make the alien understand what he wanted? Then, amazingly, the problem was solved by Chisel, who told the green being to, "Take us to where your boss sits on his ass."

Ah! Now *that* the technician understood.

"Follow me, sirs," said the little alien, and he smartly turned left. The Deckers moved stealthily along the corridor, weapons at the ready, when suddenly—from what the street gang had wrongly assumed were air shafts—there began to pump a thick purple sludge that hissingly ate its way into the plastic floor, revealing the shiny metal deck underneath. Trell's ears stuck straight out from his head in raw terror. By the Prime Builder's Testicles—*OMEGA GAS!*

"WHURR!" the alien howled like a goosed chainsaw. "Quickly! To the air locks!"

The Bloody Deckers hadn't the slightest idea what that weird glop on the floor was, but from the way the little green bozo was acting, they ran, too.

"Don't let it touch you!" screamed the seemingly boneless technician as he bounced more than leaped over the rivers of purple ichor. Though weighted down with their booty, the street gang did their level best to keep up with him and comply with the, no doubt, intelligent request.

Breaking to the right, Trell disappeared down a corridor and the humans hurried along behind him, zigzagging through a maze of passageways. Another right brought them to a *cul de sac*, where a man-sized silver oval decorated the end wall. Rapidly, Trell touched the air lock in four specific places, the door dilated, and the Bloody Deckers plowed into the room beyond, crushing the technician beneath them. Fighting his way free from the pile of bodies, the rubbery alien reached up to slap a black spot on the oval's frame. The air lock door irised shut. Darkness enveloped them for an instant, then the internal lights came on.

"Safe," sighed Trell, sliding to the floor. "Safe."

The room they were in was a plain rectangle, made entirely of what looked like unpainted steel. Lockers lined both side walls, and identical ovals faced each other from the opposite ends. Aside from the Deckers and Trell, there was nothing else in the place.

"You sure we're safe?" asked the panting Drill, his laser rifle searching the cubicle for new dangers.

"For the moment, yes," said the box on the alien's belt. "The Omega Gas cannot reach us in here." He tapped the metal door with a nailless finger. "Airtight. No organic parts. The gas can't get through."

Hammer snorted in contempt. "Gas? What gas?" he

demanded. "You mean that grape jelly out there?"

Even through translation, the poetic allusion was not lost. "It is a gel, now," gasped the technician. "Because they released it too soon. The gas is cold. But when it heats up . . . *pft*, you're dead."

Crowbar curled his upper lip into a sneer. "Oh, swell," he said sarcastically. "C'mon, let's blow this dump!"

"Yeah," said Chisel, so frightened that the only reason he was still in his boots was because they were a size too small. "Let's go."

"Shut up," growled the ganglord. "We ain't going nowhere."

Chisel stuck his chin out. "Yeah," he said loyally, doing a fast reversal. "We're staying."

Crowbar turned to face Hammer, the butt of the stolen laser braced on his hip. Protectively, the rest of the Deckers moved in close, ready to kill the ex-biker, but their chief shut them down with a glance and boldly stepped in front of the man's energy gun.

"Well?" asked Hammer, his voice dangerously low.

The ex-biker tried to out-stare the man and failed. As he shifted his eyes, Hammer took advantage of the lapse to shove his own rifle into Crowbar's gut. The big man grunted in pain. This was not working out as planned. Direct confrontation had never been Crowbar's style. In stages, Crowbar lowered his rifle, and after a moment Hammer did the same.

"We got guns like nobody has ever seen," argued the gang member, trying to be reasonable. "And now we got a chance to get outta here. So what are we waiting for? You heard him," he jerked a dirty thumb at the technician. "That purple crap out there will kill us faster than drinking a drain cleaner daiquiri. So why stay? Let's get while the getting's good."

"Nobody ices a Decker and lives to brag about it," stated Hammer as a hard fact. "Those martian mothers aced two of us, and you wanna take a hike? You chicken bastard, you gonna walk away from Decker blood?" The ganglord knew that Drill and Chisel were with him a hundred per cent, but he wanted Crowbar, too. With Whipsaw dead, the ex-biker was the strongest man they had. In a hand-to-hand fight the guy would be invaluable. That is, as long as Hammer didn't turn his back on the bastard.

Crowbar knew that Hammer was planning something, but couldn't quite figure out what, so he decided to play it cool and smooth through the gig.

"Hey, man, you're right," he said, amending his position with a forced grin. "Nobody can mess with the Bloody Deckers. We gotta take these geeks."

"Glad you agree," said Hammer with a sneer, as Drill and Chisel flanked him, their weapons prominently in sight.

"You. What's your name again?"

Suddenly, the alien realized the conversation was directed at him once more. "Trell," he replied, respectfully rising to his feet. "Trell-desamo-Trell-ika-Trell-forzua, Jr."

The ganglord chewed that mouthful over. "I think we'll just call you Trell," he decided wisely.

In resignation, the alien shrugged. It was better than Junior.

"Okay, Trell baby, what would happen if that Omega Gas got in here? Could we like hold our breath or something?"

Trell shuddered, a gesture that meant the same thing to his race as it did to humans. "You don't have to breath Omega Gas," he explained. "It touches your skin and you die. *Pft!*"

Pft again. "Okay, can we go outside and circle round to the bridge? Climb in through a window maybe?"

"No, sir. Robot weapons would atomize us the moment we left the ship. To use Omega Gas the ship must be at Defense Level A. Escape is impossible."

"So much for taking a hike," said Drill snidely out of the side of his mouth. Crowbar ignored him and tried to remain cool.

"Trapped like rats," whispered Chisel, genuinely scared. Oh, he thought, if only I still had my lucky bowie knife with me, the one Mother had tried to kill Father with.

Hammer gave the boy a friendly pat on the shoulder. "Okay, then, we attack," he said taking charge of the discussion again. "You! This air lock got any space suits?"

Trell's translator relayed the word as mobile environmental armor. "Of course, sir."

"Show me."

The technician thought he knew what the hairy Dirtling was planning, and explained that it wouldn't work. "The space suits can't resist Omega Gas for very long. Eventually, the vapors will eat though the joint compounds."

Hammer barred his teeth in his best Bogart impersonation. "Long enough to get us from here to the bridge?" he drawled.

Trell dilated his nose. Ah! Darn clever these Dirtlings. The technician shuffled to his feet and started rummaging through the equipment in the wall lockers, in the process finding his lost bottle of window cleaner. So that's where it had been hiding!

*   *   *   *   *

Pursing his lips, Leader Idow spat in Boztwank's soil. The mushroom recoiled in disgust, his floating pot smashing into the metal edge of his tech-station. For the first time in years the fungi was speechless, utterly speechless. Idow, however, was not.

"YOU FOOL!" he throated. "YOU CONTEMPTIBLE FOOL! *Cold* Omega gas? We want to kill them, not annoy them!"

"And they live," said Gasterphaz without frills. "They have taken refuge in air lock #4. Trell must have shown them how to access the hatch."

"Trell," panted the engineer, ready to explode with anger. "This is all his fault!"

Leader Idow crossed the control room and viciously back-handed the mushroom across his fleshy dome. Boztwank reeled under the blow, and the blue alien hit him again, and again. Seething, the mushroom lunged forward, his force field hands reaching for Idow's throat. But the alien commander had already activated the defense shield generator on his belt, and he laughed cruelly at Boztwank's futile efforts to claw through the immaterial barrier—which was the prime reason why everybody aboard this ship wore the device.

Knowing this, the hate-engorged fungus raced back to his tech-station, turned his grapplers up to full power and ripped free the dented metal panel. With a stentorian shriek, Boztwank hurled the dura-steel square at his taunting blue commander. Unhindered, the metal panel passed through the defensive energy field and stopped, centimeters away from Idow's throat, caught by the rocky hand of Gasterphaz. The mighty Choron crumpled the steel plate like paper and then deposited it on the floor with a ringing crash. Bodily, he stepped between his warring shipmates, a living stone wall. The combatants glared spitefully at each other around him, so nobody happened to notice a light come on at Gasterphaz's board, saying that the door to air lock #4 had just opened and closed.

"First we kill the Dirtlings, then each other," toned the protector in a voice that brooked no discussion.

Reluctantly, everybody returned to their posts, including Squee, who had been preparing to join the fight and help Idow. This did not go unnoticed by Boztwank, who was almost warm with fury. Forever unable to reach that blissful culmination of his species' existence and sporulate, a lifetime of denial had long since taken its toll, and even by his own race's standards Boztwank was insane.

Sullenly, the mushroom inspected the exposed circuitry of his tech-station for damage and pinked himself. He would gladly kill them all if he had the opportunity. Then Boztwank secretly grinned, for weren't opportunities like light bulbs—made, not found?

Leader Idow sank into his chair. "Gasterphaz, send your warobot to air lock #4, with instructions to kill everybody it sees, but if possible to save Trell." The rocky giant started to speak. "I know those are rather complex orders for the machine, but at least it gives Trell a fighting chance."

"Yes, my Leader."

Outwardly, Idow was unruffled by what had just happened,

but inwardly he was still seeing blue. When they finally got away from this accursed planet, he was going to kill that mushroom in the slowest, most excruciating manner that his torture-loving race had evolved after thousands upon thousands of years of dealing out pain and suffering. Leader Idow wondered where he could find a piece of string and a small fruit?

*   *   *   *   *

Only five space suits were hanging in the closet of the air lock, one for each member of the crew, and thus, one for each member of the gang, as Trell was coming along as their native guide.

The helmets were made entirely of a clear, hard plastic that rang like fine crystal when tapped. Trell strongly advised the gang not to do any whistling near them. The boots and gloves of the suits were made of jointed metal, while the body was a stiff woven material, rough and scratchy on the outside, silky smooth on the inside, and in the damnedest shade of electric neon orange that the humans had ever seen. When Drill asked about the strange color, the technician explained that it was to make workers easier to spot against the hull of the ship. The gang member grunted in reply. Logical enough, he thought. At least the freaking suits weren't white.

The Bloody Deckers looked ridiculous in their borrowed space suits as only Idow's had been even vaguely human-sized and Hammer had claimed that for himself. It smelled weird, but fit him okay.

Unfortunately, the rest of the gang was not that lucky.

Crowbar's draped off him in folds. The space suit was human shaped, but much too large. He was like a child in his father's overcoat. An analogy he didn't use, never having met his father or even knowing the man's name.

Chisel's space suit was snug in the waist, there weren't enough fingers in the gloves, and there was a stupid sleeve hanging off his butt which he kept tripping on until he tied it around his neck like an ascot.

Drill got the really bad suit, though. His space suit was a

pressurized dome that had three legs, and something kept
squirting him in the face with a pink liquid. Trell told the
unhappy man that the reddish fluid was vital to the lifeform
for which the suit was designed and could not be shut off. Air?
Food? guessed the gang member. No, replied Trell. They just
liked it. Ah, reasoned Drill. Drugs! Not at all, refuted the
technician stiffly. They simply enjoyed being "pinked." At
first, Drill tried to dodge the watery stuff, but invariably the
fluid struck him anyway. Soon he found himself enjoying its
soothing chromatic effect and happily awaiting the next dose.
Why, pink was lovely!

"Ready?" asked Trell, the mechanical voice of his translator
muffled by the adamantine fabric of his space suit.

"Ready," grunted the ganglord, fumbling with his rifle. It
was hard to keep a grip on the weapon with these goofy metal
gloves.

The technician dilated the air lock door, and purple mist
flooded in, filling the room. Everyone braced themselves, but
when nothing happened, they relaxed and filed into the corridor. Swirling Omega Gas was everywhere.

"Stay close to me," said the little alien, and off they went.

Speed was important, as the war gas would soon eat its way
through their space suits. The street gang had only a short
while in which to find the starship's control room and end this
matter for once and for good.

Trell was now wholly allied with the humans. His ex-
shipmates, on top of everything else they'd done to him, had
tried to kill him this time. Him! Master Technician Trell! A
being can only forgive so much. Could Pounding Metal Imple-
ment and his Life Fluid-Coated Floor People treat him any
worse?

Relying upon his intimate knowledge of the starship's construction, Trell led the Bloody Deckers through the vapor-
filled corridors. The street gang trailed along behind him,
keeping close, like brilliantly-hued ghosts on parade. The purple gas was getting thicker as they progressed deeper into the
ship, and it was getting more and more difficult to see.

"Turn here?" asked Hammer, inclining his helmet at a right passageway of a branching corridor.

"No, this way," corrected Trell, and the Deckers went to the left, vanishing in a billowing eddy of the purple war gas.

Seconds later, from the corridor they had not entered, there glided a dark behemoth. The armored treads of the robot's tanklike base rolled on the floor with the sound of distant thunder. Obediently, the machine scanned the hallway ahead of it, ready to kill anything that moved, especially Trell, as the warobot prowled the ship on a seek-and-destroy order. The deadly Omega Gas flowed unnoticed over its metal body and the battledroid, faded from sight as it relentlessly moved toward air lock #4 and certain confrontation.

* * * * *

Acting casual, Crowbar moved up alongside Hammer in the misty passageway. "So what's the plan, boss man?" he asked rhymingly.

"Find the bridge, blow the door, and kill everybody we see."

"Good plan," said the gang member, and he dropped back in line. Let Hammerhead take the lead in this, he thought smugly. People often get accidentally shot dead in battles. Like seriously dead.

Swapping positions with the biker, Drill scuttled in close to his chief. "Hammer," he said in a warning tone.

"Yeah, I know," growled the ganglord. "But we need him at present. Afterward, though. . . ."

"Check," said Drill, pausing to skillfully catch a pink squirt on his face. Ah!

After what seemed like endless trudging through foggy miles of spirals, corridors, tunnels, and ramps, Trell stopped his human caravan, apparently in the middle of nowhere.

"This is the place you requested," squeaked the technician, expansively waving a hand at the corridor they were standing in.

In puzzlement, the gang looked at their surroundings. True, this passageway was different from the others in the ship.

Instead of featureless white walls, this corridor was lined with a multitude of pipes, tubes, wires, cables, and flat square boxes. All white, of course. But there was no sign of a door or any other type of entrance. Just the purple mist and the orange gang.

"You jivin' me?" inquired Hammer, grabbing the little alien by the collar of his space suit and lifting him into the air. Trell's translator failed totally to translate the remark, but the meaning of the action was clear enough.

"No, no, I swear!" his belt babbled in fear. "This is the bridge thing that you wanted." Trell wriggled helplessly in Hammer's grip. "It is not a wall, but a door. There is a phony-trick-illusion."

"Camouflage, eh?" deduced the street tough, remembering an old war movie he had seen once on the late, late show. Trell bobbled his head yes. "Well, okay, then."

None too gently, the ganglord planted the alien on the floor and motioned to his men. They gathered around, and on Hammer's command, twisted the energy boosters on their museum pieces. The quietly humming lasers began to throb with power, and Trell's translator stuttered incoherently.

"Anywhere?" questioned Hammer, raising the crystal rifle to his shoulder. "Or is there someplace special we should—"

"Shoot!" screamed the terrified technician. "Security monitors will soon sense your weapons." The alien pointed at a plain, cream-colored box on the wall. "There! It is the locking mechanism. Now shoot! SHOOT!"

* * * * *

Gasterphaz stiffened at his board. "Idow, someone is in the immediate vicinity of the control room with energy weapons."

The blue being frowned," You don't suppose it's the—" And at the base of the control room, the door exploded.

Burning metal embers filled the air as the space suited street gang invaded the control room, firing their weapons willy-nilly. Scurrying for cover, the alien crew dove from their chairs, but the scintillating energy beams caught each of them in mid-step and the control room filled with the light of a rainbow gone mad as the personal defense fields of the aliens battled it out with the Deckers' stolen weapons. The antique rifles had been set on maximum discharge, and the field generators raced frantically to compensate. Flickering on the point of extinction, the sparkling auras around the aliens shrank and then triumphantly expanded as the force fields tapped directly into the starship's reactor for additional power. Their own beams fed back to them, the lasers shut off rather than explode, and the street gang found themselves holding futuristic paperweights.

Idow barked an unintelligible command, and the mountainous Choron rose to the attack.

Christ! The damn thing was bigger than the whole gang put together! Hammer grabbed his Army .45 from the fumbling hands of Chisel and fired the manstopper pointblank at the rocky giant. The steel-jacketed bullets musically twanged off Gasterphaz's rocky chest. Bravely, the street gang raised its rifles like clubs, determined to at least go down swinging— when the first smoky tendrils of Omega Gas drifted into the room, passed unchecked through the energy fields of the alien crew, and touched their living flesh.

With high-pitched screams, Idow and Squee faded into the purple mist, rapidly disappearing in a nauseating series of stages—hair, eyes, skin, muscle, organs, and finally bones— and then their deserted uniforms limply collapsed into empty boots. The rocky casing of Gasterphaz broke into pieces and avalanched down as his carbon-based internal bracings dissolved. Spinning out of control, Boztwank's electronic pot circled around the room, then with a click it settled to the floor, only a foul-smelling hole left in the dark soil to show where the crazed mushroom had once stood.

Confused, the Bloody Deckers found themselves alone in the control room of the starship, with just Trell and Omega Gas as company. As fierce as the battle had been, it took the gang a while to realize what had happened. They'd won!

"Sonofabitch." Drill smiled, and leaned against a white wall in relief. "Son-of-a-bitch!"

10

Twelve seconds of arc above the orbit of Pluto, remaining equidistant from the planet Dirt and its sun, there floated in the starry blackness of space a small golden cube—in essence, a globe that had been squared off to the aforementioned refrigerator shape. To the uninformed, it was quite innocent-looking. But its color alone was enough to identify the mighty starship to any starfaring being in the Milky Way. Due to the direct relationship between color and speed in hyperspace, that superfast hue belonged exclusively to the Great Golden Ones, Guardians of the Galaxy.

Regularly, the sleek patrol ship swept the solar system with its powerful sensors, searching for any unauthorized intrusion, its vast array of weapons held ready for instantaneous use: the hyperdrive nullifier, which could bring a fleeing planet to a screeching halt (supposing anybody got one hot-wired and in first gear); the omnipotent force shield dampers, which could crush a fortress like an egg or an egg like a fortress, depending upon the circumstances; and the telepathic *STOP THAT* cannon, which had brought legions of hardened space scum to their knees (if they had any), begging and pleading not to be sent to the ice mines of Galopticon 7 (a fictitious planet of horrible environment and ravenous life-forms that the Great Golden Ones had the whole galaxy believing actually existed). When the criminals sentenced to Galopticon 7 instead found themselves being stuffed into a nuclear furnace, they figured their lawyers had managed a last-minute miracle of plea bargaining, and that they were sure getting off easy this time.

If this weren't enough to scare any would-be criminals witless, secreted in dark asteroids throughout the galaxy were the Great Golden Ones' Planetbuster Bombs and Nova-grade lasers. These were never used, but perfectly capable of annihilating an entire solar system faster than you could say, "Just kidding!" Legitimate dread of these weapons no doubt caused the Galactic League to recognize the authority of the Great Golden Ones.

It was on the strength of their mythic and their known devices that the Great Golden Ones patrolled the star-lanes, keeping the galactic peace.

This particular starship, X-47-D, had been assigned to protect the planet Dirt and its indigenous population from unwarranted intervention. The two-being crew of the interstellar craft believed that this was a punishment for laxness in their duties (it was), that there was nothing they could about it (there wasn't), and that they were merely marking time since everything on Dirt was as quiet as ever (no comment necessary).

The crew of the vessel was also bored to tears, having little else to do other than search for illegal aliens. But because of their hypnotraining, their subconscious forced them to keep busy by polishing and cleaning the ship until it shone like a surgical instrument. As a result of this hypnotraining, crewmen who retired from the Great Golden fleet made extraordinarily good domestics.

In the kitchen of the golden cube (level five—section

three—down the hall and make a left at the armory), amid
spotless golden cabinets and racks of gleaming yellow utensils,
the ship's avantor paused in her task of distilling the evening
meal and lowered the flame under the complex maze of spiraling tubing, retorts, and beakers that was their equivalent of a
toaster oven. Possessing a remarkably humanoid body, the
female stood a good two meters tall, and her well-muscled figure proudly announced the excellent state of her health and
mammalian heritage. Her skin and the long, flaxen hair that
she wore loose about her shoulders were the exact same shade
as her singlet uniform, and, in fact, it was difficult to tell where
one stopped and the other began. Only the avantor's eyes proclaimed her unearthliness, as they were abnormally large, solid
black, and had no discernible pupils.

Drying her hands on a lemon-colored dishtowel, Avantor—
for that was her name as well as her title—turned to the chim-
ing communicator on the wall behind her and touched the
speakplate beneath the tiny video monitor.

"You'll have to wait a bit more for dinner, 17," she said in a
pleasantly husky voice. "I'm not nearly the proficient cook
that you are."

With a rainbow swirl, the stiff face of her primary assistant,
The 17, appeared on the screen. Formally, the short, golden
male gave her a salute, and the avantor promptly lost her ban-
tering air.

"Report," she commanded sternly.

"My liege, we have received a priority message beam from
our orbital sentry about the planet Dirt. A functional stardrive
has appeared on the planet's surface. Wave form analysis tenta-
tively identifies it as the *All That Glitters*."

"Idow's ship," whispered Avantor, turning buttery in color.
"Oh, no. How in the Prime Builder's name did they get past
us? Aren't our scanners working? How sure are you it is
them?"

Her assistant answered the questions in order. "I don't
know, yes, and the computer gave it a probability factor of
ninety-nine and ninety-nine hundredths per cent."

Grimly, the female warrior nodded. Good enough. "What's our power status?"

"Nine over nine and steady, my liege."

"Insufficient. Bring us up to 20/20 and start drive mode. Punch up the file on *Glitters* and feed it to me on my way to the control room."

The 17 saluted her. "Affirmative, my liege."

With a deep breath, the avantor braced herself and added, "Plus, prepare for a short jump."

"What? Ah—I mean, affirmative, my liege." With another salute, The 17 clicked off. The avantor allowed herself a smile. She appreciated his concern, but the inconvenience would be well worth the trouble if they could catch Idow and his villainous crew in the act. Swiftly, the female warrior left the kitchen and made her way through the twisting golden corridors of the X-47-D toward the control room. En route, the computer implant in her brain began to receive data on that most infamous of starships, *All That Glitters*.

****

computer ready.
BEGIN TRANSMISSION.
data flow commencing. access which Idow file?
   :full technical history: running time—184,000 seconds.
   :military analysis: running time—1 second.
   :theories and wild guesses: running time—994,000 seconds.
   :synopsis: running time—300 seconds.
SYNOPSIS, PLEASE.
Once, a long time ago, there was a very nasty boogum named Leader Idow. Oh, was he scary . . .
ADULT VERSION.
. . . and it is interesting to note that Idow and his gang in their various incarnations have wreaked more havoc on the galaxy than a supernova gone wild. They are perverts, sexual degenerates who get their jollies by watching sentient beings die violent deaths and by causing the downfall of civilizations

on a regular basis. Their "fitness test for the Galactic League" is a curse on the lips of many an anthropological team who have linked them to the demise of many outwardly reaching young planets.

While, from time to time, his latest collection of degenerates have been captured or killed, Idow himself has always somehow managed to escape and find a new ship and crew. The Great Golden Ones estimate his age at 2,000 planetary rotations, but don't know for sure. The file room of his hometown was destroyed by a "mysterious" chemical stick explosion. A—

STOP. COINCIDENCE?

probability factor zero.

CONTINUE.

—cruel and vicious race by nature, Idow's people, the Sazins, revel in torture and suffering to a degree that leaves most races ill. Their music is the modulated screams of the slowly dying, and the less said about their mating habits the better. The only reason they are tolerated is that the Sazins usually practice their sick pain games on members of their own race, and have the uncanny ability to design really great music systems, although everybody throws the demo disc into the garbage.

To his blue brethren, Idow is revered as a minor god, his glorious infamy bested only by the inventor of the rack.

In one of their more highly laudable acts, the Great Golden Ones stripped the Sazins of every spaceworthy vehicle, because, as staggering as it is to contemplate, Leader Idow was personally responsible for all three of the worst incidents of First Contact gone bad.

case history #1—The Koolgoolagans were a peaceful, leafy race of intelligent mobile plants. They had developed into an incredibly noble, non-violent race who didn't even have words for murder, lie, or income tax. The treeoids seemed destined to become the greatest race of doctors in the history of the universe as their saplike blood appeared to be a near-universal antidote/antibiotic, and their branching limbs slimmed from strong, broad tentacles down to hair-thin manipulators of fantastic delicacy that enabled them to perform the most difficult types of surgery without the need of cumbersome masks, microscopes, or even instruments. (see medical text #474.)

Unfortunately, the gentle race was discovered by the crew of *All That Glitters* and after several of the innocent doctors were tortured to death in the usual manner, the Koolgoolagans were horrified to discovered that they had been pronounced "too violent" for galactic society. The resulting wave of shock and shame that swept through the populous caused them to wilt, turn colors, lose their leaves, and die *en masse*. The fall of the Koolgoolagans was as pretty as it was tragic. (see botanical text #1,259—"The Greatest Disaster," and literary text #138—"Idow Is A Fink," an anonymous epic poem.)

The Great Golden Ones arrived days after the fact. A valiant attempt was made to revive the race, or to locate any surviving sprouts. But it was to no avail.

medical note: During the massive raking, it was accidentially discovered that if you smoked a cigar rolled from Koolgoolagan leaves, years would be added to your life and many minor ills cured.

law enforcement note: Nowadays, it costs a fortune to smoke a Koolgoolagan cigar, and many confidence tricksters have become millionaires by selling phony Koolgoolagan seedlings.

case history #2—The RporRians are a rather unpleasant race of evolved cockroaches, who nevertheless, had developed a high level of biotechnology when Idow and his crew dropped in to say hello. As did everybody else, the hive dwellers "failed the tests." But, instead of meekly waiting for doomsday in the form of a vast nonexistent warfleet, or foolishly committing mass suicide, or ruining their ecology forever by building a planetary GO AWAY! sign like the Feppathorgans, the terrified insectoids hastily constructed organic starships and skittered out into the vastness of space in a crazed attempt to hide between the stars. When they were finally contacted by the Great Golden Ones and told the true story of their predicament, the bugs went nuts, vowing vengeance on the race that had so cruelly tricked them. But, since they had no precise idea just who in particular had done it, they decided that everyone was to be held accountable and declared economic warfare on the galaxy.

finanical note: The RporRians have no constraints when it comes to turning a buck. They will finish breakfast, seize control of a corporation, milk it dry, put millions of sentients out of work, and shatter a world's economy by lunch. Afterward, they have a dummy corporation buy the now-worthless business before pouring billions of credits back into the company to save it, thus reaping a truly staggering profit with which to spring for dinner.

psychological note: These sort of amoral antics are extremely confusing to most sentient races, but highly effective. The age-old concept of debugging your business computers soon took on a new and horrifying relevance.

"If it makes money, do it!" is the RporRian's credo—from selling primitive worlds non-working versions of their hyper-space drive, to running Three Card Monty games. The RporRians have cut an economic swath through the normally prosperous galaxy that make the sad event of business executives leaping from their office windows a daily occurrence.

But, the last straw came when the insectoids began selling counterfeit Koolgoolagan cigars, which cut into the monopoly of the Great Golden Ones. With a real-life armada to rival Idow's mythical dreamfleet, the star police booted the pesky bugs back to their home world of RporR and erected a robot space blockade to keep them there. The blockade is three planetary rings deep with orders to shoot on suspicion of sight. (see military text #2—"Don't Annoy The Great Golden Ones.")

The RporRians still escape occasionally, but they have assumed the status of a minor nuisance. Business has since returned to normal, and the galaxy breathed a heartfelt sigh of relief.

case history #3—The worst example of a bad first contact happened very long ago, but the staggering side effects of it are still felt today.

Like so many others, the peaceful planet of Gee had been visited by the space-going perverts. But when they failed the tests and were warned of their imminent deaths, the genial, courteous Gees—who up until this event had had no higher interests than group sex and playing the nose flute—armed themselves to the teeth and boiled out into space in crude, nuclear-powered steamships, ready to fight to the death to protect their beloved planet. Each minute that passed without Idow's all-destroying warfleet showing was exploited to the utmost. With frantic haste they built bigger and better ships and armor-plated their moon into an invincible space fortress. Virtually overnight, they molded their race into a crack military force of four billion strong, laid a field of controlled black holes around their solar system, and trained their grandmothers in psychokinetic warfare.

Finally, they developed their own brand of hyperdrive technology and so, the peace-loving Gees stormed into the Void, ready to attack their attackers before they themselves were attacked.

Finding no resistance at first, they established supply lines and built adamantine fortresses in every solar system that surrounded their home star. Along the way, the Gees began encountering other space-going races and, hesitantly at first, began forging mutual defense pacts. Eventually, more and more systems fell within their sphere of influence, and the process rapidly gained momentum. (see political text #19— "Building A Galactic Society: An Evolutionary Process?")

"When at last they learned the truth of the cruel deception, it was too late. Their armed patrol ships were scattered throughout the stars, and the Gees discovered within themselves the heretofore unknown desire to stick their nasal units into other people's business.

And thus were born—the Great Golden Ones, the unasked for Guardians of the Galaxy.

end synopsis.

please rewind.

****

"And, the Prime Builder knows, we don't want that kind of an event ever to happen again!" noted the avantor to herself.

Disconnecting the computer link, she stepped off an ever-moving stair strip and purposefully strode along a golden corridor that dead-ended at the pumpkin-colored security door which led to the control room of her starship.

Calling the location a room was an act of pure politeness. A broom closet would have been a more correct description, as it was scarcely large enough to hold the two Gees at the same time. The walls and ceiling were a deliciously cool shade of blue to aid their concentration, and a wide bank of video monitors ringed the cramped room at head level—Avantor's when she was sitting, The 17's when standing. In the middle of the alcove was a square metal pedestal with a short bench bolted to the front and topped by a complex control board. Standing next to that was The 17, his gold uniform more clean and pressed than his hypnotraining deemed necessary. Had the avantor known the human word, as she should have, she would have deemed him a martinet. But then, making job-related mistakes was why the two of them had been sent here.

Set alongside the pedestal was Avantor's goal, the squat, immobile command chair: a heavily cushioned recliner from which she literally flew the ship by the seat of her pants.

As the avantor seated herself, The 17 gave a little bow and then saluted.

"We are proceeding toward Dirt at our maximum sub-light speed," he reported crisply. "Arrival in 57,600 seconds."

"Unacceptable," she replied, feeling the itching sensation of the command chair's neural links passing through her clothing and delicately entering into her body. "Prepare for a jump."

"At your command."

In proper military fashion, The 17 began throwing switches and shunting power to the starship's dimensionally unsure Q-coil enginettes. During this procedure, the joining process was finished and the avantor interfaced with her vessel, seeing through its cameras, breathing with the air plant, and feeling her heart beat to the pulse of its reactor. With a mental command, she formed a glowing 3-D grid in the air before/inside her, spacial equations scripting along the bottom. Next to/inside her, The 17 activated his navigational controls, and a pair of blue dots blinked onto the grid.

"From here . . . to here," he suggested with a pointing finger.

"We agree," said the female/starship, then Avantor closed her eyes and concentrated. From the eight corners of their golden cube, streamers of invisible energy ripped apart the Time/Space continuum, and once again she felt the omnidirectional sucking sensation as the starship dropped out of normal space and into the hot, gray nothing of hyperspace.

To Avantor's enhanced senses, hyperspace was a painful tingle. Not lethal per se, just terminally unpleasant, much like asking an RporRian for a loan. But this was what the job of an avantor entailed, so the female warrior gritted her teeth and forced the interstellar craft onward through the endless thermal void.

"You're two degrees off course," warbled a voice from somewhere. "Correct and maintain."

"Affirmative," she heard herself reply and redirected her ship by the sheer willpower of her artificially enhanced mind.

Despite the bizarre nature of the medium, some of the galaxy's leading scientists seriously postulated on the possibility of life-forms evolving in hyperspace. So far, no proof of their existence had been found. That was one of the main problems with hyperspace: the only people who could really examine it closely were the avantors—the dedicated navigators who guided starships through the featureless expanse by the sheer power of their living minds. They were far too busy working to take note of any interesting scenery—were there any to be noted.

Second after agonizing second ticked by. The avantor rigidly kept her ship on course, and The 17 carefully monitored her vital signs. Soon, the tiny blue dots on the grid met, a chime sounded, and with a sweating gasp Avantor disengaged the struggling enginettes as the craft phased back into normal space.

Gratefully, she accepted a glass of chilled fruit juice that The 17 offered, letting her ship continue along its original trajectory and slowly radiate away its excess heat.

Now, filling their forward viewscreen was the planet Dirt, an attractive world. This time Avantor and her 17 had a good chance of catching Idow and friends so that it might remain that way.

On the other hand, if they let those space criminals get away, and another species tumbled down the fiery hole of global destruction . . . then the Galactic League would probably order the Great Golden Ones to *build* a real Galopticon 7, just to have a fitting place to exile the two of them for punishment.

11

Wisps of purple gas floated past Hammer, clinging hungrily to his visor and obscuring his view of the control room. Annoyed, he tried to wipe the deadly moisture away, but his metal glove only succeeded in smearing his faceplate.

"Is that it?" he demanded of Trell, the adrenaline still pounding through his veins. "Is that the lot of them?" The little alien squeaked, yes. All of their enemies were dead.

Muffled hurrahs came from the gang, and one voice in particular triggered a response in the ganglord. "Not quite," said Hammer as he met Drill's gaze.

With a nod, the two men attacked. Spinning, the locksmith kicked the laser out of the hand of the startled Crowbar. The weapon hit the wall and discharged, its bolt of polychromatic fire vaporizing a chunk of the floor. Hammer ducked beneath the big man's roundhouse swing, and punched him hard in the stomach. Then Chisel blindsided the biker, tackling him from the rear. Crowbar stumbled, but didn't fall, and back-handed the boy. Chisel arced away from the biker and hit the wall, his helmet ringing from the blow. That was when Hammer and Drill moved in for the kill.

Remembering their lessons in the air lock, the youths jabbed the space suit with their fingers, triggering the opening sequence. The front of the suit split apart, exposing the man inside to the deadly mist. With a bitter curse, Crowbar stabbed out with his knife, determined to take somebody with him. But the act was never finished. As silent as a prayer, his suddenly vacant suit crumpled to the floor like so much dirty laundry.

Contemptuously, Drill snapped his fingers at the empty space suit, and Chisel spat at it, momentarily forgetting that he still had his helmet on.

"*Now* all of our enemies are dead," stated Hammer dryly, exchanging the thumbs-up sign of victory with his friends.

Trell swallowed a small intestinal organ that had unexpectedly risen into his throat during the slaughter. Obviously, Prying Metal Bar must have outlived his usefulness to the gang, and so . . . *PFT*! Well, by the Prime Builder, Trell-desamo-Trell-ika-Trell-forzua, Jr. wasn't going to outlive his!

"I will disperse the Omega Gas now, sir, if I may," he said to the ganglord, submissively lowering his head.

Impatiently, Hammer waved him on. "Absolutely, dude, go earn your keep."

My intention exactly, thought the technician as he crossed the room to punch the appropriate commands into Gasterphaz's control panel.

Imperceptibly at first, the swirling purple fog took on a new pattern, slowly re-entering the vents from which it had issued. Like a lake mist, the heavy gas stratified in the air, the layers dropping lower and lower in the room until, hugging the floor, the last traces of Omega Gas flowed back into the hall. The air appeared clear. Trell checked a monitor and indicated that it was safe to de-suit.

"You first," said the ganglord brusquely.

A slightly paler shade of green than was normal for his race, the technician undid the seals on his helmet, lifted the crystal dome just a bit, and gingerly sniffed the air. When he didn't drop dead, the little alien relaxed and began removing the rest of his suit. Judiciously, the surviving Bloody Deckers did likewise, and took Trell's suggestion of storing the space suits and extra rifles in a wall closet.

Drill freed himself from his suit and stretched gratefully. Then a horrifying thought hit the locksmith, and with sure fingers he removed the squirter mechanism from Boztwank's space suit and clipped it to his leather jacket just in time.

With the toe of his metal boot, Hammer nudged Crowbar's lack of remains. "You got a garbage chute around here?" asked the tall human with a sneer.

"Of course, sir," replied Trell, weighing his next words carefully. "Should I take care of that before or after I turn the ship over to you?" There was a pause, and slowly the street gang turned toward him. Yes, he thought that would catch their attention.

The ganglord tried to speak, but found he couldn't. Turn the ship over to us? he thought. Holy spit, it hadn't occurred to me that this spaceship was now ours! We own a spaceship? A freaking bloody spaceship!

"Deckers!" proclaimed Hammer, taking a dramatic stance. "We have hit the big time at last!"

"Right on!" cried Drill enthusiastically, shaking his laser in the air above his head. "The Bloody Deckers in space! Look out NASA! Who-wee! We gonna be bad. Badder than the baddest! Badder than . . . than the freaking Angels!"

That was sacrilege to Chisel. Badder than Hell's Angels? Nobody was badder than the Angels! Why, the Hell's Angels motorcycle gang was like having to take a leak, or rush hour traffic—an unstoppable force of nature. But, if Hammer says so, then it must be true. The boy grinned from ear to ear. Wow. Badder than the Angels. Gosh!

"So, what we gonna do first, chief?" asked Drill eagerly, slinging his rifle over his shoulder.

Do? The ganglord's plans hadn't evolved that far yet.

Scratching his neck, Hammer surveyed the bullet-shaped room with its incredible array of controls. What could a starship do? Fly to the moon? Who cared? That wouldn't put money in your pocket. This called for some serious thinking. Hammer sat down in Idow's deserted chair and rested his boots on top of the control board. Trell rushed over to neutralize the controls before the human accidentally pressed the wrong button with his feet and blew something up, most likely them.

"Hey, Trell baby," asked Drill, copying the position of his chief. "Can you fly this ship for real?"

Even to the humans, the expression on the face of the alien crew member said that he was insulted. *Fly* the ship? Trell thought scornfully. I'm a master technician! Why, given time and materials I could *build* a starship!

"Chill out," commanded Hammer, lacing his hands together atop his greasy mane of hair. "The man was only asking."

While rooting through the clothes of the dead aliens, searching for something to steal, Chisel found three metal belts made of woven silver strands, each having a weird ornate buckle covered with bumps and lumps. Controls, the boy deduced, his brain almost exhausting itself from the strain. Buckle and unbuckle, he decided and pressed a random bump to see if he was right. A sparkling bubble sprang into existence around him. The frightened youth threw the belt away and the bubble went along with the belt, leaving Chisel behind.

With a clang, the metal belt hit a panel near Hammer's feet, startling the ganglord. Grudgingly he turned. "What the hell are you doing now, pinhead?" he asked, annoyed.

"It bit me!" whined Chisel, with his finger in his mouth, using his standard phrase for anything not working as expected.

"Yeah, sure." Hammer rose from his seat and retrieved the belt from the floor. The twinkling light field readily admitted his left hand. But his right, holding the laser rifle, met stone wall resistance. The ganglord switched hands and the same happened.

"Hey, Trell, what is this thing, anyway?"

"Personal defense field," sighed the disappointed alien, who had not planned on telling the Deckers about the devices, a bit of insurance against their wrath. "It is what my ex-shipmates used to cowardly defend themselves from your brave attack."

Drill lifted an eyebrow. "Laying it on a little thick, ain't he?" asked the locksmith sarcastically.

Amused, Hammer sneered. "So what? I happen to like having my boots licked."

As Trell explained the operation and limitations of the devices, the Bloody Deckers strapped on the field generators and playfully tried clubbing each other over the head with the lasers. The exchange of blows got spirited, and Trell scurried over to the ruin of the security door, not willing to chance being crushed to death by these—to him, at least—lumbering giants.

"Ah, gentlebeings. There are many delicate instruments in here, so perhaps it would be wise to desist?" he suggested, taking another step into the outside corridor. "Or move your exercising to the arena?"

"Enough, then," agreed Hammer with a chuckle. "Cool it, guys."

Panting from the exertion, the gang broke apart, and Trell hesitantly re-entered the room, staying close to the wall.

"Goddamn!" gasped Drill, mopping his brow with a red and white bandanna. "These are great!"

In careless abandonment, Chisel flicked the sparkling defense field's ON/OFF switch. "Yeah," agreed the boy happily. "Neat!"

Hammer cinched the flexible metal belt tighter around his waist. "Only good against energy weapons, though. Right?" he asked, and the alien technician repeated his earlier statement. Useless, decided the ganglord. Cops don't carry lasers, and wearing this thing wouldn't protect me from a gun or a club. But Hammer decided to keep his anyway. You never know, you know?

Drill strolled over to Trell and rested a friendly arm about the alien's scrawny, green shoulder. "Answer me a question, dude, will ya?"

Dubiously, the technician glanced at the human towering next to him. "If I can, sir."

"Why the hell is everything so freaking white in here?" asked the gang member in exasperation. "Walls, floors, ceilings, doors—shoot, boy—white paint cheap where you come from, or what?"

This was a tough question to answer, but Trell did his best. Keeping to the most basic of terms, he told the gang about hyperspace, and he covered the relationship between colors and velocity in that weird non-dimension. He kept mathematics out of the discussion entirely and described things as simply as he could, but it still took him quite a while to cover everything. Throughout his speech, the alien's translator remained silent. When he was finished, it spoke to the waiting street gang using the most advanced scientific terms they could understand.

"Big juju," declared the box on Trell's belt. "Much magic. Ship no fly fast, if not white."

Blandly, the Bloody Deckers accepted this information and returned to their examination of the control room.

Trell was stunned beyond words. Impossible! The entire theory of chromatic space travel boiled down to two sentences? *Gak!* The technician quickly reversed his opinion of the Dirtlings. Obviously, they were nowhere near as primitive as he had originally believed.

A blinking light on Squee's old board had Chisel nervously summon Trell. And to the alien's surprise, it was an incoming transmission.

"Oh, Hammer, sir," he called respectfully, indicating the flashing blue button. "Do you wish to answer this call?"

"A call?" the ganglord sounded surprised. Confused, he fingered the array of controls before him. Now how do you . . . um . . . er . . . aw, to hell with it. Answering the phone was Trell's job, he suddenly decided. "You do it, Mr. Master Technician."

With a straight face, the alien touched the blinking button, which activated the viewscreens. They swirled and cleared to show a large room with wood paneling and five computer consoles, behind which sat what the gang would classify as Big Money types. There was a football player in a general's uniform, two college professors—a gray-haired guy in a blue suit, and one with glasses and a moustache in an expensive three-piece job—a hot looking Oriental chick in a flowered dress, and a skinny dark guy in somebody else's suit. The gray-haired professor started to speak and the viewscreen speakers crunched and hooted like an elephant raping a Volkswagen.

"Well, the same to you, fellow!" retorted Drill, hostilely sticking out his tongue at the screen.

That stopped the translator cold. Swiftly, it harmonized itself with the operating being and started again. This time it performed the arduous processes of translating English into English.

Hammer glared at the viewscreen belligerently. "Okay, who are you clowns?"

* * * * *

The FCT exchanged perplexed looks.

Ceremoniously, General Bronson removed the cigar from his mouth to speak everyone's unspoken question. "And since when," he growled, "do street punks talk like the damn Prince of Wales?"

"I REITERATE," demanded the wall monitor. "PLEASE IDENTIFY YOURSELVES."

Taking charge, Sigerson faced the monitor squarely. "I am Professor Rajavur, in command of the United Nations First Contact Team." He motioned to the people about him. "And this is General Bronson, Dr. Wu, Sir Courtney, and Dr. Malavade. We are the official representatives for Earth in this situation. Are you all right? What has happened to the aliens?"

"WE ARE UNDAMAGED . . . AND THE PRESENT SITUATION IS UNDER CONTROL . . . FIGHTING IN SELF-

DEFENSE, MY ASSOCIATES AND I WERE FORCED TO DESTROY THE CRIMINALS WHO HAD KIDNAPED US . . . THE ALIEN MENACE HAS ENDED . . . THIS STARSHIP IS NOW UNDER OUR CONTROL."

With these words, the world rejoiced, the previous communications blackout forgotten with this overwhelming good news. Earth had been saved by the Bloody Deckers! Hooray! Hurrah! Historic enemies hugged and kissed each other, cops and crooks, blacks and whites, Arabs and Jews, Democrats and Republicans. The glorious sounds of popping champagne corks, car horns, and church bells filled the globe as mankind celebrated their deliverance from what had been almost certain doom.

Deep in their underground command bunker, the FCT did not join the revelry, as their cerebral teeth were buried in a puzzling mystery. Via their throat mikes and earphones, the team held a fast conference.

"The translation device?" postulated Dr. Malavade scratching his chin. "Could it still be in operation?"

Dr. Wu made a rude noise.

"I agree with Yuki," sub-vocalized Sir John. "If so, then why is it converting the street gang's idiomatic subtongue into colloquial English?"

"Broken?" guessed Bronson, adjusting his necktie. "Damaged in the Decker's no doubt violent takeover of the ship."

"Logical," whispered Rajavur. "But, no, I do not think so."

"Telepathic, then," offered Mohad softly as explanation. "And the machine has tuned itself to its new . . . masters." Now there was an unpleasant thought. Did the street gang realize just how powerful was their position?

Dr. Wu reached for the phone on her console but the instrument rang before she could touch it. The scientist listened intently for a moment, and then sullenly replied, "No."

Snorting in annoyance, Nicholi hung up on his colleague. There had been hope on his part that Russia's ion cannon could breach the force shield surrounding the alien ship. The general was fast running out of options, and it was possible that nothing in his arsenal but nuclear weapons could penetrate the immaterial energy blister. But, no, those weapons were the court of last resort. Crisply, a military voice whispered in his ear about something, and he told them to go soak their heads.

"Well, then, why don't you lower the force shield and come out?" enticed Rajavur pleasantly. "You're heroes! The entire world is waiting to honor your brave gang." Hammer's face stated he didn't quite believe the man, so the diplomat smoothly added, "And then, of course, there's the matter of the reward."

"REWARD? . . . INDEED . . . AND HOW MUCH IS THIS REWARD?"

The Icelander did a fast mental calculation, then said to heck with the budget. "A million dollars apiece for you and your men—as compensation for your troubles and emotional disharmony."

* * * * *

"Wow!" gushed Chisel, trying to count to a million on his fingers and failing. "Gee!"

"Chicken feed," snorted Drill. Hammer agreed.

* * * * *

"INSUFFICIENT COMPENSATION . . . WE DESIRE FIVE MILLION EACH."

Prof. Rajavur had to mull the suggestion over. The secretary-general would throw a fit if he said yes. Of course, that was a point in its favor. Hmm. . . .

"Bargain with them," advised Sir John's voice in his ear. "If you make it too easy, they'll become suspicious."

"Two million," said the leader of the FCT firmly. "And that's my final offer."

"FOUR."

"Three," the diplomat countered. "And you receive full amnesty for any crimes you have committed up until this moment."

There was a short pause. "SUFFICIENT . . . WE SHALL EXIT THE SHIP IMMEDIATELY."

STOP THAT

The mental command exploded across New York, and people shook like Vegas dice under its power. Glasses shattered, guns went off, cars crashed, murders were halted, burglaries canceled, illicit love affairs stopped/started, and thirty-seven politicians resigned from office.

Tear-filled eyes uncrossed just in time to see a shiny golden cube about the size of a two-bedroom house landing end-first in the soil of Central Park, right alongside the white sphere. The strange pair strongly resembled a brown sugar cube sitting next to a soccer ball. Then, every viewscreen/monitor/television set on Earth began showing the beautiful golden, unsmiling face of the avantor.

"WE ARE THE GREAT GOLDEN ONES . . . GUARDIANS OF THE GALAXY . . . EVERYONE IN THE WHITE STARSHIP IS UNDER ARREST . . . LOWER YOUR FORCE SHIELD AND COME OUT WITH YOUR PSEUDOPODS RAISED."

* * * * *

"Waste products!" screamed Trell in terror, clutching at his chest. "It's the Great Golden Ones!" He scampered beneath his chair attempting to hide. "AIYEEE! We're doomed for sure!" Ultrasonically, he wailed at the top of his lungs, his belt translator merely relaying the word, "Sob."

Hammer was out of his chair and across the room in an instant. "What the hell are you talking about!" he demanded, shaking the little alien like a can of spray paint. "Who are they? The star cops?" Weeping uncontrollably, Trell burbled yes, and the street tough released him. God*damn*, he screamed silently. What a day this was turning into!

Hitching up his pants, Drill got tough. "Okay, chief, what's the attack plan?"

The ganglord clenched and unclenched his fists. "Gimme a minute. I'm working on it."

Inspiration brightened Trell's sad green face. "I know what to do," he exclaimed happily. "Let's shoot ourselves with the lasers! Death before Galopticon 7!"

Hammer turned to Drill. "You're closer. You hit him."

Smack.

"But they just offered us . . . you know . . . amnesty," said Chisel in confusion.

"You dope!" snarled his chief angrily. "These are the star cops—not our guys. They don't give a damn about anything we agreed on. They only want to kill us and eat our brains."

Trell blinked in confusion. "What? They want to do what?"

"God's truth," said the ganglord in total seriousness. "I saw it in a movie."

Grabbing the front of the alien's uniform, Hammer lifted the burbling technician into the air. Okay, greenie, what are our options. Can they get through our force shield?"

"Easily," lamented Trell, his boots dangling inches from the floor. "They invented the shield type we use."

"Damn. Is their force shield up?"

Twisting about, the alien consulted a sensor on Boztwank's board. "No, sir, it's down."

"Great! We got anything to shoot them with?"

The alien's jaw dropped as he was roughly deposited in Gasterphaz's super-firm chair. "You—you can't be serious! Shoot the Great Golden Ones? Why that's—"

The barrel of a laser rifle snugly entered his left ear.

"—a wonderful idea! Activating Proton Cannon. . . . Can we at least give them a warning shot?"

"FIRE!" bellowed the human at the top of his lungs.

"Yes, sir. Firing, sir."

*   *   *   *   *

From the curved pinnacle of the white starship there lanced a blindingly bright power beam that sliced the golden ship in two like a cube of cheese. Sluggishly, the top of the golden ship melted into the ray, disappearing in torrents of superheated steam, vaporized steel, and hard radiation that would cause some very unusual plants to grow in Central Park for years to come. Lowering its angle, the acidic beam moved on, disintegrating the rest of the craft until the very ground it had rested upon slagged into a boiling pool of red hot lava.

* * * * *

"Right on!" Drill exclaimed, grinning his widest grin. This was more fun than robbing a church.

"Neat!" seconded Chisel, bouncing in his seat. "Let's do it again! On anything!"

Trell felt ill and braced himself weakly against the silver edging of the control panel. "But you don't understand," he protested lamely. "We just shot the Great Golden Ones. *The* Great Golden Ones!"

"Big deal," said Drill, cavalierly dismissing the protest with the sure knowledge of a nineteen-year-old. "A cop's a cop."

Hammer resumed his earlier position in Idow's seat. "Any more of those star cops out there?" he demanded to know.

"Thousands . . . millions," mumbled the unhappy alien, slumping in despair. "And when they arrive they'll destroy this world. Nobody sane shoots at the Great Golden Ones." And for one awful moment, Hammer wondered if Trell was right. What did he know about star police and crap like that? Hammer was from the Bronx.

Thoughtfully, Drill scratched at his curly black hair. "Maybe those UN guys will still give us the money and amnesty, and by the time more star cops get here we'll be gone," he said hopefully.

Hammer brushed that idea aside. "No way, Jose. If these star dudes are that bad, then those government bastards will turn us in faster than jackcheese just to save their own hides." Then the ganglord remembered something Trell had said. "Wait a minute, nobody attacks these guys—right? It's unthinkable, like . . . like moving to New Jersey. So they ain't gonna be expecting anything. They'll just keep sailing in and we'll keep blowing 'em away! Easy as rolling a wino."

Trell's throat constricted. It was insane! It was impossible! It might just work at that.

"But that means we gotta keep the ship," said Drill, his leather jacket creaking as he crossed his arms. "And those fat cat government-types were going to give us plenty for this metal snowball."

"Yeah," whined Chisel with a pout. "I was gonna buy a car."

Hammer rolled his eyes. "Don't you idiots get it? You saw what we just did to the star cops. So, to keep us from blowing this city away, the government will pay us millions. Millions? Ha! Billions! Hell, boys, the sky's the limit!"

Confidently, he joined Trell at the controls and studiously scrutinized the complex array of round dusky white buttons, square ivory buttons, hexagonal silver buttons, switches, trip-bars, dials, knobs, levers, meters, lights, indicators, slots, keys, and gauges.

"Show me how to fire this thing," he ordered the alien.

12

The First Contact Team was in an uproar: with Mohad hunched over a computer printout, Bronson talking on two phones at once, Dr. Wu conferring with her associates at Princeton and Beijing, Nicholi struggling with the nincompoops at EmComTac, Sir John saying reassuring nothings to the world press, and Prof. Rajavur making coffee for the team—the domestic chore aiding his contemplation of the matter. Dutifully, Prof. Rajavur added cream and sugar to everybody's cup but his own, and carried the heavily loaded tray over to the consoles. Unnoticed, he dispensed the steaming drinks. They had been that close—*that close*—to settling this whole matter amicably. But now . . . though raised Catholic, Prof. Rajavur didn't believe in miracles. Sinking into his own chair he sighed, sipped, and waited for his team to report.

Soon, General Bronson cleared his throat and took a gulp of the hot coffee, only briefly wondering where the drink had come from. "SAC and NORAD confirm the report that the golden cube was invisible to radar," he stated loudly. "There could be a whole fleet of the damn things orbiting the Earth, and we'd never know it."

Sir John put down his empty coffee cup. "In my opinion, the two amber-colored beings that we saw were exactly what they claimed to be: the interstellar police. Here, watch the monitor." With his left hand, the sociologist flicked a switch and the giant-screen TV gave a repeat showing of the avantor addressing them. "Notice the way she handles herself, the demeanor of the male behind her, and their uniforms. Authority figures, without a doubt."

"Observe the radically different design of their vessel from Idow's flying behemoth," said Dr. Wu, changing the picture to the landing of the golden craft. "Sleek, compact, efficient. The corner points are perfect for defensive fire."

"I concur," stated Nicholi from behind his glass wall. "Definitely a military craft. The crew, however, was inexcusably lax."

The sciologist nodded. "Yes, and that aspect of it rather bothers me. They acted as if their very presence should have been enough to cause a surrender. They are either very stupid, which I doubt, or they have a formidable reputation." He glanced at the smoking pool on the screen. "Unfortunately, a reputation is only an effective weapon if your enemy is aware of it."

Politely, Mohad waited for everybody else to finish before speaking. "The broadcast we heard was telepathic in nature. None of my devices were able to record a single word. And the message was perceived as far away from us as thirty kilometers. Interestingly enough, it also affected the dolphins at the New York Aquarium."

Dr. Wu added this to her list of things-to-check-into-if-we-don't-die, while Rajavur mulled over the information. A telepathic broadcast. He was impressed. Those weren't even *theoretically* possible for modern science.

Silently, out of respect for the dead, the FCT watched the recording of the gold ship being destroyed again. Then

Dr. Malavade cried out, stopped the tape, rewound, and played it again in slow motion. After a moment, he froze the videotape and pointed at the screen with a stiff finger. There, clearly visible on the wall monitor were two shimmering black dots ejecting from the top of the craft. He started the tape again, and the dots floated downward, landing in the trees. The glowing effect disappeared, and two tiny humanoid figures dropped to the ground and scrambled into the brush.

"It appears that we have a few more uninvited guests," remarked Dr. Wu dryly.

General Bronson grunted assent. "I'll send NATO Intelligence out searching for them," he said, phone receiver to his ear, and fingers punching a number into the phone. "N.I. will find them quick enough."

"GENTLEMEN AND LADY . . . ARE YOU ATTENDANT?"

Heads spun at the sound of Hammer's voice.

"Yes, we're still here," stated Prof. Rajavur. Briefly, he wondered what the reaction of the street gang was going to be. The firing upon the golden craft could have been done by an automatic weapons system, it need not have been a deliberate hostile action on the part of the Deckers. It was possible, but unfortunately, not likely. He had hopes, though.

"I MUST INFORM YOU THAT THERE HAS BEEN A CHANGE OF PLANS."

Wu groaned to herself. "Oh, what now?" said the scientist *sotto voce*. "The moon on a string?"

"WE HAVE DECIDED TO KEEP THIS STARSHIP FOR OURSELVES."

"I was afraid of this," sub-vocalized Sir John. "A megalomania-power rush. We're in trouble now."

"Now?" chided Bronson.

Ignoring them, Prof. Rajavur talked fast. "Needless to say, we can appreciate these new developments, and are fully prepared to increase our offer to the originally requested amount of five million dollars."

"ACCEPTED . . . BUT THERE ARE A FEW OTHER

THINGS THAT WE DESIRE."

"Such as?" he prompted, with a beguiling smile that had convinced many a poker player into foolishly betting the maximum. What could these simple children of the streets want? Clothes? A job? Better housing?

"WE'LL START WITH DRUGS," The translation device was brutally honest in its re-telling of the youth's request. "MARIJUANA IS WHAT WE LIKE . . . TEN OR TWELVE TONS SHOULD BE SUFFICIENT."

"T-tons?" goggled the Icelander. Had the lad said tons?

"No problem," whispered Bronson's voice in his ear. "The NYPD burns that much in a week. What kind do they want?"

Rajavur struggled to regain his composure. "Ah . . . what kind would you, ah . . . ?"

"THAI STICK WOULD BE NICE . . . AND NO STEMS OR SEEDS, EITHER . . . UNDERSTAND?"

"Of course," agreed Rajavur amiably, though he had no idea what they were talking about. "Only the finest. Anything else?"

"YES . . . A ROLLS ROYCE FOR EACH OF US . . . COMPLETE WITH AM/FM STEREO, AIR CONDITIONING . . . THE WORKS . . . PLUS, A FULL TANK OF GAS."

The professor hid a smile. "I think we can manage that. Any particular color?"

"ANYTHING BUT WHITE."

"Done!" He smiled openly now. "So, when can we come and take possession of the ship?"

"NEVER."

Sigerson's smile was still friendly, but he had to use force to make it stay that way. "But I assumed that we were negotiating for the return of the alien craft."

"INCORRECT . . . WHAT WE WERE NEGOTIATING OVER WAS WHETHER OR NOT MY ASSOCIATES AND I WILL BLAST THIS PLANET INTO RUBBLE."

"Told you so," whispered Courtney's voice. "Temporary insanity."

Prof. Rajavur spread his arms in an appeal to reason. "But

surely you don't plan to live in the ship," he said to the hairy
youth.

"AND WHY NOT? . . . ITS CERTAINLY LARGE
ENOUGH . . . A BIT OF PAINT, SOME POSTERS, AND IT
WILL BE MOST COMFORTABLE . . . ANYTHING THAT
WE HAPPEN TO NEED I AM SURE YOU WILL BE HAPPY
TO DELIVER PROMPTLY."

Following that statement, a bolt of blue fire spat from the
ship and a stand of trees in the park violently disintegrated.

"CORRECT?"

A shaken Rajavur could only nod. "We'll start assembling
your tribute immediately."

"AND DO NOT FORGET THAT PARDON YOU MEN-
TIONED EARLIER."

Automatically, the diplomat corrected him. "You mean
amnesty. A person can't be pardoned for a crime unless first
he's been convicted."

"NO TRICKS . . . WE WANT A PARDON!"

"It's yours! It's yours! No problem."

"SIGNED BY THE GOVERNOR."

"In triplicate!" contributed the professor, trying to appease
the ganglord.

"THAT'S THE TICKET . . . OH, BY THE WAY . . . THERE
IS ONE MORE THING WE WANT."

Maintaining his poker face, the man sighed. Oh, what now?

"HOW ABOUT SOME LUNCH?"

The leader of the FCT picked up a pencil from the tray near
his high-security hot lines. He hadn't done anything like this
since his college days. "Shoot, I mean, go ahead."

"A PIZZA WITH EVERYTHING, AND I DO MEAN EVE-
RYTHING . . . FORGET THE MUSHROOMS AND I LEVEL
ENGLAND . . . NO ANCHOVIES OR GOOD-BYE GERMA-
NY."

* * * * *

Trell touched Drill on the arm. "Excuse me, sir, but how far
away are these places?" he asked curiously.

"Thousands of miles," answered the gang member, vaguely remembering a geography lesson he had accidentally attended. "They're other countries."

The alien shook his head. "Then I'm afraid we can't do it, sir. The proton cannon only has a line-of-sight range."

"Shut up, fool. Do they know that?"

Ah! Clever, these humans.

*   *   *   *   *

" . . . AND A CASE OF IMPORTED BEER . . . COLD."

There was a changing of personnel on the communications monitor.

"GREETINGS, PEOPLE! I, THE MIGHTY DRILL, DO HEREBY DEMAND A DOUBLE ORDER OF RIBS FROM LOUIE'S BAR-B-CHEW OVER ON EAST FORTY-SECOND STREET . . . TELL HIM THEY'RE FOR ME . . . AND A CASE OF CHIVAS REGAL."

Dr. Wu's teleprinter started chattering at that moment, and with the flick of a finger she put it into hush mode. "At least the alcohol with help cut all that grease from his system," she commented, as an aside.

"So he dies of a heart attack in ten years. Who cares? Our problem is living until tomorrow," growled Bronson. "Wrap it up quick. We've got company coming."

Rajavur blinked. Company?

"HELLO . . . MY NAME IS CHISEL . . . HEY, MA, LOOK! . . . I'M ON TV! . . . I'LL HAVE A TRIPLE CHEESEBURGER . . . A COLA—NO ICE—AND A SMALL FRIES."

*   *   *   *   *

"That's what you order?" stormed Hammer, brandishing a clenched fist at the boy. "Don't embarrass me, you creep!"

*   *   *   *   *

"*LARGE* FRIES . . . OH, AND A BUCKET OF CHICKEN, EXTRA CRISPY, PLEASE. . . . THANK YOU."

A new face came on the monitor.

"GREETINGS, DIRTLINGS."

The FCT straightened at their consoles as Trell appeared. So, at least one member of the alien crew had survived the transition of power. That explained how an uneducated street gang was operating a starship.

Green and hairless, noted Wu, typing some additional medical notes into her computer file. Some sort of plant life? No, she thought, not with those teeth. He was an omnivore. Curious.

Mohad tried to locate the alien's ears. Courtney studied his clothes. Bronson and Nicholi drew diagrams of the control room behind him.

"And what can we get for you, astronaut?" asked Rajavur in his most gregarious manner.

Obviously, Trell was pleased to be greeted as a "star voyager." He liked that! "HAVE YOU ANYTHING WITH A DOUBLE BENZENE RING, SLIGHTLY RADIOACTIVE AND ENRICHED WITH ELEMENTAL BERYLLIUM?"

That stopped the professor for a second. "Ah, no . . . I don't think so. Sorry."

"OH . . . THEN I'LL JUST HAVE SOME OF THEIR CHICKEN."

Hammer returned. "THAT'S IT FOR NOW . . . HAVE OUR TRIBUTE READY IN ONE HOUR . . . OR ELSE. " With a swirl, the monitor reverted back to an aerial shot of the white ship and the steaming lava pool next to it on the ground.

"Well, Wayne?" asked Sigerson, turning to face him.

The American general paused to light a fresh cigar. "As you told them," he puffed contentedly. "No problem. Everybody on Earth heard the demands those yahoos made and are more than anxious to help us in harvesting the ransom."

Briefly, Rajavur considered having the food poisoned, but rejected the notion as implausible. What spacecraft wouldn't have automatic analyzers in the air lock? Heck, NASA did.

"So, what's this about company?" he asked Bronson.

In response, the American soldier hit a button on his console, and the wall monitor switched to an inside view of the front lobby of the United Nations building above them. A squad of NATO soldiers and several plainclothes police were herding two humanoid beings in gold uniforms toward the elevator bank.

"The aliens from the cube?" guessed Sir John, as he cleaned the papers off his console, hastily stuffed the documents into a file draw, and locked it shut.

"Yep. NATO troops found them hiding in a public bathroom," said Bronson humorlessly. "Interpol is delivering them. They're max security. Should be here any minute."

Dr. Wu pivoted in her chair. "Then you had better mirror your wall, Nicholi," she advised him.

Wholeheartedly, the shoeless general agreed with her and flipped a tripbar on his console. The overhead lights dimmed and his bulletproof glass wall silvered over, becoming an effective one-way mirror. Then, from a drawer, he pulled out his personal defense weapon: a barrelless pistol stock with a telescopic sight and a cable attaching it to a jack on his console. In the command bunker, gimbal-mounted, .50 caliber machine guns positioned inside a false ceiling were slaved to that pistol, turning as it turned and pointing where it did. A press of the trigger, and from diverse angles, two hundred steel-jacketed rounds a second would annihilate anything in his sights. Comrade General Nicholi Nicholi had specific orders not to trust anybody, which he considered moronic. Telling a Russian not to trust a stranger was the height of redundancy.

From his console, Wayne opened the doors that fronted the elevators, and carefully watched to ascertain that only the aliens came inside the antechamber and the rest of the Interpol agents returned to their assigned posts. The familiar floor-shaking boom of the door as it closed was clearly heard by all, and soon faintly echoing footsteps came down the concrete hallway that led to the bunker's inner door. On Bronson's command, the steel portal mechanically swung aside admitting the humanoid beings.

Humans stared at Gees, who stared right back at them. A historic meeting this. The first peaceful contact between Earth and an alien species. Unobtrusively, the FCT straightened their clothing and hair as the Great Golden Ones walked closer.

The female stood six feet tall, a good twelve inches higher than the male. Both were well-proportioned, though Wu noticed a few odd muscle arrangements. Their eyes were large and solid black, seemingly without pupils. But even more striking than that was the color of their skin and hair, which perfectly matched their body-hugging uniforms—a muted tone of gold. Coming to a halt, the two beings stood stiffly at attention, shoulders ramrod-straight, with their hands behind them. General Bronson had the unreasoning urge to tell them "at ease."

Prof. Rajavur bowed to the Gees, who did the same to him.

"In the name of the planet Terra, I greet you," he said sincerely, as the Icelander had done a thousand times before in practice sessions before his bathroom mirror. Then to Dr. Malavade. "Honestly, I don't suppose they can understand a word of what I'm saying. Mohad, could you enable your computers for inter-bunker translation?"

"Most certainly," said the linguist, and he busied himself at the controls.

"There is no need for such complexities," said the female in husky tones. "We have our own translation devices that allow us to converse with any sentient species."

"Excellent. That will certainly facilitate matters," said Rajavur, recovering nicely from the shock of being addressed directly. Formally, he introduced his team, using their full rank and titles. The golden beings bowed to each of them in turn.

"I am Avantor," said the female, gesturing to herself. Then she pointed to the male next to her. "And this is my 17."

The FCT's sociologist just couldn't restrain himself any longer. "Forgive me, Avantor. But is that your name, title, or job description?"

"Yes," she answered obligingly.

Hmm. "And you, sir?" continued Courtney doggedly.

"Not a bit," said the male, proudly throwing out his chest and tilting his head to display his fine, wide nostrils. "You see,

I am our ship's 17."

Sir John paused a moment before replying, "Of course."

Casually, the two beings strolled about the command bunker, taking advantage of the opportunity to study its facilities.

"Strange," Avantor said to her assistant. "In here, they exhibit a much higher level of technology than we believed possible. Interesting. Most interesting."

Bronson and Wu exchanged smiles.

"Yes, my liege, but who is that man behind the glass wall?" The 17 asked, pointing unerringly at Nicholi. "I see he holds a weapon of some sort. Your guard, I presume?"

The Russian general cursed under his breath, but did not relinquish his grip on the pistol. The phrase "powers and abilities far beyond those of mortal men" came unbidden into his mind.

Dr. Wu intently studied the alien's black eyes. "You must see farther into the infrared spectrum than we do," she deduced correctly. If so, the mirror would only be frosted glass to them.

Seriously displeased by the security breach, Bronson unconsciously began tapping the pistol at his hip. The 17 noticed the motion and prudently stepped between the American and the avantor.

"Our physiology is not important," said Avantor, the circumspect action of her assistant not going unnoticed. "What is important is that we apprehend the criminals in that starship as soon as possible."

"Yeah, well, we're working on it," grumbled Bronson.

"And what are your results so far, General?" the golden female asked.

"Nada, zilch, the magic goose egg."

Avantor blinked. "I do not understand."

Suddenly, Dr. Malavade began to gesture wildly. "Incoming transmission!" he warned the room.

Unresisting, the aliens allowed Sir John to herd them over by Nicholi's mirrored wall, where the video cameras on the monitor could not focus on them. Courtney scurried back to his console just in time for the swirling effect to clear and:

"AND ANOTHER THING," said Hammer without any preamble. "WE WANT NEW EPISODES OF STAR TREK PUT ON TV . . . WITH THE ORIGINAL CAST, MIND YOU . . . THE FORMULA FOR COCA-COLA, AMERICA TO BE RENAMED ZIP-A-DEE-DOO-DAH-LAND, AND ALTERNATE-SIDE-OF-THE-STREET PARKING IN NEW YORK CITY TO BE SUSPENDED FOREVER . . . MORE LATER."

Sneaking a peek at the wall monitor, the aliens were upset by this transmission as much as the humans.

"That was not the Sazinian we seek," observed the avantor as she stepped forward and assumed a military stance. "Where is Leader Idow?"

"That depends," replied Sir John. "Are you religious?"

Brusquely, Rajavur took over the conversation. "Idow and most of his crew are dead. The people controlling the ship are the test subjects they brought aboard. A group of young Earth criminals that we call a street gang."

Primitives in control of a starship? Both of the aliens felt their knees go weak, and gratefully they accepted the chairs Sir John brought over to them from the kitchen area. The sociologist knew the theraputic value of sitting down after a terrible shock.

General Bronson agreed with the alien's response and thoughtfully rubbed his prominent jaw. Clearly, things were getting out of hand. "Maybe . . . ," he reflected aloud, glancing toward Nicholi.

"If you are planning on using nuclear missiles," interrupted the avantor hastily, "I would advise against it."

"Why is that?" asked Prof. Rajavur curiously.

"Because of the simple fact they would not work. Even if you had a fusion bomb powerful enough to penetrate their force shield, nothing could damage the ship itself." She frowned. "Deflector plating, you see. Absolutely impervious."

Bronson and Nicholi's ears pricked up at that. Fantastic! It was the ultimate armor. Whatever country controlled the substance could rule the Earth. Then the two generals glanced at each other and nodded. Each would make sure the other recieved full technical information. There would be no monopoly. The balance of power between their nations would be maintained.

Nonchalantly, The 17 touched the hand of his commander, the woman's distended nerves made contact with his, and telepathically the male asked her: *What the Void are you talking about? There is no such thing as deflector plating.*

17, What is the first law?

To protect.

And the second?

. . . ourselves.

Correct. The fusion missiles of these primitives will obliterate the All That Glitters, but the blast will also kill us. I say we take the ship by guile and live to tell our version of the story. Agreed?

"Deflector plating," said The 17 heartily. "Toughest thing in the universe. Nothing can harm it."

Prof. Rajavur was both delighted and perturbed by this news. In their present situation this deflector plating was a major obstacle to overcome, but afterward, a defense like that could mean an end to the threat of nuclear war. Somehow they must get a sample of the material for analysis to assure the survival of humanity.

Meanwhile, Dr. Malavade filed his tape recording of the Gee's incredible statement under a triple security seal and electronically sent a copy of it to every member of the United Nations, and Dr. Wu began to amass notes on the theorical construction of energy-repellant matter.

Strolling over to the wall monitor, the female Guardian of the Galaxy studied the picture of the huge white ball. "17, can you identify the model of that starship?"

"Affirmative, my liege. It's a Mikon #2."

"How familiar are you with the Mikon series?"

"Totally," he replied confidently. "I have the complete blueprint for every spacecraft used by known criminals memorized."

Avantor smiled at him. "Excellent. How may we enter the ship?"

The 17 pursed his lips. "Doors and hatches access only from the inside. Mostly they use the teleportation beam, although it is slow."

Her face shifted into a frown. "That's not what I asked."

The golden male squirmed uncomfortably under her stern gaze. "Yes, of course, my liege. Hmm . . . I would have to build an override key, but yes, it could be done."

"Splendid. " She turned to the FCT. "Prof. Rajavur, do you have access to any military personnel?"

General Bronson answered instead. "We have our pick of the United States Army, Navy, Marines, and Air Force; CIA; FBI; Secret Service; city, county, and state police; National Guard; NATO; French Surete; KGB; Royal Canadian Mounted Police; Interpol; and one guy named Remo. What do you need?"

"What we need is for your street gang to lower that force shield," she countered. "If only for an instant. The problem is—how can we make them perform the desired action?"

That was the crux of the matter. A problem indeed. Then a cough sounded from the loudspeaker in the corner and everyone in the bunker turned toward Nicholi as he de-mirrored his wall.

"I know how to make them lower the shield," stated the Soviet flatly. "It is simplicity itself."

13

"You do?" inquired Prof. Rajavur, surprised. "How?"

Nicholi swiveled his chair away from his console to face them directly. "It is easy," he said with a smile. "What we have to do is—"

"Shut up," ordered. Dr. Wu, her attention riveted onto the read-outs of her console. Wisely, the room did so, her uncharacteristic rudeness clearly announcing that something was amiss. "I don't like this. My sensors are indicating a mobile radiation source in Central Park."

Like melting butter, Avantor frowned. "Impossible," stated the female warrior bluntly. "The *All That Glitters* is not atomic powered."

"I said it was mobile," snapped the scientist irritably. "It is moving toward the white ship." She paused, meticulously rechecking the testimony of her dials. "Nicholi, I think you'd better alert the troops. There's a Snoopy in the park."

A lightning bolt exploding across the bunker couldn't have

produced a more startling reaction than the woman's words.

In a very undignified manner, Bronson dropped the cigar from his mouth. "A Snoopy? You sure?"

"Yes, damn it! There's a mobile radiation source approaching the alien craft at walking speed. Now do something!"

"Jesus, I'll try," he said, grabbing his phone, flipping open his code book, and punching in an emergency number that he had seriously thought he would never have to use.

The two aliens were plainly puzzled. "A what?" asked Avantor, with a quizzical look.

"This is unpardonable!" stormed Prof. Rajavur in moral outrage. "Who authorized this insanity?"

"Who could have?" asked Sir John, his face flushed with ill-controlled fury. "Only you and Nicholi have that kind of power now, Sigerson."

"None of my Snoopys are missing," averred the Russian from behind his wall of glass. "But I will double check."

"Do so," ordered Rajavur.

Holding an earphone with his left hand, Dr. Malavade snapped the fingers of his right hand for attention. "Perhaps it was the secretary-general," suggested the philologist sagely. "He has been most unhappy with our performance so far and has already demonstrated his willingness to take matters into his own hands."

"And order an assault on the starship?" Sigerson shuddered at the possible implications. "The fool! Mohad, get me Geneva on the phone. Fast!" Obediently, the communications expert flew to the task.

The 17 took a hesitant step forward. "I beg your pardon," he said. "But . . . a Snoopy?"

"Yuki, give me the location," interrupted Bronson. "I've got a man who can handle the situation, but he needs to know precisely where the device is."

"Vector 4, section 3 on your map of the park," Dr. Wu replied crisply. "Over by the statue of . . . ." Her voice faded away to nothing, and then returned strong. "What the Hell is that?"

An astonishing sight filled the wall monitor. A full division of tanks flying handmade Greek flags were crashing through the greenery of Central Park, the metal juggernauts smashing trees into kindling under their heavy treads. With obvious intent, the indomitable war machines headed for the alien starship, their 200mm guns and armor-piercing rockets aiming straight and true.

"Nicholi . . . ," threatened Sir John in a low voice.

"Not me again," protested the general in innocence. "Those tanks forced their way through my cordon, nearly killing several of my people. They're NATO troops, but operating independently. I have no control over them." With a grimace, he touched his earphone. "My men want to know if the orders still hold about non-interference, or if they should join the assault on the ship."

"Please, have them do nothing," requested the frantic diplomat. Just then, Dr. Malavade gave him the go-ahead, and Rajavur snatched at his phone. "Hello . . . Switzerland?"

Discreetly, The 17 touched Avantor. *They act concerned, and yet refuse to talk to us. Could this be a trick of some kind?*

No, she replied telepathically. *Observe their faces. Whatever is going on is urgent, and simply too important for them to waste time with us.*

"Yuki, what's its power?" asked Courtney, enabling the calculator function of his computer.

Engrossed in her work, the Chinese scientist answered him without lifting her head. "At a guess, half a kiloton. It depends on how advanced a model they have."

"Then it can't harm us down here," he muttered, thinking aloud. His dancing fingers tapped in figures. "But, everyone on the surface within, say a kilometer—that's twenty city blocks—Wow. Nicholi, those tanks must be a diversion just to keep the street gang from noticing the real attack. The bomb!"

"Oh, thank you, John," mocked the Russian general in a syrupy-sweet tone. "I never would have figured that out myself. Now go teach your grandmother how to suck eggs. I'm busy."

Bomb? Kiloton? At last, Avantor understood. "This 'Snoopy' you keep referring to is some form of atomic weapon?"

"Hmm?" Rajavur glanced away from his phone and saw the aliens as if for the first time. "Ah, yes. Yuki, do you mind?"

Formally, the Chinese physicist stood. "It's a portable fusion bomb of the type built during the Cold War. Weighing approximately twenty-two pounds, the device fits inside a normal attache case." Dr. Wu reached under her console and retrieved the briefcase she carried her daily newspaper in. "Quite similar in size and shape to this."

The aliens were scandalized. An atomic weapon that you could carry like a lunchbox? What level of madness was necessary to create, much less build, such a horror?

"The tanks have ordered the Bloody Deckers to surrender or be fired upon," said Mohad in shock. "But this is lunacy. They must know their shells cannot penetrate that force shield. Are men to die just so the Snoopy can get close to the alien ship?"

"How close?" demanded Sir John practically. "Yuki, how close should it get for maximum effect?"

"Touching the force shield would be optimum," she replied, fine tuning her sensors to even greater sensitivity. "But the bomb has been in firing range ever since it entered the park."

"Wayne, how goes it?" asked Nicholi in concern, over the loudspeaker.

The American general laid aside his phone and lit a fresh cigar. "Who knows, my friend?" he puffed. "I've done what I can. But if I were a religious man, I'd start praying right about now."

*   *   *   *   *

Whistling a Broadway show tune, a slim, nattily dressed man calmly strolled beneath the leafy green trees of Central Park, with the equivalent of five hundred thousand pounds of TNT swinging in his right hand. The park grass, dried from the summer heat wave, crunched beneath his polished shoes. Each step raised a cloud of dust that dirtied the legs of his otherwise spotless uniform.

For this mission, Agent Taurus was dressed as a major in US Army Intelligence. That got him past the NATO cordon easy enough. Now all he had to do was find the force shield surrounding the alien invader and release the handle of the attache case he carried. Mother Nature, with a little help from Albert Einstein, would do the rest.

Filling his horizon, the mammoth white ball towered over him, a sight to intimidate anyone, but this man smiled. What he held in his grip was greater than the alien invaders: the power of a miniature sun locked inside eight hundred sixty-four cubic inches, and his to command. During his rushed briefing session, the secretary-general had advised him to get as close as possible to the ship to maximize the bomb's effect. He had also been warned that the renegade FCT might try to stop him, so in case of trouble Taurus was to detonate the Snoopy immediately, no matter where he was.

Faintly, from the other side of the gigantic ship, he could hear the diversionary tanks ordering the murdering criminals inside to surrender. Soon they would open fire and—

Suddenly, someone in a policeman's uniform dropped on Taurus from the trees, locking a muscular arm around his throat. Contrary to what he would have liked to do, Taurus offered no resistance to the killing attack. Instead, as ordered, he released his grip on the Snoopy.

Or rather, he tried to, as the policeman had his own hand wrapped tightly around the handle, preventing that very action. Taurus was infuriated. A nuclear counter-agent! Betrayed by one of his own kind!

Locking two of his fingers together, the man jabbed them directly into the eye of his enemy. But the crippling blow was deflected by the back of a hand, that then circled into a fist and punched for his face. Taurus grabbed the hand in an iron grip, and for a moment the two men stood there, locked face-to-face, neither able to move.

"Taurus," grunted the phony Army officer, straining to crush the policeman's bones.

"Virgo," replied his adversary, struggling to return the favor.

The amenities over, Taurus kicked the man in the groin, but only hit the thigh as the counter-agent dodged to the left. Virgo butted with his head. Pain blinded Taurus as his nose broke. Blood flowed into his mouth and he spat it out. Brutally, he buried a thumbnail into Virgo's wrist, crushing a nerve center. The man gasped in agony and released him. Without wasting a second, Taurus chopped down with his free hand and the arm holding the bomb snapped, but the stubborn policeman held on. Then his own ribs cracked from Virgo's fist. Panting for breath, the two agents broke apart, joined only by their death grip on the leather briefcase. One was determined never to let go, the other unwilling to relinquish control and fail his mission.

In the background, the NATO tanks began their attack, the rockets, missiles, and shells exploding harmlessly on the alien ship's impenetrable force shield. But they created the kind of racket nobody could fail to notice.

* * * * *

Inquisitively, Trell tapped a power meter with his finger. No, it wasn't a minor fluctuation in the reactor. They were under attack by the forces of Dirt. How amusing. He activated the viewscreens to show the pitched battle to the gang, and to Trell's surprise their reaction was quite different from his.

"Holy spit!" cried Drill, nearly falling out of his chair. "There's a goddamn army out there!"

The blood drained from Chisel's face. "What we gonna do, Hammer? Surrender?"

"Deckers don't surrender," the ganglord angrily reminded him. "Besides, they'd kill us on sight." Nervously, he cracked his knuckles. "Trell, how long can that force shield hold?"

"Against this sort of attack?"

"Yes, you freaking idiot! How long?"

The alien technician shrugged. "Oh, I don't know. Thirty or forty of your years."

"Thirty—" said Chisel.

"—or forty—" continued Drill.

"—years," drawled Hammer, finishing the sentence.

Trell nodded in agreement. "Depends upon whether or not we turn on the air conditioner."

"Then they can't hurt us?" cried Chisel happily.

Scornfully, the alien exhaled. "Not with those toys."

Relieved, Drill returned his feet to atop the control board and reclined in Gasterphaz's old chair, his one hundred and eighty pounds of hard muscle not even creasing the cushion. "Well, okay then."

Almost against his will, Hammer grinned at the viewscreen, the light flashes from the explosions nearly hypnotizing him. *So, this is what being invulnerable feels like. No wonder Superman was always smiling.*

"Okay, Trell, get on the horn and tell those UN creeps that they get this try for free, but only this one." He chuckled at the alien's lack of comprehension. "Don't worry about it, stud, they'll understand." Hammer narrowed his eyes. "But just to make sure, let's show them what a starship can do." Leaning into the screen, the ganglord looked over the armored division like a housewife picking ripe tomatoes. "I think we'll start with . . . him!"

*   *   *   *   *

As the last Greek tank melted into a glowing steel puddle, its gun crew dashing about, frantically beating their pants to extinguish the fire, Dr. Malavade snapped his fingers at his teammates. "The Bloody Deckers say that if we try such an action again—"

"—they'll do horrible, nasty things to us," finished Dr. Wu for him in gallows humor.

Startled, the linguist blinked. "How did you know?" he asked her innocently.

"I'm psychic."

"She can read lips, too," explained Sir John, spoiling the effect. He was in no mood for jocularity of any sort, even though he understood its therapeutic value in tense circumstances such as these. The Scotsman supposed that his own nerves were cracking a bit. His job was to relay and analyze information. Against a direct physical threat there was nothing he could do. A sense of futility welled within his throat like bile, and he forced it down with a swallow of tepid Icelandic coffee.

"Hello? . . . Geneva?" asked Rajavur stiffly. "Let me speak to the secretary-general, please. . . . Yes, it is an emergency. . . . Thank you. . . . Emile? Sigerson here. I formally place you under arrest for crimes against humanity. . . . Eh? You're already in the custody of Interpol? *Good*! Hope you enjoy the color gray, you rock-headed buffoon. See you in fifty years, Emile. Au revoir."

* * * * *

Chop, block, jab, thrust, kick, punch. The life or death battle between the two nuclear agents went on and on, each man fiercely fighting for what he truly believed was right.

This is getting us nowhere, thought Taurus, gritting his teeth against the pain. They were too well matched. So in a desperate gamble, he tried the unexpected and released his hold on the Snoopy. Caught off guard, Virgo stumbled backward. That was when Taurus launched his final assault. Summoning every ounce of his remaining strength, he lunged forward in a double-hand chop, a martial arts move not meant to hurt or maim, but kill an opponent. Designed as a last resort, the attack could fell a moose. And there was no known defense, except for not being there when it hit.

It hit—

—the Snoopy, which the crippled Virgo had swung in front of himself for protection. Built to withstand anything short of its own detonation, the briefcase went unharmed. Taurus fell screaming to the ground with virtually every bone in both of his hands smashed. Then the terrible pain overwhelmed his training and the man fainted, broken at last in body and spirit.

The three linear miles of street that surrounded Central Park were jammed full of boisterous people just aching to get closer to the giant white spaceship, but the diligent NATO troops firmly kept the civilians at bay through the efficient use of sandbags, concertina wire, and a thousand armed troops with orders to shoot any troublemakers.

Patiently waiting behind their defensive perimeter, the UN soldiers watched as a sweating New York City police officer slowly shambled down a bike trail toward them. In his oddly twisted left hand, he held an ordinary briefcase. With his right hand, he was dragging the limp body of an Army Intelligence officer behind him, the unconscious man's shoe heels gouging twin tracks in the loose gravel. General Nicholi's orders strictly forbid anyone but authorized personnel from setting foot in the park, so the NATO troops stayed exactly where they were. But once the bloody couple were on the sidewalk, they were within UN jurisdiction.

Exercising extreme care, the soldiers relieved the crippled policeman of his attache case, and then bodily carried both of the battered men to a waiting military ambulance. The briefcase surreptitiously shifted into the hands of another nuclear agent, who deactivated the weapon and deftly tucked it inside a specially designed compartment of his pushcart, never pausing in his sale of ice cream sandwiches to the civilian onlookers.

A random pair of UN soldiers in the cordon around the park watched this operation to completion. Then the Canadian private scratched under his helmet and spoke to the British corporal next to him. "Hey, Sam, what do you think that was, eh?"

"Haven't the foggiest," said the woman, shifting her assault rifle to a more comfortable position. "Maybe that Army bloke was actually a nuclear secret agent sent to destroy the alien ship, and the cop was a counter-agent sent in to stop him. The two of them battled it out, with the lives of everyone in Manhattan hanging in the balance. Just in the nick of time the policeman coshed the army blighter, saving us from dying in an atomic fireball."

The man considered what his friend had said.

Yeah, ask a stupid question, get a stupid answer.

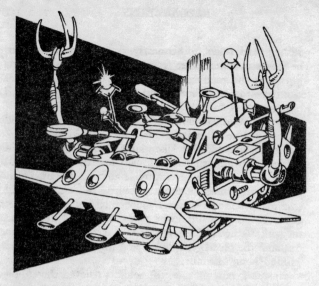

14

With thirty minutes left till lunch, the triumphant Deckers spent their time getting further acquainted with the operation of the starship. The proton cannon (the only weapon the ship carried) was, of course, the first item on their agenda. The Deckers spent a joyous few minutes vaporizing trees and benches around the ship as they learned how to aim and fire its deadly beam. Central Park was fast resembling Dresden after the bombing.

There was a tug on Trell's uniform. He turned, and Chisel asked him where the john was. After a confused moment or two, the alien got the general idea and sent the boy down the hall to the left. Trell also instructed him to be sure to press his palm firmly against a square metal plate next to the door so the facilities could adjust themselves to his life form. With a nod, the boy left, and a few minutes later somebody resembling Chisel walked into the control room. But this was obviously an impostor because this Chisel was clean, from the tips of his

polished black boots, to his neatly trimmed, coiffured hair.
The food stains were gone from his T-shirt, its rips expertly
sown shut, the toolbox design on his black leather jacket
looked newly painted, and even the boy's buck teeth gleamed
healthily.

Dumbfounded, Hammer and Drill asked what the heck had
happened to him. Chisel replied that he walked into the bathroom and it had bit him. Upon closer inspection, it seemed
that the boy and everything he wore were spotlessly, almost
antiseptically, clean. Even his knives had been sharpened.

To the gang's puzzled demands for information, Trell had
no answer. It was a bathroom. What did theirs do?

As excited as kids at Christmas, Hammer and Drill dashed
off to try this technological marvel for themselves; returning in
a short while, scrubbed, washed, polished, pressed, and
thoroughly—to the bone—clean. A condition that none of the
gang had ever been in before. It was kinda nice.

As the laughing Deckers examined each other's laudable
condition, Trell took the opportunity to re-tune the tech-
stations in the control room to their new masters—Hammer as
leader, Drill as protector, himself as engineer, and Chisel as
communicator—as the communication board was partially
sentient and did most of the work by itself.

Deciding how to ferry the tribute on board turned into a
lengthy discussion. Hammer insisted that since he and his
gang had been teleported aboard the starship, so should the
tribute.

Trell argued against that on the grounds that the tribute
would be much more massive then six Dirtli . . . humans, he
corrected himself. The equipment couldn't handle that large a
load in one shot, and the device took a hundred thousand seconds to recharge. Much too long. Better to lower the shield for
a moment, let the trucks across the boundary, and then raise it
again. For those few seconds everybody would be watching for
trickery, with Drill's ready finger on the proton cannon's firing
switch.

Grudgingly, Hammer agreed. It was a gamble, but the

Bloody Deckers had taken bigger risks than this just going to the movies on Forty-second Street.

If lunch was late or the UN tried anything stupid again, Drill resolved that the first building to go would be the World Trade Center. The locksmith had always been fond of the Empire State Building, and those snotty bastards had built the twin towers seven stories taller just to be spiteful. But, if he focused his beam on the base of the buildings, one small zap and . . . down they'd go! Drill wondered if he could angle the fall to make them take out the mayor's office. Or better yet, police headquarters!

Just then, out of the corner of his eyes, Trell noted a meter flux and focused his scanners onto the indicated area. "Sir, there's a large party approaching our ship from sector 12," he announced.

"Show me," commanded Hammer, reclining in his formfitting chair. His viewscreen swirled into a picture of the war-torn park.

Meandering through the mountains of dirt, splintered trees, and glowing lava pools was a conga line of vehicles headed by four silver-blue Rolls Royces, followed by several armored bank trucks and flatbed wagons filled with bales and bales of a leafy, dark green material.

"Yee-HAW!" whooped Drill, exuberantly smacking the uncushioned arm of his steel chair. "It's a freaking parade! Goddamn it, chief, the government is actually paying us off!"

"And there's our gold," whispered Chisel, the illuminated controls of his tech-station brightening in harmony with their master's heightened emotional state. "Gold. . . ."

Not a bank truck, Hammer noted with misgivings, but a convoy of five. He didn't like that. There was too much stuff out there. Much more than they'd asked for. Some subtle instinct, honed true in a thousand street fights, warned the youth of treachery, but for the life of him the ganglord couldn't figure out from where.

"This is more tribute than you asked for, isn't it, sir?" asked Trell, twisting about in his seat. "Are your people trying to—"

and he spoke of a practice common to his race of giving a victorious enemy many gifts to soften their feelings toward you. His translator merely said the word "bribe."

After a moment, Hammer nodded. Yeah, that made sense. The world was scared spitless of his gang and they were trying to buy the Deckers' goodwill. The government was always paying people lots of money to behave themselves. It never seemed to work, but they kept trying. Greedily, he rubbed his hands together. Well, he certainly appreciated the habit.

"Trell, steer them over to the loading bay and prepare to lower the shield." He scrutinized the caravan of goodies closely. "You sure the loading dock can hold all of that junk?"

"Easily, sir. Vehicles included."

"No problem?"

"None."

Drill's face broke into a grin. "She-et, our own personal bank trucks. Say! Could we—" and the locksmith stopped talking in mid-syllable, his mouth and eyes forming a triangle of *O*s. Hammer and Chisel swiftly followed suit.

The caravan had reached the assigned spot outside the force shield and the drivers were disembarking. Women. They were all women. Beautiful women. Gorgeous women. Redheads. Blondes. Slim, long-legged, busty women who were mostly dressed in lacy bits of gossamer that hid none of their charms. Timidly, a few of them waved at the starship. A gorgeous redhead in a micro-mesh bikini bent over to examine something from the ground, and the three males swallowed hard.

"Goddamn," said Drill in awe. "Now that's what I call tribute!"

Chisel tried to close his mouth, while Hammer removed his tongue from the viewscreen. Trell also observed the scene with interest. Ah, lunch!

"Lo-lower that force shield," ordered the ganglord, having trouble speaking. "Get that—those—get them aboard!"

"Women," said Chisel, drooling slightly. "Hubba-hubba."

"Oh, we party tonight!" stated Drill for a fact.

Unaffected by the display of shapely human females, the

alien technician remained ever vigilant, watching the sensors constantly sweeping the starship's perimeter, as he carefully lowered their main defense.

* * * * *

A dry twig propped against the force shield fell to the ground, and a crudely built black box in the hands of a NATO trooper beeped. "The shield is down, sir," said the corporal to his commanding officer.

"Then go-go-go," whispered Col. Robert Weiss into his throat mike, and a nondescript pile of smashed trees disgorged a platoon of heavily armed soldiers.

Keeping low to the ground, the soldiers swiftly crossed those critical meters separating them from the force shield's boundary line. The last man used a leafy tree branch to brush the ground in their wake, obliterating their tracks. Unfelt sensors from the starship tracked the soldiers' every step, but the alien warning system did not announce their presence to Trell as the signal was nullified by a small black box that the NATO trooper carried. Quickly, the thirty men scrambled up the loose mound of dirt at the starship's base, making infinitely less noise than the caravan of trucks and cars on the other side of the interstellar craft.

Avantor and The 17 were not with the assault team, but had remained in the FCT's bunker, as Prof. Rajavur considered their technical knowledge of alien weaponry much too valuable to risk in a firefight. Reluctantly, the Gees had agreed with the request, their hypnotraining forcing them to accept the prudent course of action rather than go for the more fulfilling act of personal revenge.

As the commandos safely gathered in the cool shadow beneath the curved hull of the gargantuan ship, Weiss pulled a slim rod of burnished copper and hastily soldered microchips from his shirt, the override key hastily built by 17. Pressing the activating switch, he waved it at the vessel's hull. Anxiously, the assault team waited. The Gee techncian could only guess at the override code to open the starship's hull. If The 17 guessed right, fine. But if he guessed wrong . . . well, the NATO troopers were not afraid to die, but they did fear a useless death and the subsequent reprisal of the angry street gang on their defenseless world.

The men allowed themselves to breathe again as a meter-wide section of the hull disengaged itself and swung aside, allowing a pile of alien trash to tumble out: bones, bottles, wrapping paper, half-eaten fruits, busted bits of junk, and one thoroughly dead Quatralyan. Heroically, the soldiers pretended to ignore its ominous presence. Then, as quietly as possible, they began ascending the sloping tube, their rubber-soled footwear aiding their climb up the slick metal. When the last trooper was safely inside, Weiss pressed the activating switch on the jury-rigged key again. At the bottom of the pipe the hull cycled shut, and darkness enfolded them.

"Visors," whispered their sergeant, and the men pulled the front of their helmets down. Through the infrared-sensitive glass the darkness disappeared, to be replaced by a black and white view of their fellow soldiers and the awful-smelling metal tube. Somebody muttered a comment about defecating backward and was sharply reminded of the no-talking rule by an eloquent rap on the head.

"All present and accounted for, sir," said Lieutenant Nealon, nodding his head and feeling awkward about not saluting. But he was bracing himself against the low ceiling with his right hand, and saluting a superior officer with your left was the supreme insult in the military, a matter duels were fought over.

Weiss thanked him and briefly consulted the map that The 17 had drawn from memory of the starship's construction. Straight ahead of them should be a power junction for the garbage tube's security sensor. Raising specially modified binoculars to his visor, he found what he was searching for, a hexagon jutting out from the distant wall. Slipping in the alien muck, Weiss and his soldiers cautiously approached the sensor. The trooper with the black box scanned the dirt-smeared hexagon and received a reassuring beep. Tenderly, as if defusing a bomb, the service panel was removed. A private commenced cutting wires and bypassing circuitry cubes so that when the troops exited the tube, the control room would know nothing of the occurrence.

Colonel Weiss bit his cheek in concentration as another wire was snipped. One wrong move here could cause their immediate death. And this was the easy part.

*   *   *   *   *

The last truck rolled across the force shield's boundary, and Trell flicked it back into existence. Safe once more. Thumps and curses caught his attention and he turned. Twirling Metal Spiral was pounding on his viewscreen.

"What is wrong, Drill?" asked his translator.

"This freaking thing is busted!" stormed the gang member. "I can't see the broads no more!"

"They have gone beneath the curve of our hull," the alien explained. "Our cameras can't operate that close." Lithe green fingers prodded a control lever and the viewscreens shifted to a picture of the loading bay: a tremendously large room, with weird alien machinery adorning the, as always, white walls.

"Ramp extended," said the technician formally, twisting an ivory dial and punching a clear plastic button. "Opening main doors."

Like an internal view of an egg being cracked, the white wall broke apart, and the split expanded until the afternoon sun flooded into the loading bay. Engines roaring, the cars and trucks rolled along the ramp and into the cavernous room. True New Yorkers, the drivers parked their vehicles anywhere they wished, in no discernible order. The women disembarked, gawking at the bizarre machinery, a few shivering in spite of the room's warmth.

Without a sound, the titanic white door cycled shut.

"You ready, Trell?" asked Hammer, his eyes glued to the female smorgasbord on the screen.

"Yes, sir."

"Then do it, dude."

A throbbing yellow light filled the loading bay with its probing rays. The energy beam minutely examined the women. Bolt by bolt, the limousines and trucks were scanned, the thick armor of the bank trucks no more resistant than air to the questing rays. There were no hidden weapons, no poisons, no explosives, no radio transmitters, no . . . no . . . no. . . .

"Clean, my Leader," announced Trell, thankful that the ganglord's solar flare of a temper would not be invoked. "They are as they seem. Predominantly naked females of your species and petroleum-burning motor carts." Petroleum-burning! Hot Void, he hadn't thought of that. The alien thumbed the switch on the microphone of his viewscreen.

"TURN THOSE ENGINES OFF!" boomed the technician's voice from the ceiling of the loading bay. The women rushed to comply. Trell *snorked* in disgust. Probably have to scrub the place by hand to get the stink out.

"Can we go and greet them, chief?" asked Chisel shyly. Women had always been a mystery to him—what to say, when to say it, how to get them to stop screaming . . . a mystery that he fervently hoped would soon clear up. Along with his complexion.

"Let the bitches come to us," said Drill, his hungry eyes never leaving the viewscreen for an instant. He had never seen women like this before, not even in movies or magazines!

Trell advised against it, though. "That would be unwise, letting them see the control room. Why don't you meet them in the pleasure room, and—"

"The *what?*" asked Hammer incredulously.

The little alien repeated himself. A pleasure room . . . the idea intrigued Hammer. These alien dudes did themselves okay.

"Trell, you tell them where to go, and then show us how to get to this pleasure room, too."

"Affirmative."

The ganglord stood and smiled. "You stay here and keep a watch on things, while the boys and I get down."

"Yeah," said Drill, licking his chops. "Get down."

The technician spoke to correct their mistake. "But sir, the pleasure room is above us. . . ."

Hammer waggled a finger. "Just tell us the way there and— No, on second thought, I don't want you here by yourself." The hairy youth loomed over the alien like death itself. "I don't want you getting no fancy ideas. You're coming with us."

Somehow, Trell managed to smile. "Of c-course, sir." But all he was thinking was *Oh, Void.*

* * * * *

Once out of the garbage chute, the soldiers unzipped themselves from their coveralls and tossed the soiled garments aside. While Colonel Weiss checked their location on the map, they closed the door behind them and prepped their weapons. Then, in double-time hush, the troopers hustled down the clean white corridor as fast as their combat sneakers would allow.

The interior of the starship proved to be an intricate maze of branching corridors, passageways, ramps, and spirals. Soon, the colonel realized that his map didn't exactly match this craft, as a left turn put them in the kitchen rather than the reactor room. Terrific. While it was true that without Avantor and her 17's help, Earth would be in even worse trouble, it was also true that if the two of them hadn't let Idow and his crew get here in the first place, none of this would have happened. Or maybe that was just sour grapes on his part.

A corporal tugged on his sleeve. "Sir," whispered the man. "There's a Y-intersection here that's not on the map. Which way do we go?"

"Left again," he told the man, mentally crossing his fingers, and the troops marched on. Thanks a heap, Great Golden Bozos.

* * * * *

In the corridor to their right, beyond the curve of the ship, a huge, tanklike robot ceased its endless pacing to and fro in front of air lock #4 and rotated a massive armored turret. *Rrrr?* A noise. And with its weapons primed for action, the warobot sauntered down the passageway to investigate.

* * * * *

As the twelve women hesitantly entered the pleasure room, they gasped in astonishment, just as the Bloody Deckers had done only minutes before.

When the street gang had first entered, they hadn't been very impressed. It was just another big white room. But as Trell palmed a glowing panel on the doorjamb, the walls and domed ceiling had darkened into a rich sky blue, with a holograph of cheerful orange clouds passing serenely overhead. A green carpet of living moss sprouted from the floor, each downy-soft blade literally begging for the touch of their bare feet. The gang was ill at ease with talking grass, but after a brief experiment they rather enjoyed stomping the masochistic moss and its subsequent cries of joy.

While this went on, big comfortable divans seemed to flow out of the walls; plush couches that adjusted themselves to any position their occupant took, as the delighted Chisel soon discovered. Tastefully displayed on cut crystal tables that dramatically dropped from the clouds without any apparent damage were artifacts from a thousand worlds: gently humming vases of translucent metal, an ice statue of a bolting seven-legged creature that neither melted nor ran, and a cheap plaster cockroach with a timepiece in its stomach.

Rotating out of a corner of the room was a library of videospheres containing the stereophonic death throes of a hundred different test subjects. Hoping to find a porno flick or rock concert, Drill pulled out a sphere at random and tried to fit the rainbow ball into the play unit but was unable to make the alien contraption work. Frustrated, the locksmith ceased his fumbling and pinked himself as the women entered. Lustfully, he gave them the eye of a professional girlwatcher. Oh, man, he thought, these foxes are so hot they should have set off the fire alarm.

With his right ankle on the left knee, Hammer sprawled on a red velveteen couch and, like a king holding court, waited for the women to approach him. Making himself comfortable, the youth had doffed his black leather jacket and folded it neatly onto the moss by his boots, his activated laser rifle lying conveniently nearby. In his tight denims and sleeveless T-shirt, the boy's muscular form was readily apparent, as were his many scars.

Timidly, the bevy of semi-naked beauties stayed clustered near the doorway until a tall blonde spotted Hammer and deliciously undulated over to the ganglord.

"Greetings, Hammer of the Bloody Deckers," she addressed him, obviously quoting from memory. "The United Nations of Earth salute you and your brave men for the capture of this alien vessel and hope that you will accept this—" she had the grace to blush here "—additional tribute in the spirit it is given."

"That's cool," said Drill, barely controlling his rapine impulses. Sitting on the edge of the couch, the embarrassed Chisel crossed and re-crossed his legs.

Seductively, the blonde smiled, as if reading their thoughts. "I'm Amanda," she said introducing herself. "And this is Roxanne, Ruth, Alice, Julie, and Cynthia." Cynthia smiled bewitchingly at Drill, and he leered at her.

"And over there," continued Amanda, pointing to the second group of ladies, "is Joyce, Deborah, Lynn, Stacy, Wilma, and Laura."

Laura, a tiny blonde with an astonishing bust line captured the immediate interest of Chisel. Why, he was actually taller than her! New sexual vistas suddenly opened for the boy and he felt his face burn red.

Full of curiosity, the wide, bedroom eyes of Lynn glanced about the room. "I thought there were four of you?" she said, finger teasingly in mouth.

"There are," said Drill, jerking a thumb toward Trell. The bored alien was sitting over in the corner sullenly twiddling his thumbs.

Mate and get on with it, the alien ordered them mentally.

Lynn's eyes remained guileless. "Four humans," she corrected herself.

Hammer furrowed his brow. So, they thought the traitor was still alive, eh? Instinctively, he lied.

"Crowbar's in the control room," he said loud enough for the other members of his gang to hear. "Making sure that nobody tries nothing stupid."

Amanda shrugged, sending erotic waves through the more prominent portion of her anatomy. "That's okay. We could send a girl to keep him company so he wouldn't feel left out."

Hammer snorted. "Screw him."

The willowy blonde dimpled. "That, too."

"I mean, forget it. I don't want my man getting distracted, like from his work." The ganglord smiled then and mentally undressed the woman, which took very little effort on his part. "And you sure could do that," he admitted. "Come here, babe."

Submissively, the woman did so. Hammer rose from the couch, pulled her close and kissed her on the mouth. She resisted him at first, then molded her body against his and returned the investment with compound interest. When they finally parted for necessary air, three more females gathered about the ganglord and began caressing his body.

Food from the delivery trucks was brought in by a team of squat, menial robots that strongly resembled a self-propelled waiter's cart with a pair of black metal arms, and the repast was spread out on a blue crystal table. Rock music pounded from an amazingly fancy AM/FM stereo/cassette player. Trell stared at the device with ill-concealed amusement. What was it? A machine for sound reproduction or a missile launching system?

"Time to par-ty!" yelled Drill, a woman on each arm. Chisel had his clinking jacket stripped off him by an oriental girl, who then nestled in his lap and wiggled delightfully. Speechless, the street punk heard Lynn and Wilma whisper incredible things into his ears and then seal the messages with hot kisses.

"I used to be an exotic dancer," confessed Cynthia to the panting Hammer as she warmly rubbed against him.

"Well, then, show us, lady!" commanded the sweating ganglord. "Show us!"

Drill boosted the volume on the stereo. The statuesque blonde spun to the middle of the room, kicked off her shoes and proceeded to twist her supple body and kick her long legs high in the air to the beat of the music. The walls of the pleasure room absorbed the harmonic tones and threw them back at the revelers cleaner and clearer. Soon, everybody but Trell was dancing on the green floor, shouting and laughing and stomping the tender moss into trembling ecstasy.

The alien restrained himself from summoning a medrobot, deducing that this strange ballet must be part of the humans' mating ritual. How primitive. Why didn't the men just club the women unconscious like civilized people? More bored than ever, Trell consoled himself by eating a bucket of fried chicken, bucket included. Daintily, he licked his fingers clean. Delicious! The technician found a second bucket, emptied out the chicken, and gleefully began munching on the greasy waxed cardboard. By the Prime Builder, could these Dirtlings cook!

Soon, Trell's translated laughter joined that of the cheerful, dancing throng.

*   *   *   *   *

Colonel Weiss's first indication that something was amiss came in the form of a chattering assault rifle from the rear of his squad.

"Back!" he ordered his troops, and the point men came running. The NATO soldiers dashed around a corner and into a scene from Hell itself.

At the far end of the corridor, the monstrous warobot had found the intruders at last and was rolling toward them in a manner that the NATO manual would definitely have described as hostile—its jointed metal arms tipped with whirring blades, snipping shears, or very nasty looking blue glowing balls. Wasting no time with subtlety, Colonel Weiss ordered the immediate use of rockets.

Promptly, both bazookas reached out with fiery fingers to strike the meter-wide tread of the robot, violently reducing the armored links to mangled metal trash.

Annoyed, the mechanical paused for a moment, then activated its cumbersome belly jets. In a wash of warm air, the behemoth slowly lifted a foot off the ground and began gliding forward. Immediately, a dozen grenades bounced down the expanse of the passageway to explode underneath the alien machine, but the triphammer blasts only made the machine bobble a bit in its flight. Without waiting for orders, the bazookas spoke again, destroying a huge section of the passageway directly in front of the armored horror, forcing the robot to clear away the wreckage before it could advance.

Privates Angelo and Peters pumped their grenade launchers and fired, the 40mm shells of high explosive impacting smack on the domed head of the warobot and causing it to blink. A hail of shrapnel flew back at them, and ricochets thumped into bullet-proof vests. A man cried out and fell, blood on his uniform. Lieutenant Nealon triggered his flame thrower, the arcing spray just reaching the distant machine to hose it with liquid napalm that clung like burning honey to its metal hide.

Unstoppable, the warobot floated on, it's collection of weaponed arms dripping flame.

Colonel Weiss frowned. They didn't have the time or resources for a pitched battle. "B Squad, delay that thing!" he yelled over the din of combat. "A Squad, to me!"

The troops split apart. B Squad dug in their heels and took defensive positions. The colonel and A Squad raced on, knowing full well that the fate of the world rested on them finding the control room and subduing the street gang. The corridor before them Ƚd. According to the map there should have been another Y-intersection coming up. But as the soldiers turned the corner, they found themselves at a dead end. Damn map was wrong again! Weiss touched the wall. Under his fingertips he felt it shift to the left and lock. The map wasn't wrong this time. They had been sealed off.

"Benson! Kaminski! Blast a hole in that partition. Gelfand, Lutzman, assist them. Everyone else back!" Weiss herded his troops away from the wall.

* * * * *

But, the colonel had left B Squad an ace in the hole, a corporal who carried an experimental prototype from the UN Weapons Lab—an Atomic Vortex Pistol, whatever that was—and Christ alone knew what the thing could do. It had been brought on this mission just in case of an emergency.

Well, if stopping this robot isn't an emergency, thought Lieutenant Nealon, then Daniel Webster has just changed the definition.

"AVP Fire!" Nealon ordered, and the corporal unleashed his death-dealing maybe. Blinding heat filled the length of the corridor and somebody screamed.

* * * * *

Trell's happy grin wilted as his translator subsonically told him what was happening on deck 6, relaying the information to him via Boztwank's tech-station.

"Alert! Alert! We have been boarded," said the beige box on his belt in English. Nobody seemed able to hear him over the deafening music, so Trell lifted the tape player up high and brought it smashing down on the crystal table. In the silence that followed, his translator calmly repeated its message.

Rudely, Hammer shoved the women off his lap and grabbed his jacket and laser. "Come on boys! We got some killing to do."

Drill stopped the man with a shout. "Hold it," he said, feeling inspired. "I got a great idea!"

Already at the door, the ganglord pivoted. "What?"

"How about using that Omega Gas stuff?" asked the locksmith. "Hey, Trell, we got any left?"

"Yes, there is!" cried the technician enthusiastically. He joined them by the door. "Lots! We can stop them cold!"

"Stop them *hot*, you mean!" snarled Hammer in correction, and he gave the alien a push into the hallway. "Get going greenie! We're gonna flood this ship with boiling Omega Gas and kill their asses dead!"

Garbled as that was, Trell got the general idea. Yes. They must kill these unknown invaders and their beasts of burden.

"What about the girls?" asked Chisel, jacket on, laser in hand, but still encircled by his allotment of scantily clad beauties.

Just bait in the trap, Hammer realized. But he excused himself for not figuring it out sooner, as this particular trick had never been played on him before. A pretty slick trap, too, he had to admit. Keep the gang busy with broads while the cops raided the place, literally catching the Deckers with their pants down. Should he kill these women and order some more? Nyah, what a waste. That Amanda, yum!

"Stay close," he ordered them. "And keep your mouths shut. Or else. Got it?" Terrified, the women meekly nodded and tagged along behind the racing street gang as best they could.

Minutes later, everyone was crowded into the control room and Trell manually closed the newly repaired security door, using a magnetic lock to hold it in place. Then as an afterthought, he wedged Boztwank's heavy pot against the door.

"Who's out there, anyway?" inquired Drill, only casually interested in who they were about to slaughter. "The FBI? The Army?" Then he blanched. "Not those star cops again!"

"Who freaking cares," snapped Hammer, taking his seat and throwing what few switches he knew how to use. "Trell, where are they?"

"Deck 6 . . . 5 . . . no, deck 4!" shouted the alien listening to his belt translator and hurrying over to his post. Whoever the invaders were, they were getting uncomfortably close to the control room.

Then a tremor shook the floor and suddenly there were no more working sensors in that part of the ship. What the Void was going on down there? "Deck 4," Trell repeated. "Deck 3 sensors indicate projectile weapons, chemical explosives, some kind of an energy weapon, and a large, metal—Why, they're battling the warobot!" Trell was astonished. "It must have been hunting for us ever since you escaped from the test chamber." *Gak!* The alien shuddered when he realized they'd probably passed right by the robot on their journey to the bridge, hidden in the Omega Gas.

"A war robot?" asked one of the women, and Hammer told her to shut up.

Frightened, the ladies exchanged nervous glances. They could only imagine such a machine as a horrible metal monster with an armored tanklike body and a dozen weapon-tipped arms. All they got wrong was the number of arms. There were a hundred.

"Our enemies battle our enemies," muttered Drill, sliding into his ponderous chair. "Like, biblical, man." Hammer grinned at his lieutenant. Always the intellectual, he thought.

As if for protection, a brunette pressed herself against Chisel, and he shoved her away. No time for that now. This was business.

"How hot we gotta make the gas?" asked Drill, punching buttons and pulling a lever. Trell reached past him and pushed the lever back a notch.

"Eight times your body temperature," said the translator on the alien's belt, doing a fast conversion. "That will take about four thousand seconds." Then Trell smiled. "No! Only one thousand seconds. The Omega Gas is still warm from before!"

Another tremor shook the starship and a patch of lights on the protector's board went dark.

"Trouble?" questioned Hammer.

"Only for them," snapped the angry technician. He hated to kill anybody, but the instinct for self-preservation was strong in his species.

Hammer scowled at his console. "What button do I press?" asked the ganglord. The alien pointed, and Hammer poised a thumb over the glowing indicator.

"You just tell me when," growled the human through gritted teeth. Rule #1 for the universe: Nobody messes with the

Bloody Deckers and lives.

Trell shouted agreement and checked the panel gauges. There would be no mistakes this time. He was going to wait until exactly the right moment and then release scalding hot Omega Gas into the corridors, peeling the very paint off the walls and killing everything organic it reached.

* * * * *

Deep within the bowels of the starship, the deadly Omega Gas bubbled and steamed in a metal caldron, the growing pressure accelerating the heating process until the war vapor was straining at the release valve, struggling to be set free.

But it had been commanded to wait.

Nine hundred seconds to go.

890.

885.

880.

15

Streamers, stars, and swirls gradually faded from their eyes and sight returned to the NATO soldiers of B Squad. Fifty meters away sat the warobot, an inert black mountain, its multiple arms dangling like metal wind chimes. Deep scars were burned in its prow from the energy cone of the Atomic Vortex Pistol. Raggedly, the men cheered in triumph, then stopped, as every inch of their exposed skin was painfully sunburned. Medical packs were opened posthaste.

"What does that weapon fire again, corporal?" asked Lieutenant Nealon, applying first aid cream to his blistered hands.

"A controlled nuclear tornado, sir," replied the soldier, dressing his own burns.

Somebody laughed. "That? Controlled?"

"Hey, what about radiation poisoning?" asked a worried soul.

"According to the manual there's no harmful fallout," stated the corporal, pointing to his hip where a leather-bound book the size of the Manhattan Yellow Pages hung from his belt.

"Enough chitchat," growled a sergeant, slapping a fresh ammo clip into his rifle. "We still got a job to do. Let's move out."

Groaning, the soldiers got to their feet and prepared to rejoin their companions, when something creaked behind them. They spun around to see the alien machine down the passageway tremble, its arms stir, and once more lift off the floor and begin moving forward, as though nothing had ever happened. Lieutenant Nealon cursed. Good Lord, what did it take to stop that thing, a court order? The AVP had only stunned the wardroid. Okay, how about more of the same?

"Visors!" the lieutenant shouted, and the troops rushed to obey, knowing what to expect. "Fire!" he ordered, tapping the AVP man on the shoulder.

Dutifully, the gunner raised the weapon again and pulled the first trigger. The scarlet beam of a tracking laser shot out from the tiny cylinder clipped to the underside of his cumbersome, multi-barreled weapon. With a gulp, the soldier then squeezed the second trigger, and a twisting lance of burning energy vomited from the bulbous muzzle of the AVP with a bucking recoil. Searing yellow light blinded the humans as the spiraling cone of atomic flame stretched horizontally down the length of the corridor to strike the frantically backpedaling warobot.

Violently, the alien machine shuddered as the stabbing tip of the nuclear tornado skipped across its prow, leaving ugly, glowing furrows in the black armor. Electrical discharges danced along the robot's massive frame, and drops of molten metal sprayed the walls. Then, as the AVP ceased its outpouring, the warobot went dark and slumped to the floor, its assortment of blades and probes and drills punching holes in the soft deck. In the blissful calm that followed, the toasted NATO troopers said a fervent prayer . . . and then groaned in disappointment as the running lights of the robot brightened, its massive head swiveled toward them, its clanking arms assumed a defiant posture, it rose into the air, and resumed gliding toward them.

Lieutenant Nealon grimaced. The damn thing shook the charge off faster this time, he noted unhappily.

"Fire!" the sweating man commanded.

Panting, the corporal shook his head. "No go, sir. The battery pack needs time to recharge."

"How long?"

"Sixty seconds."

Sixty lives was more like it, Nealon thought grimly. But every one of them bought A Squad precious time. "Open fire!"

Bullets streamed from assault rifles, probing the robot for a weak spot. Screaming rockets slammed into the distant walls, the ferocious blasts piling up mounds of material to delay the warobot's approach. The battledroid outmaneuvered the humans by reaching out with a pair of huge metal claws to crunchingly grab hold of the low ceiling and ponderously swing itself over the massed wreckage. No mindless automaton this: the robot learned from its mistakes.

That chilling sight prompted the troopers to fire their weapons with renewed determination. The starship's ventilators efficiently cleansed the smoke from the air, giving the NATO forces a clear shooting range. But for what? Thermit, grenades, napalm; so far the only thing to even hamper the machine was the Atomic Vortex Pistol. Fat lot of good it did.

A thunderous explosion sounded from around the corner and billowing smoke heralded the arrival of coughing men who thirstily drank in the clean air and stumbled away again. Colonel Weiss was among them.

Unbelievably, the dividing wall still stood, and was only spiderwebbed with cracks. Benson and Kaminsky expertly slapped more of the doughlike plastique on the barrier, jabbed in time pencils, and twisted off their ends. The soldiers scarcely had taken cover when the charges blew. As the fumes dispersed, curses sounded louder than the plastique. The fissures were wider, big enough to put your arm through, but before their eyes, the gaping cracks began to close like a wound in living flesh.

"Again!" Weiss ordered the demolition team. "This time with everything you've got!"

Pounds instead of ounces of explosive were smacked onto the wall, and time pencils broken. The concussion shook A Squad to the floor. Lying prone, Colonel Weiss rolled over, his assault rifle ready to add its pittance of destruction to the job. But the wall was gone, blown to smithereens.

"A Squad," he shouted triumphantly. "Move out!"

Effortlessly, the soldiers hopped over the remains of the wall and raced off. A zigzagging turn brought them to another dead end, and the locking click of the self-healing wall was clearly heard by everybody present.

Furiously the colonel thought, thirty years of battlefield training coming to his aid instantly.

"Search for an air vent," he ordered them, but alas, none were to be found. Only one thing left to do then, he decided, retreat and try to battle their way past that armored tank B Squad had been delaying. By God, they'd fight it hand-to-hand!

"Charge!" shouted Weiss, and without question the NATO troopers reversed direction and bravely advanced to the rear.

* * * * *

Two levels above the fighting, Amanda closed the front of her gossamer-thin nightie and approached Hammer. Gently, she touched the ganglord on the shoulder. "Hammer?"

"What?" he snarled out of the corner of his mouth, not taking his eyes off Trell.

"Where are we?" she asked, in her throaty voice.

"This is the control room, bitch, and we are in control."

Uncertainly, the woman glanced about the strange, white room, and the incredible profusion of controls at each of the tech-stations that the Decker's were occupying. "What happened to Crowbar?"

The ganglord raised an eyebrow. "Eh? Ah! Hmm. He's out taking a leak."

"Oh." She seemed to accept that. "Can you really kill off the cops with some kind of gas?"

Hammer grinned at the tall blonde evilly. "Freaking-A, lady, they're already history! This Omega crap dissolves you like sugar in water. *Pft!* You're gone. Super-dead."

"Wow." A sparkle came to her eyes. "Then there's no danger to us. You're still in charge?"

"We're in charge of the world!" roared Drill, raising a clenched fist into the air like the revolutionaries on television always did. "King Deckers!"

The lovelies whispered among themselves, and the gang preened under their fearful respect. Yes, the Bloody Deckers were kings of the world.

"King of the world," said Amanda reverently. "But a king needs a queen," she suggested, drawing herself close enough to Hammer so that a warm breast lightly brushed his cheek.

"Queens," he corrected her, his attention drawn away from his controls and to her cleavage in a momentary rush of lust. "Lots of 'em. At least a dozen."

"But one's got to be his first lady," she murmured, stroking his astonishingly clean mane of hair. "Can I?" the woman asked him softly.

The street tough smiled. "Can you what?" he asked in return, thinking of a thousand things that she could do. And he read *Penthouse Forum.*

"The cops," she said, breathing deeply, which produced spectacular results. "Could I kill the cops? Please? I always wanted to off a bunch of pigs." The ganglord hesitated. "Pretty please with sugar on top?"

With a laugh, Hammer slapped her on the bottom and she squealed in delight. "Okay, fox, you off the pigs. You just gotta press this button here."

Amanda's expression showed her amazement. "Really? Just press that button?"

The street tough nodded. "Yep. That's it."

"Why . . . thank you, lard-for-brains."

It took Hammer a good second to react to that. Angrily, he

spun his chair toward her, and she raked the boy's face with her nails, digging bloody furrows in his flesh, just barely missing his eyes. With a curse, the ganglord lunged at her, swinging a haymaker that would have caved in her skull had it connected, but she swayed out of the way and gave him a short punch in the throat. Hacking for air, Hammer stumbled backward.

Cries from his companions showed that they, too, were under attack. Blindly, Hammer shot a fist out, accidentally connecting with Amanda's pretty nose, shattering it. The girl went down, her face bloody. Hammer vaulted from his chair and turned, just in time to avoid having a spike heel driven into his brain by the long-legged Joyce. With murderous intent, he grabbed for his laser, only to discover the weapon was gone.

Suddenly, he realized that the women had split up into teams. Three babes in black lace and fishnet stockings were piled on top of Drill, pounding him with their fists. And three in peek-a-boo mesh body suits had surrounded a bewildered Chisel, who apparently had a patch of his hair yanked out. Standing, with his back to his console, the disheveled kid swung his left hand in a glittering defensive pattern, while he sucked at a vicious bite mark on his right wrist. Hammer judged that the boy was in shock, but even as he watched, Chisel's face took on a feral look and the knife began to slice instead of defend. The half-naked women hastily moved away from him.

They were not bait in the trap, the ganglord realized, correcting his previous appraisal, but spies sent to protect the invaders downstairs. Hammer contorted his face into a snarl. Well, tough tittie, bitch, it hadn't worked!

Vindictively, the street tough punched a button on the console and . . . the empty chair sank out of sight, the floor closing over the hole. He blinked and glanced at the bank of identical white buttons. Hellfire, he'd forgotten which one it was!

Desperately, Hammer raked his hands across the control board, pushing dozens of buttons at once. Pictures of different planets appeared on the viewscreens. Wall panels opened and

closed, disruptors tumbling out. Ion clusters got a ring job.
The turbo-lift went into reverse. Toilets flushed. Dinner was
started. Starch was added to the laundry. An unnameable alien
device stopped doing its unnameable alien function. And the
ship was renamed *Ezrlptxy*.

Trell had come to some disquieting conclusions about Dirtling mating practices and discreetly took refuge behind a small
pile of stony rubble that had once been Gasterphaz. Even in
death, the Choron protected.

Their long blond, black, and red hair streaming in the air
behind them, several of the women dashed over to snatch the
disruptors that fell out of the wall. But they were dismayed to
find that only the lasers taken from the Deckers were activated.
They tried pulling this and twisting that, but to no avail.

Barking a warning, the three women with working laser
rifles assumed a firing stance, holding the weapons with anything but trepidation. The other girls drew aside, modestly
drawing the remnants of their ripped clothing together, their
voluptuous bodies smeared with blood. Instinctively, Hammer
grabbed the dazed Amanda and held her in front of him as a
living shield.

"Try it, and the bitch dies," he growled threateningly, and
then added a few phrases that people in polite society would
never utter in front of a lady.

The blonde awoke at his shouts and smashed a high heel
directly onto Hammer's instep. With a howl of pain, the
ganglord released the woman, and she threw herself to the
floor. Without hesitation, Wilma, Alice, and Lynn fired their
lasers. Triple beams of searing energy lanced out from the
rifles, and the polychromatic rays struck and clung to the sparkling defense fields that had sprung up around the Deckers.
But the earlier conflict of laser and shield repeated itself as the
fields shrank, trembled, and then expanded. And the women
were just as surprised as the Deckers had been when the lasers
shut down rather than consume their own beams and be
destroyed.

Switchblades snapped into action, and the gang moved in

for the kill, with no thought of mercy for the fairer sex. They had been betrayed and the women would die. Their blood would be just drops in the ocean already spilled by the gang. It was four-to-one odds, but the women were virtually naked and unarmed.

As the Deckers attacked, the three women in bikinis expertly dodged the clumsy knife thrusts and jabbed out with their appropriated rifles, the butts smashing male teeth. Small fists smacked into pockmarked faces, breaking noses and jaws. Shapely knees met elbows. Bones cracked. Switchblades dropped from nerveless fingers and were kicked away. Drill's squirter was chokingly wrapped around his neck. Alice and Wilma punched opposite sides of Hammer's head at the same time, scrambling what little brains he had. The ganglord slumped to the floor. Chisel was drop-kicked on top of him by the beautiful but deadly Wilma Fisher, U.S. Secret Service.

The fight over, Lt. Amanda Jackson of the New York City SWAT team fired off orders to her mixed-bag of commandos. "Fisher, Webbert, guard these morons. Kill them if they move. Cohen, Bentley, find Trell and have him turn off that gas. Everybody else, with me."

Through sheer force of will, Trell tried to make himself turn invisible. Failing that, he prayed. But the women found him anyway, crouching behind his makeshift barricade.

"I am not of your species!" he shrieked as they hauled him wriggling into view. "I didn't mate with you! DON'T EAT ME!"

UN security guard Alice Bentley bared her teeth at the alien crew member and snarled, "If you don't turn off the Omega Gas and stop that robot immediately, I'll bite your head off and *then* mate with you!"

Trell turned a nauseous shade of aquamarine and lunged for the control panel. Wildly slapping buttons, he reversed the Omega Gas process. He then turned to Gasterphaz's tech-station and froze. The controls were destroyed: wires, switches, and relay cubes melted into an unrecognizable mess. A laser must have splashed its beam across the panel. And there was nothing he, nor anyone else, could do to effect repairs outside of a week's hard work.

Dejectedly, he faced the crazed female Dirtlings. "I hope I taste just rotten," said the technician as his last great act of defiance.

Lynn Cohen grabbed a fistful of the alien's uniform. "And just what do you mean by that?" demanded the Interpol operative, her bedroom eyes now spitting fire.

"Stop the robot?" squeaked Trell's translator. "Hot Void, I can't even talk to it."

"Try anyway!" ordered the petite brunette, licking her chops suggestively, and the little alien obediently fainted.

Efficiently, the gang was stripped and their clothing distributed among the women. Everybody was given at least two knives from Chisel's seemingly endless assortment. The huskier of the females wore the gang's leather jackets and were armed with motorcycle chains. The three women in ripped bikini's had donned t-shirts to cover their nakedness. They also sported the stolen laser rifles.

Lieutenant Jackson, in her peek-a-boo black lace body suit, stuffed torn bits of handkerchief into her nose to stop the bleeding. With professional expertise, she checked the clip on Hammer's Colt .45, duly noted the number of bullets left, slammed the clip home, and worked the slide on the automatic pistol, chambering a round for immediate use. On her orders, the door of the control room was forced open and Assault Team C moved out.

Their decorative, but unbattleworthy, high heels were discarded, and as the Decker's boots had proved too large for any of the team, they ran barefoot along the starship's main corridor. The soft floor felt oddly warm and almost alive to their bare feet.

Chosen by the FCT's computers for their physical beauty, courage, and military training, none of the women faced the upcoming fight with anything but grim resolution. The avant-garde soldiers knew the desperate strait their male counterparts were in, and that the laser weapons they now carried could be the deciding factor in the battle's outcome. But, like the street gang and Trell, they were unsure where the fight was located. At a branching corridor, they paused.

"Which way, sir?" panted the Swedish airline security officer that Dr. Malavade had personally recommended for this assignment, knowing her fondness for trying new, exciting things.

Amanda cocked her head. "The noise does seem louder in this direction." But the sounds of battle dropped off sharply as they neared a four-way intersection.

"Damn," sighed a zaftig Green Beret, stopping in the act of using a discarded fishnet stocking to tie off her riot of ash-blond curls. "We're too late."

"Can it, sister," barked the U.S. Secret Service operative, wishing that she had her trusty .357 Magnum with her instead of this souped-up alien flashlight.

Coyly, a buxom KGB agent tucked a well-shaped breast back into the flimsy lace bra it had inadvertently popped out of while they were running. "Perhaps if we tried the next level down," she suggested in flawless English.

"You tell us how to get there, comrade," snapped the poster girl for the United States Air Force, a rocket-jockey of a test pilot who was as famous for her impatience as her fabulous pneumatic shape.

Down the corridor to their left, one of the women on point seemed to be listening to the wall. "Mandell! What in hell are you doing?" demanded Jackson, walking over to her.

Stacy Mandell, a martial arts instructor and ex-Miss Nude Connecticut, removed her ear from the vibrating white wall and waved her commander back. "Clear the area!" she shouted in a surprisingly husky voice. "Scram! Beat feet!"

As the women staged a tactical withdrawal, a high-pitched squeal became evident. Rapidly, it grew in volume, reaching higher and higher in tone and tempo until the squealing drove them to the brink of screaming. But the female soldiers gritted their teeth against the horrid noise and took the punishment, unwilling to yield another foot of the corridor. Obviously, something was coming through the wall, but they were not going to retreat. The team would stand and fight, if only to avenge the brave men sent to assist them. Whatever came through that wall was going to be hit, and hit hard, by beams, bullets, knives, chains, hands, and feet.

The devilish noise reached its painful crescendo and the wall disintegrated in a blinding flash of light and heat; the spray of vaporized metal stung every inch of the womens' exposed skin. A rain of fused, black robot parts closely followed the explosion. Four metal arms loudly clanged off the opposite wall, a whirling blade cut a jagged trench in the white material, and the robot's head embedded in the floor like a cannonball hitting a snow bank. After a moment, the starship's hidden ventilators whisked away the pungent smoke, and from the gaping hole in the wall a coughing man in a NATO uniform stumbled into view. Amanda rushed to assist him.

"Are you okay?" Weiss and Jackson asked each other.

As the women helped the bedraggled soldiers into the corridor, their respective commanders took the opportunity to report.

"The Bloody Deckers are in our custody," said Lieutenant Commander Jackson with a salute. "We are in control of the ship. No personnel losses to report, although each of us would like to be disinfected and then shower for a week." A twinkle entered her blue eyes. "I see you got your robot."

"Don't even mention a shower to me," laughed the colonel, mopping the sweat from his flushed face. "And, yeah, we beat the damn thing. But I'm going to have some strong words with the scientists in the NATO weapons lab."

"Why's that?"

"They never told us that the Atomic Vortex Pistol only had a kill range of three feet." To the woman's puzzled expression he added, "I'll explain later."

16

Less than an hour later, in the underground command bunker of the FCT, the humans and visiting Gees were gathered around the linen-covered poker table to closely examine some of the more interesting artifacts taken from the *All That Glitters*.

Meanwhile, what remained of the Bloody Deckers was hauled off in chains to NATO HQ for a thorough debriefing and a jail sentence that could only be measured in radioactive half-lives. However, in the weeks to come, a statue would be erected in Central Park honoring the gang for saving mankind from Idow and his crew; a monument that was regularly defaced by the New York citizenry—and cleaned by the local branch of the Hell's Angels Motorcycle Club.

Contemptuously, Sir John tossed the defense field generator onto the table with other belts, laser rifles, bits of warobot, and the remains of Boztwank's squirter. "A toy," he declared in an annoyed tone. "Useless. It was foolish of the aliens to depend on such a limited defense."

Dr. Wu took her accustomed seat between Bronson and Nicholi. "True," agreed the Chinese physicist. "A force shield that was proof against both energy and material weapons, similar to the dome that protects their ship, would have used a great deal of power. More than the field generators in the belt could readily supply. But since you could link either the shield or the field to the starship's reactor, who cares?"

"Lack of mobility?" guessed Prof. Rajavur, fingering the woven metal hem of the belt.

"How about a compromise, then," suggested General Bronson, grinding out his cigar butt in an ashtray. "A defense shield. Literally. A round disk, say . . . a meter in diameter, anchored directly in front of you. Crouch down and you'd be safe from frontal attacks."

"Plus, you could stand and run, firing around the edges," added Nicholi, smiling broadly at the American general. "I like it, Wayne. I like it!"

Using a lint-free cloth, Dr. Wu wiped a smear of dried blood off the translucent crystal barrel of one of the laser rifles. She inspected the weapon's breech, and then held it to the overhead light. The barrel cast a rainbow pattern of colors across her face. "I wonder what a full laboratory analysis will reveal about the beam-focusing mechanism? Is it an electromagnetic prism assembly like Prof. Richard Hill of Boston University is working on, or something entirely new?"

Mentally, Rajavur made a note of the name so that he could requisition any available information on the man's research for her. Then he paused. On second thought, knowing Yuki, she had probably already requisitioned Hill himself as a lab assistant. "How long before you can make a report?" the Icelander asked his scientific advisor, hiding a smile.

"Twenty-four hours for the preliminary," she replied, primly crossing her legs and wondering what the gray-haired man found so amusing. "Sooner, with any luck. Interpol is sending an armored truck to collect these small items and carry them to the UN laboratory in Long Island."

With fingertip pressure, Mohad turned one of the defense fields' *ON/OFF* switches. "The results will be most enlightening, I am sure," quipped the linguist.

"Will you and Yuki be conducting the experiments?" asked Nicholi, luxuriating in his old poker chair and carefully stretching his arms so as not to impolitely smack any of his teammates. Czar's Blood, he was glad to be out from behind that sheet of glass.

"No," said Dr. Malavade. "For a while at least, Dr. Wu and I will be living in the alien starship with an international team of scientists overseeing its complete dissection. Why, the communications equipment alone—"

"I want to see those engines," stated Yuki flatly.

Rajavur countered with, "You mean the medical facilities."

"No, the shield generators," interjected Bronson.

Eagerly, Sir John leaned forward. "Trell is what I'm interested in," he said in scholarly passion. "There's so much that he can tell us about galactic society and the way it works. Why, even what he *doesn't* know can be informative. You see—"

Nicholi lifted a restraining hand. "Please, Johnathon, no lectures today."

"Be sure to clear everything through Wayne," the diplomat sternly told them. "He's in charge of security for the whole project. The brand new secretary-general of the UN has placed the entire matter in our, quote—highly competent hands—end quote."

The bunker rang with easy laughter as the First Contact Team relaxed after this most hectic of days. Unnoticed by the humans, the two golden beings standing over by the kitchen unit nervously exchanged meaningful glances, put down their mugs of buttered and salted coffee, and briefly touched hands. Seconds later, the avantor stepped forward to say, "Unfortunately, we cannot allow you access to any of this information."

Everyone stopped laughing.

Maintaining a diplomatically neutral face, Rajavur laid aside his huge coffee mug. "And why is that?"

"Yeah," puffed General Bronson suspiciously from behind a freshly lit panatela, Comrade General Nicholi closely flanking him on the left. "What gives?"

"After all, we can probably improve upon your designs," said Dr. Wu in tactless truth.

"Most likely, Doctor," agreed the female avantor. "But it is strictly against the rules."

"*The Galactic League Handbook*," piped in her loyal assistant. "Chapter Nine: *Codes of Conduct*, sub-section 3: 'Regulations Referring To The Dispersal Of Technical Information To Non-Member Planets.' Item one: DON'T."

"This is ridiculous!" snapped Bronson, plainly nettled by the outrageous statement.

Avantor was unruffled by his outburst. "A fact nonetheless, General."

Unable to stop the Gees without resorting to physical violence, the FCT watched helplessly as the two aliens collected the items taken from the starship and placed them in a storage box supplied by the humans. Avantor locked the box tight. The 17 broke the key in half, and both Gees hid a piece in a seamless fold of their golden uniforms.

"But surely, the mere fact that we already know of these devices' existence eclipses such an action on your part," observed Sir John.

Score one for our side, thought Mohad smugly. Then he froze as a strange hand began groping his knee under the table. Eh? he thought. What was going on here?

Avantor wiggled her ears in dissent. "The rule book disagrees. And personally, I believe your race is simply too violent to be allowed scientific knowledge of this level."

"We're too violent?" stormed General Bronson, removing the cigar from his mouth and jabbing it at the two alien beings. "And what the hell were Idow and his crew, galactic Girl Scouts?"

Hoarsely, The 17 coughed into his hand and fanned the air before him. No Koolgoolagan cigar, that. "On the contrary, they were criminals. You, though, are not."

Not openly anyway, thought Rajavur as he continued to tap a message in Morse code on Dr. Malavade's knee. The communications expert squeezed the diplomat's hand in acknowledgment, politely excused himself from the table, and left the bunker by the main door.

Sir John marshaled his powers of debate and rallied to the attack. "Well then," he said, taking hold of the lapels of his gray tweed suit and assuming his best lawyer stance. "You must be ignorant of the effect that your presence has had on Earth. Peace has broken out like the common cold. China, Russia, and America have signed an unprecedented peace treaty. England and Ireland have come to terms. Israel and the PLO have joined as one nation. So have North and South Korea, East and West Germany. . . ." The sociologist spread his arms. "It's pandemic! A new feeling of Earthly brotherhood has enveloped our globe. Such an unconditional reaction on our part *must* cause you to reconsider."

Avantor was unswayed by his argument. "No," she repeated.

Comrade General Nicholi Yuriavich Nicholi coldly regarded the guardian of the galaxy in the disapproving manner that Russian generals seem to have patented. "If we were indeed the savage primitives you think," he said rationally, "would we. not simply take the machines and deny you use of the starship that you so desperately need to return home?"

Lovely, noted Courtney, mentally applauding the general. Not a threat, per se, but merely the acknowledgment that a threat could have been made and wasn't. Crafty old bear. Maybe . . . perhaps . . . ?

With inhuman control, the avantor turned her expressionless black eyes on Nicholi. "Comrade General, we are in constant communication with our home world. Any unwarranted acts on your part would result in eventual retaliation by our Great Golden Fleet. The starship *All That Glitters*, its equipment, and sole surviving crew member, belong exclusively to us. Do you really wish to test your military prowess against ours?"

Angry, General Bronson removed the cigar from his mouth, noticed that everybody was staring at him, paused, and then returned the stogie to its normal position, his thoughts unspoken.

"Well, if that is your unalterable position," sighed Prof. Rajavur, his voice trailing off in resignation. "Are you sure there is nothing we could say to change your minds?"

The golden female shook her head in the accepted Dirtly gesture. "Sorry, Professor, no."

Sadly, the diplomat shrugged and rose from his seat. "So be it. At least you will allow us to see you off in the manner deemed proper for visiting dignitaries? We could assemble the leaders of our world here in less than . . . two days."

Bull, thought Nicholi keeping a straight face. We could have the entire UN General Assembly here in less than two hours. What was the Icelander plotting?

Avantor remained unyielding. "Expedience dictates our immediate departure. We mean you no discourtesy, but we must return to our headquarters with all due speed. Prior orders. I'm sure you understand."

The two generals nodded in agreement. Yes, orders were orders. A universal rule. Like never pulling on a busted straight. Or volunteering for anything.

"But of course," agreed Rajavur in sympathy. Gallantly, he offered his hand to the aliens and they shook. "You don't mind if we personally see you off, do you?"

At last, the avantor smiled. "A pleasure, Professor. My 17 and I would consider it an honor."

* * * * *

This conversation, relayed *en toto* to Great Golden Ones Headquarters, was judged to be fitting and proper. Avantor the avantor and her 17 were to be congratulated on a job well done.

Later, under harsher scrutiny, it was decided that this is where the two made their big mistake. But at the time, who could have known?

* * * * *

Night had come to Central Park. The electric towers of New York City brightened the horizon while powerful floodlights illuminated the area about the colossal white ship brighter than the sun. In relative peace, the FCT bid its guests adieu while thousands of unseen eyes kept close track of their every move. The noisy civilian crowds were hundreds of meters away behind the military cordon, and the NATO troops had just recently been reinforced by a special crowd control unit from the NYPD. Why, during a rock concert, this small a group was the lull the police relaxed in. Heck, nobody was even drunk!

The street gang's tribute had been long since removed from the starship and the confiscated alien artifacts replaced inside the cargo bay. Standing near the base of the loading ramp, Avantor and The 17 checked over the inventory of items, making sure that nothing from the ship was missing. But, The 17 quickly noted a major discrepancy and bluntly asked the attending humans where Trell-desamo-Trell-ika-Trell-forzua, Jr. was.

Resplendent in his red diplomat sash, light gray morning coat, and black silk top hat, Prof. Rajavur feigned surprise. "Gosh, I thought the ambulance would have delivered him already."

Avantor chewed over the human word. "Ambulance," she repeated. "A medical emergency vehicle? Why would the technician have need of such a transport? Was he damaged in the fighting?"

"Killed, actually," said General Bronson, trying to sound embarrassed. "While trying to escape. Our troops were understandably a bit trigger-happy."

Thoughtfully, the female alien turned her eerie black eyes on the Earth soldier. "And why wasn't I informed of his demise earlier?" she inquired, her voice the temperature of liquid methane.

Bronson shrugged, making his chest full of medals tinkle. "You didn't ask," he replied truthfully.

"Where is Trell's body located?" interjected The 17, boldly stepping forward, his electro-clipboard and stylus floating rigidly in the air next to him.

Comrade General Nicholi, who was as equally decked out as his friends in full dress uniform, sash, ribbons, and metals—none of them for good conduct—answered the golden male's question. "He's across the street in a mobile UN lab undergoing total dissection. Is there a problem with that?"

For a moment, Avantor and her 17 touched hands. "Produce his remains immediately," the female alien ordered. The unspoken words "or else" were heard clearly by everyone present.

The FCT exchanged a round of glances as Nicholi muttered something to the military aide standing beside him. The UN soldier nodded, saluted, and spoke briefly into his walkietalkie. In less than a minute, the civilian crowd parted and through the NATO barricade rolled a military ambulance. The aliens strode over to the white car as armed UN guards opened the rear doors for them. On the rubber matting of the floor was a styrofoam container, and inside that, nestled in a foggy bed of dry ice was an ordinary tin janitor's bucket with a snap-on plastic lid.

The Gees stared at the pail, each other, the pail again, and then The 17 gingerly lifted the lid. In dismay, they saw that the bucket was filled to the brim with a thick green mush the consistency of overcooked pea soup.

"Trell?" squeaked The 17, as if half expecting an answer from the emerald puree. Swirling about, Avantor angrily opened her mouth to speak when Dr. Wu interrupted her.

"*Total* dissection," said Yuki, her hands neatly hidden in the flowing angel sleeves of her heavily embroidered red and black formal Chinese robe. The avantor closed her mouth with a snap.

Impeccable in a cream-colored nehru jacket and turban, Dr. Malavade noted that accidents will happen.

"Chalk it up to scientific fervor," said Sir John, dressed in an incongruous, but historically accurate tam-o'-shanter, wisket, family tartan kilt, knickers, and silver-buckled shoes. Only alien beings—and other Scotsmen—would think his outfit dapper.

Studying the humans' expressionless faces, Avantor briefly wondered if something was decaying in the land of cheese makers.

"Verify that it is him, 17," she commanded.

As ordered, the golden male stuck a finger into the warm glop and put it in his mouth. Hmmm, not bad actually. Modified vegetable fiber, slightly radioactive, enriched with elemental beryllium and benzine. Check, that was the physiology of Trell's species, all right.

"It's him, my liege," he reported erroneously.

Satisfied, the avantor wheeled about and marched into the ship, The 17 following close on her heels with the covered bucket. Seconds later, the door to the loading bay closed behind them.

Almost immediately, a harsh buzzing sound filled the air and the white ship lifted up, as easy as a child's balloon, compressed dirt falling from the bottom of the sphere as it floated into the nighttime sky. Heedful of the people below, Avantor kept the engines at 10/10, barely sufficient to lift the enormous vessel, until they were well away from the planet's surface. Then The 17 boosted the reactor to 20/20. With an explosion of power, the ship vanished into the starry black of space.

Shortly, NASA signaled Dr. Malavade on his pocket communicator that the alien craft had shunted into hyperspace, and he happily announced the fact to his compatriots.

"Well, well," smirked Nicholi, feeling very pleased with himself and the world in general. "We did it."

Dr. Wu took off her ceremonial robe and folded it over an arm, exposing the floral print dress she'd been wearing earlier. "Yes, it does appear that way," she said in agreement.

"How long do you think it will take them to realize that they've been tricked?" asked Bronson, as a night breeze tugged on the lighter flame he applied to his latest cigar.

Prof. Rajavur shrugged. "With any luck, never. But we're planning on lift-off in a month."

General Bronson exhaled a stream of smoke. "Is that possible? To build a starship from scratch in thirty days?"

"With the resources of the entire world behind us?" asked Sigerson, removing his red sash and tucking it into his silk hat. "Most certainly."

"What was in that bucket anyway?" Mohad asked as he unraveled his turban. Silly thing, turbans, but girls seemed to like them. Made him appear taller, at least.

Yuki gave him a tired grin. "Minced asparagus bombarded with gamma radiation, then laced with powdered beryllium and a dash of cleaning solution. I based the formula on what Trell had asked for lunch."

"I am so glad this worked," said Sir John, doffing his tam-o'-shanter and stroking his moustache. "But just in case, I had a duplicate of Trell waiting in the wings, so to speak. I based my plan on that scenario we played out four years ago, in the event it became necessary to disguise humans as aliens. Why, I even had duplicates of Avantor, Idow, the Bloody Deckers, and us."

General Nicholi raised an eyebrow. Another Yuki? Impossible.

Dr. Wu frowned. Another Nicholi? No thank you.

Deep in thought, the six members of the defunct First Contact Team turned away from the crumbling edge of the lake-sized hole in the ground. Taking their time, they strolled back to their waiting limousine and the fantastic task ahead of them.

"Where is Trell anyway?" asked Sir John, after a while.

Rajavur smiled. "Right now? Aboard a stealth jet, en route to Kennedy Space Center, telling us everything he knows about starship engines, force shields, proton cannons, hyperdrives. . . ." Sullenly, the diplomat kicked at a clod of dirt in his way. "Seems a pity, though."

"What does?" asked Nicholi, genuinely surprised. "Our plan has come off flawlessly."

Prof. Rajavur stuck his hands in his pants pockets. "Almost. You see, Trell claims to know nothing about deflector plating."

Dr. Malavade stopped walking and lifted his head to look at the twinkling points of light above the city, stars that were no longer so distant or unreachable.

"As you say, a pity."

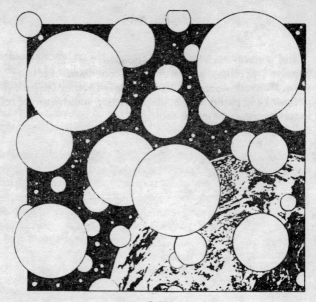

17

Like a yo-yo on a string, the Cape Kennedy technician hung suspended from a steel cable and body harness rig high in the air alongside a nearly completed starship. Grimly, the woman concentrated on her welding, since the fate of Earth might well rest on the quality of her work. Warm sea breezes gently tugged the woman's hair free from her cap. Visibly annoyed, she tucked it into the collar of her sweat-stained uniform. There was little time for food and rest, and none for laundry if she wanted to stay on her rigid work schedule.

On the distant horizon, across a thousand flat acres of ferro-concrete, the towering space shuttle assembly buildings appeared like doll houses, and yet they seemed to look fatherly at the starship taking form before them. Pride of accomplishment overwhelmed any negative feelings about NASA's state-of-the-art technology becoming obsolete virtually overnight.

Wary of pinching her fingers, the woman judiciously lowered the last armored section of the starship's hull into place and activated her hand-tool. Carefully, the technician guided a molecular softening beam along the joining line of the metallic plates, causing their atomic structures to intermingle and form a single, unbroken mass. The entire hull of the colossal starship had been formed this way out of thousands of curved adamantine sheets that not even a nuclear laser could have heat-welded.

With her right hand, the woman artfully cold-fused the pieces together, while her gainfully employed left hand held the internal components of the alien tool in place. The hastily assembled device had been built under Trell's adroit direction.

Over the last thirty days, NASA, backed by the money and power of the UN, had completely retooled its Florida base. They slapped together devices and machines with unheard of abilities as fast as they could. Time was paramount. Every second saved was more precious than gold—a word that left a sour taste in everybody's mouth these days.

Also in the past month, the First Contact Team had abdicated its position of power and returned the world to autonomy. The United Nations politely thanked them for a job well done, awarded the team a wheelbarrow full of medals, then disbanded the unit and reassigned its members to new, top priority duties. Then, when nobody was looking, the UN Security Council took swift steps to assure that such an incredible upsurpation of authority would never happen again. Among other things, they set fire to the FCT's mainframe computer, filled the command bunker with concrete, and welded the door shut.

Meanwhile, thanks to their improved scanning devices, (courtesy of Trell, again), Earth knew precisely when the Great Golden Ones had started moving in their mobile space forts to form a blockade around the planet. Subsequently, the final countdown for launch had been advanced. Spaceworthiness was the top priority—the internal work could be finished once the ship was in flight.

With a satisfied nod, the technician tucked her hand-tool away and turned on the air tank of her scuba outfit. Under constant visual observation, this act told her superiors that the work was completed. They immediately cut the support cable.

Down through the air the woman dropped, expertly angling her fall to swan dive into a huge vat of thermal jelly that had been waiting six stories below her. With a loud clang, thick steel shutters slammed into place, sealing off the top of the vat just in time. Searing gouts of green flame washed over the launch site, cracking the ferro-concrete apron and melting every unprotected item. Smoothly, humanity's first starship lifted into the clear azure sky.

But after a kilometer or so, the ion drive of the vessel began to sputter and cough, causing the interstellar craft to wobble erratically. And, extending for hundreds of meters around the ship, its poorly tuned antigravity field started liberating countless volumes of turbulent air, which quickly formed a hurricane about the comically bobbling globe. This only made the huge, ungainly starship doubly visible from space. Promptly, the Great Golden Ones dispatched a sleek war-cube to intercept the sluggish escapee.

* * * * *

Aboard the golden flagship of the spaceborne armada, Avantor, now a junior grade avantor, and her primary assistant, The 16, sternly stared at the bow monitor. Only the extenuating circumstances of the situation had given them another chance to safeguard the primitive planet and protect their pensions. The Budget Department had wanted to send the two inept guardians back to Dirt in a Class 2 garbage scow, but Tactical had overridden that suggestion, although it was fitting, and equipped the pair with a Class 10 superdreadnought, along with an even thousand robot space forts. This was done out of a wish to see the job done properly, as well as the desire just to insert a dead tree branch into the sight receptors of Budget.

Avantor's new ship was not a globe or a cube, but a mighty centihedron, a multi-planed sphere with one hundred sides and one hundred and fifty points, each of them armed with energy weapons of frightfully destructive abilities. While it was many times the size of their old ship, the superdreadnought was still only designed for a two being crew, since the gargantuan Choron reactor took up so much room. The crew's personal suites were pleasant enough, though, and the brig was nice and large.

When asked, their new megacomputer had given a ninety per cent plus probability of the Dirtlings trying something dramatic before finally accepting defeat. So it was no great surprise when The 16 spotted a near duplicate of Idow's captured ship struggling to reach the freedom of space.

Avantor wiggled her eyebrows in professional admiration at the remarkable sophistication of the craft, crude as it was. They must have some extraordinarily good scientists down there to deduce so much of galactic technology after so brief a glimpse, she thought. It's a pity about the quarantine order, but such a violently robust species must be kept to their home world until they learned social restraint and some proper respect for galactic law.

"What's our situation, 16?" asked the woman, relaxing in her new formfitting command chair, serenely positive that everything was under control, and just as incorrect as she had been the last time.

"Something appears to be dreadfully wrong, my liege," said the male, touching the bald spot in his golden hair where his new remote computer control had been implanted. "I am receiving reports from our space forts of not merely one, but numerous launches from all over this planet. Twenty, forty . . . no, fifty ships have lifted off!"

"Show me," commanded the avantor, leaning forward in her seat.

The technician tilted his head and the walls of their control room filled with holographic views of the planet below them. Everywhere, flocks of giant blue balls were struggling to reach beyond the planet's atmosphere.

Humorlessly, Avantor grimaced. A mass escape, eh? Damn clever these Dirtlings, but the trick would not avail them.

"Activate the color tracker, 16," she loftily commanded.

Her assistant nodded to her, almost inadvertently causing the life-support equipment to turn itself off. "Affirmative, my liege."

Then something on the monitor caught the avantor's attention. She blinked and thoughtfully scrutinized the dozens of bright red globes floating above the planet. Hadn't those vessels just been blue?

"The Dirtling ships are changing color!" exclaimed The 16, confirming her fears. "My liege, we won't be able to track them through hyperspace if they can do that!"

Stiffly, the female warrior rose from her command chair. "That does it," she snapped irritably. "Activate the force shield damper and prepare to fire our main cannon. I hate to destroy sentient beings, but we warned them about this. Now let them learn that the Great Golden Ones are not entities to be trifled with."

"Affirmative, my liege," grunted The 16, as unhappy about this as his leader. Staring at the bow monitor with his pupilless eyes, the short male lowered his head and from point thirty-four of their geometric craft there reached out a shimmering gold pencil of destruction that struck the nearest of the Earth vessels. Capable of coring a small moon, the dispersal ray was unstoppable by anything short of pure neutronium. So, it was a great shock to the Gee soldiers when the deadly energy beam bounced harmlessly off the smooth hull of the green ball and ricocheted back to vaporize the support drone flying next to them.

"Impossible," gasped the junior avantor, limply collapsing back into her golden chair. "That was a dispersal ray, a full power dispersal ray. How could they have just shrugged it off?"

"M-my liege," stuttered the pale technician, even paler drops of yellow moisture glistening on his forehead. "You don't suppose that the Dirtlings could have . . . by themselves . . . invented . . ." And Avantor's eyes flew open wide, her mind flooding with comprehension.

"Deflector plating," they wailed in unison. "*OH NO!*"

* * * * *

Of the fifty purple globes rising from the surface of the Earth, only the starship from Florida held a live crew. The rest were multi-million-dollar decoys, robot ships whose sole task was to confuse the Great Golden Ones by getting the manned craft lost in the crowd. A nearly precise duplicate of Idow's Mikon #4, the manned vessel was well over half a kilometer in diameter and had an eighty person crew: seventy-nine human beings and Trell. The little green opportunist had been happy to collaborate with the FCT, telling them everything he knew. Trell had even invented something called deflector plating out of thin air when they flatly insisted that he do so. In exchange for this, they didn't turn him over to the Great Golden Ones. It was a mutually beneficial arrangement, because nobody, especially Trell, wanted to see him shipped off to Galopticon 7.

Internally, the starship was a mess, with empty packing crates, excelsior stuffing, spare parts, bedding, food, and mounds of supplies piled everywhere. In fact, the vessel carried almost enough spare parts to build another starship. But this was an absolute necessity, as the craft would be a long way from home and anything might happen.

Aboard the human-built starship, Planetary Ambassador Rajavur, Trell, and a platoon of the brand new UN Space Marines nervously crossed their fingers and prayed. They were very glad indeed that the Gees had only fired a warning shot across their bow. Hopefully, the space police wouldn't have time to unleash any real weapons before they were long gone.

Impatiently, the diplomat, soldiers, and alien waited for the moment when their Swiss captain would twist together a pair of electrical wires and activate the shipboard computer. The machine would then drastically shrink the size of their gravity field and boost their flabby drive flame into a raging inferno of power, exponentially increasing the ship's speed. Hopefully, this would enable them to catch the Gees off guard and get far enough away from Earth to be able to shunt into the dubious void of hyperspace.

It was a brave, almost foolhardy plan, and the grand representatives of Earth honestly had no idea if they could actually smash through the impressive space blockade. Or, if they did, if the captain could then find the real Galactic League and Rajavur successfully argue their case for admittance. Everybody aboard the stout craft only knew a single fact for certain.

That the brave crew of the UNSF *Hector Ramariez* was sure as Hell going to try!

BOOK TWO
IN SPACE

NEW *DRAMATIS PERSONAE*

CREW OF THE UNSF RAMARIEZ

Dagstrom Keller: captain.
Abagail Jones: first mate.
Paul Van Loon: chief surgeon.
Martha Soukup: navigation.
Purity Lilliuokalani: communications.
Marvin Hamlisch: sensors.
John Buckley: weapons.
Abduhl Benny Hassan: spaceman first class.

UN SPACE MARINES: "HECTOR'S HELLCATS"

Kurt Sakaeda: lieutenant.
Tanya Lieberman: master sergeant.
James Fuerstenberg: private.

THE REST

(unpronounceable): Queen/Mother of RporR.
Einda: prostitute.
Silverside: criminal ganglord.
The Galactic League.
The 3000: supreme commander of the Great Golden Ones.
Bachalope Thintfeesel: news reporter.
Jose de San Martin: secretary-general of the UN.

18

With a dazzling pyrotechnic display, the *Ramariez* shunted into hyperspace, escaping just as the Gees were about to unleash another superweapon, leaving the aliens with nothing but a viewscreen full of zigzagging drones and the certain knowledge that they had failed yet again.

* * * * *

As the black of space was replaced by the featureless gray of the hyperspacial void, the bridge crew of the *Ramariez* broke into wild cheering. They'd done it! Success!

"All right, settle down," ordered Captain Keller after a few minutes of therapeutic pandemonium. "That was the easy part. Snap to! We've still got a job to do."

This sobered the crew immediately, and as the sailors went busily to work, the starship captain glanced at the digital clock in the left arm of his chair. Four minutes to go.

Blond hair, blue eyes, square jaw, six feet tall, and darkly tanned, Dagstrom Keller more resembled a movie star playing a professional boxer than a naval officer. Actually, Keller had boxed during college and had been considered an Olympic hopeful. But he had been forced to withdraw from competition as the training interfered with his studies. He still occasionally boxed these days in Swiss naval tournaments. In point of fact, he was well known as "Ol' One-Two Keller," both for his devastating left-right combination attacks and, unfortunately, his bedroom prowess.

The UN General Assembly had never heard of Dagstrom Keller until the FCT promoted him as their candidate for captain. Dag himself had been surprised. But upon due consideration, the man seemed perfect for the assignment. Keller was the youngest captain of a nuclear aircraft carrier to be decorated four times for bravery. He had graduated from the Zurich Institute of Technology *magna cum laude* and read science fiction, the latter a hobby the FCT believed might give the man a certain advantage in any bizarre situation that cropped up on his quixotic search for the Galactic League.

As ratings scurried about with their arms full of plastic boxes and chief petty officers meticulously swept the deck clear of excelsior, the captain pinched together two wires inside the open right arm of his chair, ignoring the slight electric shock that tingled in his fingers. "Power room? This is Captain Keller. I want a read-out on the spacewarp generator."

"Sorry, Captain," said a voice from the tiny speaker dangling in the rat's nest of wires. "But we can't do that."

"And why not, mister?"

"Haven't unpacked the gauges yet."

Oh. "Well, do your best and report when ready."

"Aye, aye, sir."

Twelve levels below, in the center of the great ship, protected by hundreds of feet of dura-steel and lead, Trell clicked off the power room's intercom and dutifully returned to his work.

Ever since he had been rescued from the Deckers, the little alien had been worked like a *Thurstd gik*, a phrase that had no human analogy, aside from sticking a fountain pen into an electric pencil sharpener.

Hard work? Yes. But the little technician had never been happier. Unlimited amounts of material and assistants had been placed at his disposal. He had been awarded every Ph.D., doctorate, and scientific award that humanity had possessed, and been paid a truly staggering lump sum for his time and effort. Something no *gik* got.

On board the *Ramariez* (a name that filled him with shame, even though he'd had nothing to do with the murder), Trell sported the official rank of master technician, and was second only to the leader . . . ah, captain, in authority. Plus, NASA had allowed him to design the light blue jumpsuit his team of engineers wore: the directors of the space agency knew that within the heart of every engineer lurked the soul of an artist.

The little alien had done them proud, too. Once the extra set of arms had been edited out, the purely functional outfit was extremely comfortable for humans, possessed over eighty pockets of varied and assorted sizes, was certified stain resistant, and naturally smelled like beer, which saved the power room crew the trouble of constantly consuming breath mints. It was quite accidental that blue was the alien's favorite color and complemented his green skin tone.

Under Trell's watchful eye, wrenches, spanners, laser torches, and hammers were applied with artistic fervor to the ever-growing complex of machinery in the center of the giant ship. Soon, the army of workers had assembled the equipment into a more coherent shape and they were at last able to remove a smoking brassiere from the innards of a power relay. A fast-thinking tech had saved the day by using it to lift and separate a pair of red hot ion thrusters without losing a hand.

The entire engineering crew had applauded the act, half for the woman's ingenious solution to the problem and the rest for her superb structural integrity.

*   *   *   *   *

With a musical ding, the unpainted steel doors of the elevator opened on the bridge and out strode the ship's doctor, Paul

Van Loon. Slightly balding, with an enlarged nose, the tall, athletic Dutchman was considered a perfect choice for this post as he was an accomplished NATO surgeon who had served two tours of duty in the Middle East, held a minor degree in veterinary science, and was an amateur botanist.

This was his first real visit to the bridge, and the physician took the opportunity to look around. This ship was going to be home for quite a long time.

Located near the top of the globular craft, the round room that housed the bridge was reduced to a half circle by a dividing wall in which a turbo-lift, elevator, emergency spiral stairs, and a fireman's pole were located. NASA redundancy at its peak. Tech-station consoles lined the outer walls, with the front of the room dominated by a staggeringly huge triptych-shaped viewscreen. The captain's command chair was strategically positioned on a small dais overlooking the freestanding navigation, communication, and weapon consoles. Suspended from the ceiling was a video camera that recorded everything that was done and said for an eventual review. The Roddenberry Design Studios had created a functional masterpiece.

Picking his way through the litter on the deck, the physician noted the incredible vista of swirling gray visible on all three of the forward viewscreens. Casually, he glanced at a working meter on the environmental console and was surprised to find the outside temperature well over a thousand degrees Celsius. No wonder the aliens used hyperspace as a swear word. Nothing could live in that dead, sterile void.

And that was probably going to be the extent of his work on this ship, realized Van Loon. Observation. The UN computers had accessed the personnel files of the world to choose their complement of eighty from the teeming billions of Earth, so it was no surprise that everybody, from the captain down to the lowliest marine private, was in perfect health, a college graduate, combat veteran, a specialist in a dozen different fields, and could probably sing and dance as well. It made the physician feel uneasy to realize that he was probably the dumbest person on board the ship.

Casually, the Dutch physician strolled over to and took a seat at the vacant weapons console. "Okay, sir, we made it to hyperspace, what's next?"

With a start, the captain regarded the man. "Don't you know?"

"Sorry, I was too busy organizing my equipment and staff to attend any of the final planning sessions."

Keller nodded. Those last few days in Florida had been truly hectic, what with everybody working around the clock at a fever pitch, skipping meals and losing sleep. It had rather reminded him of finals in college.

The captain glanced at the clock. Two minutes. "According to Trell, the best way to travel through hyperspace is by using an avantor. Unfortunately, in spite of an exhaustive search of every self-proclaimed mentalist on Earth, we couldn't find one with a perfect six-dimensional sense of direction."

"Six?" queried the doctor.

Captain Keller nodded as he lifted his feet for an enlisted man to sweep under.

"Yes, six. This means we have to use the cumbersome method of computer guidance, as most races do." He lowered his feet as the rating passed by. "But in order to do even that, we need a hyperspacial navigation cube. And while Trell could tell us how to build such a device, he doesn't know any planetary coordinates. Not even his own home world. They're just too complex to remember—thousands of integers long. Thus, in order to travel to the Galactic League, we've got to get an HN cube first."

Just then, a swarthy machinist mate with the name HAS-SAN on the breast pocket of his dirty blue coverall ambled over and began to install a bank of push-button controls in the gaping hole in the right arm of the command chair.

"So, we're off to find a cube?"

"Exactly, Doctor."

"But how?" asked Van Loon, standing for a moment so a rating could bolt the chair he was sitting in to the deck. "We can't blindly jump around the galaxy hoping to find a friendly race who just happens to have a couple of spare navigational cubes lying about. They must be very expensive."

"Extremely so," agreed Keller. "But we are not thieves. The *Ramariez* will pay market value for any goods received."

"There's something you're not telling me," stated Van Loon after a pause.

Captain Keller nodded, his blue eyes never straying far from the clock.

"That's part two of our escape plan. You see, we know the exact location of one, and only one, HN cube."

At first, the Dutch physician didn't understand, but then as comprehension dawned, his face sagged. Oh no.

* * * * *

The right, Honorable Jose de San Martin, the new Argentinian secretary-general of the United Nations of Earth, felt a cold rivulet of sweat trickle down his back as he prepared to greet the avantor. His staff had delayed taking the Gee's call for as long as they dared, but the aliens had forced his hand.

Seconds after the *Ramariez* escaped, the Gee's had released a salvo of incredibly small missiles, each only about as big as a flashlight. And one by one, the zigzagging, unmanned Earth drones had been hunted down and destroyed in a nuclear flash that the sensors indicated was an antimatter explosion. The lemon-colored missiles punched through the deflector plating like it was paper—a fact that cheered nobody on Earth. Apparently, there were various degrees of invulnerability.

"Sorry to keep you waiting, *senorita*," apologized the secretary-general as he displayed a politician's smile to the video camera set above the monitor on his desk. "I was indisposed."

"Unacceptable," snapped Avantor, radiating hot-buttered fury from every pore of her body. "Tell me where that ship went or I shall destroy every satellite and space platform orbiting your measly excuse for a planet."

To Jose's way of thinking, this conversation was breaking down far too quickly. "Surely, you don't mean that," he demured. "Many of those platforms are manned, and besides—"

The view of the Gee was instantly replaced by a shot of the nighttime sky above North America and the blackness became filled with pinpoint explosions. Then, in a blinding flash of light, twelve astronauts, eight cosmonauts, and one very surprised-looking chimpanzee were suddenly teleported into the secretary-general's office.

"We are not murderers," noted Avantor in somber tones as the video monitor returned to a picture of her.

"But you had no right!" blustered de San Martin as everybody but him dashed for the door. "Some of those were private property! You're no more than a common criminal!"

The golden female frowned. "Incorrect. My assignment is to erect a blockade about your planet and to ensure that your race does not gain unauthorized access to space travel. How I do so is my concern. You have just lost the right to use any orbital platforms for the next ten solar rotations. Do you wish to lose your suborbital privileges as well? I am fully capable of grinding your transportation system right down to surface level!" The stern face of the Gee swelled to fill the video monitor. "Now, for the very last time, *where did they go?*"

As a trained politician, the lies flowed smoothly to de San Martin's mouth. "Acting as they are, without the official consent of our organization, how could I possibly know their destination? It seems unreasonable on your part to assume—"

"The human is stalling, my liege," interpreted The 16 with a scowl.

Avantor agreed, and as her finger descended to press the button that would annihilate every operating airplane Dirt possessed a transdimensional hole erupted into existence and the *Ramariez* burst out of hyperspace inside the force shield of the Gee's centihedron superdreadnought—for the alien craft was the only known location of an HN cube.

With a clang the starships stridently slammed together. The avantor was ripped free from her command chair and thrown against the forward viewscreen, while half of the systems in her vessel shorted out. In the dim orange glow of the emergency chemical lights, the woman limply slid down the wall to land on her head, a dazed expression slackening her golden features.

"My liege!" cried The 16 weakly from the corner of the room, amber blood dribbling from his nose. Ignoring the pain in his brain from the howling feedback of the damaged computer, the disoriented Gee forced himself to crawl across the deck and tug his commander into a sitting position. Her golden head wobbled like a balloon on a string as she attempted to focus her attention on him.

"Of course," burbled the avantor incoherently. "They didn't go anywhere . . . couldn't . . . no cube . . . come to steal ours." She began to pitch forward. "Stop them, 16! Don't let the Dirtlings get the cube. Eat the device if you have to—" And the woman slumped unconscious to the deck.

But the damage had already been done. While her intentions had been good, Avantor's choice of words had been disastrous. Even in its present condition, their warship was still quite capable of defending itself, but only if it was told to do so. Locked in the unbreakable grip of his hypnotraining, The 16 was forced to crawl out of the room, unable to stop himself from heading for the navigational computer or even make himself pause for a moment at the kitchen to grab a bottle of organic vegetable flavoring.

* * * * *

Within the air lock of the *Ramariez*, apparently unaffected by the titanic collision, stood twenty burnished statues poised and waiting. The hulking metal brutes were not inert decorations, but highly mobile battle suits—sort of a hybrid between a space suit and a tank. They were armored by two inches of molecularly reinforced dura-steel, powered by a series of stretchable servo-motors, and energized by a miniature atomic battery. The wallet-sized power cell, containing over a thousand kilowatt hours, was not a contribution of Trell, but an invention of Norway, which had kept the atomic battery a state secret for the past decade, as they had had no military use for the device except for running mobile government saunas.

Protected by their NASA/SRI built life-support systems, the marines could comfortably fight in vacuum, underwater, amid lethal radiation, almost anywhere. The strength-amplifying servo-motors in their exoskeletons enabled the soldiers to run for a hundred kilometers without tiring, or rip a Cadillac in half—a more than fitting end for the oversized gas guzzlers. Plus, an inner cushion of mini-force-field bubbles let the troopers withstand pointblank cannon fire or survive a fall of eighty stories onto concrete; hence their total lack of reaction to the violent ramming. As long as the power was maintained, the marines were virtually indestructible.

But, not content with mere passive defense capabilities, NATO also armed the space troopers with an unnamed assault rifle that fired 5mm, armor-piercing bullets, sported a pump-action, 20mm grenade launcher, two "Church Key" class anti-robot missiles, and a polycyclic laser. In addition, the rifle exploded if anyone other than a crew member tried to fire it. It was a cute trick that had led to some interesting strategy sessions over beer and pretzels.

Standing patiently in the air lock, crowded shoulder to metal shoulder, the marines waited in their half-ton uniforms for the go code. Every trooper was a combat veteran, most of them holding the rank of master sergeant, or even higher, in their home country's military, but each more than glad to become a lowly dogface again for the sake of this special mission.

Their appointed leader, Lt. Kurt Sakaeda, was a devilishly handsome American of Japanese descent who held the rank of colonel in the United States' much touted, but rarely seen Delta Force, a supersecret group of ultra-tough fighters who were supposed to be able to eat Green Berets for breakfast. Oddly enough, though, Sakaeda was a quiet, scholarly man whose sole interests outside the military seemed to be the stock market and chasing women.

As the white starship continued to revolve about the gold,

trying to align their air locks, a private near the rear of the group broke the self-imposed radio silence.

"Sir? Lieutenant?"

"Yeah? What is it, Higgins?"

"How about 'Satan's Taxicab' . . . 'cause it's hell on wheels?"

It took Lieutenant Sakaeda a moment to realize that the soldier was referring to the matter of their weapons having no pronounceable designation, much less a nickname the troops liked. "That Damn Gun" didn't count, although considering how often generals had stuck their heads into the UN labs and asked: "How's that damn gun coming along?" it was running a strong second.

"Later, Private."

Sigh. "Aye, aye, sir."

With a clang more felt than heard, the rotating spheres locked into position and Sakaeda told the troops to get ready.

Breathlessly, the soldiers watched and waited as the metal halves of their air lock parted to reveal the outer hull of the alien ship, its air lock tightly closed.

Upon Captain Keller's command, the *Ramariez* computers began to flash all of the 914 possible override signals that Trell had postulated might open the Gee's main access portal. But, unknown to the humans, due to damage caused by the collision, the Gee computer was receiving every signal, including the correct one (#675), as pure gibberish. As a result, the air lock remained firmly locked.

Trell suspected radio interference, and, from the bridge, advised the marines to manually tap in the medical evacuation code—which he believed was their best chance anyway. Sakaeda pulled a crystal rod from his belt pouch and waved it at the ship before them. Silently, a small panel on the golden hull swung aside to reveal a keypad. Quickly, a thick metal finger tapped in the proper sequence of symbols. But once again the computer received the information as a flood of meaningless signals and did nothing.

Lieutenant Sakaeda was becoming worried. Time was running out. Why they hadn't been attacked already he couldn't understand. The Gees must be setting up an ambush. His growing unease was felt by the rest of the marines.

Suddenly, a private, acting upon twenty years of combat experience, played a hunch and turned his assault rifle on the keypad, hoping to blow the lock. Ricochets filled the air lock, and instinctively the soldiers hit the floor. The metal keypad was undamaged by the fusillade of bullets. However, the random pattern of strikes was blithely transmitted to the harassed computer which accepted the onslaught of signals as a slightly misspelled surprise inspection tour notice and, with a clicking hiss, politely opened the outer air lock door.

From the floor, the marines exchanged glances. Well, heck, can't argue with success.

At the noise, Lieutenant Sakaeda stopped shaking the trigger-happy trooper. "Nice going, Corporal Fuerstenberg."

"I'm a private, sir."

"Not anymore."

"Thank you, sir!"

The inner door to the Gee ship had a simple hand lever, and soon the squad was peering into the ship. Ahead of them stretched an innocent-appearing pale yellow corridor. On the floor before them was a small mat emblazoned with a square made of broken lines—the universal symbol for *Welcome*.

In unison, the soldiers chuckled. Subtle, real subtle.

With a tap of his chin, Lieutenant Sakaeda activated his suit radio. "Mainhardt!"

"Sir?"

"Sweep that hallway."

"Affirmative, Lieutenant."

Clumsily, the soldier set the tripod of her ungainly weapon, adjusted the focus to wide angle, thumbed off the safety, and squeezed the primary trigger. From the three prong muzzle of the Atomic Vortex Rifle there lanced out a swirling cone of blinding radiation that exploded down the empty passageway. As the nuclear hurricane filled the passageway with its turbulent energy, the welcome mat exploded into a cloud of flechettes that melted in midair, laser beams lashed out from the door jamb and died as their circuits exploded, panels in the roof opened, and nasty-looking robotic devices fell to the deck, twitching ineffectually as smoke erupted from their mechanisms. The entire middle section of corridor slammed together three times with a force that rattled the marines inside their power suits before the giant motors hidden in the walls burned out. As the searing power bolt reached the end of the passageway, it punched a small glowing hole in the lock of the far door. With a creak, the metal portal began to slowly swing open.

"*Gott en Himmel*," whispered a private over his suit radio. "Dat is some—"

And from behind the door a smiling robot butler with a wide gash in its chest fell face first into the hallway, dropping its tray and spilling a collection of gold cups, their liquid contents splashing on the floor. None of the marines were surprised when the environmental meters in their helmets swung to lethal.

There was a click and Lieutenant Sakaeda addressed his troops. "This was too damn easy. Watch yourselves."

With dry mouths, the point soldiers took their assigned positions, and the platoon began to weave its way through the ruin of the corridor, the double set of air locks behind them automatically cycling shut.

Following the stronger of the life readings on their sensors, the marines easily located the control room. The only incident worthy of mention was a slight mishap with an escalator that tried to eat their unauthorized feet halfway between levels. But the heavy metal casings of their boots easily destroyed the gnashing robotic teeth and they continued undefeated.

Suspicious at the ajar door, the troopers acted by the book; two soldiers dove into the room to draw fire, while the rest of the squad pivoted out from the sides, their weapons at the ready. The action was smartly done, but inside, they found only a small pool of what resembled honey and the unconscious Avantor.

As Lieutenant Sakaeda gazed upon the supine female, the

soldier felt his heart skip a beat. She was every bit as beautiful as when he first saw her on television a mere month ago.

"Lieutenant?"

Sakaeda snapped back to reality. "Yes, Sergeant?"

Tanya Lieberman waddled forward, a squat golem of steel in her UN power suit. The short, mousy blonde was a captain in the Israeli army and reputed to be the best rifle markswoman in the world.

"No sign of the male, sir. The second life form reading we have is down that passageway."

"Check. Privates Tausz, Sowards, front and center! Guard the avantor. Call the ship. Tell them she'll need medical attention."

The troopers acknowledged the command.

Lieutenant Sakaeda shifted the grip on his rifle. "Everybody else, stay with me!"

Tracing the electronic blip of their sensors, the marines were led through a maze of twisting hallways until they reached a locked door emblazoned with three overlapping rings in a triangle pattern: the universal symbol for *Authorized Personnel Only*. Lieutenant Sakaeda grunted and glanced at his sergeant. Well, they were authorized, just by the wrong side.

An adroit application of plastique unlocked the portal to the main computer room, and the marines rushed in to see a pair of wiggling golden legs sticking obscenely out of the side of a towering computer bank.

"Get him!" snapped Sergeant Lieberman.

Shouldering their weapons, two of the metal-clad marines grabbed the Gee and hauled him into view, just in time to see the small male swallow a fist-sized crystal cube covered with black squiggles.

With a burp, The 16 felt the grasp of the hypnotraining leave him. As his mind cleared, the Gee reached out with his computer implants to focus awesome weapons of power that would vaporize the invaders. Then, Corporal Fuerstenberg rushed forward to grab the alien and began to apply the Heimlich maneuver. However, the well-meaning soldier forgot that he was wearing strength-amplifying power armor until he noticed The 16 turning brown in color. Quickly, the space marine released the wheezing alien and the Gee collapsed to the deck in a dead faint.

"Nice going, Private," Lieutenant Sakaeda chastised the man.

"Ah, that's Corporal, sir," corrected the barracks lawyer.

"Not anymore."

Wisely, James Fuerstenberg turned off his radio before sighing. Oh well, easy come, easy go.

19

"Close, please," instructed Dr. Van Loon, peeling off his stainless surgical gloves. The tentacled garbage can next to him squeaked yes and began efficiently sealing the belly incision of the peacefully sleeping 16 on the multi-level table. Slowly, the three dimensional holograms of the patient's intestinal tract faded from the air above the surgical platform, and the human physician shucked his gown, depositing it in what he correctly assumed was a waste basket, where the cloth disappeared in a brief flash of atomic disintegration. Dr. Van Loon turned to take a final glance at the recumbent Gee and gasped as he saw a robot nurse light what appeared to be a slim, green cigar and stick it into The 16's mouth. Every instinct cried out to the physician to run and remove it, but during the operation he had gained an almost religious faith in the bizarre little machines.

As he watched, a small tube looped out of the robot's side and deftly sucked up the accumulating cigar ash as if it was something precious. Puzzled, the doctor shook his head and exited the room. A religious rite? Or was it actually medicinal? When Van Loon had time, he would have to check into that.

As the double set of doors closed behind him, the middle-aged man stumbled out into the corridor and leaned against the golden wall to catch his breath. It had taken all of his skill as a surgeon, veterinarian, botanist, and roadside car mechanic to pull that operation off, but miraculously, it appeared to be a success. The Gee was just fine and probably wouldn't even have a scar. Thank God for those self-programming robot nurses. Without them, this would never have been possible. They had done ninety per cent of the actual work. The Dutch physician had never even postulated the existence of reverse scalpels, sourceless lights, or blood plants—flowering bushes that manufactured any desired type of biological plasma by the gallon and delivered it via their own thorn-tipped vines. Through their built-in translators, the robot nurses had informed him the plants were a primitive ancestor of the legendary Koolgoolagans. Whoever they were.

During his hurried reading of the Gee's medical texts on the different species of the galaxy, Van Loon had discovered that it was a good thing he was not going to work on a Choron, as the rocky giants didn't have doctors, per se. They had, more precisely, structural engineers specializing in explosives and plumbing.

Out of the corner of his eye, Van Loon spotted a distant group of cursing crew members struggling to drag an enormous plastic crate toward the air lock and he smiled.

Shamelessly, the physician had ordered the confiscation of every surgical instrument on board the Gee's ship, including the blood plants. The futuristic devices made his equipment on board the *Ramariez* seem as outmoded as stone knives and leeches. When engineering had some spare time, they could analyze the intricate workings of the complex machinery. If the *Ramariez* made it back to Earth, the ship would bring home the seeds of the greatest medical breakthroughs since sterilization.

"Hello, Doctor."

Van Loon glanced up to see Abagail Jones, the first mate of the *Ramariez* standing before him. It was hard to believe that the statuesque redhead was Australia's top astronaut. Considering the pre-contact state of that country's space program, she'd had plenty of time to branch out, and had become an expert on military strategy. The three monographs on theoretical space warfare she had written, one of which had been confiscated by her government for reasons of national security, were more than enough to bring her to the FCT's attention.

When Jones had heard that the position of first officer on the starship was available, the astronaut had done everything in her power to get the berth. And while not on the original list of candidates for the position, the directors of NASA were so impressed by her qualifications, determination, and choice of blackmail photos, that they unanimously awarded her the post.

Stiffly formal, as always, the first officer had the jacket of her duty uniform fully buttoned over her jumpsuit and highly polished lieutenant's bars shining on both collars. Flanking the officer were a pair of marines in power armor, squat no-name assault rifles cradled in their metal arms.

Unknown to the officers standing in front of them, the soldiers were holding a private conversation over their radios, wisely deciding that "The Dispos-All" was a dumb name for the rifle, along with "Blast Master" and "X-Caliber."

"Well," inquired Jones impatiently. "Did you get it?"

"Ya, sure," sighed the doctor, and he pulled a lump of white cloth from his uniform pocket. Gingerly, he unwrapped the layers of sterile gauze and passed the cloudy crystalline box to the first officer.

Turning it about in her hand, the tall woman inspected all six sides of the crystal. Only a few of the black squiggles on its milky surface were intact. "Is it supposed to look like this?" she asked in concern.

The doctor shrugged. "How should I know? First time I saw the thing it was nestled inside a man."

"Not a man," the lieutenant corrected him curtly. "A member of the Great Golden Ones. An alien. Remember that."

Usually, Van Loon found the woman's xenophobia faintly amusing. In fact, many of the command personnel were starting to tell alien jokes just to tease the woman. But now he found himself filled only with exhaustion and disgust at the necessary evil. The woman had been assigned to the ship as a dissenting voice to help balance the overwhelming goodwill among the crew toward non-humans. Even the most highly trained of their personnel sometimes treated aliens like pet animals or toys, a stupid practice that could jeopardize their entire mission and the future freedom of Earth.

Lieutenant Jones pocketed the alien artifact. "Come on, let's not keep the captain waiting."

As they began walking along the corridor, Van Loon glanced at the two hulking soldiers and could hardly suppress a smile.

"Expecting trouble?" he asked curiously.

"No. But I'm prepared for it." she replied. "This cube is much too valuable to risk."

Hesitantly, Dr. Van Loon agreed. They had certainly gone to enough trouble to get the device.

The officers and marines paused for a moment at an intersection, held up by a minor traffic jam of crew members wheeling carts of equipment over to the *Ramariez*.

"It looks like you're taking everything not nailed down," noted Van Loon.

"Only what is needed," sighed Jones with a trace of bitterness in her voice. No sailor of the seas, or space, liked the idea of piracy. "And we are leaving payment in exchange for our acquisitions."

Payment? "Ah, the thulium," remarked Van Loon in understanding. "Is there enough to cover the medical supplies I confiscated?"

By way of a response, the lieutenant pointed to a marine in power armor coming down the passageway carrying a half-ton steel safe in his hands.

Jones nodded. "We're leaving them one thousand galactic

standard pounds."

That deserved a whistle, so the doctor obliged. That was almost sufficent funds to purchase the golden ship and the planet it had been built on.

To the horror of the international banking association, and most jewelers, the element thulium proved to be the base of the galactic economy, and not silver or gold. And for excellent reasons: steel was stronger, platinum prettier, aluminum lighter, silver a better conductor, and arsenic tastier. In point of fact, there wasn't a single property that the metal held which another element didn't do better, faster, or cheaper. The stuff was virtually useless, but extremely rare, which made it the perfect currency. Thulium's value was rigidly linked to its atomic weight. One galactic ounce, slightly less than a Troy ounce, was a good month's wages and the *Ramariez* had in its hold over ten metric tons of the stuff, equal to 320,000 ounces. It was enough to bribe the Galactic League if necessary. A possibility that had not been overlooked.

Upon reaching the air locks, Jones returned the guards' salutes, and the four sets of doors automatically opened in front of them and closed in their wake.

"How is the avantor?" asked Van Loon, as they entered their home ship. "I sent a corpsman to examine her during the operation.

"Still unconscious," answered the lieutenant. "But resting comfortably in our brig."

Forcibly, Dr. Van Loon spun the woman about to face him. "The brig? And why the hell isn't she in sick bay? Or with The 16?"

Lieutenant Jones stared pointedly at the doctor's hand on her shoulder, and the soldiers behind her stepped closer. Self-consciously, the physician let go of her arm. She turned and continued on her way.

"Avantor and The 16 will soon be reunited," replied the first officer as if nothing had happened.

It took the physician a moment to understand. "You're putting them both in the brig? But they're supposed to be treated like honored guests! That's why we're bringing them along, as observers."

"I've had video monitors set up in their cell," said the first officer calmly. "They won't miss a thing that happens on the bridge."

Van Loon gawked at the woman. Xenophobic or not, there were limits. "I'm going to report this to the captain!" he told her in cold fury.

"Please do, Doctor, and while you are at it, inform him that the being with the most experience regarding the Great Golden Ones, Master Technician Trell, feels that we are endangering our mission merely by allowing them within two light years of this ship. It is his considered opinion that we should drop them into the nearest sun." She cocked her head. "I am merely attempting to strike a happy medium."

With that, the starship officer and her guards walked away, leaving the good doctor standing with his mouth hanging open.

* * * * *

When all personnel had been accounted for, the starships disengaged and the *Ramariez* again jumped into hyperspace, taking a slow spiraling course to nowhere, as they waited for Trell to transcribe the cube's contents to the *Ramariez* computer.

Captain Keller was reviewing a manpower report when the first officer entered the bridge.

"Well, Lieutenant?" asked Keller, handing the clipboard to a rating, who scurried away with the paperwork. "Were we able to retrieve the information we needed off of the HN cube?"

"Yes and no, sir," she sadly reported. "Unfortunately, the digestive juices of The 16 had enough time to seriously damage the device. In fact, as far as Trell can determine, everything but the coordinates for six star systems has been wiped from the cube."

Pensively, the captain gnawed a lip. "I suppose it's too much to ask that any of those are the coordinates to take us to the Galactic League?"

"I'm afraid not."

"Are they at least six useful systems?"

"Unknown, sir. Trell is still correlating the data."

Keller grunted. Damn. Well, his next move was obvious.

Deftly, he lifted the hinged top to the right arm of his chair and unclipped a tiny microphone set next to a laser pistol. Also in the cubicle was a coffee butler, a paperback novel, and two buttons. The left button summoned his yeoman; the right would vaporize the ship as their engines boosted to 100/100 for a brief, shining microsecond. He was always very careful not to get the two confused.

Shutting the lid, Dag lifted the wireless mike to his mouth and pressed a switch on it marked with a bit of sticky tape that bore the pencilled word "intercom."

"ATTENTION. YOUR ATTENTION, PLEASE." His words rang in every room of the great ship, and people paused in whatever they were doing—tying their shoes, eating a sandwich, picking a lock—to hear what the man had to say.

"CAPTAIN TO CREW. THERE WILL BE AN IMMEDIATE MEETING IN THE WARD ROOM OF EVERY DEPARTMENT HEAD. PLEASE BRING YOUR STATUS REPORTS." He gave them a minute to absorb that. "AND UNTIL FURTHER NOTICE THE SHIP IS ON YELLOW ALERT. MARINES TO REMAIN ARMED, SHIELDS ON FULL. THAT IS ALL. KELLER, OUT."

Returning the mike to its proper position, Captain Keller spoke to his waiting first officer.

"I talked to Dr. Van Loon, Lieutenant."

"Sir?"

"The Gee's are to be accorded every comfort and courtesy. And as soon as the avantor is awake, I want to be notified of the fact."

Jones nodded. "I understand, Captain."

"See that you do."

A pregnant pause followed, during which each of the officers listened carefully to what the other was not saying aloud.

Satisfied, Keller rose from his chair. "The bridge is yours, Lieutenant. Try not to crash us into a moon or anything."

She saluted. "Aye, aye, sir."

As the doors to the turbo-lift closed behind the officer, Abagail took her place in the command chair with a heartfelt sigh of appreciation. Ah, at last.

* * * * *

The turbo-lift deposited Keller on the appropriate level with a minimum of fuss, and Dag stepped out with a smile on his face. God, he just loved these things. Elevators could only go up and down, while turbo-lifts could also travel horizontially and diagonally. Increase the speed, add bells and colored lights, and the contraption would make a fabulous carnival ride.

As the captain strode into the ward room, he spotted a lone technician tightening screws on the underside of the oblong conference table. The rating began crawling out to salute, but Keller told him not to bother and the man kept on working.

The ward room was hexagonal in shape, for no particular reason other than aesthetics. The carpet was magenta, and the wood-paneled walls were dotted with framed cityscapes of Geneva, Orlando, and New York.

With almost unlimited power at their command, it had been an easy matter for NASA to arrange for the function rooms to be equipped with laser holograms of wood paneling and colored carpeting that became activated only when the lights were turned on. This made for a much more relaxed atmosphere to work in and only the ultra-delicate speedometer on the navigation console could detect the minute loss of velocity. Of course, in combat situations, the walls and carpet reverted to white.

Strolling about, Captain Keller noted something wrong with the room and turned to address the rating who was climbing out from under the table.

"Excuse me, sailor. . . ."

"Hassan, sir," said the youth with a flash of gleaming white teeth. The dark-skinned teenager stood, dusted himself off, and then hastily saluted. "Abduhl Benny Hassan, sir. Spacer first class. Engineering division."

"Yes. Fine. Thank you. Where are the chairs?"

Hesitantly, the technician pointed to a pile of flat cardboard boxes leaning against the wall near the door, their edges indenting the wood panel hologram. "That's them, Captain. I thought I should do the table first, in case you wanted to establish a preliminary psychological zone of authority about yourself for the meeting."

Keller stared at the boy.

"Just trying to help, sir."

"Appreciated," said the starship captain. "Carry on."

As the youth went busily to work with pliers and screwdriver, Captain Keller reminded himself that his crew was the best Earth possessed. Instances such as this were sure to become commonplace, God help him.

While waiting for his staff to arrive, Keller leaned against the edge of the table and began to toy with the good luck piece he kept in his shirt pocket—a silvery metal coin about the size of a Swiss franc, or an American half-dollar. The front bore the emblem of the United Nations of Earth, the reverse had a six-pointed star with a circle in its center, the universal symbol for "One hundred per cent pure thulium—honest!" It was the first such coin minted, and just prior to lift off, the remaining members of the FCT had scratched their initials on the coin wishing him luck. Keller appreciated the gift, although the Swiss astronaut knew that when numismatists heard about this, the purists among the coin collectors would curse their names forever.

The door to the ward room swung open, and in walked Lieutenant Sakaeda. The marine was dressed in a tan duty uniform with a holstered laser pistol, his black hair still damp from a shower. Keller forgave the man for that; he knew how sweaty you could get working inside a power suit. Dag had endured long training sessions in them himself.

Next came Prof. Rajavur in a three-piece, charcoal gray suit and holding a mug of that drain cleaner he had the audacity to call coffee. The diplomat was closely followed by Dr. Van Loon, in proper ship's uniform, and finally Trell, who scowled when he saw there were no chairs.

"Somebody put you in slow motion, Abduhl?" chastised the little alien.

"Hey, chief, I only got two hands," complained Hassan from inside a jungle gym of chair legs, struts, and seat-backs.

At that, Trell puckered his face and burst into laughter. Ha! Two hands. Wait till he tried that joke on an Oolian!

Captain Keller cleared his throat. "Okay, gentlemen, take your . . . ah, assume your places."

As the officers and civilian positioned themselves about the table, it occurred to Dag that his crew was a true cross selection of every racial subspecies that the planet Earth had to offer, with the notable exception of Greece.

"Here's your seat, sir," said Hassan, wheeling the chair over to him.

Keller thanked the man and, after adjusting the spring tension, sat down at the head of the table.

"Let's have your report, Master Technician," he directed.

"Our initial plan has failed," Trell told them sadly. "Due to the heroic throat capacity of The 16, the HN cube was damaged and is totally irreparable."

Shocked murmurs greeted that.

"So the raid was a bust?" asked Lieutenant Sakaeda, removing his cap and stuffing it into a pants pocket.

"Female sex glands were not involved," denied the alien. "However, we did manage to transfer all useful information in the Gee's cube to our own blank."

"And?" prompted Captain Keller.

Trell made a face. "We received only six complete sets of navigational coordinates. There were hundreds of partial coordinates, but I decided to filter those out as they were worse than useless."

"How so?" inquired Van Loon.

"We might jump out of hyperspace and land on the planet we aimed for—at ten thousand kilometers a second."

The Dutch physician was forced to agree that would seriously hinder their mission.

"Couldn't we finish the partial integers ourselves?" asked Prof. Rajavur as he took a sip from his new cup, which bore the legend: "I HELPED DEFEND THE EARTH FROM ALIEN INVADERS, AND ALL I GOT WAS THIS LOUSY COFFEE MUG."

Amazingly, Trell told them yes. "Dirt . . . ah, Earth . . . no, Terra (the official name) has excellent calculating machines. The computers we have aboard ship are some of the best I've ever seen, considering their lack of sentience. Working together they won't take more than a lunar rotation for each coordinate."

"A month we cannot afford to waste," said Keller sternly. "Okay. We have six places to try and find an HN cube. That doesn't sound too bad."

Trell waved his hands in a pattern of negation. "It's worse, sir. Two are maybes, one is an unknown, and the rest are totally undesirable."

"What are the three we can't use?" asked Van Loon curiously. Then a hooting siren split the air.

Frantically, everybody tried to recall their training sessions and identify the noise. Fire? Flood? Vacuum? Engine overheating? Breach in the hull?

"Jailbreak!" screamed Lieutenant Sakaeda, as he tumbled backward over a half-built chair and dashed out of the room in a single motion.

*   *   *   *   *

Shouting a martial arts *Kia*, the avantor kicked aside the remains of the door to her cell and boldly stepped through. The dura-steel lock had been reduced to molten scrap with a single psychokinetic blast, a trick that her grandma had taught her.

With a snort of contempt, the Gee ripped off her paper

hospital gown and proceeded naked down the hallway, searching for The 16.

Momentarily, her attention was caught by the sounds of frantic movement in a nearby cell. But when the guardian of the galaxy looked in through the grill, she saw that it was only some humans cowering behind the cell's sparse furnishings. Timidly, they waved hello at her. The avantor's eyes narrowed to slits as recognition hit her and they ducked back down. Oh, them. She moved on.

Through the grill of the next door, Avantor spied a room full of equipment stolen from her ship. No uniforms or handweapons, though. Mostly it appeared to be medical supplies. Odd.

The following cell yielded her goal, but the Gee's delight turned to horror as she saw her primary assistant lying unconscious on a bed. The mystery of the medical supplies was solved.

Disposing of the door took only a moment, and she rushed across the room. The 16 lay peacefully sleeping on a waveless water bed, covered to his neck in white sheets, the contrast lending a bit of color to his cheeks. On a small table nearby was an RDP monitor and a blood plant whose leafy vines reached under the covers.

Softly calling his name, the avantor knelt on the floor and touched his hand. His pulse was strong, breathing steady, but telepathically the woman felt the disorientation in his mind and the soreness in his stomach.

Shamefaced, Avantor remembered that she had done this to him with her fumbling words, and realized that he had almost died. Ingesting an HN cube would kill a professional Choron weight lifter.

Dimly, she could feel his disjointed memories of the operation, dominated by images of the bald human doctor struggling to remove the cube. But the golden female felt no gratitude for the act. The Dirtlings had been more interested in getting the cube than in saving a life.

Drastically, she revised her plans. The 16 was too ill to move.

Avantor would have to take over the vessel herself. Training video #460/B—"How to Capture a Starship When You Are Naked, Unarmed, and Alone"—flashed through the woman's mind and she reviewed the pertinent points. Check. This shouldn't take more than nine hundred seconds.

Leaving the door ajar, she left the cell and turned to see a guard in power armor clumping toward her.

"Wait!" shouted Private Fuerstenberg over the external speaker of his suit. "We need to—"

Talk, was the word he was going for, but the Gee cut him short with a psychokinetic bolt that slammed the hapless man backward, embedding him into a steel bulkhead, and really putting the inner force field cushion of the power armor to the stress test. With a tremendous groan, the battered marine went limp, but stayed where he was, his metal boots dangling inches off the deck.

Like a glorious golden halo, the avantor's long hair flared out from her body by the secondary static-electric charge of the mental blast, her magnificent bosom heaving from the exertion. But she did not stop to catch her breath. The main door to the brig proved to be a simple magnetic lock/dead bolt/pry bar combination, and moments later she stepped into the outside corridor.

Ready for anything, the two uniformed guards in the passageway relaxed and holstered their guns when they saw who it was exiting.

"Are you okay?" asked the first marine, and the other started to doff her uniform jacket to give to the naked woman. Like golden rods of steel, the avantor's fists shot out and crashed into the humans' jaws, and the guards toppled to the floor.

As Avantor bent down to take their energy weapons, the turbo-lift at the far end of the hallway opened and out came Lieutenant Sakaeda and a squad of soldiers in power armor. Four marines in the center of the group were lugging a hunk of sewer pipe with a glowing crystal sphere on the end—the sight of which made the guardian of the galaxy go pale. Oh Void.

Halting some ten meters away, the soldiers pointed the

cannonlike weapon at her and the ball on the tip began to glow
with power.

"Avantor, don't do it. We can explain everything," said
Lieutenant Sakaeda in his most soothing tones. "There is no
need for violence."

"*Szorklop!*" spat the warrior, pulling the two laser pistols
free from the guards' holsters.

It was then Sakaeda realized that neither of them were wearing translators. A critical mistake. Damn, nothing else to do.

"Riflemen, hold your fire!" he cried. "Cannoneers, *let her
have it!*"

STOP THAT

With a shudder, the Gee dropped the guns and stumbled
backward into the brig under the pointblank blast of the *STOP
THAT* cannon liberated from her own ship. Gasping for
breath, she fell sprawling to the floor. Lieutenant Sakaeda
grinned in satisfaction and started forward.

Struggling to her knees, in a most provocative pose, the
avantor focused her awesome mind powers and blew a hole in
the wall alongside the cannon crew, bits of steel ricocheting off
the armor of the marines. She scowled in annoyance. Missed!

Grimacing, Sakaeda touched his stinging cheek, his hand
coming away covered with blood. Okay, goddamn it. That was
quite enough of that.

"Cannoneers," he shouted. "Fire! Fire! Fire!"

It took five more of the psionic blasts, each hitting the Gee
like a baseball bat, until, at last, Avantor slumped unconscious. Only the fingers of her right hand managed to cross the
threshold of the door, which was a whole lot farther than anybody had ever dreamed she would get.

As the marines cautiously clunked into the brig and a medical team came running out of the elevator to their left, a low
moan sounded over their suit radios.

"Where's Fuerstenberg?" asked Lieutenant Sakaeda.

It didn't take the soldiers long to find their bruised friend, but freeing him was another matter entirely.

*   *   *   *   *

"Well?" demanded Captain Keller gruffly to his wrist transceiver.

"Avantor is back in her cell, sir," reported Sakaeda's voice. "A maintenance crew is repairing the damage she did. The *ST* cannon has been positioned in front of her cell door and wired to the lock. The next time Lady Godiva tries to take a walk, she won't get very far." He paused. "We also gave her a jumpsuit and a translator."

"Acceptable, Lieutenant," said Keller. "Report to the ward room as soon as you are finished."

"Aye, aye, sir." With a click, the soldier signed off.

"I warned you about the Gees, my Captain," Trell reminded the human. "Nobody has ever successfully kept one prisoner."

This interested Dr. Van Loon. "You've tangled with them before?"

"Yes, when I was with Leader Idow."

"Meaning no disrespect, Trell, but why were you with that bastard? I have come to know you fairly well and you're not the criminal type."

Prof. Rajavur knew the answer to that, but remained silent and let Trell tell his tale.

"I was with Idow by necessity, not choice," said the alien calmly, not offended a bit by the question. His tour of duty aboard the *All That Glitters* was not the high point of his life, but neither was it something he was ashamed of—even though very few of the memories were pleasant. Then his face brightened as he remembered that Boztwank was dead. "My parent was a gambler, but, to my misfortune, not a very good gambler . . . and got deeply into debt. The only honorable solution was selling me into slavery to pay the bills." Trell dilated his nostrils. "Not an unusual practice on my world."

Captain Keller raised an eyebrow. "Parent, singular?" he asked curiously.

"Yes, indeed," chimed in Van Loon, unable to resist the temptation to wax didactic. "The Mormanzumas, Trell's people, don't procreate by fertilizing an ovum in a female like us, but by budding. That is, controlled cellular fission which results in a duplicate being. But not a clone. The new entity has its own unique personality." During this, Trell averted his eyes and blushed. Sex talk always made him uneasy.

"Interesting," mused Keller. "Then why does he look so human? Trell, did your race evolve from primates like ours?"

The alien wiggled his ears. He had no idea. His race was not interested in history, only technology. Nobody cared who did what to whom or when, unless it resulted in an invention.

At that point, Lieutenant Sakaeda appeared in the doorway and saluted the room. "Sir!"

"Come in, Lieutenant," acknowledged Keller, returning the salute. "I see you were wounded."

The Delta Force agent touched the bandage on his right cheek. "Just a scratch, sir."

"Good enough. Have a seat."

Closing the door behind him, the lieutenant walked to his chair, pausing for a second to throw a crumpled piece of paper containing another suggested name for their weapon into a golden waste basket, where it disappeared in a flash of atomic disintegration. Assault Rifle #666, because it beats the hell out of you. Geez! He was going to have a serious talk with the troops about this nonsense real soon.

"To continue," said Captain Keller, returning to the original thread of conversation. "We have only three places to try to get an HN cube without resorting to piracy again." He consulted a list. "Our top choice is Darden—an agricultural world of horse-drawn carriages and steam engines. Apparently high technology goes against a tenet of the local religion, sort of like our own Quakers. They may have a cube to sell us stored away in the old barn that serves as the planetary starport."

"Doesn't sound very encouraging," noted Van Loon gloomily, taking notes in his pocket medical journal.

The captain agreed. "Next choice is a real long shot, the

planet 'Oh, Yeah?' A radioactive cinder of a world that has
become a memorial to the stupidity of war. There are dozens of
dead starships in orbit about the planet, and Trell believes
there is a remote possibility that we can find a functioning
cube among the wreckage. But it is highly doubtful."

Nobody made a comment about the distastefulness of grave
robbing, their mission eclipsing such mundane considerations.

"And the last coordinate is a world Trell doesn't know a
damn thing about."

Lieutenant Sakaeda stopped scratching at the red-stained
cotton gauze square on his cheek. "Nothing?"

In his own defense, Trell pointed out that there were millions of inhabited planets in the galaxy. He admitted that these
coordinates sounded vaguely familiar, but so did many others.

"An outside chance, at best," said Keller in frank honesty.

Thoughtfully, Prof. Rajavur took a sip of his coffee, its excellent quality dispelling that old myth about ship food. Faintly,
he wished Yuki and the rest of his old team were there to share
it with him. "To repeat Dr. Van Loon's earlier question, what
are the worlds we can't use? Underwater colonies? Orphan-
ages? Prisons?"

Captain Keller consulted his list. Even though the words on
it were typed, the contents were still a little hard to read. The
interfacing of Trell's translator with the ship's computer and
laser printer was not yet perfect. "The first is the planet RporR.
Trell, am I pronouncing that correctly. R—pour—R?"

A green nod. "That's right, sir. Although everybody else in
the galaxy does tend to spit the name a bit more."

The starship captain ignored the rhetoric. "It's a forbidden
world. Nobody may enter or leave." A faint smile. "RporR has
a blockade around it just like Earth."

"Excellent," said Sakaeda with a grin that put the taste of
salt in his mouth. Quickly, he returned his lips to a neutral
position. "Then they're potential allies."

In the strongest possible terms, Trell told the soldier he was
absolutely wrong. RporRians weren't the allies of anybody—
except maybe assassins and garbage collectors.

"The second is a secret criminal base that Trell knows about from his association with Leader Idow. It is the center of operations for a stolen starship ring. We can definitely get a hypernavigational cube there, but we have broken enough laws already. Our mission is to ingratiate ourselves into galactic society, not purchase stolen equipment."

However annoying that decision might be, the room had to agree with the thinking behind it. Too bad, though.

"What is number six, Captain?" asked Rajavur.

Keller scowled at the paper in his hand and then tossed it aside. "The planet Gee, headquarters of the Great Golden Ones."

"No, we don't want to go there," observed Hassan from the floor as he put the finishing touches on the last chair.

"Thank you, sailor," stated Captain Keller coldly. "Your work is finished here. You may leave."

As the embarrassed technician shuffled out of the room, Keller surveyed the faces of his executive staff. "Any further discussion? No? Accepted then."

Rising to his feet, the Swiss officer walked over and activated the intercom on the wall. "Bridge? This is the captain . . . Have navigation turn the ship white, straighten our flight plan, and feed in the coodinates for the planet Darden."

"Acknowledged," squeaked Lieutenant Jones's voice from the box. "Any further orders?"

"Tell you when I get there. Keller out." Dag rapped his knuckles on the polished tabletop. "Meeting adjourned, gentlemen. We reconvene on the bridge in six and a half hours."

"And may the Prime Builder grease us with his own ear wax!" cried Trell, climbing on top of his chair and brandishing a green fist in the air.

The precise meaning of that phrase was unclear to the human officers, but the tone was positive, so they cheered along with him anyway for the sake of solidarity.

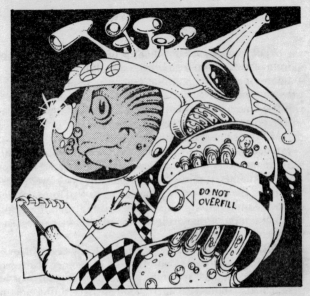

20

Centuries ago, when the Galactic League was formed, it had been decided, for major political reasons and minor military ones, that the league should not be placed on any existing planet and thus elevate that race above others. So, an uninhabited star system was arbitrarily chosen, and in a historic feat of engineering, a sphere of metal was slowly built about the local sun, totally encasing the solar body. On Earth, the structure would have been called a Dyson sphere, after Freeman Dyson, the American scientist who first postulated the mind-staggering concept. The rest of the galaxy simply called it impressive.

Inside the sphere, houses, cities, parks, forests, lakes, and buildings-buildings-buildings were constructed at an astonishing rate. Then the population of a dozen worlds poured into their new homes. But with nine hundred quadrillion square kilometers at their disposal, overcrowding was a word that would never be used on the artificial construct. Even now, with the population at twelve trillion, people often rode to work alone in the car of their monorail train during rush hour.

Interestingly enough, the debate over what to name the titan sphere raged for less than a planetary rotation when a particularly sentient sapient suggested it be called Big, for, notwithstanding its many other qualities, that one could not be denied. The name was readily accepted.

Extending like a spider web into the heart of the flaming sun were mighty solar energy cables—coal black superconductor ribbons, kilometers thick, that collected the raw power necessary to run the contra-gravity generators, so vital to an upside-down community, and the distance-annihilating telecommunicators that made the smooth operation of a galactic society possible.

On the outer hull were continent-wide clusters of Nova-grade lasers; batteries of giant dispersal ray cannon that used multiple thermonuclear bombs just to blow the dust out of their barrels; million-kilometer-long quasar-spitting antennas; force shield towers, each built from a small planet; docking facilities for a hundred million superdreadnought starcrafts; and one fast food outlet run by a sluglike being who was very rich indeed.

As hard as it was to believe, Big was not an original invention of the league. At the other end of the galaxy (second spiral arm, fourth sun to the left) another solar body had been found enclosed in an artificial globe of metal. When a team of eager young explorers landed and entered to greet the builders, they found a dark and deserted interior—with a smaller sphere inside. Obviously, the inhabitants had constructed it as the sun had shrunk from usage—a natural phenomenon that would take several billion planetary rotations. Bravely entering the second sphere, the explorers found another sphere, and another, and another, and . . . after two hundred and nine of the things, the team of explorers (now quite old) finally gave up and went home.

The current theory is that the mad builders are still in there somewhere, but nobody is particularly anxious to meet them.

There were quite enough amateur loonies in the universe, no need to bring in professionals.

On Big, amid the sprawling grandeur of the upside-down megatropolis, at the mathematically chosen north pole—longitude 0, latitude 0—was a small, stone amphitheater. The open air structure was brightly illuminated by the dominated sun in the overhead sky. The architect had claimed that this was a purely dramatic touch, and it had won her much acclaim. But honestly, the auditorium's rooflessness had been done just so the plant wouldn't have to stop work every few hours and go outside to eat.

A thousand seats filled the amphitheater, each facing inward toward a raised stone dais in the center, where a simple podium of solid gold stood. This was the audience chamber of the Great Golden Ones, where the guardians of the galaxy released bulletins to news reporters or sought the counsel of learned beings.

Today, it was reporters—a hundred gatherers of news from as many different worlds. A true cornucopia of beings who bore only a faint resemblance to Earthly: tugs and rugs, rats and bats, apes and grapes, logs, fogs, dogs, lizards, birds, rocks, and even the occasional humanoid or two. The reporters had been brought here on a double star, alpha prime, ultra-emergency summons, which meant interstellar war, the sun was about to explode, or a truly major party.

Floating in the sunny air above the crowd were thousands of shiny metal balls. Most of them were remote broadcast cameras, some were reporters from machine cultures, some containment vessels for energy beings. Nobody was exactly sure what the heck a half dozen or so of the things were.

At the sound of a gong, a muscular golden male in a flowing amber tunic walked out onto the dais, and the murmuring crowd grew quiet. Bracing himself, The 3000, the supreme commander of the Gees, once again wondered whether or not it was really worth his while talking to these idiots. Reporters, the bane of his existence.

"Attention, gentlefolk," said the tall humanoid into the

force field microphone floating invisible in the air before him. "I bring you news of a shocking and most unpleasant nature."

The reporters grew tense. They knew what this meant—no party.

The 3000 cleared his throat. "A race of violent primitives has escaped from the blockade about their world and is loose somewhere in the galaxy."

For a moment there was shocked silence at this unprecedented announcement, and fevered images of the RporRian plague flashed through everything's minds. Then came the expected barrage of questions.

"Do they have pets?" asked a reporter in the front row, shouting over the ruckus.

Startled, the Gee blinked. "Ah, yes, they do have pets."

"What kind?" persisted the news gatherer.

"Various kinds, I believe—"

"Insects? Do they keep insects for pets?"

"Yes-yes! They keep insects for pets!" snapped the golden male. "Now can we—"

"SLAVERS!" screamed the hysterical spideroid, its eight arms and legs undulating wildly. "My people must be set free!"

"Non-sentient insects," said The 3000 loudly over the commotion. Just like you, he added privately.

"Oh." The reporter averted all of his eyes and blushed. "Never mind."

A potted plant next to the arachnid kicked it with a convenient frond. "Come on, grow up," chided the evolved rutabaga. "It's not like they eat vegetables or anything."

Wisely, the Gee said nothing.

"Do they have a use for dried proto-yeast?" asked something from the rear of the room.

The 3000 forced himself to smile politely. "We are getting away from the main issue. These criminals—"

"What is their opinion of the *Thurstd* problem?" asked a translucent balloonish creature who was strapped into his chair by elastic bands to prevent him from drifting away on the morning breeze.

"But they don't know anything about it!" stormed the Gee, starting to lose control. "How the Hot Void could they?"

"New race pleads ignorance to the plight of the *Thurstd gik*," said the reporter into the soft plastic recorder on its clear, pudgy wrist.

The 3000 tightened his jaw and in a practiced motion drew a wide-barreled pistol from inside his tunic. Ruthlessly he swept the assemblage of reporters about him with the weapon's ethereal rays. Instantly, the news gatherers were motionless, and even more importantly, quiet, as the telepathic command to *SHUT UP* reverberated in their brains. The psionic pistol was a special modification of the *STOP THAT* cannon and was authorized by the Gee Security Council solely for use at these infamous meetings.

In the ensuing still, the wall behind the Gee swirled with color and changed from a holographic view of the galaxy into a magnified picture of the Galactic League herself. The regal reptiloid smiled benignly at the crowd and every reporter in the amphitheater saluted the video monitor in their own way. Even the metal globes in the air did a little dip of respect.

"Your Excellency!" gasped The 3000 in surprise. "I'm honored!"

"Thank you, 3000. It has been a while since we last attended these gatherings." Royally, the female gazed over the assembled throng. "Now, are these dangerous primitives flying blind through space or do they have a hypernavigational cube?"

"Yes! They stole it!" said the golden male in righteous fury.

"Indeed. From whom?"

Oops. He had not been expecting a cross-examination—especially by the league. The 3000 mumbled something that sounded strangely like the word *us*.

Daintily, the amphibian lifted an eye ridge. "Could you repeat that, please?"

"Us. They stole the cube from us," admitted the Gee, with a woebegone look. "They raided the superdreadnought orbiting their world, then stole a cube and the crew."

A silence more hushed than before filled the room. Primitives took over a Gee superdreadnought? Zow! Wow!

"How?" asked the league, getting to the heart of the matter.

"That information is not privy to public consumption," said 3000 stiffly, placing his hands behind his back.

"Understandable," said the scaly female on the monitor. "Still, they must be fairly advanced to build a starship, even one without a cube. Perhaps they are advanced enough to join the league."

"But they didn't invent the starship," said the golden male hotly. "They stole the engine design!"

"From whom? Not you again?"

The 3000 had trouble getting this out. "Leader Idow."

A shocked gasp was heard from the reporters, and the league narrowed her bulging eyes in anger. "They are aligned with Leader Idow? Then I authorize the immediate destruction of their entire solar system, from the sun out."

"Well, they're not exactly aligned . . ."

"Explain; please."

The Gee was trapped and he knew it. Before the near hypnotic gaze of the Galactic League it was worse than useless trying to lie, or even shade the truth. The story of X-47-D's incompetence could no longer be kept secret. "The humans killed him and copied the engine design before we could stop them."

The reporters wrote furiously. Leader Idow was dead? This was real news!

"When is the parade?" called out a catish reporter.

"How much is their reward?" asked a newshound.

A mass of granite raised its stony head. "Where will the monument to them be built?" boomed a Choron. Rocks were his people's favorite subject to read about.

"How do you spell 'human'?" queried the spideroid.

"Interesting," mused the Galactic League, her throaty tones echoing over the amphitheater's PA system. "They destroy the greatest threat the civilized galaxy has ever seen, and you blockade their planet. Why?"

Eagerly, the assemblage leaned forward. A good question that. The league could have been a reporter. Each news-being waited, stylus in manipulatory appendage.

"They are dangerous primitives, Your Excellency. A threat to the peace of the galaxy!"

It sounded to the league like the Gee was desperately trying to cover up a monumental blunder. The Great Golden Ones had been making quite a few of those lately. "Dangerous, you say? Did they kill the crew of the ship they raided?"

"Well, no. . . ."

"And?"

The 3000 sighed in resignation. Hot Void, you couldn't get anything past the Galactic League. "And they left behind a bag of thulium. One thousand pounds."

Startled mumblings came from the crowd.

"Only a most unusual thief leaves behind enough to buy what they steal," noted the reptilian female. "It is our opinion that before any further punitive measures are taken, we will speak to these 'humans.' Find that ship, 3000, and bring us the crew, unharmed."

The Gee saluted. "I will do my best, Your Excellency."

"We want them alive. Remember that."

As the picture faded from the wall, The 3000 touched his forehead and in a blinding flash of light teleported away. Instantly, the reporters burst from their seats, fighting to reach the doors. The dignified amphitheater quickly resembled a video theatre in which somebody had shouted the words 'radiation leak.'

But, remaining seated in the front row, seemingly unaffected by the clamorous departing of his fellow news gatherers, was an aquatic creature whose prominent dorsal fin was covered with telecommunication devices. Crimson-colored, the fishy biped was dressed in a wide assortment of clothing, none of it coordinated, except possibly against each other.

His name was Bachalope Thintfeesel (Bach to his friends,

which were few, rarely sober, and mostly wanted by the Gees—like the friends of any good reporter). He was a freelance news writer who made his living by being the first with the most at every major event. And this was just about as major as they come. Piracy! Kidnapping! Blockade running! The death of Leader Idow! And now an interstellar thing-hunt under the direct order of the Galactic League.

Surreptitiously, Bachalope used a four-fingered hand to check on a sophisticated sound recorder disguised as one of his less flamboyant belt buckles. Good. He got the entire discussion on wire, including the mass exiting. Now, if he could just locate the primitives before the Gees did, he would have the story of the century! But, with an entire galaxy to search, how could he possibly find them?

Then he smiled toothily. Yeah, that ought to do it.

*   *   *   *   *

Back at Earth, squadrons of Gee superdreadnoughts sent by The 3000 were supervising the positioning of an armada of drones to encircle the planet, and strategically placing a flotilla of mobile space forts whose batteries of antimatter missiles could easily stop any conceivable mass escape.

The UN fought back by grounding every aircraft, docking every boat, and stonewalling any Gee attempt at communication by filling the entire radio spectrum with gigawatts of rock-'n'roll music, canned laughter, and the song of the humpbacked whale. The aliens translated the mix as "Oh, baby, I'm so hot tonight! Hubba-hubba. Let's do it. Let's do it now. Oh, baby. Oh, baby. Want a fish?" Which seriously annoyed them. Everybody hates elevator music.

Meanwhile, the remnants of the FCT were scattered across the globe hard at work. Generals Nicholi and Bronson were at Star City in Russia assisting the proletariat to design a super-fast, anti-drone ICBM. Dr. Wu was in Australia at Port Woomera, aiding and abetting the construction of Earth's first starfleet. Dr. Malavade was in the desert of New Mexico busily adapting the gigantic radio telescopes there into a battery of quasar-grade pulse transmitters which humanity would use to try and communicate with somebody out there other than the damn Gees. And from Rockefeller Plaza in New York City, Sir John Courtney was constantly bombarding the masses of the world with carefully worded news announcements (propaganda, actually), that kept the populace at a fever pitch and insured their full cooperation.

Humanity was doing everything it could think of—from trying to improve deflector plating and flashing searchlight beams into space in a hypnotic "GO AWAY" pattern, to sticking pins in golden voodoo dolls.

But the Great Golden Ones were also unleashing the full might of their peacekeeping forces, and there was little doubt that the strategic balance would be in the Gees' favor.

* * * * *

Meanwhile, on the planet Darden, the crew of the *Ramariez* were sadly informed by the farmers that no HN cubes were available, but they were invited to wait a planetary rotation or so, when a drone cargo ship from Big would land to take on their yeast harvest. The locals felt sure the robot crew would have no objections to signaling the Great Golden Ones and asking them to bring a replacement. Captain Keller politely declined the offer and the *Ramariez* left post haste, only seconds ahead of the landing of an Emergency Data StarCapsule which brought the news that the humans were wanted criminals to he held at any cost.

Jumping to the burned out cinder of "Oh, Yeah?" the starship crew found numerous hyperspace navigational cubes in the riddled hulls of blasted vessels circling the dead planet. But every piece of equipment aboard the spacecrafts was so highly contaminated with atomic radiation that the cubes were totally useless.

As the *Ramariez* left the ominously silent planet, her captain was forcibly reminded by the grim specter of ruin that theirs was a mission of peace, and violence was to be used only as a last resort.

A short hop through hyperspace later, as the *Ramariez* approached the third choice on their short list, the crew was struck by the similarities of the unknown planet and Earth. Roughly the same size and distance from the sun, both were mostly water and had a single moon.

"Just like home," said a crew member wistfully.

Dr. Van Loon agreed. "The inhabitants will most likely be very similar to us in general build."

"Or dinosaurs," noted Chief Petty Officer Buckley, his Royal British Marine moustache stiffly abristle, but still cut short enough to fit into a space helmet. "They were on Earth long before us."

Hiding a smile, the physician stated that the possibility was extremely remote.

"Captain?" called out Ensign Hamlisch from the sensors console.

Keller turned from his examination of the internal circuitry of the hydroponics station and lowered the console top into place. "Yes, what is it?"

"Sir, scanners indicate that there's a golden egg orbiting this world."

"A what?" asked the Swiss naval officer, joining the pale, bony man at his board.

"An egg, sir," stated Hamlisch. "Honest. It's of very advanced design. It's beyond the abilities of my instruments to analyze the thing."

Scowling over the ensign's shoulder, Captain Keller peered at the tiny four inch monitor. "Put it on the main screen, please."

"Aye, sir." The picture of the blue and white planet before them zoomed in close. There, filling the screen, was a tapering, oval spheroid, yellowish-brown in color, twirling about its vertical axis. Data about construction, size, and speed scripted along the bottom of the screen. Twenty eyes scrutinized its form and shape.

"About the size of a refrigerator," muttered an ensign.

"The bridge is no place for levity, mister," snapped Keller

and the woman flinched. "Your opinion, Doctor?"

Van Loon stepped closer to the viewscreen, carefully studying the rapidly rotating object. "None worth mentioning, sir."

Captain Keller squinted an eye. It was time to call in their resident expert. "Ensign Lilliuokalani, summon Trell, please."

"Aye, aye, sir." The Hawaiian communications officer pressed a button on her console and spoke into a fixed microphone. "Master Technician Trell to the bridge. Master Technician—sir, incoming signal!"

"From the planet?" asked Keller, climbing into his command chair.

"No, sir, the egg."

The captain buckled on his seat belt. "Translate and put it on the main speakers, mister."

"Aye, sir." Deftly, the astronaut flipped switches and the ceiling-mounted speakers crackled to life.

". . . ARNING TO ALL STARSHIPS. LEAVE THIS SYSTEM IMMEDIATELY. STATUS OMEGA. REPEAT: STATUS OMEGA. WARNING TO ALL STARSHIPS . . ."

The speakers went silent.

"It's a closed loop," reported the ensign.

As Keller chewed the information over, the doors to the elevator opened and Trell walked in. Or, at least, he started to enter, but when the alien saw the planet on the forward viewscreen, he gasped and went light green.

"Something wrong?" asked Captain Keller, swiveling his chair about at the sound.

"Leave," the alien somehow managed to say. "Now. There is nothing for us here. Go. Depart."

As in a daze, Trell stumbled forward, and the captain kept abreast of him by slowly rotating his chair.

"You said you knew nothing about this world," noted Keller.

"I said I didn't recognize it from the coordinates," explained the shaking technician. "Let's go. Please?"

"Sir," called out the communications officer. "Message from the planet."

Keller nodded, and the overhead speakers crackled once more.

"SO, POND SCUM, YOU RETURN," thundered a voice dripping with hate. "WELL, YOU WILL NOT TRICK US THIS TIME, IDOW. PREPARE TO DIE!"

Eyes popped across the bridge crew. *Idow?*

Captain Keller whirled about, grabbed Trell by the collar, and lifted him off the floor—a practice the little alien was starting to get used to.

"You've been here before, haven't you?" growled the starship officer. The technician bobbled his head yes. This was a planet Leader Idow had visited when Trell was a new member of the crew. Thousands of days ago. That is why the coordinates had been vaguely familiar to him. Captain Keller released the alien with a curse.

"Red alert!" barked Dag frantically. "Shields, full power! Navigation, dead stop! Communications, tell them this is not the *All That Glitters*. We simply look like them. And—"

"Incoming!" shouted the weapons officer, and from an orbital platform above the world a blue-hot plasma bolt lanced out. Seconds later it struck the ship with triphammer force, bouncing the bridge crew out of their seats, but no consoles were shorted and the lights did not dim.

As the humans scrambled back into their chairs and buckled on safety belts, a black cloud of missiles rose from the surface of the planet, leaving no doubt as to their destination.

"Shields?" demanded Keller.

"Holding," reported CPO Buckley, fighting to keep his voice steady. "But not against many more of those."

The missile salvo drew closer and another plasma bolt was fired in their direction. The starship captain made a fast decision.

"Reverse course," shouted Keller and then did a double take as he saw the moon near them split apart and its hollow interior disgorge seemingly millions of fighting ships—that charged straight toward the innocent *Ramariez*.

"GET READY TO DIE, IDOW!" screamed the voice on the

speakers. "YOU SCALELESS, EGG-EATING—"

"Shunt!" bellowed the captain, as the helmsman stabbed her finger on the proper button. In a burst of light, the *Ramariez* jumped into hyperspace, only moments before countless missiles, plasma bolts, lasers beams, and nuclear mines flooded their previous location, exploding with such horrific, space-twisting, mind-shattering force, that even in the non-dimension of hyperspace the *Ramariez* felt a slight tremor and the lights momentarily dimmed.

"Ship's status!" snapped Captain Keller, as the room brightened and telltales began winking on every board and console. A few minutes passed while information was hastily gathered and processed. As the reports came in and Keller became satisfied that his ship was undamaged, he dropped their status to yellow alert. Then the captain ordered the forward speed cut to dead slow. In essence, the *Ramariez* was now drifting in hyperspace.

"The Gees are going to have real trouble with those guys," remarked Dr. Van Loon dryly as he left the medical console. Sick bay was fine. Nobody hurt. Avantor and The 16 were both undamaged and resting confortably.

Keller agreed with the physician wholeheartedly. Those folks had a real bad attitude problem.

"And they probably don't have a hypernavigational cube, either," noted Trell pragmatically.

Lost in rumination, Captain Keller reclined in his chair and rubbed his dimpled chin. The operating perimeters of the situation were rapidly deteriorating. As a duly appointed officer in the United Nations' space navy, he had taken an oath to obey galactic law to the best of his ability. Dag grunted. Unfortunately, the only course left open to them now was totally illegal, plain and simple, and no amount of bickering or word-twisting, could change that fact. So, what he had to decide was: should the *Ramariez* commit trespassing or receive stolen goods? A misdemeanor or a felony? Hell, no contest there.

"Helmsman, set course for RporR. We're going to see how

well this crew can run a fully established blockade."

"Aye, aye, sir!"

The soft thud everyone heard following that statement proved only to be Trell fainting.

21

"Queen/Mother! Queen/Mother!" cried the RporRian guard, pushing aside the beaded curtain and dashing into the throne room. The excited insect paused only for a moment to toss a silver piece into a simple clay pot already half-filled with the coins, that being the standard surcharge for delivering a message to Her Most High, Divine Loveliness, Gatherer Of The Taxes, Guardian Of The Treasury, Master Breeder, and Expert Penny Pincher, (squeak-squeak-thromb-squeal-chatter-gnash-grunt), The Fourth. The absolute ruler of RporR.

The corpulent female was supine upon a pile of coins in a dark, moist alcove of the cavernous room, sedately enjoying a snack of crystallized sweet moss. Her lesser limbs slowed in their constant, mindless counting of the coins, and the wall-mounted organic laser cannons flanking her tightened their focusing coronas and tracked the approach of the advancing male.

Lazily, she raised four eyelids to gaze at the small male dancing excitedly on the marble floor before her.

"What is it (hiss-spit)? Another buy-one-get-one-free sale?"

"No, Your Majesty! A starship approaches!"

"A scout returning home?" she asked, raising another set of eyelids and beginning to show some faint sign of interest. That damn blockade of the Gee's was a clever trap. RporRians could check in, but they couldn't check out.

"No, Your Greediness. It's a blue Mikon #4!"

"Aliens?" For the barest moment her sub-hands paused in their eternal work, and she laid aside her clawful of moss. "Oh dear, what do our sensors tell us about them?"

The messenger rattled with pleasure. "Thulium, Queen/Mother, and lots of it!"

"Wonderful," she sighed and removed a ceremonial rasp from its long-undisturbed compartment to begin filing her bargaining claws. "Then let us prepare a welcome for our guests."

"A parade, Beloved Assessor?" cried the guard, clapping his forelegs together with the sound of castanets. "Could we hold a parade?"

She smiled widely, the act almost breaking her head in two. "That sounds like an excellent idea (hiss-spit). Yes, they should have a parade."

"Yippee!" cried the messenger/guard as he started to skuttle from the room.

"Oh, and (hiss-spit)?"

Breathless, he paused by the door, the reflected light from the glass beads casting a thousand tiny rainbows across his twitching, gnarled features. "Yes, Your Avarice?"

"Take that fake silver piece out of the pot and put in two real coins or I will make you stand on a stepladder." She was no longer paying attention to him, but her vestigial kneecaps crackled ominously.

Fearfully, the male swallowed hard. "B-by, your command." Gee, was she a Queen/Mother, or what?

* * * * *

As the *Ramariez* drifted through space, the green dot on its forward viewscreen rapidly grew into a picture of a lush, tropical world. However, the details were obscured by a thin gray fog that seemed to blanket the planet.

"Dead stop," ordered Captain Keller, and the ship eased to a halt. He studied the screen before him, trying to get a glimpse of the Gee's blockade. Nothing.

"Tactical, Mr. Buckley."

"Aye, sir," The CPO fiddled with the dials on his console. A vector graphic formed on his monitor and information began flowing across the bottom of the screen.

"Class K star, no sunspot activity. Eight planets in the system: three before us, five aft. Nothing in our vicinity but a few asteroids. No divergent courses. Getting a high metal reading from the planet, indicative of an advanced civilization." He tapped a meter with a finger. Hey, wait a minute, he thought, those readings were going right off the scale! Hell, right off the planet!

"Sweet Jesus," whispered the Irishman, crossing himself.

"Report, mister," barked Keller, the whipcrack tone achieving the desired effect.

"At first I thought the fog around the world was a dust storm, or maybe pollution," said the chief petty officer, a calm professional once more. "But the cloud is not even in the atmosphere."

Seated at the scanner console, Ensign Hamlisch worked to slave their monitors together. "You don't mean. . . ?"

"It's the Gee blockade," confirmed Buckley, barely able to believe it himself. "A swarm of gray metal pyramids that completely surrounds the planet."

Captain Keller snorted. "Visible at this range? Impossible. There would have to be millions of them."

"Ninety-seven million," corrected Chief Buckley, staring at his flashing gauges. "And still counting."

Keller managed to maintain his facade of calm, with only

the slight crunching of the plastic of his chair arm to reveal the tension this news produced. When the Great Golden Ones put up a blockade they didn't fool around. Just calling it a blockade didn't do the construct justice. It was staggering. And this was what the Gees had been in the process of erecting around Earth. For the first time, the starship officer fully appreciated what it was they were defying.

In contemplation, the captain glanced at the viewscreen at the front of the bridge. The left panel was in data mode, scrolling mathematical equations; the right screen displayed the planet highlighted by computer-generated color splotches indicating chemical composition and thermal activity; the middle showed a magnification factor-ten picture of the world framed by a gray metal cloud.

"Why is the blockade thinner directly in front of us?" asked Ensign Soukup, stating the captain's unspoken thought.

"Checking," said Hamlisch, manipulating his scanner controls.

"Well?" demanded Captain Keller after a minute.

Ensign Hamlisch flipped a switch and frowned. "Because, sir, as far as I can tell, we are in a spiral passageway that goes through the blockade to the planet." He nodded at the middle viewscreen. "The only reason we can see RporR this clearly is that we've come out of hyperspace somewhere near the end of the spiral."

"A passageway?" mused the captain. Then he snapped his fingers. "Of course! We must be in the Gee safe route through this mine field."

"Makes sense, sir," conceded Soukup. "Considering whose coordinates we used to get here."

"Skipper," announced the communications officer, touching the wireless receiver in her ear. "I have just gotten a warning from a sentry device shaped like a golden beehive on the other side of the planet."

"Ordering us to leave?"

The Hawaiian turned to face him. "No, sir, just strongly advising us not to land. Or, if we must, then not to breathe the air on the planet."

"The atmosphere does not register poisonous," stated a nurse at the medical console, in a thick Russian accent.

"Air tax," said Lilliuokalani, face deadpan.

Captain Keller wondered if the woman was trying to be funny.

"Let me get this straight," said Dag, leaning forward, elbows resting on knees. "It is only prohibited for an inhabitant to leave, but not for somebody to visit unless they pay a tax?"

"Apparently so, sir."

With a sigh of contentment, Keller reclined in his command chair. Great. They were still semi-legal then.

"But this is much too simple," ventured Ensign Soukup, swiveling her chair about. "Surely the locals must see ships coming in. Why don't they just try leaving the same way?"

"They probably do," conceded Buckley. "But the drones are so arranged that thirty per cent of them can fire in unison on any target."

"What kind of power does that entail?" asked Lilliuokalani.

Ensign Hamlisch looked apologetic. "Sorry. My gauges don't go that high."

Captain Keller grimaced.

"Should we erect shields, sir?" inquired Chief Petty Officer Buckley, fingering the proper button.

"Unnecessary," decided the starship captain. "It appears that as long as we don't have any RporRians on board, we're safe."

"Aye, sir."

"Anything directly from the planet, Mr. Lilliuokalani?" asked Keller.

"Negative, sir."

The captain considered that most odd. Surely they knew the ship was coming in for a landing.

"Follow the spiral in, Ensign Soukup," he ordered the woman. "And approach with caution."

The helmsman gulped. "Affirmative, sir."

To the nervously watching crew, it appeared as if the ship was floating through an endless bank of mist, the sheer number of the Gee drones swamping the visuals.

"Entering atmosphere," announced Ensign Hamlisch as the viewscreen began to change from foggy gray to a clear blue. In the distance, puffy white clouds lined the horizon.

"Where should we land, sir?" asked Ensign Soukup.

Attentive to detail, Captain Keller studied the continent. Most of the land was either vast farms or smoke-belching factories, the two historical adversaries oddly intermingled, almost as if the effect of pollution on crops was unknown. Or perhaps the locals enjoyed the taste of smog. Anything was possible with an alien race. Both of the coasts were sparsely settled, and only three major cities were discernible; two resembled a military complex, and the third an amusement park.

"There," said Keller, pointing to the left. "That city over there, surrounded by what resembles a roller coaster. It fits the description of their planetary capital."

"Scanners indicate docking facilities for starships to the west of the capital," reported Ensign Hamlisch crisply. "Change course, six degrees, north by northwest."

"Affirmative," replied Soukup, adjusting her controls.

"Belay that order!" snapped Captain Keller. "Land us at that park in the middle of the city. According to Trell, it's public property and available for anybody to use for free."

"Free?" asked SFC Hassan from his engineering station. "Are you sure about that, sir?"

Keller told the man yes, and to shut up.

"Ensign Lilliuokalani, have the landing party assemble in launch bay #1," directed the starship commander. "The first team will consist of Ambassador Rajavur, Sergeant Lieberman, and six marine guards armed only with pistols. We don't want to appear threatening or discourteous."

"Affirmative, sir."

"If anything goes wrong, the rescue squad is to be led by Lieutenant Sakaeda with every remaining marine fully armed and in power armor, backed by our hover cannon, laser batteries, and the ship's main gun."

Just the thought of the awful weapon made the Hawaiian uneasy. "Aye, aye, Captain."

* * * * *

"No, we're not going to call it that either," said Sergeant Lieberman, resting a polished boot on the edge of a bunk, the shiny leather toe making a dent in the otherwise mathematically flat cloth plane. "Look, what's wrong with calling it the UN Assault Rifle Mark One?"

"But, Sarge," complained a private, scratching her ear. "That's boring!"

Lieberman scowled. "And what would you call it, Griggs? 'The Iron Rug,' because it can't be beat?"

"How about, the D-20?" suggested a tall, bony private, in a radio announcer's booming voice.

Sergeant Lieberman braced herself. "Okay, I'm ready. Why?"

"Because, as we charge into battle we'll yell: Die! Die! Die! Die! Die! Die!—"

"Thank you, Fuerstenberg," she said cutting him off. "We get the idea."

"Why is that knucklehead here?" whispered a private to the corporal next to him.

At that moment, the wall speaker chimed and began announcing the personnel assignments for the intended landing.

"Later," said the noncom as she and the other chosen marines broke for their lockers and began strapping on equipment.

* * * * *

"RporR," sighed Trell, gazing at the small, wall-mounted auxiliary viewscreen in launch bay #1. His earlier journey to the floor had given him only a brief reprieve from the awful knowledge of what they were about to do—land on RporR of their own free will. This was probably the last free thing any of them would ever do before they landed in one of the bugs' infamous debtors' prisons, which were filled exclusively with off-worlders who thought they could outsmart the insectoids. Proof that stupidity was a universal trait.

"What's wrong with the place, anyway?" asked a private, strapping an extra ammunition belt about his waist. "Seems nice enough to me."

After the master technician had given the marines a short, at times near-incoherent synopsis of the insects' career, even the New Yorkers among them were impressed with the bugs' amoral greed. Those guys would put a Cuban drug smuggler to shame.

Located just below the equator of the huge starship, on the port side, launch bay #1 was a curved rectangular room whose plain steel walls had yet to be painted. Luminous yellow lines sectioned off the center of the room into twenty squares, and inside those were sleek silver aircars.

Designed purely for atmospheric travel, the vessels strongly resembled a conventional bus with the roof removed, plenty of seats, one driver, and no cargo space. All that was missing was a "No Smoking" sign, a change box, and gum on the floor.

Unlike the spacegoing shuttle craft, which were named after astronauts, the aircars were christened in honor of atmospheric flyers, both real and imaginary: Icarus, Wang Ping, Verbo, D'Amecourt, Count Zepplin, Orville & Wilbur, Kal-el, and so on.

Equipped with Rolls Royce-built antigravity generators and belly turbines for lift, and heavy-duty Choron ion thrusters for drive, the amazing crafts could lift an army tank full of lead and still travel at over 800 kph. The versatile aircars could also float in water for days, and had studded, puncture-proof tires for emergency ground transportation. However, the marines considered the things little more than flying deathtraps, as the aircraft had no armor to speak of and maneuvered like a dead whale on roller skates.

Dressed in tan duty fatigues and combat boots, each waiting marine was armed with a laser pistol with five extra power packs, an HK 9mm automatic with nine extra ammo clips, and in a bulky shoulder holster, a single-shot 40mm grenade launcher. Just like the captain had ordered, sidearms only. Personally, the marines wished they could bring some real weapons with them.

"How's it coming, sir?" asked Sergeant Lieberman, ambling over to their assigned craft, *The Icarus Express.*

"Done, Sergeant," said Trell, closing the hood of the aircar while wiping his lower hands clean on a rag. "I charged the antimatter accelerator, aligned the photovoltaic disc, balanced the gyroscopes, and changed the wiper blades.

Pause. Smile. "Great."

Over in the far corner of the bay, a maintenance technician stopped her mopping of the floor. "Photovoltaic?" she asked. "But surely the DRL assembly is electronic."

"Nonsense," replied the man next to her, pausing in his scrubbing of the wall prior to painting. "The magnetic lens must be controlled by fiber optics. It would eliminate any possibility of negative feedback."

"Yeah," said the janitor, studiously reapplying her mop. "That makes sense."

Leaving the alien to his work, Sgt. Lieberman called for her troops, and the soldiers came running. As they gathered around, the noncom gave them a cursory inspection and nodded in approval. They were hard, lean, and mean. She paused. Sounded like a Marine law firm. Hard, Lean, and Mean, attorneys-at-war.

"Security has got to be tight on this trip," said Lieberman, working the slide on her automatic to chamber a round for immediate use. "The RporRians will do anything to get their people off this planet, and the drones have orders to shoot to kill. The locals don't have communication satellites anymore, or use airplanes. Too risky. The drones keep shooting them down."

"No kidding, Sarge?" asked a private, checking the load on his grenade launcher.

"It is true," said Trell, neatly arranging his tools in a folding metal box. "Some of the more cowardly of the bugs don't even dare stand up straight. Minor criminals are often punished by making them stand on tall things in the outside."

"Really? And what do they do with felons?"

"Breed with them."

The three word reply was delivered with such disgust and hate that it conjured nightmarish visions, and shivers ran along the spines of the marines. Some things are best not known.

"Okay, time to board," said Lieberman, glancing at her watch and deliberately breaking the mood. "Take only window seats, but don't get comfortable. I want everybody alert and ready for trouble. But the first person who acts without permission will get a unidirectional boot in the ass."

As the marines tromped onto the aircar, the janitors across the room chuckled. Tanya Lieberman snorted at them. *Maybe the lenses were controlled by fiber optics*—sheesh! Didn't they know the magnetic flux of the aggie generator would distort any such primitive maser relay? The dopes. But then, that was why they were the cleaning crew.

* * * * *

As the harsh buzz of its drive softened to a muted snore, the *Ramariez* came to rest a rigid two meters above a large grassy plain, with gentle rolling hillocks and several lakes. The pastoral locale was the Mid-City, Tax-Free, Outdoor Recreational Center of (gargle-choke-burp) the capital of RporR.

The local population had scurried away at the starship's approach. In fear, the humans supposed. But within minutes the natives were back, hastily assembling plastic sales booths about the ship, taking photos and hawking goods—not to each other but to the humans inside. Such esoteric items as: edible postcards, Gee dart boards, Koolgoolagan cigars (fake), and bags of genuine souvenir dirt.

Standing in front of the main viewscreen, Captain Keller studied the banners fluttering above the inflated booths. Most of them bore a broken triangle, the universal symbol of "FOR SALE." Quite a few had the triangle and double circles which translated as "BARGAIN." And one even had three circles, which the starship officer supposed meant "CHEAP." Nowhere did he see just a broken circle, the symbol for "FREE SAMPLES."

"Are you sure about this?" Keller asked the wall.

"Positive, sir," replied the voice of Trell. "The ship is too low to need a flying permit and to high to require a parking fee."

"What a crazy world this is," remarked Hamlisch softly.

Ensign Soukup readily agreed. "Aren't they all, my friend?"

* * * * *

"Here he comes," observed the driver in a measured tone.

Sergeant Lieberman scowled. "About time."

Holding onto his silk top hat, Prof. Rajavur ran across the metal deck of the loading bay toward the waiting aircar. The Icelander was dressed in his best tuxedo and platinum translator, and sported a red silk ambassador's sash. His shoes were polished, his iron-gray hair combed into obedience, and he had even gargled with sugar water to be more pleasing to the insects. As Sigerson hurriedly climbed into the transport, he was dismayed at the profusion of weapons among the marines. But he wisely acknowledged their necessity should things turn ugly. The RporRians did have a bad reputation.

"Sorry I'm late," apologized the diplomat as he took his seat next to the driver. "But I had to assemble the honorarium."

"No problem, Mr. Ambassador," lied Tanya, who was used to dealing with dignitaries and VIPs. At least he was polite. "Driver, notify the bridge we are ready."

"Aye, sir," said the marine, and he unclipped a mike from the dashboard. "*Icarus* to *Ramariez*, permission to lift."

"Permission granted," said the captain's voice. "Godspeed and good luck."

"Roger, wilco," he replied and returned the mike to the dash.

"Respirators on," ordered Sergeant Lieberman, pulling the elastic strap of the modified gas mask over her head. Muffled grunts sounded in acknowledgment. "Okay, Private. Let's go."

"Aye, sir," murmured the pilot, operating the vehicle controls by litany. "Running lights . . . check. Safety interlock . . . go. Atomic batteries to power. . . . Turbines to speed. . . ."

With a blast of warm air, the *Icarus* lifted from the deck, floated over its sister vehicles, and maneuvered out the opening doors of the launch bay, which promptly closed behind them.

Sprawled in front of the humans was a glittering metropolis with a thousand buildings of various shapes and sizes. In the distance, Rajavur could now see that the roller coasterlike structure encircling the city was made of tremendously thick metal beams and huge slabs of stone. He was astonished the thing didn't sink into the ground under its own weight. The diplomat wondered what the erection could be.

Taking its time, the *Icarus* descended into the greenery of the park, giving the marines plenty of opportunity to plan a ground-based offense, in case it should prove necessary.

Slowly, the aircar glided between stands of giant ferns and out over the legions of sales booths, the blast of its belly turbines causing a great commotion, blowing the tacky merchandise everywhere. Disappointed hoots and angry chirps sounded in their wake.

Once beyond the economic obstructions, the UN craft assumed a more sociable level and proceeded down the main thoroughfare at what the driver guesstimated to be walking speed.

Every building in sight was low to the ground, never more than four stories high, and mostly made of a creamy white material not readily identifiable. Flaring towers of silver lace dotted the wide sidewalks, fluted grooves in the ground served the obvious function of streets, and parking meters were commonplace.

The city appeared to be infested with curious onlookers who jammed the sidewalks and chittered noisily at each other. As the aircar slowed at an intersection to watch for cross traffic, a fat cockroach broke free from the crowd and dashed forward to run alongside the humans.

"An ounce of thulium for the secret of the passageway!" offered the bug, withdrawing a coin from its wicker belly bag.

Prof. Rajavur was unprepared for that particular question, so he played his instincts. "What secret?" he asked innocently, his words echoing slightly inside his respirator.

The bug paused in his speaking, but not in his running. Oh, they knew how to dicker, eh? "Okay, two ounces of thulium, but that's my last offer."

"Sorry."

"Four ounces," countered the treadmilling insect. "And I'll throw in a picture of my sister."

That made the Icelander blink. "I beg your pardon?"

As an incitement, the bug showed the humans in the aircar a full-color 3-D hologram of his nude sibling erotically dripping green ichor. Gagging noises ensued. Puzzled, the RporRian tapped his discount translator with a foreleg. The device must be malfunctioning again, those almost sounded like insults.

Just then, the silver towers began to ring with a clear tone, and the buildings disgorged thousands of insects. An incredible parade began to form about the *Icarus*.

Gaily flowered floats in the form of spaceships and planets came out of disguised garages and moved into position fore and aft of the aircar. Precision drill teams snapped and jerked their spears to a hard cadence count. Nimble teams of acrobats leaped and flew through the air with amazing agility. Eight armed jugglers tossed about glowing glass balls, two-headed axes, flaming torches, and live squirrels. Insects with white-painted bodies—mimes—performed all of the standard works, and then did a few indecipherable routines which the marines could only guess at the meaning of, like "Eat The TV" and "Wind The Baby."

A barrage of brilliant fireworks arced skyward from every rooftop, filling the air with pyrotechnic grandeur and making the drones very nervous. Confetti rained down as balloons went up. Then came the *piece de resistance*, as a huge marching band in crimson leather uniforms and feathered hats seemed to well from the very ground around the vibrating air-car. The string, wind, and percussion instruments sounded remarkably like any Earthly high school band—full of vim and energy, but slightly off-key. The tumultuous crowd of bugs laughed, cheered, shouted, and sang. It was wild, wacky, wonderful, and very, very noisy.

"Sir. . . ," shouted Sergeant Lieberman, holding hands over her ears and putting a wealth of meaning into the word.

Nearly deafened, the diplomat could only nod. They could only take a few more seconds of this, and then they would be forced to retaliate. Whatever the consequences.

22

Back on the *Ramariez*, a violent explosion rocked the cafeteria on Level 19, throwing people, chairs, and food to the floor, and from the smoking hole in the metal deck poked the angry, golden head of Avantor.

Grabbing a convenient table leg, she started to climb out when the only crew member on his feet brought a fully loaded dinner tray crashing down on top of her head, spraying beef stew, biscuits, and beer into the air. Only another Gee could have told the woman's eyes crossed under the impact before she limply dropped out of sight.

"Medical to the brig, stat!" ordered Lieutenant Jones into her wrist transceiver while getting to her feet. "Engineering team report to Cafeteria B, pronto. Security to both places, now!"

Dripping spaghetti and garlic sauce, Jones turned to the crew member who was still holding the dented, vibrating tray. "Good work, Corporal," she commended him.

"Private," the marine responded sullenly.

The lieutenant smiled tolerantly. "Not anymore."

PFC James Fuerstenberg sighed down to his boots. Maybe he should just have the stripe put on with Velcro this time.

* * * * *

Judging now to be the time, Prof. Rajavur rested an arm on the cushioned metal siding of the aircar and tapped a nearby marching bug on the shoulder, getting its attention.

"By the way," said the human in a friendly manner to the insect. "We have no intention of paying for this parade."

In ragged stages, the music stopped and the parade ground to a halt.

"W-what did you say?" asked a startled cook holding a saxophone, a food-stained apron still encircling his abdomen.

"We're not paying for this," repeated the diplomat, his words ringing loud and clear in the sudden still.

As quickly as it had formed, the parade disappeared; the performers breaking formation, the floats returning to their docks, the laser holographs of fireworks turned off, and the balloons reeled in on tethers. Soon the streets were deserted, without even a stray alien dog to keep the humans company.

Sigerson had deliberately waited till the very last moment to tell the insects this, to give them a taste of their own medicine. In a briefing with Trell, the diplomat had been told that once visitors set foot on the Grand Plaza Of Haggling they were then legally liable for the cost of any entertainment incurred along the way. But, if you couldn't meet the demanded price in thulium, or some equally valuable goods, it was off to the work prison with you for the rest of your natural life. Many off-worlders caught in this insidious trap tried to escape, and even though the RporRian police were a joke, the Gee drones in the sky were not.

Apparently, while the main job of the pyramids was to keep the insects planet-bound, the drones also served as auxiliary officers for the Great Golden Ones, and the Queen/Mother could call upon them for assistance to deal with any criminal.

A sobering thought. But to Rajavur, also a warming one. The Gees were not evil stormtroopers oppressing the masses, but merely police officers enforcing existing laws.

Sergeant Lieberman gestured. "Okay, let's move on."

Accelerating, the *Icarus* continued along the vacant main road of the city, passing blocks of apartment colonies, shopping arenas, and body waxing parlors.

The humans made faces when they spotted a movie theater with a huge, garish poster depicting a drooling male humanoid carrying off a delicately built bug in a torn silk dress while some robots gave chase. The marquee read: INVASION OF THE FLAT-EYED MONSTERS! The logo on the poster was: *They wanted our women!* And in smaller print underneath: *Not even money could stop them!* It made the crew members feel proud to know that Hollywood had never produced such godawful tripe. Well, not often, anyway.

Eventually, the aircar slowed as it reached a flat hexacre of stone situated directly in front of a staggered series of lumpish domes piled on top of each other—the Imperial Hive. This was their goal, the only authorized point for trading with offworlders—the Grand Plaza Of Haggling.

"I'll get out here," said Rajavur, disembarking, the motion making the aircar bob like a boat on water. "Follow me, but not too close."

"*Yasher koach*, sir," said Sergeant Lieberman, showing a thumbs up. Rajavur's translator relayed the Hebrew phrase as: "Have strength."

With the diplomat walking before them, the *Icarus* cautiously floated through an archway of giant plastic mandibles and entered the dreaded Colosseum of Commerce.

The circumference of the plaza consisted of wooden bleachers whose seats went horizontal at the deposit of a coin. But the mechanism had to be constantly fed to forestall the inevitable vertical dump. Most of the huge attending crowd was standing. The earlier throng had not left for the day, but merely relocated here, eager to see the Queen/Mother teach these upstart mammals a lesson. It was fabulous entertainment, highly educational for the children and, most important, free.

The only ornamentation in the place was a life-size statue of a RporRian male standing on a small dais. It was the actual mummified remains of (hiss-burble-cough), the famous poet, who, for a single copper unit, would robotically recite his immortal words:

> Thulium,
> thulium, thulium,
> I'd kill my own children for a bag of thulium.

The sentiment of the piece lost nothing in translation.

While patiently waiting, Prof. Rajavur rubbed the tip of his shoe across the strange gritty substance that formed the plaza. "What is this stuff?" he asked out loud. "Some form of concrete?"

"Checking," replied a voice from the communicator on his wrist. "Negative, sir. The material is primarily organic. A base epoxy, mixed with bone dust and powered silicate."

The diplomat couldn't stop himself from asking. "No spit?"

Pause. "That's the truth, sir."

Cutting his laugh short, a trumpeting horn sounded from the Imperial Hive and the crowd parted to admit a squad of smartly marching soldier bugs holding electric whips and quivers of crystal snakes. The soldiers advanced to the center of the plaza and parted to each side. Then, a hairy sedan crawled through the middle, walking on eight jointed legs like a cross between a tarantula and a lounge chair.

It was then that Prof. Rajavur remembered that the bugs were adept in biotechnology. That certainly explained the trickle of clear water running down the middle of the fluted streets. The organic cars must be too simple-minded to litter-box train and the water was used to flush away any of their involuntary by-products. The diplomat approved. It was neat, efficent, and sanitary. In spite of their fanatical devotion to greed, the cockroaches were not barbarians.

Twinkling merrily in the sunlight, the body of the ambulatory sedan was resplendent with clusters of jewels and silver filigree. The Queen/Mother herself was mostly hidden in a pool of dark shadow caused by a bone and membrane umbrella supported by the sedan's scorpionlike tail, on top of which was a special flashing light of royal blue. All the humans could see of her was large, lumpy, and leglike.

* * * * *

"What do you make of that sedan, Doctor?" asked Captain Keller, gazing at the main viewscreen. When he did not receive an answer, Dag glanced about the bridge." Where is Van Loon?"

"Conducting an experiment, Comrade Captain," somberly replied a nurse at the medical console.

"An experiment?"

The beefy woman nodded. "*Da*, commander, something to do with the Gee medical supplies."

Keller *humphed*. Must be damn important for the physician to miss this. "Are you recording everything for him, nurse?" he asked.

"Of course, sir."

"Very well, carry on."

* * * * *

In the aircar, a private leaned forward in his seat and tapped Lieberman on the shoulder. "Hey, Sarge, what will we do if the professor can't make a deal?"

"Leave," said Tanya succinctly.

"Retreat?"

The sergeant grimaced. "Look around you, Andrews. If we take a threatening step toward the Queen/Mother, every bug on this planet will rally to her defense."

Uneasily, the private observed the thousands of bugs watching their every move, and noted the wide assortment of mandibles, claws, and stingers. Yeah, he guessed she was right. Nobody wanted to reenact Little Big Horn, especially when you had to play the part of Custer.

With a blare of trumpets, the living carriage stopped in the center of the plaza, and a RporRian guard, naked but for the ever-present belly pouch, walked toward the humans holding a cast iron pot.

Remembering his lessons, Prof. Rajavur dropped in enough silver for everybody in the party. The drone chose a coin at random and submitted it to a primitive, but effective, test of authenticity: he bit it.

At his nod, the Queen/Mother chattered for a while.

"I bid thee greetings," said the translator hanging from a hairy strut of the living carriage. "Identify, please."

The diplomat bowed with a flourish of his hat. "Ambassador Sigerson Rajavur from the planet Terra." He deliberately did not introduce the marines, on the belief that soldiers in an insect culture would be, at best, second class citizens.

"We come in peace, and as a token of respect, offer a few meager gifts unworthy of Your Majesty." The professor had originally planned to compliment the Queen by calling her Your Loveliness, but just couldn't bring himself to do it.

A marine handed him a heavily laden silver tray, which Rajavur then passed on to a drone. On the tray were: a cut glass jar of Egyptian honey, a box of Belgian chocolates, a silver Chinese dagger in an ornamental sheath, and a fine collection of necklaces depicting cultures from every nation on Earth. Wisely, none of the offerings were made of gold, or were even yellowish in color, except the honey.

Daintily, the Queen/Mother smiled, displaying only a few hundred of her daggerlike teeth.

"Gladly we accept these gifts," said the platinum-edged box. "And I decree that, for the rest of your stay, you may breathe freely of the air of my planet."

Rajavur bowed again. "Thank you. Does this invitation also extend to my associates?"

Ah, the dance had begun. "Of course."

"Thank you, Your Majesty."

Happily, the humans removed their respirators, and then were sorry they had. Pollution was pretty bad, and only the smokers in the group didn't mind the thick chemical taste to the air. It was worse then Bombay, India, in the summer.

"Lovely," said the professor, trying not to gag. "Thank you for allowing us to share it."

An elderly bug in the crowd stepped forward to ask the mammal if it would like to buy some air, but a guard pushed the impetuous entrepreneur back into place. Heckling was not allowed.

"What purpose has brought you noble beings to my humble world?" asked the corpulent insect, toying with the candied skull of an ex-lover.

"Curiosity," said Rajavur. After a ten-second pause he added, "Plus, we need some supplies."

The Queen/Mother demurely oozed a bit of ichor at those words, and her bargaining claws extended. "We are not a metal-based culture. But I am sure that, for a small fee, we can deliver anything you might need."

Sigerson had a feeling that her phrase "a slight fee" meant something along the same lines as "the check is in the mail" did on earth.

"Our hypernavigational cube has developed a crack and we seek another to compare coordinates with."

Apprehensively, the Queen/Mother glanced at her chamberlain, and he whispered in her ear-hole. "Yes, we do have such a cube available for purchase," she replied via the box. "The sale price is the total destruction of the blockade around my planet."

The Icelander went cold. Wow. She caught on fast. The captain had asked to be consulted on any difficult decisions, but Rajavur didn't need to bother the man about this. "I am sorry, but, no."

"Your vessel lacks the necessary armaments?" she asked inquisitively, her lower limbs doing a pantomime of strangling a rabbit.

"Our ship does not carry any weapons," lied Rajavur with a straight face. "We are as peaceful a race as you are generous."

The RporRians went stiff at that and started chittering among themselves. Sergeant Lieberman wondered if the diplomat was wise in insulting the bugs, and told her troops to get ready for trouble.

A thrilling laugh came from the translator. "Amusing. I will give you an HN cube if you will take ten of my people in your ship and release them on any planet." On cue, a swarm of insect children were brought out from behind the sedan, the adorable infants endearingly intent on sucking flavor sticks.

The ambassador gave the matter serious thought. What harm could ten baby bugs do?

Over the radio Trell asked Lieberman if the children had a green sheen to their thorax or chitlin, and the marine replied yes. "They're pregnant queens," the technician frantically told her. "Release them and within a single solar revolution the galaxy would be spleen-deep in the horrid monsters."

"Room is severely limited on our ship," stated Sergeant Lieberman in a loud voice for the professor's benefit. "Ten additional beings would strain our life-support to the breaking point."

Prof. Rajavur appreciated the assistance, and the Queen/ Mother blithely accepted the obvious lie.

"Perhaps we could *buy* the cube from you," offered the diplomat as if he had invented the concept. "Say . . . for sugar?"

Coyly, (squeak-squeak-thromb-squeal-chatter-gnash-grunt) oozed a bit of green. This was so exciting. "Your ship isn't large enough to carry sufficient sugar," she informed him.

"Well, how about thulium?"

Ah, the dance quickened. "What do you offer?" she asked putting the skull of her brother into a refrigerator compartment at the base of the sedan's armored tail.

He decided to start with the fair market value. "A pound."

The Queen/Mother almost choked on her own laugh.

Rajavur took that as a no. "Five pounds."

"We are a primitive race," apologized the corpulent bug. "My people believe that any number lower than ten is evil and will bring pestilence to the land."

"Mine are even more primitive," counter-apologized the diplomat, "and cannot count higher than five. Plus, in accordance to our religion, our priests would have to examine the cube for its holiness prior to the exchange of material."

"Examining the cube would be an insult to its maker, my scientist son," said the translator, "and would require an additional five pounds of thulium to appease his artistic temperament."

"Does that include all relevant taxes, levies, fares, surcharges, import fees, export duties, tithes, and royalties?"

The Queen/Mother clicked a claw in respect. The mammal danced well. "The price is inclusive."

Prof. Rajavur smoothed back his wiry crop of hair. Fifteen pounds for a real cube, eh? The price was outrageous, and they would have to beware of a last-minute switch, but . . .

It started like a dog crying, but then built in tempo and volume until the very air was tangible with the strident howling.

"Raid!" yelled a bug, and the screaming crowd frantically dispersed in every direction.

"Alert!" said Lieberman, touching the earphone of her radio. "A Gee superdreadnought is coming down the spiral."

Rajavur was silent as he hopped on board the aircar. This was twice the Great Golden Ones had interrupted him in the middle of a successful bargaining session. They were really starting to honk him off no end.

Somehow the lumbering craft managed to execute a razor-sharp U-turn in the confines of the plaza, and the vessel took off in a blast of green flame that washed over the empty bleachers, setting fire to stray bits of paper and the mummified statue. The Queen/Mother and her entourage were long gone. Unannounced invasions by the Gees were an annoying, but constant occurrence.

With the flip of a switch, the *Icarus*'s autopilot precisely retraced its journey down the main road at near Mach speed. Everywhere throughout the city, bugs were diving into any open doorway or window. Incredibly, the buildings then started to sink into the ground. As they did, the roller coaster structure about the city began to visibly rise. The purpose of the mysterious erection at last clear.

"It's a counterweight," cried Rajavur, loosening his grip and losing his silk top hat to the wind.

Hanging on to the dashboard for dear life, Sergeant Lieberman squinted against the hurricane force distorting her vision. "By God, you're right!" she cried.

"Impressive!"

"Let's hope we live to tell somebody about it!"

Putting a bat out of Hell to shame, the aircar rocketed through the park, uprooting the sales booths. The side of the *Ramariez* welled before them like the white cliffs of Dover and the passengers prepared to die in a terrible crash, when the landing bay doors opened, and the human pilot landed them as softly as a feather on the metal deck. With a resounding clang, the bay doors slammed shut, and the starship immediately launched.

* * * * *

"Rendezvous with the superdreadnought in two minutes," said the sensors officer.

"Shields on full, main gun primed," reported the weapons officer.

"What course, sir?" asked navigation.

Captain Keller bit a lip. He had no wish to fight with the Gees, but if the *Ramariez* tried to fly through those drones, their amassed firepower would put more holes in the ship than a political speech. *Think fast, space ranger!* the captain silently quoted from one of his favorite books.

Keller made his decision. "Navigation, set course for ninety degrees to ground zero."

"Straight up?" gasped Trell from his console. "Are you mad?" Only the alien could have said it, even though most of the bridge crew was thinking the same thing.

"Hardly," drawled the starship commander. "Ensign Soukup, on my order I want maximum possible velocity, that means every engine we have operating at full thrust, plus the emergency chemical boosters."

"Aye . . . aye, sir."

As the *Ramariez* rapidly neared the edge of the blockade, the drones locked their awesome weapons of destruction on the ship, but not satisfied with that, the Great Golden Ones also unleashed every weapon in their arsenal that could operate at that distance.

"Sir!" cried Buckley, pounding on his console. "Both shields are down!"

"Hyperdrive nullifier in effect," reported Ensign Hamlisch crisply. "We can no longer shunt into hyperspace."

"Engine #1 is dead," added Trell, frantically throwing switches and pressing buttons. "There goes #2 . . . and #3!"

The captain strapped on his seat belt and pulled it as tight as possible against his lap. "Lilliuokalani, shoot that centihedron with the *STOP THAT* cannon. Navigation give me full power. Weapons, turn this ship gold!"

* * * * *

With a smug expression of triumph, The 34 released her grip on the control stand of the Gee centihedron and turned to the bearded amber male rising from the command chair.

"We have them trapped, my liege," she said with a smile. "There is nowhere to hide on the planet, the drones will destroy them if they go any higher, and we block the only exit."

Solemnly, the avantor stroked his beard and nodded. "Excellent, 34. This will mean promotions for both of us. Well, let's go gather our prisoners. Open hailing frequencies and—"

STOP THAT

Unexpectedly hit by their own weapon, the Gees were blown off their feet by the psionic strike. Weakly rising to their knees, the pair tried to stand when their minds were scrambled by yet another slamming blast, followed quickly by two more. Meticulous as always, Ensign Lilliuokalani had read the report about Avantor's attempted escape from the brig and carefully noted the crucial number of shots necessary to induce unconsciousness.

Writhing on the deck, The 34 somehow managed to flop an arm around and touch the sweaty hand of her commander.

S-suggestions, my liege?

Prayer, 34.

And blackness overwhelmed them both.

Which really was a shame, for in that condition, neither of the Gees were able to see out their viewscreens and thus appreciate the subtlety of what happened next.

* * * * *

Relentlessly, the drones moved in for the kill, half a million proton cannons locking on target. But then, at the very last moment, just before the outpouring of a trillion gigawatts of subatomic death, the onrushing starship impossibly changed color.

Startled, then embarrassed, the pyramids quickly disengaged their weapon systems and swerved out of the way of the golden ship. Their simple robotic brains were unable to fathom where the Gee spacecraft had come from, or remember that only seconds ago the intruder had been white. It was the proper color, and that was all that mattered. Nobody else in the galaxy would dare to use the restricted hue. The punishment was Galopticon 7.

Happily at this point, no RporRians remained above the surface to see the telling event, and thus the key to unlocking the blockade remained a secret.

At near light speed, the *Ramariez* tore through the opening in the gray metal cloud, her thermal backwash slagging any drone too slow to get out of her way. Several of the damaged pyramids reacted to that as an attack and automatically fired at the fleeing craft, either missing it entirely and vaporizing another drone, or scoring a direct hit upon the *Ramariez*. The ship's deflector plating ricocheted the beam right back at the pyramid with disastrous results.

Bursting free of the planetary blockade, with smoky tendrils of pyramids chasing after them, the Earth ship changed color again and jumped into the relative safety of hyperspace.

* * * * *

"Ha!" cried Chief Buckley, snapping his fingers at the main viewscreen in victory. Captain Keller forgave the minor breach of regulations. He felt like blowing a horn himself.

Ensign Soukup relaxed the death grip on her control panel. Whew, they'd actually made it. With luck like this, Dagstrom Keller should quit the star service and become a professional gambler. She started to speak, but had to swallow first to clear her throat. "Sir, should I plot a reverse course so that we can try again?"

"Hell, no," snorted the captain. "We barely escaped this time."

"Skipper?"

Keller swiveled to the left. "Yes, Lilliuokalani?"

"We could circle about the star system and approach from the other side," offered the communications officer. "After we first turn the ship red and constantly broadcast a fake identity code, of course. It's a variation of the battle tactics used by the Byzantine Empire against the Mongolians in the 12th century. . . ." Her voice trailed off as the captain stared meaningfully at the woman.

"Perhaps not," finished the ensign lamely.

"Very wise," he concurred. Dag was also familar with the ploy. It hadn't worked against the Turks in 1453 and he didn't think the Gees would fall for it now.

"Besides," added Keller aloud. "That ship was more than likely the advance scout for a task force sent after us. If we attempt to return to RporR, our chances of successfully getting away, much less obtaining an HN cube, would be zero."

"But, sir," said Ensign Hamlisch in concern. "Doesn't that leave us with only one course left?"

Keller frowned, his elation disappearing as fast as his ship had from the Gee sensors. "Unfortunate, but true. Navigation, set course for star system #553646. We are about to remove any question of our criminal status."

A sigh. "Aye, aye, sir."

* * * * *

Down in the brig of the Earth ship, The 16 collapsed, exhausted, onto his water bed. It had been a major effort for the Gee to boost the limited range on his computer implant to reach the robot drones, override their communication lock, and then force the machines to call Great Golden Central for help. But, once again, the Terrans had proved themselves to be fast, smart, and lucky. Yet the galactic police officer would not surrender. Eventually, his captors would make a mistake, and it would be their last.

23

Fourteen hours later, the *Ramariez* phased into normal space, its shields hard and weapons at the ready. Delicate scanners hungrily swept the empty volumes of space around the ship, searching for any conceivable danger. But the screens remained clear, and the meters did not flicker a needle. When satisfied, Lieutenant Jones signaled a step down to yellow, then green alert, and the crew breathed a sigh of relief. Safe. For the moment at least.

Snug in the command chair, Jones stifled a yawn and drained her cup of hot chocolate. It had been a long, boring shift, with little to do, but at last they were here. Made good time, too. Gold was a fast color, but white was notably safer, and she ordered the change. No sense calling attention to themselves.

Putting her empty cup aside, the woman primped her uniform, buffed her bars of rank, and fluffed her auburn hair. The bridge crew for the command shift had come on duty an hour ago, so Keller should be arriving any moment.

"Captain on the bridge!" somebody shouted.

Quickly, the bridge crew stood and saluted as Captain Keller sauntered in through the turbo-lift doors, forcing his smile into a yawn. By God, that thing was fun. After this was over, he just had to get a turbo-lift for himself, even though he lived in an A-frame.

"At ease," he said, returning their salutes, and everybody resumed their work—although sitting a bit straighter and talking less than when Jonesy was in charge.

"Morning, Lieutenant," said Keller as the woman relinquished her position in the command chair.

"Good morning, sir. Sleep well?"

"Lord, yes. Those water beds are fabulous. Made me feel like I was back at sea. Anything to report?"

"Nothing, sir. Hyperspace was quiet."

He gave her a smile. "As it should be. What's our position, Ensign Hamlisch?"

"Right on target, skipper," reported the sensors officer proudly, as if he had done it himself. "Exactly 50,000 kilometers away from the outer asteroid belt."

"Excellent. Lieutenant Jones, you are officially relieved."

"Yes, sir." The tall redhead saluted, but hesitated before leaving. "With the captain's permission, I'm not tired and would very much like to stay and observe the approach."

Dag tried to hide how much that suggestion pleased him. "Permission granted," he said formally. "Glad to have you with me, Abagail. Take over the damage control console."

"Thank you, sir." She turned. "You are relieved from duty, Mr. De Lellis. Go grab some sack time."

"Aye, aye, Lieutenant." Damn. The portly French scientist had wanted to take part in the exercise, not just watch it on the monitor in the crew lounge. Oh, well.

According to Trell, the solar system before them was not a particularly unusual phenomenon. The galaxy had quite a few similar astrological abnormalities. In its formative years, the swirling plasma radiating out from the newborn sun had not formed into huge planetary globules for life to evolve upon, but instead had coalesced into countless billions upon billions of asteroids encircling the sun in a staggered series of wide bands, jagged hunks of rock, and superhard ice that ranged in size from marbles to small moons.

Flying above the eclipse of the system, the starship approached the forbidden zone at a cautious 100,000 kilometers per hour, the Q-coil enginettes barely humming from the minor exertion. The main viewscreen of the bridge was filled with the dark splendor of the ringed sun; only the occasional glint of frozen gases breaking the majestic grandeur of the stony bands. And somewhere in that jumble was their last chance of success: an asteroid nicknamed "Buckle" and a criminal entity known only as Leader Silverside.

"Navigation, communications, weapons, medical, and sensors," barked Captain Keller. "Put your sensors on automatic trip. I want to know the instant any of those rocks register life."

A chorus of *Aye, aye, sirs* greeted the order.

"Sir, do you think it might be time to try and talk to Avantor again?" asked De Lellis, who had been walking from the bridge as slowly as possible. "She might be able to help us find Buckle."

"It is highly doubtful that the Gees would be willing to talk to us, much less give advice," stated Lieutenant Jones.

Thoughtfully, Keller cracked his enlarged knuckles, the only lasting trophy of his boxing career. "On the other hand, it can't hurt to ask. Go ahead and give it a try, Ensign."

"Thank you, sir!" Smiling broadly, the man saluted and left the bridge.

Exactly ten minutes later, the scientist returned, his hair in disarray, what remained of his uniform in tatters, and a smoking doorhandle dangling from his right hand.

"Avantor remains uncooperative," said the Frenchman, a puffy lip slurring his words.

Keller didn't know whether to laugh or cry.

"Report to sick bay, mister," the captain said as a compromise to both.

Weakly, Ensign De Lellis saluted, almost hitting his head with the handle. "Hank goo, sur," he managed to say. Stumbling to the fireman's pole, the battered scientist slid from sight.

Captain Keller sighed in resignation. "I really hate to say this, but the time has come to unleash the RAT."

"I am forced to agree with you, sir," said Jones with a frown. "Marines would be useless on this mission, as we will be dealing with criminals, not enemy soldiers. As horrible as it is to contemplate, the Reserve Away Team is our best bet, since they are the only veteran alien fighters we have."

"Unfortunate, but true."

Just then, the elevator doors shushed open and a massive metal figure emerged to lumber forward. When the armored trooper reached the captain, it saluted him with a faint whine of servo-motors and presented Keller with a clipboard. The captain deftly signed the manpower report, the UN space marine saluted, and clunked away.

"Lieutenant, I want you to personally see to their equipment. And when you open that cell door, be accompanied by at least a dozen guards like that one in power armor."

"Yes, sir. Shoot if they try anything?"

The starship commander considered the suggestion. "Only to wound, Lieutenant. For the present, we need the Bloody Deckers."

* * * * *

Surrounded by a squad of metal guys holding mother big rifles, the street gang was escorted from its cell in the brig to a ready room, where the convicts were allowed to change from their black-and-white striped prison fatigues into tan military jumpsuits with a nice wide belt and really bitchin' boots.

So far, this trip had been an easy gig for them. The food was great, and their quarters were luxurious compared to the 10x15 cell at the Nevada Maximum Security Prison, where they had been serving their ninety-seven consecutive life sentences. Bad place that. The gang had to do some serious head busting before they were finally safe from kissing their own shoes. Geez, you try and conquer the world just once and some people go crazy.

"Hey, Prof," called Drill, zipping up the front of his jumpsuit and shrugging to straighten the shoulders. "We doing this gig naked, or what?"

"There are plenty of guns for you in the shuttle craft," stated the Icelander from behind a steel wall of marines. "But be very careful how you use them. Computer sensors in the weapons prohibit them from firing at any ship personnel. And if you attempt to use the guns to remove your bracelets, both the weapon and the bracelet will explode."

Clenching and unclenching scarred fists, Hammer frowned at the smooth ceramic bands on his wrists. The ganglord looked meaningfully at Drill, but the locksmith sadly shook his head. These things had been cold-welded on them by some weirdo alien device, so there was no mechanism for him to work on. Besides which, they were supposed to explode if the gang left their cell without authorization, or went down a proscribed corridor, or hit the bracelets too hard, or . . . or . . . or. . . . No, they were good and trapped. Nothing to do but go along with the scheme and wait for a lucky break.

"What about knives?" asked Chisel, struggling to lace a boot, his mind almost overloading with the effort to remember the kindergarten poem: *First you build a house, then the man goes inside.* . . .

Lieutenant Jones had been expecting that request. "There is a box in the shuttle craft with a hundred assorted knives, hooks, and hatchets for you."

With a yank, the boy finished tying the knot and stood up straight. Only a hundred? He guessed it would have to do.

When the street gang was finished with their ablutions, an unarmed marine gave each man a heavy leather pouch.

Curious, Drill peeked inside. "What is this stuff? Canadian money?"

"Subway tokens?" guessed Chisel, sniffing a coin.

In response, Jones started to explain the intricate history of thulium, then decided against it. "Space dollars," she told them.

Hammer tucked the bag into a hip pocket. "That's cool. Chump change, folding cash, or serious bucks?"

"Think of them as flat diamonds."

"Wow," gushed Chisel drooling slightly. "We're rich!"

Unnoticed, Drill palmed a coin and dropped it into his boot.

"You understand the plan?" asked Prof. Rajavur when the gang had stopped fondling the money and was under control once more. Or, rather, what passed for control.

Running a hand over his hated prison crew cut, the lord of the street gang snorted in contempt. "Yeah, yeah. It don't take no nuclear genius to cook this scam. We go to the bar, act tough, get to see the boss, buy this cube thing, and come back here fast—or else."

Then, in spite of the guards and the fact that this situation reminded him of a classic World War II movie, Hammer took the opportunity to add, "I don't like being a freaking errand boy, you old fart, and if this wasn't earning us full pardons, my gang wouldn't do spit, you pointy-headed bug-jumper."

After RporR, the insult stung. "I understand, Melvin. Now, shut up and go board the shuttle before I order your left hand blown off for insubordination."

The ganglord turned blood red at the use of his proper name, then broke into laughter and strolled from the room with his marine guards and chuckling gang close behind.

Relaxing, Lieutenant Jones exhaled and holstered her laser pistol. "Nice bluff, sir."

"I never bluff a man who has nothing to lose, Lieutenant," said Rajavur coldly. "Hammer could have done the job just as well with only one hand, and he knew it."

It was then the Australian officer decided that someday she simply had to play poker with this man.

* * * * *

"Negative again, sir," reported Ensign Hamlisch calmly,

even though he was boiling inside. The scientist hated to fail in anything. This tenacious attitude had cost the man several friends over the years, but earned him the Nobel Prize in Physics at the astonishing age of twenty-five.

Acknowledging the report, Captain Keller drummed his fingers on the cushioned arm of his chair a few times and then loudly slapped the plasti-cloth covering. "Okay, Trell, how do we locate this place, radar sweep the entire solar system?"

"Conceivable," admitted the alien. "But usually, you do not find them, they find you."

"Meaning?"

"We hover above the fourth asteroid ring and broadcast a low power message. Upon acceptance of our transmission, Buckle will send out a tracer beam."

He nodded. Good enough. "You heard the man, Lilliuokalani. Proceed."

"Affirmative, skipper. What frequency should I broadcast on, Master Technician?"

As Trell rattled off the string of integers, the Hawaiian adjusted a slide and flipped a toggle switch.

"Is there a code phrase or password I should use, sir?" she asked, her fingers poised above the keyboard.

The alien waved a pattern of negation. "Just say something nasty about the Gees."

"Aye, sir." The communications officer typed a brief message on her keyboard and hit the enable key. A minute later, she announced incoming coordinates.

The captain woke from his musings. "That was fast. What did you say to them?"

Ensign Lilliuokalani blushed. "I said we liked to decapitate Gee babies and fornicate the neck stumps."

Keller stared at the woman.

"Too verbose, sir?"

"No, that was fine, Ensign. Just fine." Mentally, he made a note to have Van Loon keep an eye on her. Then he glanced about the room. Where was the physician, anyway? Oh, yes, still in the lab. The man was starting to live down there. He wondered what the good doctor was doing.

Following the directions, the *Ramariez* reversed course and began to move counter to the asteroid flow. The plain of tumbling mountains flowed beneath them like an impossible river of stone, an endless avalanche to nowhere.

"Why is it we can't find them?" asked CPO Buckley, his brogue deliberately asserting itself. "Faith, with our sensors we should be able to locate a single freckle in Ireland."

Trell talked for quite a few minutes, and the translator box on his belt said, "Disguised."

"Disguised how?" asked Captain Keller. "Camouflage? A jamming field? Or is it some sort of cloaking device that bends our scanner beams 180 degrees around the target?"

Once more the alien technician launched into a short science lecture to try and clarify the complex physics involved, and his translator replied, "Yes."

The captain humrphed. Might as well talk to the avantor.

"Navigation, please change course, port by keel by stern, two thousand meters," directed Lilliuokalani, touching her wireless earphone.

"Affirmative," replied Ensign Soukup, making the corrections.

As the earth ship penetrated the effect of the cloaking device, there appeared on the main viewscreen a mile-long asteroid covered with strings of lights and metal domes. In orbit about the jagged rock were a dozen starships of various shapes and sizes—every one white, of course.

"Strange how close we were to this place from our phase-in point," observed Soukup, logging the data in on her astrogation chart. "Captain, do you think the Gees know about this place?"

"You would have to ask the avantor," replied Keller sternly, and this time nobody volunteered to do so. There were lots of easier ways to get seriously hurt—like playing catch with a greased bottle of nitroglycerin in a munitions factory during a lightning storm.

"Place us in a parking orbit about the asteroid, Mr.

Soukup," directed the captain. "But with plenty of room to move if we have to leave in a hurry."

"Aye, sir."

Keeping a hand on his console, Buckley swiveled about. "Skipper, may I recommend we go to yellow alert?"

Captain Keller smiled tolerantly. He had once been a chief petty officer, too. "I was just going to do that, Buck. Ensign Lilliuokalani, yellow alert."

Throughout the ship, the command was relayed. Then Keller gave a bone-cracking yawn that was copied by the several members of the bridge crew. "And for God's sake, have the galley get some coffee in here!"

* * * * *

Sitting significantly alone in the middle of launch bay #2 was a slim, flat-bottomed plane whose gleaming white hull was made of seamless deflector plating. In bold lettering, the name *Leonov* was stenciled on her round bow.

Seemingly unaffected by the sophisticated beauty of the craft, the Bloody Deckers tromped on board the shuttle. Ready for treachery, the marines did not relax until the hatch of the vessel was tightly shut and the air evacuated from the launch bay.

Normally, the craft held enough seats for a crew of three and ten passengers, but the extraneous chairs had been removed, and ribbed plastic cargo trunks installed to take their place.

Like kids at a birthday party, the gang tore into the trunks. Aside from translators, medical kits, food packs, and other such useless stuff, the convicts found three laser pistols, with shoulder holsters. Groans greeted the familiar sight of the woven metal force shield belts, but cheers met the unexpected prize of bullet-proof vests.

The promised guns proved to be Uzi machine pistols equipped with acoustical silencers. The gang worked the bolts and checked the clips with experienced hands. These highly illegal weapons were what had earned them the right to claim Central Park as their turf. Uzis and the Bloody Deckers were old friends.

Chisel squealed with delight at the sight of the knife collection and plunged his hands into the box, unconcerned by the razor sharp steel. Hammer let the boy grab the Bowie knife sitting prominently on top and chose a standard switchblade for himself. Drill took two Japanese butterfly knives, and Chisel appropriated everything remaining. When finished, his pockets, boots, and sleeves bulged with edged death, and his body weight was increased by twenty per cent.

Smiling contentedly, the bucktoothed lad smoothed out his clinking clothes. This was the first time he had been properly dressed in a month.

Insatiable as always, Drill began roaming about the vessel searching for cigarettes. He started with the cockpit. It was as far as he got. "Hey, chief!" called the locksmith, his voice wavering.

Feeling more like a man now that he had a gun in his hand, Hammer ambled on over and froze in his tracks. There, welded to the front of the dashboard, with no attempt made at subterfuge, was a huge metal egg plainly labeled "BOMB."

"These guys play for keeps," whispered the ganglord in sincere admiration.

"YES, WE DO," said a feminine voice from a speaker under the control panel. "NOW, PLEASE STRAP YOURSELVES IN. WE ARE BEGINNING FINAL APPROACH AND WILL LAUNCH SOON."

"Then what?" asked Hammer, hating to do what he was told, but not stupid enough to disobey.

"WE WILL LAND THE SHUTTLE AT THE APPROPRIATE SPOT AND TURN THE MISSION OVER TO YOU."

The Bloody Deckers nodded. Great, that's when they could make their escape.

"WE WILL BE KEEPING A CONSTANT AUDIO AND VIDEO SURVEILLANCE ON YOU VIA OUR SCANNERS," continued the voice. "BUT YOU WILL BE AUTONOMOUS. WE WILL INTERVENE ONLY WHEN YOU SHOUT FOR HELP. IF YOU DO, THEN STAND BACK." There was a pause. "AND WE MEAN THAT LITERALLY. STAND BACK."

* * * * *

"Understand?" asked Lilliuokalani into a microphone. The Deckers murmured vague assents from a speaker on her console. "Acknowledged then. *Ramariez* out." She released the thumb switch and returned the microphone to her console.

"Ready to go, sir," the ensign reported.

Keller crumpled his drained coffee cup and stuffed its Styrofoam corpse into the disposal slot in the arm of his chair. "Take them out, Mr. Soukup."

"Aye, sir," said the woman as she plugged a miniature joy stick into her console and flipped a switch. Watching the computer graphics on her tracking monitor, the ensign thumbed the button on top of the joy stick and the shuttle launched.

Under the adroit control of the expert pilot, the shuttle craft maneuvered out of the landing bay, the thick metal doors silently closing once it was past. Little more than passengers for the journey, the street gang watched in total fascination as their ship jetted through the black velvet of space and gracefully entered the mouth of a dark cave on the pointed end of the asteroid.

In contrast to the rough, unhewn exterior of the giant rock, the tunnel they were in was a smooth tube with a gravel floor and a high, vaulted ceiling. Seven different colored light bars, like grandiose fluorescent tubes, lined the entire length of the roof and pulsed in computer binary to guide the ship.

Slowly, the *Leonov* moved through an awe-inspiring parking lot of shuttle craft: balls, cubes, pyramids—most made of white metal, but some appeared to be ceramic, a couple glass, and one in the back was obviously constructed of riveted wood. A big blue ship they passed was shaped like a clam, another like a football helmet. There was a four-story-tall baseball bat covered with tiny windows in which fish swam by, a Christmas tree ornament perfectly balanced on its teardrop tail, and even a good old-fashioned flying saucer with a sign on top consisting of a broken triangle bisected by a sine wave. Only Trell knew that to be the sad universal symbol of, "FOR SALE, BY OWNER." Probably an unlucky gambler who had lost everything at the Vis-Par tables. That was how Trell's parent had gotten so deeply into debt.

* * * * *

On the main viewscreen, Captain Keller noted creatures moving freely about the ships and was surprised to see they were not wearing space suits of any kind.

"Is that landing area pressurized?" he asked.

"Affirmative, sir," replied Ensign Hamlisch, who had been running arpeggios on his scanner controls. "Some kind of low energy force screen covers the mouth of the tunnel and keeps the atmosphere in."

"Interesting. Chief, start calculations on a jamming field to neutralize that screen."

Buckley smiled at the prospect. "Aye, aye, sir!"

* * * * *

Finding a vacant berth between a corkscrew and a doorstop, Ensign Soukup landed the shuttle and prudently shut off the engines. As the whine of the ion thrusters died away, the gang climbed out of their seats and grouped in front of the air lock. They hesitated before exiting, so Ensign Soukup cycled open both doors simultaneously from her console.

"GET MOVING."

The Bloody Deckers glanced at each other and shrugged. What the hell, if the *Ramariez* wanted them dead, there sure were easier ways to do it than marooning them here.

"Come on," said Hammer, slapping his friends on the shoulders. "Let's go kick some alien butt, Decker style!"

Lacing their courage with bravado, the gang shouted their name like a war chant and exited the shuttle.

24

Disdaining the self-extending stairs, the youths hopped to the ground, the gravel bed crunching beneath their boots. Looking around, they spotted a slow-moving conveyer belt running down the middle of the parking lot, going from the distant mouth of the tunnel to a nearby rock wall. The Deckers smiled. They knew about these people-mover things from robbing folks at airports. Hitching up their pants, the gang boldly stepped on the corrugated strip, and they were whisked away to the heart of the asteroid.

Bright lights and noise were the first things the gang registered, but as their city-trained reflexes took effect, they soon were able to discern the incredible hodgepodge that was the town laid out before them. As far as they could see, there were buildings and structures of every conceivable description: from ramshackle igloos and ivory towers, to steel skyscrapers and brick outhouses. And almost every one had an electric neon sign of some sort. Indeed, a couple of the more garish buildings *were* neon signs and had tiny wooden houses hanging out front.

The street was nothing more than a branching path of raw asteroid stone that meandered through block after block of architectural anarchy, twisting and turning like a snake on drugs.

And the people . . .

The streets were filled to overflowing with a mixture of a circus and a zoo, combined with a Grade B Horror flick and a fancy dress masquerade thrown in for flavor. Like true city dwellers, the pedestrians marched where they liked, when they felt like it, while paying no attention to each other, even when they collided, which was often. Street venders hawked bizarre goods on every bustling corner. Pungent steam rose from vents in the street, fogging the air. Unfathomable billboards dotted the rooftops. Somewhere, angelic choirs could be heard singing, throbbing drums pounded from a rattan doorway, flutes and trombones battled for supremacy inside a paisley tent, and modulated screams came out of a concrete pillbox with iron bars on the windows. In the distance, there came an explosion and a tall spire of crystal noisily crashed out of sight. Nobody seemed to notice. It was a hundred New Year's Eves rolled into one, as if augmented by a small war and amplified through the fevered brain of a color-blind madman.

"I like it," said Drill with a grin.

Hammer agreed. The place was okay. It was sorta like that movie about the android hunter. And better yet, not a cop in sight.

As the gang stepped off the moving strip, an octopus on a wheeled cart shot out of a mirrored alleyway and tried to pick Chisel's pocket. Unconcerned, the boy stabbed the offending tentacle with a stiletto, almost slicing the tip off, and continued strolling, leaving the howling creature spurting blood. The gang member had not been the least bit bothered by the anti-social act. It sort of made him feel at home, like he was in Manhattan again.

"GRAVITY HERE IS LESS THAN EARTH STANDARD,"

said a tiny voice from their jumpsuit collars. "YOUR COORDINATION WILL BE OFF, THUS YOUR MACHINE GUNS WILL SHOOT HIGH. PLEASE TAKE THAT INTO ACCOUNT."

"Thanks, mom," muttered Hammer, wishing he could lower the volume permanently on that pain-in-the-butt. The only thing he hated worse than a busybody, were people who talked during movies. Their blood always ruined the taste of his popcorn.

"So, what's the plan, boss man?" asked Drill, in the rhyming cant of the deceased traitor Crowbar. "We split up, scout the territory, and then meet back here later?"

The ganglord scowled. "Screw that. We stay together. I got a feeling this place is more dangerous than an honest cop."

"Yeah, I agree," grinned the locksmith, then he noticed something amiss. "Where'd pinhead get to?"

Upon hearing his name, Chisel reappeared from the crowd.

"Hey, I found it!" the boy shouted, excitedly pointing to the other side of a five-way intersection.

Drill craned his neck over the milling throng to see, and Hammer pushed an old, blind, crippled dogoid into the gutter for a better view. On top of a quanset hut were two statues locked in mortal combat. The ganglord nodded. Yep, that was the place they wanted, The Twin Choron Inn.

Prior to boarding, Trell had told them the story of how a drunk pair of the stone giants had gotten into a wrestling match one night, and, equally matched, they had stood motionless on the roof for three solar revolutions before they finally got sober, bored, and went home. But by then, so many patrons of the bar used them to identify the place, the management was forced to erect a statue of the beings to replace the absentees. The sculptor had done a fine job with the photographs supplied to her, and, in fact, some of the less observant customers did not know that it wasn't the dueling Chorons still up there.

Acting cool, the Bloody Deckers pushed their way through the milling crowd and strutted into the bar.

Oddly enough, aside from the customers, the place pretty much resembled an ordinary tavern. There were tables and chairs scattered about the hall, sawdust on the floor, dartboards and astronomical holographs tacked to the walls. A ten-meter counter spanned the rear of the hut, and behind the plastic counter stood a fibrous, orange humanoid in a knit leather waistcoat. The bartender was chewing on a mint-green stick and using its left hand to clean a glass decanter.

What caught the Decker's attention, though, was the strange, elaborate machine that filled the entire back section of the hut, reaching from floor to ceiling and wall to wall. The Rube Goldberg contraption was made of plastic struts, brass kettles, ceramic barrels, glass beakers, wooden vats, and a hundred zillion metal pipes, some dripping with frost and others glowing red hot. The gang had no damn idea what the thing could be.

Surveying the room for seats, Hammer spotted two at the counter, but they were on opposite sides of an albino grizzly bear who was drinking with both clawed paws. The ganglord smiled and reviewed the opening scenes from a dozen Westerns, for just the right approach. Yep, got it.

After a hurried set of whispered instructions, Hammer approached the hulking monster from the left, with Drill and Chisel flanking him.

"Hey, whitey!" called the ganglord in the most insulting tone he could muster.

The bear paused in his drinking and rotated a monstrous head to see who the creature was addressing. Surely the little brown thing was not talking to him!

"You're sitting in my favorite chair, dustbunny," snarled the youth, rapidly clarifying the situation. "Now move your moth-eaten butt, or my den gets a new rug!"

With a ferocious roar, the huge grizzly turned and reached for the neural disrupter pistol slung at its hip. But a hail of high-velocity, steel-jacketed, 9mm bullets from three machine guns lifted the unsuspecting alien from the chair and slammed it against the plastic wall, the impact sending cracks as far as the front door. Laser beams then sliced off his treetrunk arms, and a knife thudded between his startled eyes. With a mighty groan, the hirsute goliath slumped to the floor, trembled, and went still.

As the smoke cleared, the Deckers waited for reprisals, but everybody else in the tavern returned to their drinking and talking. What the hell, they each thought, the creep probably deserved it. He had.

* * * * *

However, the bridge crew of the *Ramariez* was aghast.

"I've never seen anything to rival it," gasped Soukup, even paler than usual.

Ensign Lilliuokalani could barely speak. "To kill a fellow sentient just to obtain its chair. . . !"

"Good grouping, though," noted Buckley professionally.

"It was murder," declared Hamlisch in righteous outrage. "Cold-blooded murder."

"No, it was perfect," corrected Prof. Rajavur, walking from the closing elevator.

Captain Keller turned and greeted the man. "I agree, Mr. Ambassador. They have properly established themselves as people not to be trifled with, and nobody will suspect them of ulterior motives."

The diplomat crossed the room. "Yes, and only the Deckers could have done it in so definite a manner," said the diplomat, crossing the room and taking the visitor's chair, which was located next to the sanitation console. "I only wonder why they didn't toss a grenade into the place."

"Didn't give them any, sir," said Lieutenant Jones.

Rajavur nodded. Ah, that explained it.

* * * * *

As the humans claimed their seats, over in a corner of the hut a group of bullyboys stopped ascertaining the potential of the new humanoids and returned to their hand of VisPar, the toughest, deadliest gambling game in existence. It involved cards, dice, a roulette wheel, random number generators, post-hypnotic suggestions, and high explosives.

"Hey! Let's have some service here!" yelled Drill, pounding on the counter top.

Since it was safe again, the bartender stuffed a fresh mint-stick into its slit of a mouth and moved into view. The lumpy orange creature reminded the gang somewhat of a kitchen sponge.

"Peace!" cried the Oolian, lifting four pewter mugs brimming with foam in each hand. "Will arrive soon. Only have eight arms."

A gelatinous blob laughed uproariously at the old joke, showing how truly drunk she was, and then emptied a beaker on top of her head, noisily sucking the milky white liquid in through a group of tiny mouths that ringed the base of her throat.

In a practiced motion, the sponge mopped the excess liquid that landed on the counter top with his hands, absorbing the spilled beverage and metabolizing the alcohol. In an establishment as filled with sloppy drunks as The Twin Chorons, the bartender was starting to get fat from overeating.

"Yo," said Hammer as a friendly greeting.

The sponge removed the breath-stick from its mouth. "This is a respectable joint, creature," it stated.

"Yeah?"

"Fact. You must pay us a fee for the damages and to remove the dead body."

"Fair enough," laughed the youth, and he tossed a single gray coin on the counter.

That almost gave the bartender an air tube spasm. Keeping the coin in plain sight, he laid it on a glowing sensor pad embedded in the simulated wood counter top. The analysis took only seconds. By the Prime Builder, it was chemically pure metal. Top grade thulium. "I cannot make change for this, honorable sir," said the creature respectfully.

Hammer waved the matter off and told him to credit his account and keep a gold for himself. The Deckers were supposed to make a splash, and that sounded like a good way to do it. Nothing attracts attention more than violence and money.

"What will you have, gentle being?" asked the happy sponge, a week's salary richer. He had always liked humanoids. Hairless brown ones especially.

"Whiskey," replied the ganglord.

He waited and the bartender did the same.

"Well?" barked Hammer.

"Place your hand on the sensor plate so the drink will match your biological profile," patiently explained the Oolian. "What? Have you never been in a bar before?"

"Not as nice a place as this," lied the human, playing it smooth. It never paid to annoy the bartender. He might spit in your drink, then you would have to kill him and the bouncer would throw you out of the bar. Like, seriously inconvenient.

Complying with the request, Hammer laid his hand on the glowing square. At his touch, the machine behind the bar began to make whirring noises and started to rebuild itself, pipes reconnecting into a new configuration. It rattled and whined a bit, then a lid flipped aside and out floated a shot glass full of amber liquid.

Snagging the glass in midair, Hammer took a sip, and then downed the rest in a gulp.

"Goddamn, that's the best whiskey I ever had," sighed the youthful connoisseur. "Gimme another."

Readily, the bartender complied. With an entire thul in his account, this humanoid could drink vintage Zish for the whole night and not dent his credit.

"Got anything pink?" asked Drill, a faint tingle stirring within him at the mere mention of the word.

The sponge gave his race's equivalent of a wink, and from under the counter produced a plastic atomizer. Experimentally, the locksmith depressed the bulb and out came a fine spray of reddish fluid. The next two squeezes were directed toward his face. Ah!

Chisel pressed his hand hard against the sensor plate. "I wanna a Coney Island Special."

And with those words, the always reliable, undefeatable, alpha class, Drink Master Supreme, underwent the usual alteration, paused, and then did it again, and then again. Pipes connected and disconnected at an alarming rate, some bent themselves into condenser coils, others retracted, while yet others crackled with static electricity and tried to twist themselves into the fourth dimension. Kettles began to spin. Multicolored flames spurted at irregular intervals. Ice formed on support beams, melted, and reformed. The alien device shook, groaned, whined, burped, and trembled. A crowd had gathered by then, and bets flew as to whether or not the Drink Master had finally met its match. Deep inside the machine, a laser battle seemed to take place. A steel pipe shattered, the broken bits sprinkling to the floor. Steam erupted from the top coil, blasting tiles off the ceiling. Then, in a hushed silence, the door flipped open and out floated a frosted steel mug, filled with an extra-thick chocolate milk shake, no straw.

As the crowd watched, Chisel took a sip and nodded in approval. No whipped cream, but not bad.

With a sad ratcheting sound, the Drink Master spat a gob of whipped cream and a maraschino cherry onto the counter. The Oolian stared at the mess in horror and ran to get a rag.

While chuckling at the antics, Drill noticed three doors in the background marked *Emitters*, *Oozers*, and *Squirters*. Sagely, he deduced those must be the bathrooms and decided that no matter how much he drank tonight he could hold it until they returned to the shuttle.

At the other end of the bar, inspired by the toothy humanoid, a spider in a space suit requested a dead fly with a straw in its head. Instantly, at a table across the room, a fly in chain mail ordered a spider with a straw in *its* head. Hatefully, the two beings stared at each other. Chisel snorted contemptuously at both of the creatures, and took a healthy gulp of his milk shake. Only wimps used straws.

"When do we move, boss?" asked the locksmith.

Hammer drained the glass and licked his lips. "Enjoy your drink, dude. Act sociable. Then, if we don't get what we want, we kill some customers and set fire to the place."

"Natch."

Strolling among the drinkers and gamblers of the tavern, plying her centuries-old trade, was a semi-transparent, vaguely humanoid-shaped creature. Her name was Einda, and she was a Datian prostitute. A truly universal whore, the empathic amoeba had the ability to mold herself into a sex partner for almost any race. At least one representative of her highly flexible species was considered an absolute necessity at every decent bar throughout the known galaxy.

And she had just found her next customer.

After the incident with the Drink Master, the adaptive female decided to try for the one she mistakenly identified as the toughest member of the group, who would almost certainly be the leader—the short toothy male she had heard called "Chisel." No doubt, a title of authority.

As Einda casually wandered toward the bar, she passed by a hairy blue male sitting alone at a four person table and playing with a piece of string and a small fruit, which explained why he was sitting alone in a crowded bar. Nobody smart bothered an assassin.

By the time she reached the boy's side, the anthropomorphic tart had metamorphosed into a reasonable facsimile of the well-endowed Laura—who had stolen Chisel's heart, even as the special federal agent had broken his nose during the fight on Leader Idow's ship.

"Greetings, attractive being," murmured Einda seductively, her simple words promising everything. And she had the knowledge to deliver it, too. "Do you desire my company?"

Mesmerized by the stark naked, translucent female, whom he seemed to know from somewhere, Chisel could only nod. Without hesitation, the gang member pushed the reptilian creature next to him off its chair and offered the seat to his new friend. Wisely, the scaly alien took no offense at this ejection and strolled away.

"I am called Einda," she told him, taking the stool. Her luscious lips curled at the tips in a faint smile, half in training, half from the courteous action.

"Chisel," the human managed to say, his voice husky with unaccustomed desire. "Ah—would—ah—you like a drink?"

She slipped an arm about his waist and snuggled in, warm and close. "Please."

The boy stiffened, but when he realized she wasn't going for his wallet, he felt his face burn red in embarrassment, then lust.

"Care for a sip of mine?" he asked, politely offering the lady his milk shake.

Einda was thrilled. Everyone knew that, to her race, such an act—the sacred mingling of juices—was a proposal of marriage. This humanoid with the big teeth may not be much to look at, she thought, but the manling was the first to ever ask, to offer her a ticket to respectability. She'd be damned if he would get away.

A true hermaphrodite, her race could breed with any other species by accepting a sample of germ plasma, using their super-adaptive flesh to feed the living cells and then act as an incubator for the infant. She would not be able to contribute anything to the offspring, aside from motherly love, but that would be enough. Einda sighed. Yes, it would be enough.

"Gladly," the female throated, and pressed her lips to the steel mug, accepting the offering in the spirit it was given.

Chisel was pleased by the beautiful woman's reaction and wondered if he dared to pat her shapely knee under the counter. Nyah, probably just get his face slapped.

Then Drill nudged him in the ribs, and Einda was temporarily forgotten. Time for business.

"Hey, barkeep, maybe you can help us," said Hammer, laying down his empty shot glass alongside the other four and resisting the temptation to lick the container clean.

Drill pinked himself. "Yeah, we're looking for somebody."

"Ain't nobody here," answered the bartender in a tired voice that had heard this question a thousand times before. It almost always led to trouble.

Hammer showed a few teeth in his smile. "You don't understand. We want the boss . . . guy . . . ah, thing that owns this place."

"I own it," lied the sponge, hitting the alarm button on the floor with his proto-foot.

Drill snorted in contempt. Hammer agreed with the assessment and took a more direct approach of persuasion by drawing his Uzi, reaching across the bar, and stuffing the warm barrel of the weapon into the sponge's fibrous belly.

"How many fingers you got per hand, chum?" the ganglord asked in a deceptively sweet voice.

Frightened, the creature chewed its breath-stick to a nub before answering, "Eight."

"Seven," continued Hammer, working the bolt on his machine pistol and squeezing the pistol grip safety. "Six . . . five . . . four . . . three. . . ."

"WHO IS IT THAT WISHES TO TALK WITH ME?"

The atonal voice seemed to come from everywhere, so the ex-con eased his grip, resetting the safety on his weapon. "The new owner of the *All That Glitters*," bragged the youth. "You can see it in orbit around this rock."

That statement stopped conversation dead in the tavern, and several of the more sapient of the sentients left unobtrusively through the windows, without bothering to open the portals first.

"INTERESTING," rumbled the voice. "AND WHAT HAPPENED TO MY GOOD FRIEND, LEADER IDOW?"

A la a 1950s gangster film, Hammer picked his teeth with a not-so-clean thumbnail and replied, "We ate him."

The voice laughed in disbelief. "OF COURSE YOU DID. PERHAPS WE SHOULD DO BUSINESS TOGETHER."

At this, a section of the wall near the bathrooms broke apart, revealing a stainless steel cubicle. The invitation was obvious, but the Deckers only exchanged annoyed glances. Geez, what was this, amateur night? In unison, laser beams and bullets sprayed the cubicle, igniting the shaped charges of explosives lining the walls and quickly reducing the chamber into a twisted metal wreck.

"Sorry, but no can do," drawled Hammer, slamming a fresh clip into his weapon. "Your elevator seems to be, like, broken."

The laughter sounded again and alongside the ruined elevator, a panel slid open in the wall, exposing a gray stone passageway.

"I PERSONALLY GUARANTEE THIS CORRIDOR WILL NOT CAUSE YOU ANY INCONVENIENCE."

"Good enough," said the street tough, knowing that guys like this would rather go legit than break their word. In public, that is. He had learned that the hard way.

Bravely, the Deckers walked into the corridor and disappeared off the screens of the *Ramariez*, causing a major commotion on the bridge. As the wall closed, the bartender made a noise in front of Einda and jerked a fibrous thumb toward a corner. "A customer wants to see you," he said gruffly.

"I quit," she said haughtily, and the zaftig amoeba continued to sip her milk shake, contentedly waiting for her fiance to return and wondering what to name the children.

* * * * *

Stepping out of the hallway, the Bloody Deckers entered a room that was more bomb shelter than office.

The floor was polished concrete, the ceiling burnished steel, and every inch of the walls was covered with video monitors showing an external view of the asteroid; a panoramic shot of the city inside; the landing area; The Twin Chorons; creatures playing cards, fornicating, getting drunk, dancing, repairing a hovercar; a fist fight; and a building going up. Only a handful were dark. In fact, the center screen was just fading to black as they walked in. And standing smack dab in the middle of the room was the menacing figure of a black metal warobot, its lower chassy and upper arms edged with platinum.

Wary of the alien mountain with its multitude of weapons, the gang advanced into the room, looking for this Silverside guy Trell had told them about. But there was nobody present, except for—

"You," accused Drill, pointing a finger at the robot.

With the sound of distant thunder, the wardroid rotated its bulbous armored head, its camera eyes somehow losing their mindless machine quality.

"Yes," replied Leader Silverside in a synthesized voice. "I just wanted to see how long the deduction would take you." The status lights on its trim flickered from blue to orange. "Five seconds. Much better than average."

More frigging games, Hammer thought sourly. Doesn't anybody just talk straight anymore?

"Hey, no offense," said Drill as tactfully as he could. "But I thought you robot guys were, like, just stupid machines."

Chisel was confused. There wasn't somebody inside the tank?

In response, Silverside gave a short barking laugh like a can opener gone bad. "Others of my kind are mere devices, yes. But not I. I have free will." It flipped a gleaming silvered claw in the air. "You might call me an accident of fate."

As the gang digested that bit of news, the metal behemoth docked itself into a control panel desk that rose hydraulically from the concrete floor. "And what is the business you wish to conduct?"

Hammer stepped forward. "We need a couple of parts for our ship," stated the ganglord bluntly, getting right to the point.

A metallic snort. "Then go to Mikon. This is no silver and gold operation. I only deal in high-priced items."

"Like proton cannons?" asked the street tough, adjusting the shoulder strap of his Uzi. Damn things got heavy after a while.

"Difficult, but possible," admitted the droid, replacing the safety interlock on its weapon system as it reinterpreted the gang member's action as one of comfort. "Everybody has the right to defend themselves."

"And some more Omega Gas," chimed in Chisel, and the ganglord shot him an appreciative wink.

Orange lights changed to red. "You are aware that possession of the gas is punishable by Galopticon 7?"

Without a chair to sit in, Drill crossed his arms and cocked an eyebrow. "That a problem?"

"Not a bit," said the machine. "Just telling you why the price will be exorbitant. And I run a strictly cash establishment."

"Hey, jerk, we ain't broke," declared Chisel belligerently.

"Better not be," warned the battledroid. "Waste my time and I'll sell you to the Sazins as experimental animals."

The Deckers didn't know exactly what that meant, but it sure sounded like a serious threat. Better play it smooth.

"Fair enough," smiled Hammer, running a hand over his hated crew cut. When they got back to New York, he had some serious killing to catch up on. Starting with the prison barber.

"Oh, yeah," he added, suddenly remembering why they were here. "We also want a hypernavigational cube." The street tough stumbled over the polysyllabic word.

Silverside diminished the focus of its video cameras. "You don't want much, do you?"

"Who cares? We got the thul," stated Drill, tossing a pouch onto the control-covered desk with a thump, luckily hitting a bare spot.

Using military scanners, the robot weighed the bag while reviewing its contents. Exactly two pounds of pure thulium. Obviously, these beings did not know the true value of the precious metal.

"This is acceptable," said the mechanical as it plugged into the desk and ordered the requested supplies from storage. Then the droid flipped a panel on the desk top, reached inside, and withdrew a fresh-from-the-factory, seals still intact, brand new hypernavigational cube.

"Here you are," said the warobot, using a jointed arm with a two-pronged clip to fork over the device. "The rest of your purchases will be delivered to the landing area for easy loading onto your shuttle."

"Natch . . . ah, I mean, thanks," said Hammer as he nonchalantly tossed the future of humanity from hand to hand.

The cube was perfectly transparent, about the size of an apple, and made of something much heavier than glass or crystal. Three of its sides were covered with tiny black squiggles and the fourth was embossed with the raised design of a triangle in a circle in a square. Out of the corner of his eyes, the street tough noted a smaller version of the logo etched in the metal on the prow of the robot. Idly, he wondered what it meant. But due to a minor omission in their briefing, the gang member was blissfully unaware of the fact that the staggered series of geometric figures was the exclusive symbol placed on property of the Great Golden Ones.

With a shrug, the ganglord tucked the HN cube into a pocket. Geez, so much fuss over a stinking paperweight and the stupid thing didn't even snow inside when you turned it upside-down.

Their business concluded, Leader Silverside decided to press for some more information. "I suppose the original was damaged in the take-over fight?" it inquired in a friendly manner.

Hammer chuckled. "Hey, accidents will happen."

"Think you're pretty tough, eh, mammal?" asked the warobot, always fascinated by the natural aggression of organic life.

Rocking back on his boot heels, Drill stuck his thumbs in his belt and laughed. "Geez, dude, we're the Bloody Deckers! We use Chorons as landfill."

An interesting visual. The droid was starting to like these creatures. Perhaps he could use them as agents for a tricky deal that was coming up. They would probably die, but then, what were paid underlings for?

"Yeah, nobody messes with the Deckers," bragged Hammer, trying to impress the machine and annoy the listeners on board the *Ramariez*. "Why, we even got a couple of those Great Golden guys captive in the brig."

Rrrr? Captive? Silverside mulled that word over, with all that it implied and inferred. Why should anybody brag they had taken a Gee prisoner? Killed, yes. But captive?

A cold surge of power flowed through the warobot's circuits,

and its safety interlock violently disengaged. Why brag unless
the absurd claim was real. But that meant their earlier statement was probably also true. They had killed Leader Idow—
the sweet, gentle being who had stolen the droid from the
accursed Gees, and with his own blue hands given the machine
consciousness, free will, and a name.

Then Idow had assisted Silverside in taking over the asteroid
and creating a criminal empire so the droid would always have
a home. Idow had asked for nothing in return, but Silverside
had insisted on the right to keep the Sazin supplied with whatever he and his ship needed—food, fuel, weapons, and the
occasional crew member. Graciously, Leader Idow had accepted the gifts, and, in all the many decades they had been associated, had never once insulted the machine by offering any
kind of payment for the items.

But now, the beloved liberator was dead. Dead!

The battledroid felt its belly selenoids tighten. Revenge
must be taken on these walking bloodsacks, and the *All That
Glitters* must be blown to pieces! The very notion of the vile
thieves living in the starship stolen from its savior made the
warobot shake with ill-restrained fury.

"Hey, dude, you okay?" asked Hammer in concern. The
machine seemed to be having a seizure or something.

Twin force blades lanced out from the armored prow of Silverside to slice and dice the ganglord into bloody chunks of
flesh. As the body of the youth dropped to the floor in a staggered series of thumps, Drill and Chisel recoiled from the
scene in horror. Then, a lifetime of streetfighting overcame
shock, and with an angry shout, the last remaining Deckers
sprang into action.

25

Activating his force field, Drill dove forward and made a snatch for the HN cube. But Leader Silverside rolled forward over the oozing remains of Hammer, its armored tread grinding the crystal cube in his bloody pocket into dust.

Tumbling frantically out of the way, the gang member barely managed to evade the warobot's killing path, when a stream of bullets, and then a knife, ricocheted harmlessly off the droid's metal body. Without bothering to pause, Silverside released a flight of anti-personnel flechettes, and Chisel's scream of pain informed the machine of a direct hit.

"Help! *Ramariez*, help!" yelled Drill scrambling to his feet, but his cry for help was efficiently blocked by the jamming field of the robot's private office. Nimbly, the youth dodged under a plasma bolt that vaporized half a dozen video monitors on the wall. Wisely, Drill then turned tail and darted through the sole doorway, adrenaline and raw fear fueling him to run at Olympic speeds.

Relentlessly, the machine followed the sole surviving Decker into the corridor.

* * * * *

"Alert!" cried Ensign Lilliuokalani, rising from her seat.

Captain Keller spun away from his conference with Trell at the engineering console. "Excellent, Ensign! You broke through the jamming field?"

"No, sir," said the woman. "Drill is back in view."

The bridge crew turned from their work and looked. There on the main screen was the frantic teenager, charging out of the opening in the tavern wall and yelling to be rescued.

"Sir, should we teleport him on board?" asked Trell, getting ready to do so.

"Scanners locked on target," announced Ensign Hamlisch crisply, his adroit fingers feeding the coordinates to the console of his fellow officer.

Keller squinted. "Does he have the HN cube with him?"

"No, sir, he does not," reported Chief Buckley, checking the read-outs on his board.

"Then leave him alone, and send in the marines," directed the starship commander grimly. "We must have that cube, and, by God, this time we're going to get one!"

* * * * *

As assistance had not arrived, and knowing he couldn't out-run a machine forever, Drill decided to make a stand. Leaping over the counter of the bar, he knocked the sponge out of his way and slapped his hand down on the glowing sensor pad.

"Molotov cocktail!" he shouted, unaware that the Drink Master needed no such vocal encouragement for speed. "And keep 'em coming!"

As the alien device began its reconstruction, Drill pinked himself and prepared his weapons for the final conflict. Machine gun, laser pistol, knife—damn. If only I had a grenade, he cursed silently.

Crouching behind her stool, like the majority of the

patrons, Einda suddenly understood what was happening. Flattening herself as only a Datian can, she shimmied along the molding at floor level and down into the passageway to try and find her fiance, Chisel.

"There you are!" thundered the machine in delight, his words booming in the rapidly emptying tavern. "Time to die, assassin!"

Shouting obscenities, Drill fired the machine pistol and laser together until the Molotov arrived, and then he added its fiery bid to the battle. But nothing proved effective against the armored bulk of the death machine.

As Silverside rolled unaffected through the flame, the droid began to reminisce about the many battles it had fought to forge its criminal empire and establish itself as the leader of Buckle. Each was fun, but always ended much too soon. Someday it hoped to meet a worthy opponent and enjoy a really good workout. Maybe even one that lasted more than sixty seconds.

Smashing the counter to splinters with a single swipe of its heavy-duty manipulators, Silverside gathered the struggling gang member and pinned him against the wall with three telescoping servo-arms, accidentally breaking the human's leg in the process—not that the robot cared in the least. Then a buzzsaw extended from its prow, and slowly advanced toward the wiggling man, the singing wheel of steel hovering from the end of a ferruled metal support.

"Sadly, I am unaware of how my creator died," said the machine in its toneless voice. "But I am sure that your death will be more painful."

The first swipe of the buzzsaw sliced off Drill's bulletproof vest. The second laid open his jumpsuit, putting a shallow slash across the chest. Drops of blood welled from the cut and dribbled into his clothing. Contemptuously, Drill spat on the camera lenses of the machine and braced himself for death. The man had always known he would die in a bar fight, only he had expected it to be in Manhattan. But at that instant, the tavern was washed with light and a squad of UN marines in power armor teleported in.

Lieutenant Sakaeda absorbed the torture scene in a glance, and ticked off his options with lightning speed. Bullets would be useless against the armored bulk of the wardroid, and their lasers couldn't penetrate the force field that his helmet sensors told him surrounded the machine. That left only grenades or missiles, either of which would kill Drill along with the robot. No, wait a minute, that was wrong.

"Dead volley," ordered Sakaeda over his suit radio, and the marines launched a flurry of their special, anti-robot Church Key missiles—but without arming the weapons first.

From both of the fluted muzzles at the tip of their nameless UN rifles, twenty rustling firebirds streaked across the bar to viciously slam into the tanklike body of the warobot, going up to their hot fins in the thick armor. The savage pummeling made the droid rattle and vibrate under each battering impact, but the damage incurred was superficial. Only Sergeant Lieberman's shots did the required job.

Her first missile smashed directly onto the base of the descending buzzsaw, knocking it away from Drill's exposed throat and tearing the limb free from the warobot's chassis to crash into the nearby Drink Master—which promptly burst into flames, as the obedient device was still dutifully manufacturing the gasoline-and-soap concoction requested earlier.

The second missile zoomed straight in to embed itself right between the eye-cameras of the enemy droid.

Horrified, Silverside sent off a unique signal pulse to seize control of these robots and bind them to its will forever. But instead of instantly complying like good slaves, the metal warriors menacingly advanced closer and ordered the droid to surrender or die.

Pincushioned with missiles, the desperate machine sent off the signal again and again, but the results remained the same. Impossible! No conceivable robot or computer could possibly resist the override command, especially as it had been augmented and boosted by the technical genius of Leader Idow so that even Gee military computers were helpless before the signal pulse. Unless, Silverside finally realized, there were living creatures inside those metal shells. Hostile, alien creatures immune to its control and with both the ability and the desire to do the machine serious harm.

The unsettling thought of personal combat in which the droid did not have a totally superior advantage filled its central data processing unit, and for the first time, the warobot tasted the bitter emotion of fear.

Deciding that discretion was the better part of valor, Leader Silverside released its captive and quickly retreated, backrolling straight into the corridor that led to its office, the double doors slamming shut in the faces of the pursuing marines.

"Never mind the robot, secure the bar," directed Sakaeda. The lieutenant countermanded the order when he observed that the establishment was deserted except for his troops and a very bloody Decker. "Lieberman, check Drill."

Kneeling on the littered floor, Tanya roughly shook the young convict to wake him from his stupor. "Where's the cube?" she demanded over the external speaker of her power armor.

"My leg," groaned the street tough through clenched teeth, holding the injured limb with both hands.

Bone showed through the bloody fabric, so the sergeant activated the medical kit inside her metal wrist and gave the wounded man a NATO Hot Shot right in the neck: 10ccs of morphine, cocaine, digitalis, and methamphetamine. If that devil's brew didn't put a person immediately on his feet, the army called an embalmer.

"Destroyed," gasped Drill, as a tingling wave of relief washed over him. "But there's a whole lot more of them in the office." He pointed with a not-so-steady hand.

"What about the rest of your gang?"

He coughed. "Dead. Died kicking butt. Almost got the bastard myself. Was gonna drown him in my blood." Drill managed a faint smile. "Your turn, lady," he said and passed out.

"Good work, soldier," Sergeant Lieberman said softly,

giving the highest compliment she could. Gently, the woman laid his head on the floor and stood. With proper training, the lad would make a fine marine.

"Lutzman, stay with him," ordered Sakaeda gruffly. "Kushner check the door that damn robot went through."

"No booby traps, sir," reported the advance and delay expert over her radio a few seconds later. "But the seams have been cold-fused together."

"Okay, clear the area," snapped Lieutenant Sakaeda on the command circuit. "Matulich, Berouzi, open those doors. Platoon, get ready to move!"

A salvo of rockets from the bazooka team blasted the portal to rubble, and the marines stormed in even before the reverberations ceased, bits of ceiling bouncing off their armored hides.

Nothing attacked them in the tunnel, and the second set of locked doors was disposed of as easily as the first. Stepping over the smoking debris, the troopers saw Leader Silverside spin on its tread across the bare room and crash straight through a wall of video monitors, glass shards and pieces of wire flying everywhere. Only blackness showed on the other side.

More concerned with the job at hand, the marines ignored the robot and began searching for any HN cubes. But a single glance showed the glass-walled office was devoid of anything, save a horrible mangled pile of flesh.

"Which one of them is it?" asked a private haltingly.

"Both, I think," replied a hoarse voice.

Somebody muttered a phrase in Italian and nobody needed a translation to know that it meant "yuck."

"Your opinion, Tanya?" asked Sakaeda on their personal communication channel, none of the other troopers able to hear the privileged conversation.

"We have got to capture that robot," advised the sergeant, arming the sole replacement rockets on her rifle with the twist and jerk of a safety ring. "At the very least, it knows where the rest of the HN cubes are stored."

"I agree. Let's go get the bastard."

She smiled grimly. "And kick butt."

"We're going after Silverside," broadcast the lieutenant to the rest of the soldiers." Point men, take your positions, but shoot only to defend yourselves. We need that tin can alive."

Lieberman saluted. "Aye, sir. Okay, let's move out!"

In formation, the troopers traveled down a short spiraling ramp, but their helmet lights did little to illuminate the incredible darkness about them.

"Night visors," ordered Sakaeda, and as the marines complied, they promptly found themselves in a staggeringly large underground cavern, whose dimensions took their breath away.

This, they could plainly see, was the true interior of the asteroid. The sprawling city above them only utilized a tiny percentage of the total volume of the gigantic planetoid. Mere size did not impress these marines, but what was in the cavern gave them pause.

Strapped to the curved rock walls high above them were countless gold missiles the size of battleships, and running down the length of the asteroid, becoming lost in the distance, was a colossal amber laser assembly that dwarfed the missiles to toys. The soldiers gulped. It was painfully obvious what they were standing in. The mammoth, twelve-story tall triangle in a circle in a square carved into the wall on their left was totally superfluous.

"*Ay carumba*. It's a weapons cache for the Great Golden Ones!" breathed a voice in awe.

A grunt muttered, "No kidding."

"But if Silverside is in charge of Buckle," added another soldier thoughtfully. "Then, he must know about this place."

"So, either the Gees are really crooks, which is highly doubtful, or this Silverside guy must have turned traitor for some reason and has taken over the place for himself."

"Great!" remarked somebody, checking the action on her nameless assault rifle. "Then killing the creep won't be marked against us, but will actually be a point in our favor. Why heck, we might even get a reward."

While the soldiers eagerly discussed the possible monetary aspects of the situation, Lieutenant Sakaeda fiddled with the controls in his helmet and tried the radio again. "Landing party to *Ramariez*, can you read me? Over." But only the static of the jamming field answered him.

Damn, he thought, this must be the source of the interference the bridge encountered in Leader Silverside's office. Makes sense. With the advent of modern sensors, you can't hide something anymore just by burying it under a couple million tons of rock and ore. But, without contact with the ship, we're on our own. Okay, no problem.

Sergeant Lieberman waddled forward. "Orders, Lieutenant?"

"Regardless of our location, we will continue the search for the robot," said the officer brusquely. "Our mission is to obtain an HN cube. That objective will be accomplished." The marine nodded. Sounded good, now if only they could do it.

Although not designed for speed, Leader Silverside had nevertheless made good its escape, frantically shucking missiles along the way and taking refuge in a utility closet inside one of the flange support legs of the Nova-grade laser. Lacking anything more appropriate, it barred the door with an electromop.

Feeling safe, at least for the moment, the droid took the opportunity to remove the unexploded missile from between its eye-cameras and deposit the filthy thing on a nearby shelf. The nervous machine then uncoiled its most delicate manipulators, removed a saffron-colored toolbox from inside itself, and began to patch the gaping wound in its forehead.

With good reason, the droid was scared lubricantless. In its many years of running Buckle, the robot had never before been damaged in a fight. The act of getting shot in the head with an armor-piercing missile was most unpleasant, and the droid had absolutely no intention of ever letting such a calamity happen again. Hot Void, no.

Finished with the temporary repair job, Silverside tidied itself up and cautiously rolled to the ventilation slits in the burnished door to peek outside and see what was happening. In a regular sweeping pattern, the armed humanoids were steadily advancing into the cavern. They were obviously searching for him and revenge. The abrupt appearance of the metal-clad warriors so soon after its execution of the biped mammals in its office could not be a coincidence.

Feeling defeat breathing warm on his cranial-support unit, Silverside knew it had no choice but to play its trump card and released control of the asteroid's main defense computer—a control that the robot had never let rest for a millisecond after gaining it low those many solar revolutions ago.

Finally free from the onerous rule of the renegade robot, the loyal golden computer bank immediately sent out a long-delayed priority alpha emergency call to the planet Gee and unlimbered every offensive weapon it possessed.

The marines halted as a section of the distant rock wall directly below the towering trademark of the Gee dilated, and out rolled a hundred warobots. At the sight of the humans, the dusty Gee droids promptly unleashed a barrage of invisible death from their neural disrupters and a fusillade of highly visible plasma bolts, just for good measure.

* * * * *

Meanwhile, out in space, several small asteroids broke formation and left the plane of the ecliptic. Once in position, they jetted forward and dived toward the amassed ships in orbit around Buckle, spraying them with sizzling particle beams. A half-dozen ships of visitors and customers disappeared in silent explosions before the startled crews could react. The outer force field of the *Ramariez* collapsed under the hellish load of lethal radiation, and the ship only survived the initial attack because of its deflector plating.

On the bridge of the starship, the main viewscreen brightened and then went dark as every hull-mounted video camera was vaporized.

"Red alert!" ordered Keller, wiping tears from his eyes. "Soukup, full power to the shields. Lilliuokalani, switch to auxiliary cameras #4 through 10. Trell, seal all interior hatchways and boost engines to 40/40. Hamlisch, set the laser batteries on automatic. Buckley, fire the proton cannon at will!"

Nobody wasted time to reply. They just did it.

With the element of surprise gone, the surviving starships began to defend themselves. Scarlet laser beams and green proton rays crisscrossed space in a searing network of death and destruction.

Most of the hastily aimed weapons hit their assigned targets and drilled white-hot holes in the attacking sentinels. A few of the robot craft flashed instantly into nothingness. Several more spun crazily off into the distance as their guidance systems were wrecked. But more and more rocks left the plane of the asteroid belt to join the fight, their shimmering particle beams outshining the local sun in dazzling brilliance. Soon, all of nearby space was filled with the frightful, pyrotechnic splendor of high technology war.

"Sir, should we teleport the marines back on board?" asked Trell, frantically operating his console and wishing that he had more than just four arms and one god.

"Not until they signal possession of a cube," replied the captain firmly. It was a distasteful fact, according to the mission directive, but the HN cube was far more important than any of the individual marine's lives.

At nearly light speed, a tumbling boulder rammed the *Ramariez*, disintegrating into a nuclear fireball, and the ship shook under the stupendous blow. The rebuilt outer force field dissipated again, but the inner shield held. Telltales flashed on everybody's boards, and the starship commander nervously cracked a knuckle. This was obviously no time for half-measures.

"Belay my last order and prime the main gun," he directed the weapons officer. "Fire when ready and make damn sure you don't hit Buckle!"

"Aye, aye, sir!" cried Buckley, flipping switches and pressing buttons with gay abandonment. Faith, this is why he had joined the space service!

*   *   *   *   *

In the brig, a fast series of micro-explosions outlined a square in the white metal wall of The 16's cell, and the hot metal plate dropped to the floor with a loud clang. A moment later, Avantor peeked out of the hole. Behind her could be seen two other walls with similar breaches in them.

As she wiggled through the opening, the totally recovered 16 climbed off his sick bed, and from beneath the covers withdrew a floppy cap made of woven copper and several modified circuit boards taken out of his medical scanner. Loosely, the battery pack of the RDP monitor dangled from a wire harness.

Wordlessly, Avantor handed over her translator, and he deftly removed from it the tiny Choron relay crystal that made the device function. Only a few seconds were needed for The 16 to fit it to the electronic hat.

Removing the bandage from her head, Avantor pulled the now-functioning cap snugly into place, crossed the cell, and threw open the door. As the *STOP THAT* cannon kicked on, The 16 dropped to the floor with a groan, but protected by the handmade psionic shield (training video #23: "What To Do When Your Own Equipment Is Used Against You—Aside From Die") the avantor could only feel the faintest of suggestions from the stolen weapon.

A quick yank disconnected the cannon, and soon the two Gee officers were proceeding along the hallway, intent far beyond the simple urgings of their hypnotraining to take control of this vessel and arrest absolutely everybody within.

*   *   *   *   *

The initial volley of assorted death from the warobots was spent harmlessly against the round force shields suspended in front of every space marine. Undaunted, the soldiers then fired in return, but their heavy bullets and polycyclic lasers proved equally ineffective against the force fields and thick body armor of the rampaging droids.

Frowning, Sergeant Lieberman slammed a fresh clip into her

assault rifle. One hundred warobots against ten marines. If there was anything she hated, it was a fair fight.

"Take cover! Outgoing!" barked the sergeant on the radio. "Mainhardt, fire!"

As the troopers ducked out of the way, the Atomic Vortex Rifle cut loose, its swirling cone of nuclear energy washing over the machines with the expected results. As the machines paused to recover from the quantum onslaught, the marines released a full volley of their Church Key missiles.

In a blossoming row of fireballs, the first ten droids disassembled the hard way, hot shrapnel zinging everywhere. Uncaring, the remaining ninety war machines rolled over the burning wreckage of their fallen comrades and continued on, pinchers, drills, electro-probes, and buzzsaws extending on telescoping arms of steel from inside their bodies.

Lieutenant Sakaeda dialed his visor back to normal magnification and scowled. An entire salvo just to take out ten measly robots. Without a lot more ammunition than they were carrying, this was going to be a long, dirty fight.

"Prepare to evade!" shouted a private on the command circuit.

As his shocked companions turned to stare, Fuerstenberg raised the sights of his assault rifle and fired from the hip. The stuttering stream of bullets, beams, and rockets tore apart a center bracket for the Planetbuster Bomb high on the wall above them. Quick on the uptake, the rest of the marines followed suit and the end supports of the space missile were shot to pieces. With a deafening screech of tortured metal, the gargantuan bomb broke free and began rolling down the slope toward the massed humans with ever-increasing speed.

"On my mark, JUMP!" cried Lieutenant Sakaeda, and the marines were airborne when the spinning destroyer passed underneath, clanging and banging like a runaway trash can.

The ground-bound warobots lacked this crucial ability, however, and despite frantic evasive maneuvers on their part, the machines were unceremoniously flattened under the barreling bomb. Loudly, the megaton missile careened off the base of the huge laser and continued rolling into the distance, eventually coming to rest against a giant power booster relay, barely scratched from its brief, but hectic, journey.

"Well, this is one even Ripley wouldn't believe," joked a marine, using his helmet camera to take a picture of the paper-thin metal doilies decorating the ground.

"Eh? What ever do you mean?" asked PFC Ripley, puzzled. "I was right here. I helped do it."

A sigh. "Never mind."

"Hey, sirs!" called out a private from the bottom of the spiraling ramp. "Look here!"

Rushing over to the gesturing trooper, Lieutenant Sakaeda and Sergeant Lieberman saw that the woman had found a room of some kind hidden inside the rock wall, the door a hinged section of stone that perfectly matched the exterior. Briefly, the private explained how the vibrations of the tumbling missile had thrown the portal open and upon landing she had jammed her rifle in to keep it ajar.

Summoning assistance, the officers posted guards and directed the careful forcing of the door. Warily, the marines entered.

The square-cut cave was anything but empty. Lining the walls were hundreds of plastic shelves jammed full of white boxes adorned with perfectly ordinary appearing bar codes, and directly under a rectangular panel in the ceiling was a control board desk sitting on a hydraulic lift. It only took the troopers a moment to overcome their shock upon finding Silverside's storage closet. Hastily, the cartons were torn apart, and along with miscellaneous weapons, precision tools, force field belts, and sundry indecipherable items, they located twenty-seven pristine hypernavigational cubes.

"Jackpot!" whooped a trooper, slapping the back of the person nearest her.

"Thanks," replied the man, his servo-motors whining as he righted himself.

"Okay, everybody grab two cubes and then let's hightail it out of here before something else attacks us," directed

Lieutenant Sakaeda, shouldering his rifle.

"You heard the man," said Sergeant Lieberman gruffly. "Let's loot the place and move it, people!"

"Aye, sir!"

"Check!"

"Affirmative!"

"HELP!"

Their scanners indicated the scream for assistance had come from outside in the cavern, and the room was vacated post-haste. There, standing beside the gargantuan laser assembly, was Leader Silverside with eight metal tentacles wrapped about a struggling marine and holding the soldier as a shield before him.

"Do not interfere with my escape or this unit will be damaged beyond repair," warned the machine, its atonal voice adding just a touch of dire foreboding to the speech.

"Sorry, sir," said the prisoner, stiffly formal. "I opened a door in the leg of the big laser and there he was. No excuse."

"Forget it, Private," said Lieutenant Sakaeda soothingly. "He could have gotten any of us."

Slowly, the platinum-edged tank began moving toward the ramp. "My only wish is continued existence," stated the droid. "So I will trade life for life. On my oath of honor, this one will be released after my shuttle has launched and I am safe from your retribution."

Silverside knew it was a gamble, but the creatures might just be stupid enough to believe him. However, even without the high-tech sensors in their power armor, the marines had no problem detecting bull when they heard it.

Growling menacingly, the humans primed their weapons and started to advance, when Sergeant Lieberman noticed somebody had vanished from the rear of the group.

It took her a second to find the missing person. A trooper had used the incredible strength of the servo-motors in his UN power armor to jump almost straight up, and was at present arcing through the air far above them, a tactic only made possible by the vast size of the cavern.

"Freeze!" shouted Lieberman over the external speaker of her suit at maximum volume, and involuntarily Silverside paused. She smiled in triumph. What a shmuck.

And five hundred pounds of dura-steel filled with space marine crashed directly onto the rogue droid at 30 feet per second per second from a height of almost ten stories.

Crystal, plastic, wire, bits, hunks, chunks, and various stuff sprayed out from the meteoric landing like an explosion in a junk yard, and the trooper buried himself to the knees inside the chassis of the robot.

Though reeling from the impact, Leader Silverside swiveled its domed head and lashed out with every working arm it still possessed to rend this unorthodox invader into bloody scraps.

Ducking under the forest of lethal limbs, the soldier dove forward and rammed his fist through the patch covering the hole made by the Church Key missile in the forehead of the warobot. Silverside went berserk at the action and redoubled the effort to kill its piggyback assailant. Ignoring the brutal pounding, the trooper shoved his hand in deeper, seized the robot's brain, and closed his fingers to perform the crudest of lobotomies.

To the watching marines, Leader Silverside seemed to simply explode. Both eye-camera lenses extended to their full length, and black smoke poured from every crack in the dented metal body. Its belly tread unlinked, and every tentacle went stiff, accidentally hurling the struggling hostage away to a bruised freedom. Then spewing forth a shower of sparks, the criminal droid shuddered, its cruising lights went dark, and the machine entered into a highly deserved state of total and permanent dysfunction.

Quite satisfied with the results, the soldier pried himself loose from the tangled innards of the demolished robot and hopped down to the rocky floor. He was pleased that his life-time habit of crushing drained beer cans had finally become useful.

"Good work, Corporal," praised Sergeant Lieberman.

PFC Fuerstenberg paused before answering. "Thank

you, sir."

"And we mean it this time," she added, genuinely sincere.

Wisely, the marine remained reticent, not willing to tempt fate, or the brig, by saying a single word.

"Okay, back to the tavern before something else happens!" snapped Lieutenant Sakaeda impatiently. "Double time, harch!"

As the troops proceeded up the spiraling ramp, the ex-hostage deliberately bumped into a friend. "Hey, remember when I asked you why they keep that klutz Fuerstenberg around?"

"Yep."

"Never mind."

* * * * *

Out in space, scintillating daggers of pure energy thrust and jabbed at the robot craft, seeking the vulnerable vitals of the machinery and a quick kill. Missiles, rockets, and torpedoes were launched in clouds, not mere flights. The rockets and torpedoes lanced out straight and true, eager to meet their fiery end in the bowels of the enemy. The missiles performed complex evasive maneuvers, and then came zooming in on the enemy rocks from every side. Salvo after salvo of huge-caliber shells were fired—deadly, armor-piercing canisters jammed full of high explosives, Omega Gas, and radioactive thermit. Plasma bolts traveled serenely through the lethal battle zone, actually absorbing the energy of any destructive agency encountered en route and adding its power to their own considerable reserves, thereby increasing the already incredible violence of their detonation by some score.

But the Gee sentinels sported meters of refractory armor to the ships' mere inches, plus they had multiple layers of force field/shield combinations instead of only one of each. So in spite of everything, the offense of the inhabited vessels soon became defense under the never-ending attack of the nearly indestructible robot rocks and their ferocious particle beams.

Under the hellish onslaught of the ravenous adamantine ray,

a starship's force field would expand, running the visible spectrum as the stubborn energy barrier desperately struggled to stay erect, and finally fail. Then the doomed inner shield would fall, exposing the bare, unprotected hull of the ship itself, and yet another vessel would flash into a ball of multicolored flame. More than one craft shunted for the safety of hyperspace—where transdimensional mines homed in on the vibrations of their enginettes and violently reduced starship and crew to their component atoms.

It was horrible. It was madness. It was WAR! Worse, it was like an E. E. "Doc" Smith space battle—only more so.

Then, from the keel of the *Ramariez*, a fifteen-meter dish disengaged and ponderously swung away on a universal joint. Inside the white ceramic cup was a three-pronged barrel with a conveyer belt lined with black metal ovals feeding into it. This was the main gun of the human starship: the Atomic Vortex Cannon.

The virgin dish glowed for a moment and then vomited forth a bar of quasi-solid lightning—a burning rod of atomic annihilation that shot across the asteroid belt to punch through a cluster of rock sentinels, and several hundred innocent boulders, leaving nothing behind but luminescent vapor and charred ash.

As the blinding inferno of the vitriolic ray dissipated, the conveyer belt advanced a single notch and another thermonuclear bomb moved into position.

"Test shot completed, sir," announced the CPO briskly. "Every circuit registers in the green. Ready to commence the bombardment."

Keller adjusted the protective sunglasses on his face, as did the rest of the bridge crew. Nobody would ever again make fun of the Kremlin/Pentagon theory that "Big is Better." Whew.

"Let them eat cosmics, Mr. Buckley," ordered the captain.

"With pleasure, skipper!"

Again the dish radiated, and the seething fusion beam lanced out to move among the attacking rocks like a burning magician's wand. At its slightest touch, the sentinels flared into puffs of superheated steam and by the score they vanished; force fields, shields, and state of the art Gee armor meaning less than vacuum to the starkly indescribable fury of the mauling power ray.

Twice more the AVC spoke, and soon the main screen of the *Ramariez* showed an astonishingly large hole in the asteroid belt surrounding Buckle. Disappointed, the chief petty officer tried not to pout as the tactical screen on his control board showed only rapidly fleeing starships and no more belligerent rocks. Well, that was certainly over quickly.

With the battle obviously finished, Keller gratefully pocketed his sunglasses. "My compliments on your shooting, Chief," he said, equally impressed by the marksmanship and the performance of the weapon.

"Thank you, sir. Anything else you'd like destroyed?"

"Ah, not at the present time."

"Quite sure, sir?"

"Most definitely," stated the captain a trifle dourly. He appreciated enthusiasm, but not zealots.

The CPO shrugged and began restoring the safety interlocks as a preparation to store the weapon away. Oh, well, it sure had been fun while it lasted.

"Report from the landing party, sir," announced Ensign Lilliuokalani, swiveling from her console. "They have obtained several HN cubes. No casualties."

"Excellent," smiled Keller. "What about the Deckers?"

She touched her earphone. "Drill is wounded, but alive. Hammer and Chisel were both . . . mashed. Virtually nothing left of their bodies to recover."

"Acknowledged. Bring them home, Mr. Hamlisch, and have Dr. Van Loon meet them in the landing bay with a medical team."

"Aye, aye, skipper," said the ensign cheerfully.

Suddenly, the rear of the bridge exploded, the strident concussion nearly throwing the crew members from their seats. In unison they turned, and in through the smoky ruin of the elevator doors strode Avantor, her long hair a flaxen corona about her head.

Before anybody could move, the bridge security system automatically responded to the presence of unauthorized personnel and dropped a grenade launcher from the ceiling panel alongside the video camera. The 40mm rapid-fire was loaded with electro-chemical stun bags, able to drop a rabid elephant in its tracks. But the grim-faced Gee blew the toy away with a glance.

"You are all under arrest!" she informed them as tiny pieces of plastic and metal sprinkled to the deck.

"Avantor, can't we talk this over?" asked Chief Petty Officer Buckley, standing to attract her attention as Lieutenant Jones and Ensign Hamlisch got ready to tackle the Gee from both sides. But then, right on schedule, the overhead lights dimmed and the ever-present, soft background hum of the enginettes died away.

"THIS IS THE 16," blared the intercom in the darkness. "I HAVE TOTAL CONTROL OF YOUR POWER AND LIFE-SUPPORT. OBEY THE AVANTOR OR DIE."

As the emergency chemical lights flickered on, the crew reluctantly resumed their seats, and Trell slumped onto his deactivated engineering console. By the Prime Builder, they had been so close. Damn soft-hearted Terrans. He had told them to kill the Gees. Now it was Galopticon 7, for sure.

Momentarily, Captain Keller debated using the laser pistol in the arm of his chair. And even though he stood a good chance of success, he decided against it. Dag knew that the only way to stop the Gee would be to kill her, and that he could not do.

As Keller opened his mouth to try a plea for reason, the main viewscreen blazed with the Technicolor glory of a thousand Gee superdreadnought centihedrons phasing in from hyperspace to totally englobe the Earth ship.

Then the holographs of a thousand Gees appeared on the bridge, the etheral images of the men and women overlapping each other from lack of room, the golden light from the saffron military uniforms they wore giving everyone present a dark, beautiful California tan.

"Dirtlings, you are under arrest!" they said together in a loose harmony."

Tightening a fist so hard that the knuckles cracked by themselves, Dag reviewed the situation in his mind at a fever pitch and searched for options. Let's see, he thought. Engines shut off, shields down, weapons deactivated, Gees inside and out. Ah . . . hmmm . . . damn.

"*Pax*," said Captain Keller with a sigh, and he raised both his hands. "We surrender."

The naval officer knew when he was beaten. Sadly, the crew copied his action. So, it was finally over. Their mission was a failure and, in spite of everything, Earth had lost her bid for the stars.

And the worst part was, humanity hadn't even received a trial.

26

TRANSCRIPT #1—"Earth versus Gee." Hightlights only.
For an unabridged copy of the trial, access Recall Bubble
#45789253745, sub-sections 1-250. Recommended reading
for law students, historians, and insomniacs.

FADE FROM BLACK TO A LONG ESTABLISHING SHOT
OF A STANDARD CONTROL BOOTH. SEATED BEHIND
A TIERED CONSOLE IS A FEMALE HUMANOID WEAR-
ING A SOLEMN GREEN SHEATH WITH BLUE RUNNING
LIGHTS. SPECIES: DEMBREXIAN. PERSONAL NAME:
ORBLUK SNEEV. SHE HAS MOLDED HER UPPER HAIR
FOLLICLES INTO "WITNESS" MODE.

NEXT TO HER IS A MALE AMPHIBIAN. SPECIES:
DCONGE. PERSONAL NAME: VOCK AK-AK. HE HAS
STRIPPED HIS EPIDERMIS TO A NEUTRAL CREAMY
WHITE. ON A FLOATING TABLE ALONGSIDE HIM IS A
VAST ARRAY OF BRUSHES, STICKS, AND APPLICATORS,
PLUS VARIOUS PAINTS, POWDERS, MUD, AND FELT-TIP

MARKERS. ZOOM IN TO SEE THE FEMALE FLICK HER NOSE IN WELCOME, WHILE THE MALE BEGINS TO SLATHER A BRIGHT ORANGE PASTE OF WELCOME ON HIS UPPER RIGHT FLIPPER.

ORBLUK—Greetings, sentients! I am Orbluk Sneev. . . .

VOCK—And Vock Ak-Ak, I be!

ORBLUK—And we will be your commentators at this trial of a lifetime. The Great Golden Ones versus the inhabitants of the Sol star system. During the trial, the accused will not only be defending themselves from the incredible number of charges facing them, but will at the same time be applying for membership in the Galactic League. These guys have a great sense of timing, eh, Vock?

VOCK—(starts smearing a blue jelly on his tail) Truth you speak, Orbluk! Expect a most colorful trial, do I! Perhaps even worthy of permanent place on body. (chuckle) Due to intense interest in proceedings, discarded has been ordinary courtroom.

THE VIDEO SCREEN BEHIND THE TWO FADES AWAY TO REVEAL A HUGE COLISEUM THAT IS PACKED SOLID WITH BEINGS.

VOCK—For the first time in recorded history, the ceremonial Park of Recreation has been emptied of players, and spectators from across the galaxy have crammed themselves into its three-kilometer-wide viewing section.

EXTERNAL SHOT. PANORAMIC VIEW OF THE COLISEUM. FOCUS IN ON A GOLDEN RIOT BARGE FLYING LOW OVER THE SPECTATORS, THE LOW-SLUNG DISH ABRISTLE WITH WEAPONS. WAROBOTS RUMBLE ALONG THE COLISEUM FLOOR AND THOUSANDS OF GEE SOLDIERS ARE ON FOOT PATROL AMONG THE CROWDS, CHECKING ID BADGES AT ENTRANCEWAYS, AND MANNING CONCESSION STANDS.

ORBLUK—As you can see, the Great Golden Ones are taking

no chance on the security arrangements here. And considering some of the emotionally charged issues this trial will be dealing with, you can't blame them for perhaps being a little overzealous. (pause) Now, we will take you down onto the main area with Mogachef and LD 59, to let you get acquainted with the various participants.

CUT TO A LUMPISH FEMALE HUMANOID SWADDLED IN A SIMPLE WICKER REPRODUCTION SUIT. SPECIES: LOOOG. PERSONAL NAME: MOGACHEF. BEHIND HER ARE DOZENS OF TECHNICIANS FRANTICALLY OPERATING COMPLEX MACHINERY AND LAYING CABLES. WITH A CRACKLE OF LIGHTNING, THERE APPEARS IN THE SKY ABOVE THEM A VAST HOLOGRAPHIC PROJECTION OF THE GALACTIC LEAGUE. THE CROWD ROARS WITH APPROVAL.

MOGACHEF—Thank you. The link with the Galactic League has been established, and the trial should be starting soon.

IN THE LOWER RIGHT-HAND CORNER OF THE CAMERA, SUPERIMPOSE A DIAGRAM OF THE COLISEUM. IN THE CENTER, A SMALL RED TRIANGLE BEGINS TO GLOW.

MOGACHEF—Now, we take you over to the human sector and LD 59.

CUT TO A SMOOTH, STEEL BALL FLOATING IN THE AIR WITH A JOINTED VISION STALK RISING FROM ITS TOP. SPECIES: AN EVALUATOR FROM THE PRTHIH MACHINE CULTURE. UNIT SURNAME: LD 59.

LD 59—Transmission acknowledged. Salutations, viewers. Fact: The defendants are present and accounted for. This includes: the crew of the UNSF *Ramariez*, the First Contact Team, and the United Countries of Dirt Association, aka UN. The last group was requisitioned from Terra by a no-nonsense team of Great Golden Process Servers, who subsequently have been awarded medals of valor. (pause) The majority of the humans appear to be experiencing a form of high-level stress/anxiety. This is no doubt due to the unexpectedness of their participation at this event. I believe that we can look forward to the usual carbon-based life-form antics that we normally observe when these creatures find themselves in a prolonged life-or-dysfunction situation. Let us communicate now with the Terrans' lawyer, a.k.a. Story Weaver, Semi-Lord Tshog Brent.

SPLIT SCREEN TO SHOW A BELEAGUERED-LOOKING BIPED DINOSAUR. HIS NOSE HORN HAS BEEN MIRROR PLATED, ALONG WITH SEVERAL OF THE LIFE SUPPORT DEVICES THAT FLEX AND TURN ON HIS RIDGED BACK. HE IS DRESSED FOR SUCCESS IN FLORAL PRINT COMBAT SHORTS.

LD 59—I almost greet you, Semi-Lord.

BRENT—I nearly accept.

LD 59—You realize that your clients have no possible chance of acquittal.

BRENT—The actions my clients have engaged in will prove, under a detailed scrutiny, to have been of great benefit to galactic civilization. They will be cleared and admitted to the Galactic League as full members, or I will eat my tail!

LD 59—Brave words, indeed. Thank you. As stated, I expect a great deal of frenzy here over the next few days. We re-establish visual contact now with Orbluk Sneev and Vock Ak-Ak, to cover the opening ceremonies.

****

TRANSCRIPT #5

FADE IN ON THE 3000. HE IS STANDING ON THE TOP LEVEL OF AN OFFICIAL TABLE OF INQUIRY. ON THE LOWER LEVEL BEFORE HIM ARE AVANTOR AND THE 16, STANDING STIFFLY AT ATTENTION. NOBODY LOOKS VERY HAPPY.

ORBLUK (voice over)—We see before us The 3000, leader of

the Great Golden Ones. It is he who will formally read the charges against the Terrans. It is rumored that due to the unusual circumstances involved, he will ask for leniency to be shown if they are convicted.

CUT TO CLOSE-UP OF THE 3000.

THE 3000—The charges are: unauthorized use of a stardrive, illegal use of the color gold, harboring a known criminal, two counts of running a blockade, landing upon a restricted world, piracy, theft of Gee property, two counts of kidnapping, destruction of Gee property, speeding, littering, and resisting arrest. (pause) The majority of these crimes are punishable by death. And considering their cumulative total, I ask that the entire population of the planet Terra be sentenced to Galopticon 7. (pause) Acknowledging the harshness of this sentence, I have no objection if the inhabitants of Terra instead opt to be destroyed by a barrage of Planetbuster Bombs.

PULL BACK FROM THE 3000 TO THE CONTROL ROOM. ORBLUK AND VOCK ARE TURNED AROUND IN THEIR CHAIRS TO WATCH HIM. AS THE GEE FINISHES, THEY SWIVEL ABOUT TO FACE THE CAMERA.

ORBLUK—Well, those rumors of clemency were obviously true.

****

TRANSCRIPT #20

FADE IN ON MOGACHEF. SHE IS STANDING IN FRONT OF THE COLISEUM DIAGRAM. A SMALL CIRCLE IN THE LOWER LEFT GLOWS A SICKLY GREEN.

MOGACHEF—Today we are to hear testimony from the RporRians. They've been brought here from their home world in a surprise move by the Great Golden Ones. This could be bad news for the Terrans. We go now to LD 59 for an on-the-spot report.

CUT TO LD 59. A MICROPHONE HAS BEEN EXTRUD-ED FROM HIS LOWER HEMISPHERE AND HE IS FLOAT-ING NEXT TO A STERN-FACED GEE OFFICER.

LD 59—You are The 412, the person in charge of the RporR-ians. Why was it deemed necessary for them to be brought here? It raised the percentile risk of their escape into positive integers.

THE 412—We will use the testimony of the RporRians to determine the extent of the Terrans' crimes on their world. As for escape, we are fully aware that when we asked the Queen/Mother for this delegation, we were cheerfully sup-plied with a squad of commando fighters and pregnant queens. If they got free and infiltrated the nigh-infinite pas-sageways of Big we would never find them. But we believe that adequate precautions to prevent this tragedy have been taken.

CROSS FADE TO EXTERIOR SHOT OF METAL CON-FINEMENT CUBE. DISSOLVE INTO AN INTERIOR VIEW. INSIDE A CYLINDRICAL FORCECAN ARE SIX RPORR-IANS WRAPPED IN STRAIGHT JACKETS AND HANG-ING FROM THE CEILING IN CHAINS. DIRECTLY BENEATH THEM IS A VAT FULL OF BOILING OMEGA GAS. THE REST OF THE CUBE IS A MAZE OF SPRING-OPERATED BEAR TRAPS, MOLECULAR TRIP WIRES, AND PROXIMITY ACTIVATED NUCLEAR BOMBS.

THE 412—Incredible as it sounds, despite everything, they are still plotting to escape. But the insects have been forced to put several "givens" into their calculations. (The Gee pulls a communicator from her pocket and holds the device next to the microphone. Faint voices can he heard.)

RPORRIAN—If . . . if every Gee were to drop dead, their machines exploded, and miraculously we were given super-powers, then maybe we could . . .

LD 59—The extent of your precautions are acknowledged. When may we expect the actual testimony?

THE 412—Well, we are having a little trouble with that. The RporRians are actually demanding that we pay them to testify. Despite our abhorrence of this concept, we are negotiating with them. But, so far, they have rejected our last four offers.

LD 59—And the RporRians are reknowned for their ability to negotiate, i.e. rob you blind. Do you see this as a continuing problem?

THE 412—No. I am confident the matter will soon be resolved.

CUT BACK TO INTERIOR OF THE CONFINEMENT CUBE. AS THE FORCECAN BEGINS TO DISSIPATE, THE PURPLE FUMES OF THE OMEGA GAS RISE HIGHER AND HIGHER. FROM THE COMMUNICATOR WE HEAR PITEOUS SCREAMS OF TERROR.

THE 412—We should get everything settled pretty quickly.

****

TRANSCRIPT #25

FADE IN ON THE CONTROL CONSOLE WITH ORBLUK SNEEV AND VOCK AK-AK. BEHIND THEM IS A MR. ZISH DRINK MACHINE. ORBLUK HAS ACCELERATED THE BLINKING SEQUENCE OF HER RUNNING LIGHTS AND VOCK'S BODY IS COVERED WITH THE BEGINNINGS OF AN ELABORATE PATTERN. THE TWO ANCHOR-BEINGS ARE DRINKING BOWLS OF A HOT, MILKY LIQUID.

ORBLUK—We have just seen the surprise results of the RporRians' testimony: a dropping of the charges connected with the Terrans' visit to that waste receptacle of a planet.

VOCK—(sip) Sense to me it makes. Pressing forward with these minor charges would necessitate continued contact with the RporRians. (With a spare flipper, he smears a dirty green paste over the back of his neck.) The Great Golden Ones have obviously decided that it is not worth the risk of the bugs escaping.

ORBLUK—No dissension there, my friend. In fact, the RporRians are already back on their home world. (pause—smile) But now, we have a special treat for our viewers. A lot of sentients are disappointed that the RporRians agreed to testify. So, our Special Effects Department has created a computer simulation of what would have happened, had the bugs refused. Let's go to that now, shall we?

ZOOM IN TO THE WALL SCREEN—INTERIOR CONFINEMENT CUBE. THE FORCECAN SLOWLY FADES AWAY, AND ONE BY ONE THE SCREAMING RPORRIANS DROP IN TO THE BOILING VAT. TECHNICAL NOTE: FOR NON-LIBRARY USE, INSERT LAUGH TRACK.

****

TRANSCRIPT #37

FADE IN ON MOGACHEF, WHO HAS STEAM RISING FROM HER OUTER VENTS.
TECHNICAL NOTE: FOR THE SAKE OF GOOD TASTE, PLEASE KEEP THE CAMERA OFF THOSE LAST TWO VENTS, UNLESS THINGS GET DULL. THEN ZOOM IN FOR A CLOSE-UP.

MOGACHEF—Semi-Lord Brent has just delivered a truly inspired plea for his clients. In brief, he claims that the Gee blockade around their planet was not fully erect at the time, and that the United Countries of Dirt had never received an official notice of non-passage. Their forced boarding of the Gee superdreadnought can be argued as an act of purest desperation, and they did leave enough thulium to purchase the vessel. Plus, the avantor and The 16 were not kidnapped, but taken on board the *Ramariez* in need of immediate medical help. It was their own anti-social behavior that caused their continued incarceration. (pause) And that has been an issue raised again and again during this trial, the gross incompetence of the Great Golden Ones—from permitting Leader Idow's initial landing upon Terra, to the humans' accidental breaching of the criminal-infested weapon cache in star system #553646. An informal poll taken at a frozen Zish stand shows that many sentients are of the opinion that the Gees have degenerated into a race of incompetents. Needless to say, this is a dangerous line of thought.

INTERNAL VIEW OF THE COLISEUM. ZOOM IN A MEDIUM VIEW OF A DRUNKEN CHORON FIRING A PLASMA PISTOL WILDLY INTO THE AIR. AN AVANTOR APPEARS AND REMOVES THE WEAPON FROM HIS HAND WITH A PSIONIC BLAST. THEN A SQUAD OF WAROBOTS TELEPORT AROUND THE STONY GIANT, WRESTLE HIM TO THE GROUND, AND HUSSLE THE CHORON OFF TO A WAITING HEDRON PRISON SHIP.

MOGACHEF (voice over)—As you can see, if the Gees are fumbling has-beens, they are fumbling has-beens who still possess formidable weaponry. Let's replay that final summation of Semi-Lord Brent, shall we?

CROSS FADE TO A CLOSE-UP OF TSHOG BRENT, HIS NOSE HORN FLASHING MAGNIFICENTLY IN THE OVERHEAD SUN.

BRENT—The Gee's main objection to my clients' being granted the right to join galactic society in the first place was that humanity had failed to, quote "earn that right" end quote, by the established method of developing its own stardrive. This blindly ignores the mitigating circumstances behind their actions. To be exposed to the fact of galactic civilization, and then denied access to it, *as the Gee's blockade was meant to do*, will cause the death of this civilization, just as surely as if Leader Idow had been allowed to carry out his plans. What must they do to win the approval of the Great Golden Ones, raise the dead? I again state that the Galactic League owes my clients immediate membership status and a dismissal of all charges!

THE COLISEUM ERUPTS INTO CHEERS, HOWLS, AND

SQUEALS OF APPROVAL. AFTER SEVERAL REQUESTS FOR QUIET OVER THE PA SYSTEM FAIL, TEN THOUSAND GEE SUPERDREADNOUGHTS DESCEND FROM THE SKY AND BATHE THE ENTIRE STADIUM WITH *STOP THAT* CANNON FIRE.

****

TRANSCRIPT #150

FADE IN ON THE CONTROL BOOTH. ORBLUK IS WEARING SUNGLASSES, AND THE GARISH PRESENCE OF VOCK AK-AK IS BEGINNING TO CAUSE COLOR STREAKING WITH THE CAMERA.

VOCK—An astounding decision by the Great Golden Ones, eh, Orbluk?

ORBLUK—Truth you speak, Vock. This is a major concession by the Great Golden Ones, and quite likely directly traceable to the Terrans' outstanding achievements of killing Leader Idow, destroying the rogue warobot Silverside, and out-bargaining the RporRian Queen/Mother—factors they just could not ignore in light of the public sentiment stirred up by Semi-Lord Brent. Let's have a replay of that decision.

CROSSFADE INTO A CLOSE-UP OF THE 3000. THE GEE MALE LOOKS LIKE HE WOULD RATHER BE DOING ANYTHING ELSE.

THE 3000—It is with great reluctance that we concede that it was due to errors on our part that Leader Idow managed to land on, and make contact with, the human race. Having the knowledge and the reality of galactic civilization thrust down their air intake valves in such a fashion would have destroyed any lesser species. And yet, in the face of imminent destruction, Terra completely reorganized its government, from opposing nation-states to a unified ruling body, almost instantaneously. This is most impressive. Its subsequent actions are even more so, and would have done credit to any young, outwardly reaching, intelligent species not plagued with mental disorders.

FREEZE THE GEE.

VOCK (voice over)—Told I am that the humans wished the wording of that particular passage changed, but Semi-Lord Brent had told them to quit while they still had both feelers in the air.

UNFREEZE THE GEE.

THE 3000—As a result, we are at this time prepared to drop most of the charges against humanity.

CUT TO THE CROWD GOING WILD. BUT THEN EVERYBODY QUIETS AS A HOLOGRAPHIC IMAGE OF THE 3000 SUDDENLY APPEARS IN THE AIR AND EXPANDS UNTIL IT FILLS THE COLISEUM WITH HIS PRESENCE.

THE 3000—(booming echo) The charges we will not drop are those resulting from the deliberate and planned attack upon the avantor's centihedron M-21-3. This act of piracy we cannot forgive. We charge all of humanity with complicity in this act. For this crime, and this crime alone, we demand the ultimate penalty.

CUT BACK TO THE CONTROL ROOM.

ORBLUK—Well, I'd say that pretty much wraps it up for the Terrans.

VOCK—Truth you speak. (He glances down at his almost completed body work.) Shame, as a race they gave off much color. (With a sad air, he begins to mix a large pot of cream and liberally applies it to his body.)

****

TRANSCRIPT #151

NOTICE: DO NOT TAMPER WITH OR ALTER THIS FOLLOWING SECTION IN ANY WAY WHATSOEVER UNDER PENALTY OF LAW.

FADE FROM BLACK TO THE CONTROL BOOTH, WHERE A WILD-EYED ORBLUK AND A SMEARY VOCK APPEAR TO BE BARELY IN CONTROL OF THEMSELVES.

ORBLUK—Viewers, we have just received rumor of an incredible event taking place at the human encampment. We take you there now.
VOCK—Yes! Do now it!

ZOOM IN ON THE SCREEN BEHIND THEM. THERE STANDS A DISHEVELED MOGACHEF. HER OUTFIT HAS OBVIOUSLY BEEN PUT ON IN GREAT HASTE AS ALL OF THE SPINDLES ARE INVERTED. BEHIND HER WE SEE THE SECTION OF THE HUMAN ENCAMPMENT THAT CONTAINS THE *RAMARIEZ*. PEOPLE AND ROBOTS ARE RUNNING/FLYING EVERYWHERE.

MOGACHEF—Sentients, a monumental discovery has been made aboard the human starship, where they have been billeted through the whole trial. I am speaking now with the human responsible for the excitement, Medical Technician Paul Van Loon. Doctor, what have you done?
VAN LOON—I don't really understand what the fuss is about. The Gees were going through our hydroponics section when they seemed to go bananas . . . uh, crazy. It was just an experiment to see if I could germinate some alien seeds I'd found on the Great Golden Ones' ship. Well, I did it.

ZOOM IN PAST THE TWO TO FOCUS ON THE *RAMARIEZ*. A HUSH ENVELOPES THE COLISEUM AS A GEE APPEARS IN THE HATCH. TIGHT ZOOM IN TO SEE HIM GENTLY LEADING OUT AN AMBULATORY BUSH WITH MULTIPLE BRANCHING LIMBS, A SMALL PUCKERED BARK FACE, AND ARTICULATED FEET-ROOTS. SUDDENLY, THE SILENCE IS BROKEN BY THE DISTANT THUMPS OF THOUSANDS OF PEOPLE FAINTING.

MOGACHEF—(whisper) By the Prime Builder's heart and blood, it's a *Koolgoolagan*!

VAN LOON (voice over)—Nothing seemed to work until I got the idea of liquefying the leaves and soaking the seeds in the juice. I figured it's supposed to be this great restorative, so why shouldn't it work on its own species?

AN OFF CAMERA SCREAM. CUT BACK TO THE CONTROL ROOM, WHERE THERE IS SEEN ONLY THE SANDLED FEET OF ORBLUK SNEEV STICKING STRAIGHT UP IN THE AIR FROM BEHIND THE CONSOLE, AND A FRANTIC VOCK AK-AK WHO IS TRYING TO PAINT HIMSELF WITH FOUR FLIPPERS AT ONCE.

****

TRANSCRIPT #250

FADE IN TO SEE THE GALACTIC LEAGUE STANDING IN A SMALL POOL OF LIGHT, SURROUNDED BY A SEA OF BLACKNESS.

LEAGUE—Sentients and friends, our decision in this matter must take into account the greatest good for the greatest number. The wishes of individuals, whether individual beings or individual planets, are weighed, evaluated and, occasionally, discarded. (pause) Therefore, it is our decision that the inhabitants of the Sol star system, indigenous to the planet known as Dirt, heretofore referred to as Terrans, are cleared of all charges and are hereby granted admittance to the Galactic League. (pause) However, the crew of the UN starship *Hector Ramariez* has been found guilty of the charges brought before them. Their sentence is life imprisonment upon Galopticon 7. (pause) But, due to the extenuating circumstances involved and taking into consideration the many extraordinary actions they have performed, which will, directly and indirectly, benefit galactic society—including the actions of Dr. Paul Van Loon, which have changed the course of history—by the power invested in us, we do hereby commute their sentence to five standard years. At which time any survivors will be released. This is the decision of the Galactic League. Court adjourned.

THE HOLOGRAM DIMS AND FADES AWAY. DOLLY DOWN TO A GROUND LEVEL VIEW OF SMILING TECHNICIANS WHO ARE ALREADY BREAKING APART THE RECORDING EQUIPMENT.

CUT TO A PANORAMIC VIEW OF THE CROWD ERUPTING INTO PANDEMONIUM. THE SOUND OF CHEERING CONTINUES UNTIL THE END OF THE TAPE.

CUT TO A CLOSE-UP OF THE 3000 NODDING AND TURNING AWAY.

CUT TO PROFESSOR RAJAVUR AND CAPTAIN KELLER SHAKING HANDS AND CLAPPING SEMI-LORD BRENT ON THE BACK.

CUT TO A DISTANCE SHOT OF THOUSANDS OF GEE SOLDIERS ADVANCING ON THE HUMAN ENCAMPMENT.

CUT TO A WIDE-ANGLE VIEW OF THE HUMANS ROUNDED UP AND MANACLED TOGETHER BY THEIR GOLDEN GUARDS. SOME OF THE PRISONERS APPEAR TO BE WEEPING, BUT MOST HAVE A LOOK OF TRIUMPHANT PRIDE ON THEIR FACES.

CUT TO THE CONTROL BOOTH WHERE VOCK AK-AK IS SPRAYING HIS BODY WITH CLEAR PLASTIC. ORBLUK AND MOGACHEF ARE SHARING A CONGRATULATORY BOWL OF ZISH. LD 59 MERRILY BOBS IN THE AIR ABOVE THEM, A POWER PACK CLUTCHED IN EACH METALLIC HAND.

CUT TO A SKYWARD VIEW OF A GOLDEN POLYHEDRON PRISON SHIP LANDING IN THE HUMAN SECTOR.

CUT TO THE REMAINING HUMANS PROTESTING AS THEY ARE PUSHED OUT OF THE WAY.

CUT TO A MEDIUM SHOT OF THE CHAINED

HUMANS AS THEY MARCH ON BOARD THE POLYHEDRON SHIP. FOCUS ON EACH FACE AS THEY BRAVELY GO ON BOARD, AND PRINT THEIR NAMES ON THE BOTTOM OF THE SCREEN: KELLER, VAN LOON, JONES, BUCKLEY, SOUKUP, HAMLISCH, LILLIUOKA-LANI, HASSAN, TRELL, SAKAEDA, LIEBERMAN, FUER-STENBERG, RAJAVUR, COURTNEY, BRONSON, MALAVADE, WU, NICHOLI, DRILL. . . .

CUT TO THE PRISON SHIP LAUNCHING. TRACK IT UNTIL THE VESSEL REACHES SPACE AND JUMPS INTO HYPERSPACE. HOLD CAMERA ON EMPTY SKY FOR THIRTY SECONDS.

CUT TO A HORDE OF REPORTERS AND A DELEGA-TION FROM BIG ADVANCING TO GREET THE UNITED COUNTRIES OF DIRT. SLOWLY PULL BACK AS THE GROUPS INTERMINGLE. CROSSFADE TO AN EXTERNAL VIEW OF THE COLISEUM. ROLL CREDITS. FADE TO BLACK. FADE OUT CHEERING.

End Transcript.

27

Of course, what the citizens of the galaxy saw was a sham. The real trial of humanity took place in the private office of the Galactic League and lasted about five minutes.

* * * * *

Locked in the unbreakable grip of Gee tractor beams, the *Ramariez* was unceremoniously hauled through hyperspace to Big and forced to land at a military spaceport. A vigilant armada of centihedrons filled all of nearby space, blanketing any thought of escape, of which the humans had none. This was what they had been struggling for from the beginning—to meet the Galactic League.

Under the harsh scrutiny of warobots and riot barges, the crew disembarked and was marched to a complex of teleporters, accompanied by a heavily armed, grim-faced, trigger happy Avantor and The 16. In a blinding flash, the seventy-nine humans and three aliens disappeared—to reappear inside a long magnificent hall of polished blue stone and curved golden arches. Disquietingly, the passageway had no windows, and only a single sparkling door some twenty meters away.

"Far freaking out," breathed Drill in frank appreciation of the room's beauty. This place was even nicer than the main lobby at the Sheraton Hotel on Thirty-fourth Street! Resting on his cane, the teenager favored his sore leg. Cavalierly, he ignored the ominous tones of the one-way structure, placing his total faith in the ability of the UN marines to get them out whenever necessary. Those guys were serious butt kickers.

"Okay, what now?" asked Keller, maintaining a respectful distance from the Gees.

Avantor scowled and pointed the barrel of her neural disrupter at the man, the ghastly weapon set on its highest, most painful level of radiation: Four-Day Drunk Hangover.

"No talking among the prisoners," she ordered brusquely.

The captain shrugged, Rajavur hrumphed, and Sergeant Lieberman silently asked Lieutenant Sakaeda a question. His expression told her to wait. With a cough and a finger motion, she relayed these orders to the troops.

In spite of the fact that the smooth blue floor beneath them appeared to be made of solid stone, the whole group unexpectedly began to move along the corridor. Effortlessly, they glided down the pristine hallway, through an ever-processing energy curtain, and into a dimly lit area. As the protective portal sealed behind them, the lights came on and the humans found themselves in a small, square room.

The unadorned floor and walls were made of a nondescript material that defied visual analysis. But, as if to offset the incredible blandness of the cubicle, in the middle of the room was a shimmering, waist-high crystal pedestal with a green silk pillow on top. And sitting proudly on the pillow was a plump frog. True, a purple frog with six legs, but a simple *ecaudata batrachia*, nonetheless.

"Order: *salientia*; genus: *rana*," noted a crew member, and Trell shushed her. This was no time for a biology lesson.

"Greetings from the Galactic League," said the frog in a

high-pitched voice, minus a croak.

Holstering their disrupters, the Gees saluted and bowed, while the humans did a quick reality check.

"You're the league?" asked Hassan, dumbfounded.

The female amphibian puffed out her cheeks before answering. "Not precisely. This body is only the organic conduit through which the league communicates. This, is the Galactic League."

And like morning mist, the room about them disappeared, and the humans found themselves standing on a swatch of floor surrounded by a truly immense globe, a dark sphere whose inner wall was lined with sleeping creatures inside frosty glass tubes. Crystal rods, or perhaps beams of light connected each glittering tube to another, the resulting conglomeration ending in a dazzling display of technology so high that Clarke's Law about magic and technology seemed to be invoked.

"*Madra mia.* . . ."

"Holy. . . ."

"*Gott en.* . . ."

"Mother-jumping. . . ."

Plainly, the frog relished their reactions of awe and surprise. Even though primarily made of diplomats and scientists, many of the members of the Galactic League had a strong dramatic streak in them.

"Wait, I understand," whispered Ensign Lilliuokalani. "This represents a sample of every race in space. The individuals are placed in suspended animation, and then mind-linked together to form the Galactic League."

The rest of the group murmured assent at the deduction.

Though it was hard to tell, the frog seemed impressed. Nobody had ever figured out the operating principle of the league that quickly before. The humans were proving to be everything she had been told they were.

"Utterly fascinating," noted Prof. Rajavur. Only his fifteen years of playing poker enabled him to maintain a calm facade. "And it is most definitely the very first time I have ever heard the imperial 'we' used properly."

Via the frog, the composite brain chuckled at the witticism.

Only a robot file clerk in the Hall of Data knew that the present persona of the league was a distant grandchild of the archcriminal, Squee—more highly evolved, but just as vicious. Like so many others before it, when given a choice of becoming the voice of the league or banishment to Galopticon 7, the lawbreaker readily agreed to the former. And after its bodily functions had been stabilized and the computer link implanted, it lived a long and useful life paying for its crimes by serving the community.

"Are the people in there forever?" asked Dr. Van Loon, wondering at the possible implications of eternal servitude.

Personally, the league was very pleased with that choice of words. Not every human considered other races people, particularly not 2d Lt. Abagail Elizabeth Jones.

The frog cleared its throat. "No, the chosen members serve a term of fifty standard years and are then released. Looking, we might add, no older than when they entered. Suspended animation means just that."

As the humans reacted to that startling news, a tiny door opened in the side of the pedestal and out buzzed a fly. The Galactic League snared the insect in midair with its sticky tongue and closed its jaw with a satisfied snap.

Prof. Rajavur took a deep breath. "Getting down to business, when is our trial?"

"Trial?" asked the league. "Oh, that. It's already over."

Captain Keller arched an eyebrow. "I beg your pardon?"

It took the league a second to realize that Keller uttered an expression of disbelief and not a plea for clemency.

"Let me explain," began the frog didactically. "As you entered this room, telepathic machines read your minds, assimilated the data, and fed it to us." The amphibian rubbed a tiny webbed hand across its bumpy brow. "We must say that we haven't seen a comedy of errors to match this since the committee to name Big."

"And what is your decision?" asked Prof. Rajavur.

A leathery smile. "You will be pleased to know that Terra has been found innocent and will be immediately admitted to league status.

Relief washed over the humans, and they relaxed tense muscles and smiled. Delighted beyond words, Trell hugged himself with all four arms. Avantor and The 16 suddenly felt very foolish with their disrupters hanging out and holstered their weapons. From enemies to allies with the single flick of a froggish tongue. Ah well, that's life in the city on Big.

But, the Galactic League had not forgotten about the two Gee officers. Their punishment would come later, and in a most devious form. Oh, that dramatic streak.

"The crew of the Ramariez is also found innocent," the frog went on. "Or rather, guilty with mitigating circumstances."

I hear a but, thought Rajavur/Keller/Sakaeda.

"However," continued the league.

Close enough.

"Quite accidentally in your admirable quest for the stars, you have caused the Gees to look like idiots. A not all-together bad thing in private, but in public it could undermine the very fabric of galactic society. Interstellar crime is hard enough to control as it is. So, in order to preserve the integrity of the galaxy, a public trial must be held in which you will be found guilty and sentenced."

"To Galopticon 7?" asked The 16, who now had a sneaking suspicion where this was leading to.

"That is what we will tell the public," acknowledged the frog regally. "Actually, their place of incarceration will be someplace far more exciting."

"Where?" inquired Prof. Rajavur before Captain Keller or anybody else could ask.

The Galactic League blinked. "Why, the planet Gee, of course. Where else?"

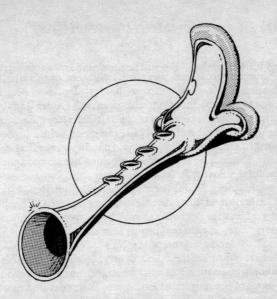

EPILOGUE

In the subsequent lunar rotations, galactic society adjusted itself like a robot automatically fine-tuning its own power plant.

First, the blockade around Earth was removed, and in a brilliant piece of diplomacy, the nation of Greece redeemed itself by giving the Galactic League the isle of Crete as a planetary landing base. The pleasant weather, lack of price, and the begging on hands and knees were sufficient inducement for acceptance.

The Gunderson Corporation went interplanetary, Ms. Bolivar got a raise, and McDougherty was fired for excessive cruelty to the employees—after which the softball team began winning games on a regular basis.

A mentally disturbed wino, claiming to be Ramariez, was adopted by a cult of Hector worshipers as their hero's reincarnation, and he lived a long and happy life indulging in wine, women, and revival meetings that culminated with egg tosses in Central Park.

Jose de San Martin, the secretary-general of the UN, found himself a very busy man, as hordes of planets had issued awards and bounties for the death of Leader Idow, Gasterphaz, Squee, and Boztwank. Unexpectedly, Earth found itself inundated with hard cash and credit, which it promptly used to modernize the planet to contemporary galactic standards: eliminating street gangs, cleaning the air and water, and building a luxury hotel on the moon.

Curiously enough, there was no bounty on Trell, as nobody had known of his existence prior to the trial. The biggest reward was for Boztwank, issued by his own world. Proof that vengeance, like charity, begins at home.

Lt. Amanda Jackson of the NYPD SWAT, and NATO Col. Robert Weiss married and opened a chain of martial arts schools, specializing in surprise attacks and misdirection.

Out of the hospital at last, Agent Taurus decided to quit his profession and retired to the suburbs of London, buying a cottage right alongside a nuclear power plant—just in case.

Dominic Mastramonico, the Italian ambassador to the UN, and the person who first conceived the idea of the FCT, was chosen as Earth's official representative to the Galactic League. The elderly gentleman had no objection to living an additional fifty years, and looked forward to dancing on the graves of his political opponents who had laughed at the idea of a First Contact Team.

On the planet Koolgoolig, Dr. Paul Van Loon (in disguise) was placed in charge of a maximum security greenhouse to help with the replanting of the Koolgoolagan race. It was backbreaking work, but the physician was content, knowing that the Galactic Medal of Smartness waited for him upon his release, as well as the position of chief surgeon in any hospital in the entire known galaxy. Including Boston.

When news of the trial finally reached him, in disgust the freelance reporter, Bachalope Thintfeesle, left the planetary system he had been so sure the humans would go to. The crimson salt-water fishoid sighed deeply. When he missed a call that was this important, perhaps it was time for him to change jobs. But, aside from working as a news gatherer, what else was the red herring good for?

The asteroid, Buckle, underwent a purge of almost biblical proportions, and the status of every other secret weapon cache was carefully checked. Many varied and interesting things were found, but happily, Leader Silverside proved to be an only child.

During the fight with Silverside, Einda had rushed into the office to find a mortally wounded Chisel. Using the adaptive proto-flesh of her own body to staunch his wounds, she carried the unconscious boy from the battle zone and escaped in a stolen starship. Hurriedly, the medical robots on board effected repairs on the human. Luckily, his wounds proved to be minimal as his accidental body armor of knives stopped the majority of the anti-personnel darts. The holes in flesh, organs, and arteries were easily fixed, along with a particularly nasty abnormality in his brain—which confused the technician no end. It almost appeared as if the child had been allowed to be born with the disorder. Now Einda realized why Chisel had proposed to her. Bracing herself for the worst, she waited patiently by his bed for the boy to awaken. The memory of the confusion on his face, and how it turned into a radiant smile when he saw her, remained with the female for the rest of their long life together.

Fleeing to the other side of the galaxy, the newlyweds used his two-pound bag of thulium to buy a small mansion and open a legitimate tavern on the nice side of a spaceport—a bar which Chisel insisted be named "McDonald's," a word he told everybody meant "a distinguished place for fun and good times" in his native language.

The *giks* staged a bloodless revolution, and won the right to disassimilate whenever they wanted to, even though nobody had ever stopped them from doing it before.

On the planet Gee, Captain Keller and the crew of the *Ramariez* took great pleasure in teaching classes to the Great Golden Ones on *Basic Evasion, Elementary Tactics* and *Com-*

bat Made Simple. The golden warriors just had to grin and take it, plus take notes. Every night, in the privacy of her cubicle, Lieutenant Jones showered and scrubbed herself from the close association with so damn many aliens. Bleh.

The sole known surviving member of the ill-fated Bloody Deckers, Drill, with a full pardon in his pocket, assumed his real name of Thomas John Glenn and joined the UN Space Marines.

In basic training, the first thing Private Glenn was taught was the proper name of his assault rifle: the Fuerstenberg. Yes, it was awkward and a bit clumsy, but deadly in combat. And it was PFC Glenn (drunk on rosé wine liberated from the locked supply cabinet in the PX), who wrote the justly famous slogan: *First in peace. First in war. Fuerstenberg.* Then, he burped and passed out.

Landing on RporR was officially made illegal and the spiral closed off.

Joyously, the FCT was reunited and began immediate work on their new job as the First Contact Team for the Galactic League, which included designing a mobile command bunker to be fitted inside the reconditioned *Ramariez.* In their off-duty hours, the humans introduced the game of poker to the Gees and did serious damage to the planetary economy before the rule of table stakes was invoked.

And then, of course, there was the terrible punishment of Avantor, the junior grade avantor, and The 16.

* * * * *

Summoning their resolve, the Gee officers knocked on the door of the office assigned to their new commanding officer. A voice told them to enter.

Dressed in casual duty fatigues, Lieutenant Sakaeda glanced up from his pile of paperwork at their approach and grinned.

"Avantor! The 16! What a pleasant surprise! Please, have a seat," he said, gesturing at a couple of chairs.

"Sir, thank you, no," replied The 16 in a stiffly formal manner, and he handed the puzzled officer a featureless sheet of thin gray plastic.

At Sakaeda's touch, cryptic symbols appeared on the sheet, and the human reached for his English-Gee dictionary.

"We have been assigned to your military unit for retraining," translated the avantor, the words stinging on her lips like lashes from a tiny whip.

The human went pale. Oh, no, Sakaeda thought, anything but that.

Avantor and The 16 felt sick to their stomachs, misinterpreting the officer's expression as annoyance. Not even aliens wanted their company after their series of monumental blunders. And who could blame them?

With a mounting feeling of helplessness, the marine scanned the plastic sheet, reading what few words he could. "If I have this right, it says here that you are supposed to report to me tomorrow at 0900."

"Tomorrow, then," snapped the avantor, and the Gees pivoted on their heels to leave.

"Wait!" cried Sakaeda franticly.

They stopped and The 16 turned. "Is it tomorrow, sir?" he asked sarcastically.

The lieutenant rose from his chair and hurried about his desk. "No, but by then it would be too late."

The 16 looked puzzled. "I do not understand."

Sakaeda ignored him. "I—I don't know how your people handle this, Avantor, but I have always been very sexually attracted to you and would like to engage in . . . *fizzlorp.*" Kurt hoped he had said that right. The medical manual that stated their races were sexually compatible did not have a pronounciation guide.

Both Avantor and The 16 blinked in surprise, and then smiled. With only each other for sex on the old X-47-D, things had been pretty darn dull. And now they were outcasts among their associates. Perhaps a mass joining with some humans was just what they needed to work off some tension and cement their new working relationship. What the Void, it couldn't hurt.

Sounds good to me, my liege.

Then let's do it, studmuffin.

"Accepted," said Avantor, feeling a preliminary rush of passion tingle through her. "Gather four of your friends and meet The 16 and me back at our room in say . . . ten Earth minutes?"

Kurt hesitated. "All males?" he asked.

Softly, the female caressed his cheek. "That would be boring," she murmured in reply.

"Definitely boring," said The 16, adding his two copper units. Hmm, he thought, I wonder if human females can *snikgorgle*? They were certainly equipped for it.

Reeling slightly from raw lust, Lieutenant Sakaeda felt his face burn at Avantor's velvet touch. Hot damn, she was his kind of woman! The marine glanced at his watch. "Ten minutes and counting!"

Excitedly, The 16 scampered from the office, and as Avantor strolled slowly away, already starting to unbutton her uniform top, the Gee added over her shoulder, "I'll bring the nose flute."

THE CREATIVE TEAM

Nicholas Angelo Pollotta, Jr. was born in Hackensack Hospital, New Jersey, in August of 1954—which makes him a God-fearing Republican with Virgo rising. In the mid-seventies, Nick was a stand-up comic and performed regularly at New York clubs like Catch A Rising Star and the Improvisation. Under the name "Nick Smith," he has had several cartoons published in publications like *Starlog* and *Dragon*® Magazine. Nick is also the creator, producer, director, and star of "The Adventures of Phil A. Delphia," a series of humorous science fiction radio plays that have been broadcast over college radio stations since 1980. Hating boredom worse than almost anything, his many hobbies include gaming, martial arts, movies, books, and guns.

In 1977, Phil Foglio won the prestigious Hugo award for Best Fan Artist. After he won again in 1978, Phil withdrew his name from consideration in the amateur category, as he had graduated that spring with a BFA in cartooning and considered himself a professional. From 1981 to 1984, Phil's monthly feature "What's New?" ran in *Dragon*® Magazine. About this time he also started illustrating Robert Asprin's "Myth" series for Donning/Starblaze. Eventually, he adapted the first book into a comic series, *MythAdventures*, for WaRP Graphics. Since then, Phil has worked regularly as a scripter on such comic books as *Dynamo Joe* and *Plastic Man*. Phil collects toy ray guns and primitive masks, and his interests include humor, poker, computers, chess, and women. Not necessarily in that order.

TSR™ BOOKS

Wondrous New TSR™ Books

The Jewels of Elvish

Nancy Varian Berberick
Author of the best-selling
DRAGONLANCE® novel
Stormblade

A tenuous alliance is threatened when a powerful ruby is stolen. Available in April 1989.

Monkey Station
Ardath Mayhar
Ron Fortier

A deadly plague sweeps the globe, causing the Macaques in the rain forests of South America to evolve faster. Available in June 1989.

DRAGONLANCE® *Preludes*

Darkness and Light
Paul Thompson and Tonya Carter

Darkness and Light tells of the time Sturm and Kitiara spent traveling together before the fated meeting at the Inn of the Last Home. Accepting a ride on a gnomish flying vessel, they end up on Lunitari during a war. Eventually escaping, the two separate over ethics.

Kendermore
Mary L. Kirchoff

A bounty hunter charges Tasslehoff Burrfoot with violating the kender laws of prearranged marriage. To ensure his return, Kendermore's council has his Uncle Trapspringer prisoner. Tas meets the alchemist who pickles one of everything, including kender!

Brothers Majere
Rose Estes

The origins of the brothers' love/hate relationship. Distraught over his ailing mother, Caramon reluctantly allows her to die. Unable to forgive his brother, or himself for his inability to help her, Raistlin agrees to pursue her last wish, an unwitting pawn in the struggle between good and evil.

FANTASY ADVENTURE

THE MOONSHAE TRILOGY
Douglas Niles

The conclusion!

Darkwell

The ultimate struggle of good and evil.... At stake, the survival of the Moonshae Isles. Tristan must forge a lasting alliance between the divergent people of the Isles. Robyn must confront an evil that has infested the land itself. Together they must decide if they will face the future together as king and queen--or as enemies, forever separated by failure and mistrust. Available in March 1989.

1987: *Darkwalker on Moonshae*
Tristan Kendrick must rally the diverse people of the Isles of Moonshae to halt the spread of a relentless army of firbolgs and dread Bloodriders.

1988: *Black Wizards*
An army of ogres and zombies guided by Bhaal threatens the gentle Ffolk while the puppet king acquiesces.

BUCK ROGERS™
ADVENTURE BOOKS

ARRIVAL

Stories By Today's Hottest Science Fiction Writers!

Flint Dille
Augustine Funnell
S.N. Lewitt
M.S. Murdock
Jerry Oltion
Robert Sheckley

A.D. 1995: An American pilot flies a suicide mission against an enemy Space Defense Platform to save the world from nuclear war. Buck Rogers blasts his target and vanishes in a fiery blaze.

A.D. 2456: In the midst of this 25th century battlefield an artifact is discovered--one that is valuable enough to ignite a revolution. This artifact is none other than the perfectly preserved body of the 20th century hero, Buck Rogers.

BUCK ROGERS
ADVENTURE BOOKS

THE MARTIAN WARS TRILOGY
M.S. Murdock

Rebellion 2456: Buck Rogers joins NEO, a group of freedom fighters dedicated to ridding Earth of the Martian megacorporation RAM. NEO's goal is to gain enough of a following to destroy RAM's Earth Space Station. The outcome of that mission will determine the success of Earth's rebellion. Available in May 1989.

Hammer of Mars: Ignoring RAM threats and riding on the wave of NEO's recent victory, Buck Rogers travels to Venus to strike an alliance. Furious, RAM makes good on its threats and sends its massive armada against a defenseless Earth. Available in August 1989.

Armageddon Off Vesta: Martian troops speed to Earth in unprecedented numbers. Earth's survival depends on Buck's negotiations with Venus. But even as Venus considers offering aid to Earth, Mercury is poised to attack Venus. Relations among the inner planets have never been worse! Available in October 1989.